Praise for Zara Stoneley's Books

'*A great treat for readers who love their books
jam-packed with sexy men and horses*'
Bestselling author Fiona Walker

'*Fans of Fiona Walker will love this book*'
That Thing She Reads

'*A delightful romp stuffed with fun, frolics and romance*'
BestChickLit.com

'*Stable Mates is up there with Riders and Rivals*'
Comet Babes Books

'*Move over Mr Grey, the Tippermere boys are in town!
Highly recommended*'
Brook Cottage Books

'*A seductive fascinating novel.
Mucking out the horses just got sexy*'
Chicks That Read

Country Rivals

ZARA STONELEY

A division of HarperCollins*Publishers*
www.harpercollins.co.uk

Harper*Impulse* an imprint of
HarperCollins*Publishers*
1 London Bridge Street
London SE1 9GF

www.harpercollins.co.uk

A Paperback Original 2016

First published in Great Britain in ebook format by Harper*Impulse* 2016

A catalogue record for this book
is available from the British Library

ISBN: 9780008194406

Set in Minion by Palimpsest Book Production Ltd, Falkirk, Stirlingshire

Printed and bound in Great Britain

MIX
Paper from
responsible sources
FSC™ C007454

FSC™ is a non-profit international organisation established to promote
the responsible management of the world's forests. Products carrying the
FSC label are independently certified to assure consumers that they come
from forests that are managed to meet the social, economic and
ecological needs of present and future generations,
and other controlled sources.

Find out more about HarperCollins and the environment at
www.harpercollins.co.uk/green

For Alex

Tippermere

Welcome to tranquil Tippermere, set deep in the Cheshire country-side. Home to Lords and Ladies, horsemen and farmers.

Set on the highest hill, keeping a close eye on the village and its inhabitants, lies Tipping House Estate. In pride of place is the grand Elizabethan style mansion, sweeping down in front of her are immaculate gardens, well-kept parkland and rolling acres that spread as far as the eye can see.

Follow the stream down to the flat below, and nestling between copses and lakes, you find Folly Lake Manor and the sprawling grounds of the bustling Equestrian Centre. The country lane in front wends its way between high hedges to the village green, the church and two village pubs. Then fans out into tributaries, follow them further and you find a small eventing yard, a scattering of country cottages and rambling working farms.

Take the road north eastwards, travel on a few short miles and soon the elegant village of Kitterly Heath unfolds before you - a village whose origins were recorded in the Domesday Book. At one end of the ancient high street a solid 14th Century church stands sentry, with an imposing school at the other, and all around sprawl the mansions old and new that house the rich and famous . . .

The Residents of Tippermere

Charlotte 'Lottie' Steel (nee Brinkley) – *disorganised but loveable daughter of Billy. In line to inherit the Tipping House Estate.*

Rory Steel – *devilishly daring and sexy three day eventer. Lottie's husband.*

Tilly – *head of the terrier trio that accompany Rory everywhere.*

Harry – *Lottie's spaniel.*

William 'Billy' Brinkley – *Lottie's father. Former superstar show jumper, based at the equestrian centre.*

Victoria 'Tiggy' Brinkley – *wife of Billy. As friendly, shaggy and eternally optimistic as a spaniel.*

Lady Elizabeth Stanthorpe – *owner of Tipping House Estate, lover of strong G&T's. Meddler and mischief maker. Lottie's gran, Dominic's mother.*

Bertie – *Elizabeth's black Labrador.*

Dominic 'Dom' Stanthorpe – *dressage rider extraordinaire. Uncle to Lottie, son of Elizabeth, slightly bemused and frustrated by both. Husband to Amanda.*

Amanda Stanthorpe – *Elegant and understated, delicate and demure. Owner of Folly Lake Manor and Equestrian Centre.*

Alice Stanthorpe – *Dom and Amanda's 3 year old daughter.*

Tabatha Strachan – *Rory and Lottie's groom. Horse mad, smitten by Rory, but suitably unimpressed by most other things.*

David Simcock – *England goalkeeper, resident of the neighbouring Kitterly Heath.*

Sam Simcock – *wife of David. Lover of dogs, diamonds and designer delights.*

Roxy Simcock – *Sam and David's 3 year old daughter*

Rupert – *Roxy's pony*

The Film Stars & Crew

Pandora Drakelow – *scheming, sneaky, man-eating star of the film. Seb's wife.*

Seb Drakelow – *Pandora's husband. Producer/Director. Hates the countryside, all things four legged and furry, or feathered, and anything North of Stratford-Upon-Avon.*

Jamie Trilling – *intern, location scout and general dogsbody.*

Xander Rossi – *Pandora's half-brother. Dashingly handsome polo player. Adviser on the film set.*

Ella – *Xander's Wire-Haired Dachshund.*

Chapter 1

Jamie Trilling had worked on enough film sets to know the sound of a shotgun being closed. It was a heavy clunk. Distinctive. The type of sound that vibrated in the still night air.

His fingers froze mid text.

Before he even had time to look up from his mobile phone there was the metallic echo of a safety catch being released and he knew he had to move. He couldn't. His tongue stuck to the parched roof of his mouth, and his throat – along with the rest of his crouched body – tightened with fear.

The shotgun barked out an unmistakable message, peppering his hands, his face, his hair with a shower of dark, peaty earth, and sending a rush of adrenalin that shocked him out of his stupor.

Jamie dived straight into the nearest rhododendron bush, catching a brief flash of a ghostly figure shimmering in the moonlight before his body hit the ground and the breath was knocked out of him.

For a moment all he could hear was the sound of his own breathing, then the crisp snap of twigs told him that whoever, or whatever, had shot at him was about to get a second chance.

He was too young to die, and if he did have to go he'd not

planned on it being under a bush in the middle of nowhere. His mother would never forgive him.

Jamie swallowed hard. If this was the movies he'd be rolling his way out of trouble and have his assailant in an arm-lock and disarmed before the next bullet had been loaded. But it was real life and his arm bloody hurt from landing on an exposed root. Lying paralysed in the greenery was so pathetic though. And for what? If he hadn't relied on bloody Pandora he'd have arrived in daylight and knocked at the door, not been skulking in the under-growth, in the middle of night, with only a camera for company.

There was another crack of brittle wood, alarmingly close this time, and a rustle of leaves and Jamie shut his eyes.

'Damned ramblers. I'll give you the right to roam, you buggers.' The unmistakably posh, and female, voice was unexpected. 'Think you own the blasted countryside.' There was the sound of a path being hacked out between him and her. He opened one eye, and through the shrubbery could just make out a green wellington boot. Not a ghost, then. 'Come out and show yourself, man, before I pepper your backside with shot.'

It was a turn of events he really hadn't expected, and it was all beginning to feel a bit surreal. A bad dream. Except it would take a better imagination than his to conjure up the painful throb in his elbow.

Jamie groaned. Two minutes earlier he'd been crouched in the undergrowth gazing at the image on his camera display like some self-satisfied goon who'd won the lottery. Now he was about to die. Or worse.

* * *

If he was honest, it had been a pretty weird kind of day, the strangest part being that his boss's wife, Pandora, was actually being helpful.

2

'Ignore Seb, dear. He's just anxious,' she'd remarked, swanning into the room just as Seb Drakelow had stormed out, after ripping a strip off him with the type of sarcasm you had to be born with. 'I can help you get back in his good books, if you like?' She'd said it disarmingly enough, but it still made him feel uneasy. Pandora was never nice to anybody. Feeling he hadn't really got much choice, he'd nodded. 'I do rather like you. It would be a shame if you were sacked so soon after starting, like the last boy.' She smiled, as sympathetically as her Botox-frozen features would allow. 'He's rather impulsive. It's his artistic side, I'm afraid. Now, what was it he asked you to do?'

Without Pandora's help Jamie would have been in trouble. Location scouting was fine when you had time on your side and knew what you were looking for. But he'd been dropped in at the deep end, with a ridiculously tight deadline, after the site his predecessor had arranged had fallen through at the last minute.

'Don't worry, I know exactly what type of place we need.' She held a hand out for his tablet. 'We did have a shortlist of places before, let me just look . . . Something like this maybe? Or this one? Oh yes, I can just imagine filming here, can't you? Although it's probably way outside our budget. Now this one,' she tapped on an image that linked to a newspaper report, 'Oh dear, they've had a fire and it looked ideal.'

Jamie looked over her shoulder. 'But that's what it looks like after the fire, isn't it? The outside still looks fine.'

'So it does, aren't you the clever one? And I suppose it might be a reasonable price if . . . Well, I'll leave it with you. I must admit though, it does look rather nice. You have a closer look and let me know.' She'd dropped the tablet on his lap, one finger to her lips. 'This can be our little secret, I won't tell Seb I helped. I presume you do want a permanent job with us?'

He did. He stared at the images, hardly noticing as Pandora left, shutting the door quietly behind her. She was right. From the few details he knew about the film it seemed to fit the bill.

In fact, the more he looked at the Tipping House Estate, the more he was convinced it was exactly what Seb Drakelow was looking for. He scanned the newspaper report, a fire, closed for business, broke landowners . . .

'You are a fucking genius, man.' An unexpected surge of triumph had flooded through him. 'A bloody genius, even if I say so myself.'

Two hours later Pandora had willingly (in her husband's absence) authorised expenses for his train ticket and practically pushed him out of the office. 'And if you fuck this up you're on your own. Seb really doesn't like failures,' had been her parting words as she'd signed the form without even looking at him.

The train journey had been a nightmare, and by the time he'd arrived at the nearest station to Tippermere it had been dark. The taxi rank had been deserted and when the station master had taken pity on him and offered the loan of a bike and directions to the estate, which was *'impossible to miss'*, it had seemed ideal. It would be a doddle – how hard could it be to find a whacking big country estate in a village?

It turned out to be harder than anticipated. There were no signs, no street lights and the names of the country lanes mysteriously changed at what appeared to be random points. He'd needed a map and he couldn't get a signal on his mobile, and his hands felt like they were about to drop off from the combination of freezing cold and juddering handlebars.

When he'd finally spotted the entrance gates to the Tipping House Estate he'd dropped the bike, punched the air and done a jig. Then he'd realised that he couldn't get in, which was slightly sobering. But with the promise of a well-paid job hovering just out of reach on the horizon he'd decided he had to be resourceful.

He'd clambered over a stone wall, torn his jeans on a barbed-wire fence, had brambles wrapped round his crotch (thank God for thick denim) and stood in more than one pile of smelly fox poo. He stank and was frayed at the edges, but he'd been proved right.

As he'd absentmindedly brushed a hand down one long denim-clad leg, his blue-grey eyes never leaving the image, he had to admit it. Tipping House was awesome. The perfect country pile. Full, no doubt, of stuck-up toffs and their horse-faced wives, but what the hell? It was the building he was interested in, not its inhabitants.

From his vantage point in the woods there was no sign of the fire damage that had caught his attention online, and even with the heavy cloak of night time, pierced only by the silver-white slivers of winter moonlight, the grand old building seemed to glow with a grandeur that spoke of majesty and pride. It shouted out, well murmured in a very upper class way, 'country estate'. It was all about *what ho's*, stiff upper lips, hunting parties and Hooray Henrys. Even the lawn was bigger than a bloody football pitch. Which was exactly what film-maker Seb Drakelow, and his demanding bitch of a wife, were after.

Jamie wasn't really into stately homes and all the pretentious crap that went with them. What he was into was ideas. And this idea was going to pay off big time. The Tipping House Estate was going to win him some points and a permanent job. Pandora had more or less said as much – although whether he trusted her word or not was debatable. But he did trust Seb, and Seb was going to be impressed.

The world might have been his oyster since leaving university, but it was a pretty cramped shell when all you were getting was the word 'intern' to slap on your CV along with an endless supply of cheap coffee and the kind of pay that didn't cover a week's worth of train fares. He desperately needed to get a place of his own. Urgently. Living with a librarian was seriously cramping his style, even if he was very fond of her. His mother. How the hell was he ever going to get a girl to take him seriously if he had to admit he'd moved back home?

It wasn't that there was any shortage of girls in his line of work, and with his loose-limbed frame, generous smile and earnest gaze Jamie had always had his admirers. But they tended to mother him rather than show any desire to strip off their clothes and drag him into bed.

There was a subtle change in the quality of the light as the clouds drifted, and Jamie focused back on the job. The clouds were clearing from over the moon – which was his sole source of light. The photographs he'd already got weren't bad, but this was his chance to get the winner. The perfect moonlit mansion. He lifted his camera to get one more shot. And that was when it all started to go wrong.

'Shit.' It was a ghost.

His mouth dried, his throat constricting, his gaze locked on the viewfinder. The figure was lit by the moon, as white as death, smack bang in the middle of his line of sight.

Except this was a solid mass, not the watery, wispy apparition he'd imagined a ghost would be. Some part of his brain told him that he should still be able to make out the mansion, through a shadowy form. That a ghost should be elusive.

Jamie knew he should run or take a photograph. But he couldn't do either. He couldn't even glance up to take it in with his own eyes. Second-hand, through the camera, was enough. He was mesmerised. The hairs prickled on the back of his neck. As he stared, transfixed, the auto focus in the viewfinder of the camera flickered, trying to fix onto and sharpen the apparition.

Which was the precise moment when his mobile phone had beeped its way into his conscience and he'd picked it up with trembling hands to find an irate '*Well?*' text message from an impatient Pandora. The sight of her profile picture had rather brought him back to reality. Then he'd heard the clunk of the shotgun.

* * *

Jamie stared at the wellington boot, which didn't appear to have moved.

'Show yourself, man, or I'll send the dogs in after you.'

'No fucking chance, you loony.' He stayed where he was, one hand clutching his precious camera to his chest. A ghost would have been easier to handle than this trigger-happy harridan.

Another shot rang out, alarmingly close, splinters of bark bouncing off the canopy of leaves that covered him, and Jamie froze. His ears picked up the clunk of the gun being reloaded, or at least that's what his imagination told him it was. In his world nobody carried shotguns or fired at strangers.

He supposed he should wriggle his way, commando style, to freedom. Not easy with a camera like a brick in one hand. And she'd probably pepper his arse with shots, or send the hounds in to drag him back. Christ, he was going to need new jeans after this. His inner action hero had obviously abandoned him.

'After him, boy, flush him out.'

'Well, Mum, I'm not quite sure this was what you had in mind when you said a degree would broaden my mind,' he muttered under his breath as the sound of snapping twigs heralded the oncoming dog. The Hound of the Baskervilles meets Miss Havisham, was his second thought as the snuffles and panting got closer. Although Havisham Hounds sounded more like a pub than a horror film. He had to breathe, calm down. Think rationally.

There was a rustle immediately to his left, the smell of sweet doggy breath, and Jamie opened his eyes – which he hadn't realise he'd shut. Whiskers tickled his cheek, above them a black, wet, shiny nose. Jamie all but giggled in relief as he realised that it was a Labrador grinning down at him. It plonked itself down on its haunches by his shoulder, tongue lolling, tail swishing through the leaves.

Jamie, who'd never heard of anybody being eaten alive by a Labrador, even though they'd eat more or less anything, offered a hand. The dog sniffed, then licked him with a noisy slurp.

'Bertie stop that, you bloody traitor.' Bertie stopped and glanced up guiltily over his shoulder, and so did Jamie. Straight into the barrel of a very old shotgun, gripped by even older, liver-spotted hands. 'And don't even think about running off. Darned safety catch, sticking again.'

Jamie wasn't even sure he could get up without help, let alone run. 'Do you know what you're doing with that thing?' He nodded at the barrel, which was a damned sight steadier than his wavering voice.

'I'm perfectly competent.'

Which he took as a yes. Despite the firearm pointed at his heart he could feel the blood returning to his extremities with a rush. His fingertips started to throb. 'It might be nice if you pointed it somewhere else.' She didn't. 'I thought you were a ghost.'

'A ghost?'

It was laughable now, but had seemed a real possibility only minutes ago. If it was minutes. He'd lost track of time, along with the feeling in one arm.

She was, he decided on closer inspection, quite an old lady. But one with a steady hand and a much firmer voice than most grannies he'd come across. More Clint Eastwood than Lady in a Van.

'Are you drunk, young man? Or under the influence of one of those new-fangled drugs you children play with?' Which was quite a good question, considering the weird direction his mind was taking him in. 'You're all the same you youngsters, need to get out in the fresh air and do some manual labour. You look pasty.'

'You'd look bloody pasty if you'd been shot at by a ghost.'

There was a glimmer of a smile across what he could now see were unmistakably aristocratic features. High cheekbones, beady eyes, a long slightly hooked nose and grey hair fixed firmly back. 'In my day . . .'

He rolled his eyes and let his head fall back onto the pillow of leaves. It was surreal, being stuck in the middle of nowhere, well, a Cheshire estate – but it might as well be nowhere, in the shadow of an amazing building, hearing the same words his grandfather threw at him on a regular basis.

'In my day nobody dived for cover. Stand up like a man, you lily-livered buffoon.'

Which wasn't quite what he was expecting.

'My estate manager will be sending a bill for any damage.'

Jamie stared up incredulously at the foliage that surrounded him. 'How do you damage a bush?'

'Fences, you fool. I know you didn't walk in through the front gate as a *normal*,' she stressed the word, 'visitor would do. You don't look like you'd be capable of damaging much, though. Far too stringy.' Her eyes narrowed and she peered more closely at him. 'Are you sure you're not on drugs?'

'No I'm bloody not. I could ask you the same. You're the one in wellies and a nightie, walking the dog in the middle of the night.' It was probably better not to mention the gun. 'Nice dog, by the way.' She harrumphed as he edged himself cautiously up onto his elbows, the dog's tail beating a tattoo against the mulch of leaves. 'Not much good at the hunting and killing, though, is it?'

'He's a Labrador, a gundog, trained for picking up game not tracking quarry.' The unspoken 'stupid boy' hung in the air. '*You* are trespassing, young man, so you're fair game.'

'I know.' He shrugged and grinned. 'Would you mind if I got out of this bush?'

'Give me one good reason why I shouldn't shoot you.'

'If you do, you won't find out why I'm here?'

'I said shoot you, not kill you.'

'Ahh. You wouldn't hit a man when he's down, would you?'

'I am more than happy to give you a five-second start, young man.'

9

Jamie was just trying to decide if she was kidding or not, as her face was scarily emotionless, when she seemed to come to a sudden decision and straightened up. 'You don't look like a lunatic. Come up to the house and make me a drink.' She lowered the barrel of the gun. 'And you can explain yourself. Now where's Bertie wandered off to? Damned sure that dog is going senile. Bertie, Bertie, come here you old fool.' Breaking open the gun, she hooked it over her arm. 'Well, come on young man, it's too cold to stand about gawping.' And without looking back, she stomped off out of the trees.

Jamie, plucking twigs from his hair and holding firmly onto his camera, ran after her. He caught up just as she reached the edge of the expanse of lawn.

'Jamie, James Trilling.'

'I'm sure you are.' She didn't even glance his way. 'Bertie, old boy, don't you even think of rolling in that excrement or you'll be sleeping in the stables.'

'Isn't it rather late for you to be out walking him?'

'Couldn't sleep. Overrated if you ask me, all this lying about. Does your mother know where you are?'

Jamie laughed. 'Why, are you going to kill me and bury my body?'

'Don't be ridiculous.' She chuckled, and he joined in. 'That is the gamekeeper's job.'

'Oh. You're kidding?' She didn't reply. 'So you live here?' They were crunching over the gravel that fronted the imposing house, and Jamie slowed his pace and glanced up. 'It's incredible.'

'It is.' Her tone softened, 'and I do. I was born in that wing,' she nodded, 'and now I live,' she paused to push open the large door, then gestured across the hallway, 'in that one.'

Jamie stared. Visiting stately homes as a kid had been part of growing up, but now, standing here in the lived-in version he wondered if he'd cracked his head while climbing over the wall. It couldn't be real. Close up, it was like something out of one of the BBC bonnet-busters that his mum loved to watch. She hated it when he called them that, or told her that the day a woman came out of the lake with a shirt clinging to her chest was the day he'd start watching them.

He supposed he should be used to places like this, just view it as another location, like the rest of the crew would do. But the only locations he'd been sent out to see since starting this job were sink estates that scared the shit out of him (Seb liked 'authentic' and was far more comfortable surrounded by concrete than fields), and deserted stretches of railway track where no doubt somebody would get brutally murdered on film. They gave him the willies, if he was honest, but this was different.

Jamie glanced at his ghostly companion as he followed her in. She couldn't be real. But with a black Labrador at her feet, the shotgun cracked open over her arm and the Hunter wellingtons on her feet, he had to admit that even in her nightie her resemblance to the portrait at the end of the hall was remarkable. 'You're, you're Lady . . .'

'Elizabeth Stanthorpe,' she finished for him, the hint of a smile twitching at her thin lips. 'Who the blazes did you think I was? You may call me Lady Elizabeth. Now, are we having that drink or not? You're not one of those feeble types that doesn't drink are you? No appetite for anything these days, you youngsters, other than fiddling with those egg box things.'

'X-box.'

She waved a dismissive hand. 'Gimmicky what-nots. All that staring at screens and fiddling with knobs. I bet you don't even have time to fiddle with girls. It's not natural.'

'Sorry?'

'Do those lap-dancing clubs still exist? They were very trendy at one time. I blame that Stringfellow chap for a lot of the shenanigans. And there were gentlemen's clubs. That kind of thing was guaranteed to raise the blood pressure. Nowadays there are no wars to fight, no hunting allowed, no sex . . . mark my words the human race will die out if the do-gooders have their way. It's all about being gay now, isn't it?' She pulled a wellington off, then pointed at his feet. 'Shoes off. Not that I have a problem with gay men. It's always gone on, that type of thing. Knew some splendid chaps who did it. But they did their duty and married the gals as well. Heir and a spare and all that.'

'People do still have sex.' Jamie wasn't quite sure where the conversation was heading.

'Jolly good. Bertie do leave those alone, there's a good chap.' The Labrador looked at her with big chocolate eyes, a boot held gently in his jaws, which he very carefully laid back down at his mistress's feet. 'He misses Holmes, don't you old man?' She patted the dog's head and his tail swung a metronome beat as he looked up expectantly.

'Holmes?' Jamie looked around, half expecting a butler to appear.

'Lab. Like peas in a pod the two of them were. Died of old age, dropped like a stone the other week as he ran out after a pheasant, daft old bugger.'

'Ah.'

'Philippa said she expects me to go the same way.' She shook her head and pursed her lips. 'Never chased a pheasant in my life though.'

'Maybe she didn't quite mean . . .'

'I know exactly what she meant. You remind me of her a little.'

He wasn't quite sure if that was a good thing or a bad thing.

'Philippa?'

'Friend of my granddaughter's. Philippa, Pip, bright girl, most entertaining. Gone off to Australia with her surfing chap and I have to say I do miss her company. She's a good girl, but I can't be doing with this sky chatting, not the same as having her here. Darned new-fangled ideas.'

'Sky chatting?' Jamie looked at her blankly. 'Oh, you mean Skype?'

'That's what I said. Do pull your trousers up properly, it's no wonder you haven't got a gal when you go around showing your underwear.'

'I never said . . .' He sighed as she marched across the oak-panelled hallway and pushed a door open. What was the point in wasting his breath? It was like some kind of test, to see what his reaction would be, although he reckoned he must have at least passed the first stage. It was a bit like playing an online game. And he hadn't a clue what her end game was, although he still just about remembered his. Even if things hadn't quite gone to plan.

Chapter 2

Lady Elizabeth Stanthorpe propped the shotgun at the side of her chair and took a proper look at the trespasser. He was more youth than man, and an untidy one at that. When he'd lain under the rhododendrons, his dirty-blond hair a splash of colour against the dark mulch, he'd looked impossibly young and innocent. Which was why she'd invited him in. 'You appear to have been rolling in fox excrement.'

He took a sniff of his jacket and grinned apologetically. 'Sorry.'

'Tomato ketchup.'

'Sorry?'

'Our old housekeeper used to swear by it. To get rid of the smell.' She put her hands in her lap and followed his line of sight.

'Is that thing even licenced?' He was staring at the gun, as though he'd never seen one before. 'Is it safe?'

'Of course it is, young man, it was one of Papa's favourites. He bagged a lot of poachers with this, easier to hit than rabbits, can't move as fast.'

'Isn't it illegal to shoot people?'

'That rather depends.' He was waiting for an explanation and Elizabeth watched him, bemused. He seemed bright, if a little confused, just like Philippa had been when she'd first arrived in Tippermere.

The girl had been a friend of her granddaughter, Charlotte, and the same age, but had soon become a firm favourite of Elizabeth's.

She had a taste for adventure, the spirit of youth. It had been nice to have a youngster around the place who was smart, but still had a streak of mischief. Her inquisitive mind, and a natural leaning towards investigation, had made her an excellent journalist and an entertaining companion. Philippa had been such fun. Unlike most of the people she came across day to day.

'Are you going to pour that drink, young man?'

'Isn't it a bit late?'

'Never too late for a tot of whisky. Keeps you warm at night. So, do I know your mother?'

'I doubt it.' He grinned and reached for the ice tongs, deciding fingers probably weren't the best etiquette.

'Don't you dare!'

Jamie jumped as the commanding tone rang out, making the cut glass sing.

'You are not ruining my best whisky with bloody ice! Which school did you go to, boy?'

* * *

Old ladies, Jamie thought, were supposed to mutter and croak, although maybe that didn't apply to the upper classes. 'Not one of the better ones, obviously.' Waving what he considered the right type of glass and the correct bottle of whisky he got a nod of approval. 'But although I may be a heathen as far as whisky goes, I'm not a rambler.'

'So I gather.'

'Or a druggie or drunkard.'

'But you were on private land so I was perfectly entitled to shoot. You could have been an armed intruder.'

'I'm a scout.'

'Aren't you rather old to enjoy short trousers and middle-aged men?' She raised an elegant eyebrow, the corner of her mouth twitching.

Jamie laughed and took a sip of the shockingly smooth malt whisky. During his train journey he'd had the chance to read a little bit about the Stanthorpes, and in particular about Lady Elizabeth. Eccentric, elegant, impoverished. Matriarchal. But none of the reports had as much as hinted about a sense of humour. 'I'm a location scout.'

'Is that what the less-savoury reporters call themselves these days?'

'God, no. Is that what you thought? I'm nothing to do with the press.'

'They aren't all bad.' Lady Elizabeth frowned. 'Philippa was always very fair in what she reported, but so many seem to be lacking in scruples as well as a grasp of the finer points of the English language.'

'Oh. So, do you get many of that type out here?'

'Only recently.'

'Since the fire?'

She ignored the question. 'And you're not from the insurance company?'

'Nope.' He shook his head.

'That fire has been rather an inconvenience, which is why I wasn't surprised to find another interloper in the grounds. You're not some kind of investigator?'

'No. Honest, nothing like that. So you've not started repairs yet, then?' He'd actually thought it rather odd, when he was taking photographs, that there was absolutely no sign of fire damage. The newspaper reports had talked about a devastating fire, about flames that took the fire brigade several hours to get under control. So he'd assumed that at least some of it must have been fixed pretty quickly, that the Stanthorpes were the type of people who could afford to put things right, even though they might still be willing to take Seb's money. But if they had, why did she think he was from the insurance company?

And yet he hadn't even noticed anything out of the ordinary since they'd arrived at the house. Apart from the very faintest trace of acrid smoke that hung in the entrance hall.

'You do seem to be asking rather a lot of questions if that's the case. But no. Not yet.' She tapped a nail on her glass and Jamie could only guess at how annoyed that meant she was. 'There appears to be a lot of bureaucracy involved.'

He zoomed in the picture on his camera. 'You can't see any damage from outside. I thought it was supposed to be a massive fire.'

'It was bad enough. So what do you know about the fire, James? Is that why you're here?'

She had a pretty piercing gaze for an old lady.

'Jamie, not James. Not even my mother calls me that. Well, yes and no. I mean I'm here because I saw the pictures in the newspaper after the fire. I'd never heard of Tipping House before that, in fact,' he grinned sheepishly, 'I've never even been to Cheshire. But I thought the place looked cool, so, er, I came for a closer look.'

'So you're not one of those developer chaps?' He shook his head. 'Swarming round like flies they were. They smell the rot. I would have quite liked to have taken a pot shot at one or two of them, but Charlotte said she'd hide the key to the gun cabinet if I did.'

'Charlotte?'

'My granddaughter.'

He racked his brain for facts, but he hadn't really been interested in reading the reports – his attention had been grabbed by the pictures. And there hadn't been a memorable picture of any attractive heiress. Maybe she looked like a horse. 'Seems sensible, you know, to stop you shooting at people. So, what happened?'

It didn't really matter as far as the job went, but he was interested. 'Was it arson, like some of the reports said? Are you after a big fat insurance pay-off?'

'Ridiculous idea.' She held her glass out for a refill, so he complied and wondered why she still looked sober as a judge when his world was wobbling at the edges. 'To answer your questions, yes, we had a substantial fire here. Yes, arson is suspected but,' she peered over her glass at him, 'some people seem to think we had a hand in it, which is quite preposterous. And to answer your final question, quite honestly the extent of any insurance pay-out is none of your business, young man.' She stared at the amber liquid. 'Such a shame when the wedding business was beginning to turn a proper profit. Awful mess, damned good job they used to build places properly. The curtains, of course, were ruined. We'd only had them cleaned a couple of years ago. Such a waste. I do hate waste.' She frowned. 'It has been suggested that a disgruntled guest started it, because he had been muttering about jumped-up toffs, but that is nothing new, is it? I do rather suspect there is more to it than that. Bloody developers, no respect.' Her voice had drifted, so maybe the drink was getting to her. Then she put her glass down on the table and fixed him with the type of look that made him feel like a naughty schoolboy, even though he'd never actually been that badly behaved. 'Mark my words, I intend to get to the bottom of it. So,' she sat slightly more upright, if that were possible, 'why were you snooping about in the middle of the night rather than arriving at a more civilised hour?'

'Well I don't usually, er, snoop, in the middle of the night. My train was cancelled.' He'd called Pandora to suggest a re-run the following day and had been told, in no uncertain terms, to make sure he took 'the fucking photos today' – so much for him suspecting she had a nice side. 'I'm working for this film producer and he's on the look out for a location. When I saw this place I thought it looked perfect, so I offered to come over.' He held his

18

camera up. 'Take some shots. I mean, I would normally just knock at the door and ask, but I got lost looking for the place. Then, when I found it, with the gates being shut and everything, I thought it was a bit late to be bothering you. I only needed a few photos of the outside and the grounds.' He shrugged. 'I just thought it would make sense to get on with it. So, I, er, got over the wall and then thought if I got a move on I'd be able to get the last train home, but . . .'

She was frowning. But it had seemed the sensible solution at the time. Now he wasn't so sure. But at least he'd met Lady Stanthorpe. His mum would be impressed, although he'd have to skate over some of the facts. 'It's amazing, the way the light . . .'

'It's dark.'

'Even in the moonlight it's fantastic.'

She didn't look convinced. 'And what are you filming? Some inaccurate historical nonsense? Why you people are too lazy to check your facts confounds me.'

'Dunno exactly, but it's not old-fashioned stuff. All they told me was that they wanted somewhere to shoot the polo bits. You know, that game they play on horses, with sticks.'

'I do know what polo is, young man.'

'They wanted a backdrop like this for it, you know, something posh, impressive.'

'One doesn't play polo in Cheshire in the winter, dear boy.'

'One would,' he grinned, 'want to do a few shots now, and most of the shoot in the spring. Apparently there's more to polo than just the beautiful game.'

'Is there now? One would hardly call it beautiful, although some of the Argentinian players have a certain something about them. My late husband, Charles, used to play when he was abroad. He was rather dashing, I must admit, although all that racing about did take it out of him as he got older. Arthritis is a bugger and I rather feel that the poor ponies suffered as the poor old fool put weight on. So much nicer for them with some slim young

19

man on board. So much nicer for all of us.' She waved her empty glass again, and Jamie wondered if she was pouring it down Bertie, who was now snoring and whimpering, his feet dancing as he chased imaginary rabbits.

'So, you say you will be filming outside?'

'Outside only.'

'And there would be substantial reimbursement?' She tapped her stick on the floor and Bertie leaned more heavily against her. He guessed this was what Elizabeth looked like when under stress. Just a twitch. 'Poor Charlotte does rather needs funds. Bloody insurance people aren't paying out yet. I've always said one was better investing one's money oneself elsewhere.'

'It is all repairable, then?'

'It is, for a price. But until then the business is at something of a stand-still. Brides-to-be are not interested in looking at scorched walls. No imagination, you youngsters, these days.'

'Well, we would pay to film here.'

'I'm not sure Tipping House, or the village of Tippermere for that matter, is ready for a film crew. You would no doubt ruin the lawns and litter the place with pop bottles, chip wrappers and people with loud-hailers.' She stared gimlet-eyed down her long nose.

'No doubt.'

'And you would scare the horses. And you do realise that we can't stop the pheasant shoot or the Boxing Day meet just to humour you?'

'I do. But all that is finished by spring, isn't it?' A Boxing Day meet was surely on Boxing Day? 'It could up your profile.' She stared. 'You know, keep you going while you're waiting for the insurance money?' The lines he'd been fed spilled out of him. She raised an eyebrow. 'Be fun?' He'd strayed from the script, but now he was pretty sure he had her hooked on that one. 'Must be pretty quiet round here. Give me a call. I've got a card . . .' He was reaching into his pocket as he spoke.

She waved a regal hand, dismissing the idea. 'I will do no such thing. You may call me after Christmas and I will decide whether I wish to pursue this matter further. The first Tuesday in the New Year will suit, at 3pm. But I'm not promising anything. I shall raise the matter with Charlotte when the time is right. Although, if I were you I'd keep this quiet, because if my son Dominic gets as much as a whiff of this kind of thing he'll raise the drawbridge.'

'You've got an actual drawbridge?' Jamie was even more impressed.

'A metaphorical one.'

'Ahh. And Dominic has the final say?'

'Certainly not. But he can be quite sniffy at times and he is rather strong-willed when he puts his mind to it.'

'I wonder where he gets that from?' He hadn't thought he'd actually verbalised the words, but it appeared he had.

The corner of her mouth twitched. 'One has to know what one wants. But he is slightly too, what is the word? Conservative for my taste. He is a dressage rider.'

She said it as though it explained everything, which to Jamie it didn't. Knowing very little about horses and absolutely nothing about dressage riders.

'Precise, controlled. The boy sorted all his books alphabetically and his cars into the most orderly of rows when he was a child.' That didn't help much either. 'Re-stabled all the horses one day because they weren't in any kind of size or colour orientation. The head groom was not amused.'

'Ahh.'

'He was very young though. He appears to have grown out of his most faddy tendencies. Too many fancy notions and picky habits aren't good for a boy. Poncey. Not quite sure where he gets it from, his father was nothing like that. If anything upset him he'd go out and shoot.'

'And so Dominic helps you run the place?'

'Oh heavens above, have you not listened to a word I've said?

Dominic is my son, but Charlotte, my granddaughter, runs the estate.'

'Ah, so Charlotte is Dominic's daughter.'

'No.' She shook her head, lips pursed. 'Dominic is Charlotte's uncle.'

'Oh. But shouldn't he . . .'

'The Stanthorpes have never liked to stick to the normal order of things; we do things our own way. Tipping House is never passed to a male heir, it is inherited by the eldest female and sadly Charlotte's mother, my daughter Alexandra, died in rather unfortunate circumstances. One day all this will be Charlotte's. You really do need to do your homework, young man.'

Jamie frowned. He'd thought taking a few pictures and selling the idea to Seb was all he needed to do. But it appeared not. The longer he was here though, the more he realised it wasn't just that he needed this job; he actually wanted it. He wanted to peep into the life of Lady Elizabeth Stanthorpe. To make her smile.

'And so Charlotte is in charge?'

'I rather think I am in charge.' Her tone was dry, but there were the crinkle lines of laughter around her eyes again. 'But she is responsible for running the estate and raising the necessary funds.'

'She's the one who set up the business here, as a wedding venue, isn't she?' Elizabeth nodded. 'And one of the punters started the blaze, so she's knackered.'

'Knackered is a word I'd reserve for an altogether different usage, young man, but she is in rather a predicament. Most of the bookings were over the summer months, so very few had to be cancelled. But she should now be taking bookings for the spring after next, and how can she? These young girls look around and want everything to be perfect, and that is not going to be achievable for quite some time.' She sniffed. 'These insurance investigators are quite tiresome. And without the income one is very much back to square one.'

'Even if you get it fixed up?'

'A place like this costs a fortune to maintain and that is something that, sadly, we don't have. That young fool of a bank manager is already starting to twitch, silly boy. But I'm sure things will sort themselves out, although I might well shoot the next person who arrives with a buy-out plan.'

'Why not just sell the place?'

'Sell?' She raised both eyebrows. 'Don't be ridiculous. Over my dead body. If they think they can turn this village into a safari park or giant amusement arcade they have another thing coming. The Marquis of Bath and that Aspinall chap have a lot to answer for, putting ridiculous ideas into people's heads. You will never see a pride of lions here during my lifetime. Utter tosh and nonsense. Right, I'm sure it's past your bedtime. Your push bicycle is by the front door.'

'Push . . .?'

'The police called in to say they'd seen it propped against the south wall,' she raised an eyebrow and he tried not to smile. 'Some chap saw you climb over, but they knew better than to follow you. More than one policeman has been peppered with shot on this estate. By accident, of course, mistaken identity and all that. One of the gamekeepers went to collect it while I brought Bertie to sniff you out.'

'You knew I was there? You didn't find me by accident?'

'What do you think I am? This estate stretches for miles, and I can't see in the dark at my age, can I?'

'I suppose not.'

'Be careful on the bicycle, you look a bit tipsy. Unlikely to meet any traffic but the ditches can be hazardous I'm told.' She stood up. 'Can't have you killed just before Christmas can we? Your mother would never forgive us. Oh, and watch out for ghosts and wolves.' And he was pretty sure that it was the whisky that made him think she'd winked.

Chapter 3

'Faster Worwy, faster, faster.'

Charlotte 'Lottie' Steel jumped as the unexpected shrill scream echoed down the hallway and her needle came unthreaded, and disappeared between the floorboards. 'Bugger.'

She shut one eye and peered down the crack, wishing that they could afford to send the horse rugs to the local saddlery for mending. Impoverished landowners might be expected to make do and mend (and she definitely was impoverished), but sewing was really not her thing. She just wasn't very good at it. She was much better at whitewashing the stables, if she was honest, and at least then she'd not be using her fingers as pin cushions.

In fact whitewashing, and mending fences, were the type of thing she'd spent most of her time doing before she'd discovered that one day she would inherit Tipping House – and in the meantime was expected to manage the day-to-day running of the estate, and remove as much of the responsibility as she could from her elderly grandmother. Not that Elizabeth considered herself either elderly or in need of assistance. It was rather Lottie who thought she needed help, especially since her wedding business had gone up in smoke, leaving them once again struggling to make ends meet.

But it was hard to imagine now that she'd ever thought she could belong anywhere else. When she was a child she'd always imagined that one day she'd follow in her father, Billy Brinkley's, footsteps and enter the world of show-jumping (or at least groom his horses and be the one that educated the youngsters), and then when she'd moved in with Rory she'd imagined herself supporting his eventing career and chasing off his female fans, and the very last thing that had ever crossed her mind was that she would instead live a life rather more along the lines of her aristocratic grandmother Lady Elizabeth and her Uncle Dominic. Although whilst it all sounded rather grand, the reality was anything but. And at times she quite honestly found it hard to believe she was related to them, even if she did feel she would die rather than give up her beautiful, but demanding, inheritance.

Whitewashing and mucking out stables, she decided, came to her much more naturally than balancing spreadsheets and sewing.

'Giddy up, horsey.'

A shrill whinny stopped her short and she forgot all about needles.

Her husband, Rory, could often be seen cantering around Tipping House with their goddaughter, little Roxy, riding on his shoulders, but he couldn't whinny like that. That sounded far too authentic. Lottie scrambled across the room on all-fours and leaned out of the doorway.

It was indeed a horsey, or rather a very fat Shetland pony, coming down the hallway.

'No Woxy, I mean Roxy. Oh for heaven's sake!' Lottie exclaimed. For a moment one of the portraits swung on the wall as the excited child caught it with a flailing arm before it came to a rest at a rather jaunty angle. 'Stop, stop. Rory, stop before Great Uncle Albert falls off the wall.'

Rory stopped. The pony didn't. It ambled on past him, reached the end of the lead rope and ground to a halt a couple of feet short of Lottie. Stretching its stubby neck out, it peered down at her through long-lashed brown eyes before snorting and showering both her and the hall rug with spittle. Roxy, who was perched like a cherry on a cake, lurched in the saddle, then giggled.

'Lot-tie.' Her blond curls trembled as she waved her hands in the air in an enthusiastic greeting and she bounced on the saddle. 'Look at me, look at me, me and Alice have got weal horseys and I'm in my best pwincess dwess. Look, look.' But Lottie wasn't looking at her. She was staring at her devastatingly dishy husband and trying to keep the cross look fixed on her face.

Rory. Gorgeous, fit Rory. Clad in the tightest of breeches and sloppy polo shirt, despite the cold winter air. He tipped his head to one side and grinned, his tawny-brown eyes alive with mischief. 'What are you doing down there, darling?'

Rory Steel loved the children, the children loved him, and as his best horses had been turned out for a rest and the ground was far too hard for jumping, he'd been glad of the diversion that a bit of baby-sitting offered. And he also loved his scatty but occasionally bossy wife, Lottie. In fact, when her assertive side emerged he found her totally impossible to resist, as that glint in her eye worked wonders for his libido. Not that he ever had a problem that way.

Rory and Lottie were widely accepted as the dishiest, and possibly the nicest, couple in Tippermere. Where Rory was lean and hard, Lottie was no size zero, but possessed rather unfashionable curves. As a teenager she'd been as leggy as a yearling, but she'd matured into a statuesque (she thought fat) woman, who appealed to the old and young men of Tippermere alike. Her gorgeous thick hair gave her a 'just out of bed' look that was irresistible, and her enormous green eyes and generous mouth made her as huggable as she was desirable.

'Rug-mending. It's not going too well though.' She stared at the row of haphazard stitches.

Rory also found her home-making activities quite attractive

too. Well, all in all, the longer they'd been married the more he'd fallen in love with the girl.

Lottie gazed up at him and couldn't stay cross. She never could with Rory, well, not unless he'd been really, really bad. Like the time he'd turned up with a string of horses and organised a jump-off at her father's wedding, in the marquee, before the cake had been cut.

She fought the smile that was threatening to break out. It had been typical Rory – mad, fun and had signalled the end of the wedding cake. When his horse had landed on it.

Then there had been the episode on the day she'd launched her wedding fayre business. He'd done a runner – and then turned up and proposed like some dashing and romantic knight.

'I'm not sure you should bring them in the house, even if they are small.'

'You're no trouble, are you girls?' He winked at Roxy, who giggled.

Lottie sighed. 'I meant the ponies not the girls.'

She had been finding it strangely therapeutic, sat on the floor sewing (even if she wasn't very good at it). Except when the needle came unthreaded. That was annoying. But maybe leaning out of the doorway was a mistake, with a pony on the loose. 'Hang on.' She clambered to her feet, the horse blanket falling off her knee, and Tilly the terrier, who'd been chewing the end of it, let go and with an excited yap launched herself down the long hallway straight at Rory. Who, forgetting the job in hand, let go of the lead rope and caught the little dog. The shaggy pony, sensing freedom, did a swift U-turn and headed for the nearest open doorway.

'Look, Lottie, I'm widing, I'm widing Woopert all by myself.' Roxy grinned, forgot about hanging on to the saddle or the reins and clapped her hands excitedly. 'Take a picture, picture for Mummy.'

'Crumbs.' Right now Lottie wasn't interested in capturing the moment for prosperity, she was more bothered about damage limitation. Sliding in her socks on the polished floorboards, she skidded after her goddaughter, grabbing the lead rope just as the round-barrelled pony opened its mouth to take a bite out of the flower display. The pony retaliated with a loud burst of wind (it could have been worse, Lottie decided, much worse) and Roxy giggled.

'Is that a new fashion statement, darling? And on the catwalk today we have Lottie in green breeches with purple horse blanket artistically attached.' Rory had wandered in to the room after them and was now leaning against the pony, one arm around Roxy, looking thoroughly amused.

'What?' Lottie glanced down, confused. 'Oh bugger.' She was towing the blanket with her. She'd been concentrating so hard on neat stitches that she appeared to have sewn right through the blanket and her breeches. And she also appeared to be towing a terrier.

Tilly, spotting a moving object, had forgotten all about her master, Rory, and had taken chase. She now had her teeth firmly attached to the end of the blanket that had been trailing on the floor.

'Should we put Rupert back, Auntie Lottie?' The softly spoken, but perfectly enunciated, words drifted through the chaos and Lottie looked up to see her little cousin Alice (though she thought of her more as a niece, due to the age difference) standing in the open doorway, her dark hair drawn back into a perfect sleek ponytail, a very solemn look pasted across her pretty features.

Although only a few months separated Alice and Roxy, they were as different as night and day. Roxy was a born giggler, the spitting image of her own mother, the gloriously over-the-top Samantha Simcock, with a dash of her energetic footballing father thrown in, but Alice saw life in a far more serious light.

The polite and shyly pretty Alice was the perfect blend of her parents – Dominic Stanthorpe, Lottie's uncle, who was precise and perfect in everything he did, and his wife, Amanda, who had always been poised and beautiful. Except when she was pregnant. Now, that, Lottie thought, should have been enough to put anybody off ever starting a family. Except poor Amanda had decided to put herself through the ordeal again and was currently back at the puking stage. Which was why Lottie had offered to look after Alice for the afternoon. Which meant she couldn't say no when Sam had asked if Roxy could join in the fun, could she?

But what had ever made her think asking Rory to assist had been a good idea?

Except he was great with kids. They loved him. In fact, she thought with a pang of guilt, he'd make a perfect father. How on earth could she ever think about having a family of their own though, when they were penniless and they lived a life of chaos, dashing between horse shows and trying to come up with schemes to keep food on the table?

'Auntie Lottie?'

Sometimes, Lottie thought, the three-year-old Alice was more mature than the adults in this place.

'That's a brilliant idea, Alice.'

'Rubbish, we've only just started.' Rory gathered the terrier into his arms and grinned. 'Do you want unstitching?'

The pony, realising that Lottie's concentration was elsewhere, nudged the vase with its stubby little nose and Roxy giggled as it rocked from side to side. Lottie put a steadying hand out and was glad that most of the stuff in their wing of Tipping House was actually either from Rory's old cottage, or rubbish. Her life really wasn't compatible with priceless antiques.

Whilst she absolutely adored her inherited home and could never, ever imagine leaving it, sometimes she thought that life back at Mere Lodge had been so much safer. At Tipping House you never quite knew what disaster was going to befall you next.

It was hard to be dignified, but Lottie was going to do her best in front of the children. Not that she really wanted them to think this was normal. 'I'm not sure you should have ponies in the house, darling.'

'Old Lizzie said we could,' Rory said with a wink.

'Shhh. Don't call her Lizzie.' Lottie lived in dread of the day when her grandmother, Lady Elizabeth Stanthorpe, overheard the diminutive of her name and planned revenge. 'Or old. You know she hates it. And I'm sure she didn't say you could.'

'Oh come on, don't be a spoilsport. It's common knowledge that your mother used to ride her pony in here.'

'That's different. We've got somebody coming to look at the place. What if it smells of horse poo?'

'Woopert poo, Woopert poo.'

Lottie ignored the little girl, who was now bouncing up and down in the saddle and no doubt increasing the chances of 'Rupert poo'.

'The last lot who came to look round said it smelled doggy.' Lottie felt herself redden at the memory of the very haughty young bride-to-be standing in their magnificent hallway with her nose in the air proclaiming that it was old and smelly and not at all what she'd expected. 'It doesn't, does it?' She sniffed as though to check.

That was the trouble these days. Since the fire, the once-imposing Great Hall had been out of bounds as it smelled strongly of smoke, charred wood and whatever the firemen had used to douse the flames. So, potential customers had to visit the Steel's own private wing of the house to discuss wedding bookings, which wasn't quite as clean and tidy as it might have been. Or as sweetly scented. However many bowls of potpourri she distributed. She really should ask the manufacturers of Glade for sponsorship, considering the amount of their products she'd distributed around Tipping House.

But she was fighting a losing battle. Horse rugs seemed to find their way up from the stable yard, because it was far too cold to repair them down there, scattering loose hair and horsey smells as the heat permeated the grease and sweat-imbued fabric. She had to admit, she loved the smell of horses and hay, but she fully accepted that it probably wasn't what a bride-to-be was looking for on her special day. And that was the problem. Lottie had built up a business selling dreams, wedding dreams. The glossy brochure promised perfection and the numerous articles in *Cheshire Life* and *Tatler* portrayed a sanitised version of life in the countryside and the old creaking mansion. When a bride-to-be came to Tipping House Estate she was buying a fairy tale not the rather less-inspiring reality.

Lottie sighed. Real life included the dirty boots that were kicked off everywhere but the boot room, the bits of damp leather that were sponged down, soaped and oiled as they sat by the fire in the evening, spreading a rather unique odour, plus the assortment of gifts that the dogs brought in with them. Some dead, some alive, and some unmentionable.

She chewed the inside of her cheek. Taking bookings for the following spring was all well and good, but would they ever have the money to repair the damage? And what was supposed to happen in the meantime? They'd all but used up the small nest egg she'd accumulated since establishing the business three years previously. The fire had been such awful timing, and her rather naïve assumption that she'd fill in one form and the insurance company would hand over a very large cheque had proved just that. Naïve.

'It doesn't smell to me.' Rory kissed his wife on the nose and took the lead rope from her hand. 'You worry too much.' He backed the pony up so that it was no longer straddling the rug. 'And anyway they aren't coming, Lots, they rang and cancelled this morning.'

'They cancelled?' She looked at him aghast, her throat tightening with disappointment. 'Oh no, not another one. Why didn't you tell me?'

'Sorry, darling, forgot. They said something about wanting it to be perfect, but really needing to see the place as it was actually going to be, and muttered some tosh about what if it wasn't ready in time. All the usual guff. Would have told you earlier but one of the horses had barged through the electric fencing again. That horse must have a hide like a rhino, or he just likes the buzz.'

'Oh damn and blast, what are we going to do, Rory?' She felt like wailing, but knew there was absolutely no point in collapsing into a pathetic heap. Off the top of her head she had no idea how many appointments had been cancelled, but it was a lot. Too many. The diary was a mass of red crossings out and was beginning to look more like a patchwork quilt than a sign of their success. At this rate, by the time they had the place refurbished and ready to go there would be no business left. They'd have to start from scratch again.

She had long ago accepted that the coming summer was a write-off and belts would need to be tightened (not that a stable full of horses understood that concept), but had been banking on a healthy number of bookings for the following year.

'This year is going to be hard enough,' she chewed the side of her fingernail, 'but we're completely screwed, sorry, messed up,' she glanced up at the children guiltily to check if they were listening, 'if we've not got anything definite for next year. I was counting on a full diary from April to September. What am I going to do, Rory?'

'Cheer up. We'll think of something, darling.'

'We'll fail. Gran will never forgive me. I've let her down.'

'Lottie.' Rory, noting the dejected tone looked down at her fondly. Although she could come across as totally scatty and disorganised, he'd discovered over the last few years just how strong and determined his wife was, and it was slightly worrying that after keeping her chin up and fighting back since the fire, she was now looking slightly beaten. 'You've never let anybody down. You took this place on and got the business going and you

32

know how proud Elizabeth is of you. We all are. Me especially. You can do this. We can do it. Together.'

'But what—'

'Are we putting them back, Uncle Rory? My pony doesn't like it on his own outside.'

Lottie had all but forgotten little Alice, who was still at the doorway waiting patiently. Just like her mother, Amanda, would have been.

'Your pony?' Lottie suddenly noticed that the little girl was clutching a rope firmly with both hands. '*Your* pony doesn't like being on his own?' She looked at Rory. 'You mean there are two? Where have all these ponies come from?'

'Lady Lizbet bought them.' Roxy bounced a bit more. 'I love Lady Lizbet, I love Lady Lizbet.' She bobbed up and down, and then stopped and grinned. 'I'm going to be her when I gwow up.'

Rory nodded confirmation. 'Late Christmas present. She thought it was time Alice started to ride, said she didn't want her behaving like her mother did around horses.'

'And didn't Amanda and Uncle Dom mind?' Lottie knew only too well how hard Amanda had tried to share Dom's love of horses, and that she had been totally relieved when he'd said it didn't matter. Lottie had never, ever, seen anybody look as petrified sat astride a horse as Amanda had been.

Rory shrugged. 'Not a clue. And she bought Roxy one too. Said it was only fair.'

'Mine's called Woopert and Alice has got Bilbo. He's black. Mine is owange.' Supplied Roxy helpfully.

Lottie stared at the pony. 'We call it chestnut, Roxy.' And then at the grinning Rory. 'And what does Sam say?'

'Wow, isn't it amazing, babe? How awesome is that? My little princess riding and everything, just like a real lady.' Rory clapped his hands together and grinned as he completed what Lottie had to admit was quite a good impersonation of Samantha.

'Mummy says I can go to Lympi next year and I'm going to

be a pumpkin.' Roxy tugged experimentally on one rein. 'Can you make me into a pumpkin Lottie? You can do sewing stuff and Mummy doesn't cos it hurts her nails.' Her face was solemn. 'I can be owange then like Woopert. I've got lots of days to pwactise.'

'Chestnut.' Lottie corrected automatically.

'She means Olympia Horse Show. She's been watching YouTube videos of the fancy-dress parade.'

'Doesn't she mean a plum pudding then? You don't see pumpkins at Christmas really, do you?' She leaned in closer to Rory and lowered her voice so the girls couldn't hear. 'Wouldn't it have been better to have given owange Woopert to Alice and let Roxy have black Bilbo? She can say her Bs.'

'Your grandmother specifically said they were to be this way round.'

'I bet she did.'

'Said something about speech impediments should not stand in the way of life decisions.'

Lottie rolled her eyes.

'What colour are plum puddings, Worwy?'

Rory never got chance to answer as a squeal of delight, and clapping of hands, had everybody turning round, apart from the pony.

'Oh my God, oh wow, aren't they just gorge? How adorable is that cute little horse?' Rushing in on her high heels, bracelets jangling, Samantha Simcock blew a kiss in Rory's direction then wrapped her arms around Lottie, engulfing her in a waft of very expensive perfume, which contrasted alarmingly with Lottie's own eau-de-horse. In fact the two girls appeared polar opposites in every visible way. Where Lottie had curves, Sam was model-slim (with the exception of her very expensive boobs), her complexion was as perfectly made-up and blemish-free as a touched-up photo of a model, her clothes the height of fashion and her blue eyes as clear as a baby's. But appearances could be deceptive and Sam was as down to earth and honest as they came, and more – like Lottie – strong willed and determined than she looked.

When Sam and her husband, England goalkeeper David Simcock, had moved into the neighbouring (and very upmarket) village of Kitterly Heath she had, for a very brief time, been lonely, but with her extrovert personality and natural warmth it hadn't taken her long to make friends.

In Tippermere she should have been a fish out of water, but she wasn't. Everybody warmed to Sam; she was non-judgemental and generous to a fault, which more than compensated for the fact that her view of life in the country was slightly unusual, to say the least. Sam's dog, Scruffy, was the only dog in the village to sport a diamante collar; she was the only girl who had ever turned up at a Boxing Day meet in six-inch heels, and she flatly refused to get on a horse on the grounds that a fall might have a devastating effect on her boob implants.

Sam had hung on to her bling and embraced the countryside in her own way – complete with high heels, hair extensions, weekly manicure and Botox.

Lottie loved every outrageous inch of her friend and couldn't imagine life without her.

'How are you doing, babe? You and Rory are just so sweet looking after little Roxy for me. Aww, come on Alice honey, don't stand in the doorway all shy. You get your little horse as well, sweetie pie, and I can take a picture of you both together. Her Ladyship is so fab, isn't she? Oh Daddy will be so proud. Our own little princess on a horse, just like the royal family and Jordan, you know, whatchamacallher, Katie.'

Lottie wasn't too sure that the Windsors would want to be wrapped up in the same sentence as an ex glamour model, nor was she sure that her gran was 'fab'.

'Maybe it would be better if we all went outside?'

'It's a bit nippy out there, babe. Did you know you've got a blanket thing dangling from you?' The stage whisper carried clearly across the room.

Lottie gave the blanket an experimental tug, wondering if ripping it off would work or whether she needed scissors. 'They're ponies. They're supposed to be outside. That's why they've got fur coats.' Lottie looked pointedly from Sam's fur to the ponies and back again. 'And the light's much better if you want to take a photo. It's so gloomy in here in the winter.'

'Aww aren't you clever? Here you are, babe. I've got some nail scissors in my bag somewhere.' She rifled through the contents of her very large tote, eventually coming up trumps. 'Come on girls.'

'Do you think we should wash him?' Alice was staring at her Shetland pony, who was waiting patiently behind her in the hallway, and was looking as genuinely concerned as her mother often did when faced with a cushion that needed plumping up. Lottie had never met a child quite like her (although she was the first to admit she was no expert where children were concerned), but found her much easier to handle than Roxy, who at three years old was already as huggable as Sam was, but twice as energetic. Rory loved her.

'I think you could brush him later.' Lottie gave Alice a hug. 'But he might turn into an icicle if we get him all wet now. Here you are, let me lift you up.' Once in the saddle, Alice was as still, upright and elegant as her dressage rider father, unlike Roxy, who was bouncing about like one of the terriers.

'Mummy, Mummy can we paint Woopert's nails so they look like mine?'

It was only then that Lottie noticed Roxy's teeny tiny nails were sparkling like diamonds. In fact they could be diamonds, knowing Sam.

'Course we can, babe, can't we Lottie? He will look so cute with pretty feet.'

'They're not real diamonds, are they?' Lottie hoped she didn't sound as horrified as she felt.

'Don't be daft, hun.' Sam giggled, a carbon copy of Roxy's. She lowered her voice and leaned in conspiratorially. 'Don't tell her but they're diamante, like Scruffy's collar, but she thinks they're the real deal.' Her voice lifted. 'Cos she's my little princess, aren't you, babe?'

'And Woopert is my pwince.' Roxy for once sounded serious, then grinned.

'It might come off quite quickly in the field.' Lottie dreaded what Uncle Dom, or her gran, would say, if they spotted a diamond-encrusted pony in the paddock.

Samantha frowned, then just as quickly smiled. 'Well we can get him a nice sparkly harness thing for his head can't we? Like Scruffy's collar. I mean he's got to look handsome when we go to Olympia and ride in front of all those people, hasn't he?'

'I don't think . . .' Lottie didn't know quite how to put this.

'We are going aren't we, babe? Dave will be so proud, just like Wembley and him playing for England. When he played in the World Cup I was so proud of him, and he'll be just as chuffed to see his little princess on her horse, won't he, babe?'

'It's not that easy. Roxy has only just started riding, and,' Lottie floundered, looking at Rory for help, wondering just how to explain that the three-year-old might not quite be ready to star at an international horse show. Whereas she often had doubts, Sam had none. She was an unstoppable force, totally confident of her own ability to conquer the world.

'Bit of a challenge for next year, Sam. Have to see how it goes, won't we girls?' Rory supplied.

Sam gave him a hug. 'Oh, you're so sensible and clever, isn't he, Lots?' She kissed him. 'The best godfather in the world, isn't he Roxy, babe?' She giggled. 'The godfather, oh that sounds bad, doesn't it? Aww and it's so nice of you to bring the horses inside. I mean it's parky out, freeze the balls off a . . .' She put a hand over her mouth and laughed again. 'Listen to me, and in front of the kiddies.'

'The horses aren't supposed to come in the house.' Lottie frowned in Rory's direction.

'Aren't they babe? Well, why?'

'Worwy said Lady Lizbet would let us.' Roxy was now fed up of sitting on the motionless pony and spotting a way back onto centre stage went for it. 'Catch me.' And before anybody could stop her, she'd flung her leg over the pony's withers and launched herself in her mother's direction.

'Isn't she priceless? Bless.' Sam kissed her daughter on the head. 'Shall we take your little pony back to his bed, then?'

'And then go shopping for nice sparkly things for him to wear?'

Sam, who could never say no to a good shopping trip, especially one that included anything that sparkled, grinned. 'Course we can, princess.'

Lottie was pretty sure that it was impossible to buy a diamante bridle in Shetland pony size, and totally impossible to buy anything horsey with diamonds on. Pretty sure. But then she'd never seen a shaggy mongrel wearing a diamond-encrusted collar and an Armani jumper until Sam had rehomed Scruffy. Oh, what would the dogs' home think of him if they could see him now?

'Come on.' Roxy tugged experimentally on the reins and the pony turned his head the other way. 'Naughty horsey.' Sam might be blond, busty and blingy (in her own words) but she was also 'bloody determined' when it suited her, and Roxy, it seemed, had inherited her mother's genes by the bucket load. Heading round to the other side, she pushed.

Rupert sighed, then yawned, showing a good set of teeth, and shook his head and neck with such vigour that he showered Roxy with what Lottie hoped was shavings, and not as she suspected, dried flakes of mud and poo. Then he rested a back leg as though to demonstrate his complete lack of interest.

Roxy waved a finger. 'I'm vewy disappointed in you.' Lottie tried to keep a straight face, but one glance in Sam's direction and she knew she couldn't keep it up. Rupert the pony, sensing that his fun might be over, didn't want to leave the party. 'Uncle Worwy, make him move.'

'Has your mummy never told you that boys don't like bossy girls?'

'Mummy tells Daddy she'll,' she grimaced, concentrating, 'make him beg for more and he likes that. It makes him do his big smile.'

'Roxanne!'

Lottie and Rory, who had never heard Sam call her daughter by her full name, tried to avoid looking at each other.

'When did you hear that?'

'When you played horsey in your bedwoom. Now I'm playing horsey widing too.'

'Rory maybe you should make him move?' Lottie didn't dare wait to hear what Roxy might come out with next.

The thing was, Rupert didn't want to move. Not even with Rory pulling, Lottie and Roxy pushing, and Sam waving the bowl of sugar lumps in front of his nose.

'Hang on.' Lottie was out of breath. 'Idea.' She held a hand up. They all waited until she could speak. 'Backwards.'

And so Rupert departed Tipping House in reverse. He very nearly got stuck in the doorway when he sped up, taking Sam with him, and nearly made her the filling in a sandwich between his hairy bulk and the door jamb, but pretty soon he was surprised to find himself at the top of the stone steps.

'Don't bring him in again, Rory. Please,' Lottie begged, hoping she didn't sound a complete spoilsport.

But Rory was too busy putting Roxy back in the saddle to hear. 'Ready to go, Alice?'

Alice who had been watching the proceedings with interest, nodded. 'I don't think he liked going backwards,' she said solemnly. 'Once he started he couldn't stop.'

'Like the wheels on the bus,' added Rory with a nod. 'All day long.' And broke into song.

'Aww bless, isn't he good with the kids? I can't wait for you two to have your own.' Sam winked at Lottie. 'And you'd make an ace mum. I mean you've had all that practice with foals and puppies and stuff.' She paused. 'I mean I know it's not my business, babe, but if you've got problems with your tubes I know this doctor.'

Lottie shook her head.

'You've got this lovely big house, you could fill it with kids and hardly notice.'

Lottie thought she probably would notice, even one little teeny tiny baby. After a particularly drunken night at the pub Sam had shown her all her baby pictures of Roxy, every last one of her through the blooming stage of her pregnancy, and most of the in-labour ones, and she'd thought Lottie was kidding when she said that quite frankly she'd rather have a puppy.

'He would make a lovely daddy, though, wouldn't he?'

'He would.' Lottie agreed, which rather took Sam by surprise. But, as she watched the trio of the man she loved and the two little girls make their way to the stables all singing about the wheels on the bus at the top of their voices (well, Alice's was slightly muted) she suddenly felt a pang. Would she ever make a good mother?

It wasn't just Sam who'd dropped heavy hints to Lottie about starting a family, these days it seemed to be on everybody's mind. In fact she'd started to feel like it was expected, her duty, and if she wasn't waving an ultrasound scan from the flag-post soon she'd be letting the side down. Even Rory had joined in and that was truly the worst part. She wanted to be there for him, to give him whatever he wanted, support him as he supported her in the running of the estate. But the mere thought of having a baby made her palms go clammier than when she was faced with a bucking youngster and a three-foot hedge.

So she'd said the same to her husband as she had to everybody else. They didn't have enough money to feed another family member. Right now, it was all hands to the pump doing the work with the horses themselves. Paying a groom was completely out of the question, so for now the only help was Tab, who worked in exchange for lessons and a horse to compete. She couldn't afford to have her feet up playing the pregnant mother. Not yet.

Lottie sighed and clutched the horse blanket to her. The part that really scared her wasn't being short of money, it was what she'd say when they'd got their lives back on track. Would the man she loved still want her when she admitted that she was prepared to do almost anything except bear his child?

Chapter 4

'It's for charity, love,' said Mrs Jones, admiring Mr August for a lot longer than Lottie thought necessary. 'Oh my, would you look at Mr July? His helmet's hardly big enough to cover his meat and two veg.'

Lottie cringed at the rush of middle-aged hormones the normally restrained shopkeeper was displaying as she waggled the calendar around. 'There's something about a fireman, isn't there, love? I wouldn't mind being rescued by Mr February and look at the way he's cuddling that puppy. I don't know which is more adorable.' She shoved the calendar under Lottie's nose. 'Maybe we need a hot horseman one. What do you think, dear? Your Rory and that lovely Mick. People would pay to see them with only their riding hats and boots on now, wouldn't they?' She frowned. 'And your dad. Although a lot of people have seen him in his undies already.'

She said it kindly, but Lottie still blushed. It was years, no, decades, since her father, Billy Brinkley, had appeared in the tabloids, but everybody remembered. And brought it up regularly. Even the village gossips. Although she supposed they were a similar age to him. Really, they were all old enough to know better.

'Sorry, love. But your old man was quite a pin up in his day.' Mrs Jones sighed and Lottie fidgeted, hoping that was the end of the conversation. 'And he was such a naughty boy, just like your Rory. Must be something to do with all that fresh air and horses, eh?' She winked. 'Your mother had her hands full, I can tell you.'

Please let the ground swallow me up, thought Lottie. Instead the tring of the little bell above the door announced another customer. Bugger, if she wasn't careful there would be a full-scale debate about what made a horseman hunky and whether Billy was still up for a full frontal for charity.

'Are you sure I can't tempt you, dear? It is for charity and it is the start of the New Year tomorrow. Where does the time go? So it's your last chance. You wouldn't want to miss a single day of Mr January would you?'

'Just the er, pint of milk and, er, yes, okay one of these.' She grabbed the calendar. 'For charity, of course.' Maybe if she took it with her that would be the end of it, and after all that the fire brigade had done for her, the least she could do was show some support. If they hadn't been on the scene within minutes of the blaze being spotted, the whole of Tipping House (and guests) could have been barbecued, not just the main entertaining rooms.

'Hang on, hold your horses, love, is that the last one?'

She hadn't moved fast enough. The booming gruff tone was instantly recognisable. Her father.

Lottie glanced up and he was standing there, large as life, in his boots and breeches, blue eyes twinkling. His thinning sandy curls were damp against his head from the riding hat that he'd just taken off (which luckily meant his horse must be tied up outside, so he wouldn't be there for long) and his arms were folded over his rather stout frame.

'I hope you're not planning on pinning that up in the bedroom to give the lad some competition.' He guffawed.

Mrs Jones joined in. 'You're a card, Billy. We were just talking

43

about you, weren't we? Those were the days when I couldn't put the newspapers out on a Sunday morning without seeing your body.'

'Dad!' Lottie felt vaguely nauseous. The conversation about her father's naked butt (and, yes, it would get onto that if she hung around) was bad enough. I mean, who wants to even acknowledge their parents have bodies, let alone ones that have been lusted over by the nation? But for him to even hint at anything going on in her own marital bedroom was just plain weird. Cringe-worthy.

Mrs Jones obviously thought it was hilarious though.

'I'm only getting it because it's for charity,' Lottie protested.

'Yes, well you can stop looking, love. Come on,' he waved a hand, 'give it here. I need that if it's the last one.'

She found she was gripping it more tightly than she'd expected when he tried to take it. 'What do YOU want with naked firemen?'

'It's a surprise for Tiggy.'

Oh God, now he was dragging her step-mum and their relationship into this. 'Here.' She shoved it at him. 'Don't say another word.'

'After a younger man is she, Bill?' There was what sounded suspiciously like a girly giggle from Mrs Jones, who appeared to be flirting outrageously as she leant her elbows on the counter, displaying an ample cleavage. 'Always a place in my bed for you if you need it, my darling.'

'No, no, no.' Lottie put her hands over her ears and hummed.

'Tigs took a shine to Mr February. She said she's thinking of doing a bit of painting again and I haven't got the time to pose for her, have I now, Molly?' Billy winked at Mrs Jones, then looked back to his daughter, who was studying the bars of chocolate avidly. 'Want me to buy you some sparklers while I'm here, love?'

Lottie looked at him, startled. Was that some kind of euphemism? Did he think her and Rory's love life needed a boost? Was

Sam now responsible for the corner shop stocking vajazzle kits as well as superior fake tan?

'We always had them when you were a kid. Thought the sprogs would want some.' She looked at him blankly. 'Sparklers for little Alice and Roxy? Fireworks? To see the New Year in with, Lottie. I know Rory's stocked up with more fireworks than they've got on the Thames, but a few of these never go amiss, do they?' He tapped the packet she hadn't spotted on the counter. 'I'm sure young Roxy could put a few to good use.'

'Oh God, yes, of course, thanks, got to go. Happy New Year.' She grabbed both packets of sparklers that Mrs Jones was now holding out, made a lunge for the pint of milk and was out of the shop faster than a starter at Aintree.

Her father's guffaws echoed round the shop as the door slammed shut behind her, and if it hadn't been for Harry's whine of surprise she would have forgotten all about the spaniel and left him still tied to the hook under the window.

'Cripes, Harry, they go sex mad after a certain age.' She would have actually quite liked to have had a closer look at the fireman's calendar, but no way was she ever going to mention it again. To anybody. 'Come on, Harry, we're off to Sam's to talk about something sensible like acrylic nails and boob jobs, and pick up the nibbles for tonight.'

* * *

'Have you seen that naked fireman's calendar that they've got in the corner shop, babe? That Mrs Jones was showing me this afternoon; said they were selling like hot cakes before Christmas. If I hadn't got my Davey I'd be after Mr October, I can tell you.' Sam pulled her leather jacket more firmly round her. 'He'd warm me up. Cold enough to freeze the brass bits off a monkey out here, isn't it, babe?' She chuckled. 'Nothing like a fireman's lift and an ogle at his hose to get you glowing.'

'Sam!' Lottie glanced over in Roxy's direction, but the little girl was too busy to hear. She was whispering into Alice's ear, no doubt trying to get her to collaborate in mischief.

'Aww bless, don't they look cute together? Roxy with them blond curls and Alice all dark and neat like Mandy. Where is Mand?' She looked round. 'She dashed off just after we got here.'

'Loo.'

'Throwing up again? She's spent more time with her head down the bog this time than she did when she was carrying little Roxy. Poor thing. Would put me off being preggers if it made me like that. I told Davey we should have at least two more, though, and I know he wants a little boy, though he says he's happy with his girls. Ooh look at Rory and Mick with them big flames, they look like Romans or something, don't they? But with clothes on.'

Lottie giggled. 'They're torches, for lighting the fireworks, I think.'

'Nothing like a big bang to see in the New Year, is there, babe?'

Lottie loved fireworks. In fact Bonfire Night had always been the highlight of the year for her – until the last one. She glanced nervously behind her at the large French windows that led from the terrace into the Great Hall.

Not that a stray firework had started the blaze responsible for destroying a fair chunk of Tipping House and wiping out her business, but if they hadn't been so busy staring into the dying embers and setting more midnight fireworks off at the end of a very drunken and noisy party, they might have realised that the flames in the window weren't a reflection of what was going on outside.

And they might have called the fire brigade before there was the sharp crack of hot glass followed by a rush of black, billowing smoke.

Sam caught the look and gave her a hug. 'Sod him, babe. Next

November we can pretend the guy on the top of the fire is that toe-rag, burn him at the stake.'

'We're not sure it definitely is him yet.' Lottie wanted to be fair and although all indications were that the bridegroom who had been celebrating his wedding at Tipping House on November 5th had, in fact, snuck out of the four-poster bed armed with a match and bottle of spirits, enquiries were still ongoing.

'Well he did say so on Facebook, so it's got to be, hasn't it?'

'You can't believe everything on there.'

'Course you can, love, all the important stuff. I don't bother listening to the news any more, I just go on Facebook.'

Lottie did love Sam, even if she could be decidedly un-PC at times. Well that was part of her charm.

'Have you got a date to get it all done up again then, babe? I do miss seeing all those lovely brides here. That one that looked like she was a big fat gypsy was amazing. You know, the one with that glass carriage. Life a fairy tale it was.'

'I miss them too.' Lottie fought the feeling of gloom. 'The insurance people are still poking around, and to be honest I'm not quite sure where I'm going to get the money from to get started again.'

'We'll sort it, babe. We can have another fundraiser, can't we, Mandy?'

Amanda Stanthorpe, who had emerged from the bathroom, was looking pale green at the edges and didn't even have the energy to flinch at the abbreviation of her name. She smiled wanly.

When she'd first moved to Folly Lake Manor in Tippermere she'd spent most of her time wishing she wasn't there; she was scared of horses, hated disorder and loathed mud, but after her millionaire husband had died she'd been touched by the support and warmth of her neighbours and now couldn't imagine living anywhere else. Especially after finding a kindred spirit in Dominic Stanthorpe. Marrying him and having his daughter had been the best thing she had ever done. Apart from the actual pregnancy part, of course, which had left her feeling like she'd been fed through a mangle. Repeatedly.

Amanda was the most organised, demure, and elegant person in Tippermere and Lottie had been in awe of her for a long time. Before discovering that the immaculate exterior was a cover for a shy but extremely kind person. She still found it impossible to believe, though, that the young Amanda had been a geeky, unfashionable kid from the suburbs who created a fantasy world to escape from her loneliness. All she could see when she looked at her Uncle Dominic and Amanda was a perfect couple who could have run the Tipping House Estate with effortless ease, had the Stanthorpes not decided long ago that it should only be passed down to female ancestors.

Since discovering that she was to inherit the estate Lottie had worried on an almost daily basis that Dominic would be distraught at being passed over, but he was adamant that he had no desire to shoulder the huge burden that Tipping House represented, but was happy to help his niece out where he could. And she had to admit that he seemed extremely content with Amanda in their rather elegant, and decidedly easier to maintain, home.

'Not missed anything, have I? I hope Alice hasn't been any trouble.'

Lottie smiled and hugged the friend who had married her uncle and become her aunt, which was a bit weird. 'Only Sam talking about firemen and another fundraiser to put the weddings back on track, and Alice is never any trouble.'

'We could have another wedding fayre.'

'Amanda.' Dominic, who had been quietly watching proceedings, stepped out from the shadow of the building and put a protective arm around his wife's shoulders. 'What did we agree about not overdoing things?' He looked down his long, elegant nose, slightly disapprovingly, in Lottie's direction and she shrugged her shoulders, doing her best to ignore the piercing

48

blue gaze that was so like her gran's and always left her feeling like a naughty child.

'Just a small event, darling, as an announcement that we're back in business.'

Lottie gave a sigh of relief as Dom switched his gaze from her back to Amanda, and it softened. He'd always seemed stuffy, serious, and slightly too aristocratic and forbidding as she was growing up (and still did sometimes, like when she was sure she'd done something he wouldn't approve of), but when he looked at Amanda he was a different man.

Well, he still made her feel a klutz – overweight, clumsy and never quite as confident as she should be – but she'd seen a softer side to him since he'd met Amanda and had been amazed by how delighted he'd been at the prospect of fatherhood.

'Big is better though, isn't it, girls?' Sam laughed heartily. 'Like them firemen on the calendar. Have you seen it, Mand?'

Amanda shook her head and Dom sighed. 'I will go and attend to the champagne, ladies.'

'Old Molly at the shop told me your dad had been in stocking up for Tiggy, saucy mare isn't she? And at her age as well. Bless, she's such a card. I reckon her and your dad are a perfect match. Well, of course, not as perfect as your mum and dad.' She gave Lottie an apologetic hug.

'They are perfect together, though she's much too nice to him sometimes. I'm not sure Mum would run after him like Tiggy does. From what Gran's said I think she was more like Roxy.'

'Aww, nobody is like my Roxy, she's a right little tinker at times. I bet your mum was lovely, just like you.'

Lottie smiled. It was hard to know what her mother, Alexa, would have been like if she'd lived beyond her twenty-fourth birthday. Everybody said she'd been mischievous, a whirlwind of energy with long curly hair and dark flashing eyes, but Lottie didn't know. She couldn't even remember her mother's touch, her presence. 'I was younger than Roxy and Alice when she died, and all I know is that her and Dad loved each other.' But would Alexa have loved her, Lottie? Had she ever even wanted children, or had she had that gnawing empty well of fear at the pit of her stomach when she'd found out she was pregnant, the same feeling that Lottie had whenever the baby question was asked? Maybe Alexa had just been doing her duty and trying to fill Tipping House with the heirs it demanded.

'Aww I've made you sad, babe.'

'You haven't, I'm fine.' Lottie grinned and tried to shake off gloomy thoughts about babies. 'I love Tigs. She's good for Dad. He was such a grumpy bugger before.'

Sam giggled. 'I've been trying to get Tiggy to come with me and get her roots done. I mean, nobody actually wants to have all them grey bits on their head, do they? My hairstylist, Bobby, would make her look ten years younger, and I reckon a bit of Moroccan oil would work wonders on her hair. Look what it's done for me.' She held a blond strand out for inspection. 'I don't think them people in Morocco should have kept it a secret from us for so long, it's amazing. Anyhow, she keeps saying she's busy. Run off her feet she is.'

Lottie knew Tiggy was no such thing, but wasn't surprised at the tactics. Her step-mother, AKA 'Tatty Tiggy', was more than happy in her own skin and Billy loved her just as she was, with her bohemian clothes, wild hair, and ample bosom. Whilst Lottie was pretty sure that nothing in life ever horrified Tiggy, at a guess she did, no doubt, think the idea of a Samantha-style makeover a huge joke. She was still trying to work out whether there was a tactful response or whether she'd be better just smiling, when a shriek of laughter made them all turn round.

'Lottie, Manda, Mummy look, look at me.' Roxy had found an old cushion and was sitting on it sliding down the stone steps that led up to the balustrade, where they were supposed to be watching the fireworks from. She was nothing if not resourceful.

'What is she like? Bless her. Davey, Dave hun, be a babe and bring her back. My heels are hell walking up and down these steps. Get one caught in a crack and I'll be A over T again, won't I?'

'I thought your au-pair was supposed to be here, Sam?'

'I've given her Christmas off, babe. So she can see her family, back in Croatia or wherever it is. Where's she from, Dave?' She carried on without waiting for an answer. Dave was busy turning his daughter upside down so that she squealed and her dress covered her head. Lottie watched worriedly as he put her on his shoulders. She was only three and he was the size you'd expect to be an England goalkeeper to be – six foot and quite a lot. Roxy, though, was fearless.

'But it's New Year now, Sam, shouldn't she be back?'

'Aww I know, babe, but it's a long way, isn't it? We can manage, can't we Davey? And I thought a proper Christmas holiday, just us,' she linked her arm through Lottie's, 'would be amazing. We've helped each other out, haven't we, babe? And the kids love being with you and Rory.'

Hmm, I know they do, thought Lottie, waiting for the inevitable subject to crop up again. Just when she'd been trying to forget about it.

'Your turn next eh, hun? Don't want your eggs getting past their sell-by date, do you? You'll only be fit for making omelettes, as my mam used to say.'

Lottie smiled. Sam was as bad as Gran; once she had an idea she was like a bloody terrier. There was no letting go, but this was one decision that Lottie wasn't going to be bullied into. It wasn't just that they couldn't afford it – it was more than that. The whole idea scared her: all that responsibility, just her and Rory and a tiny defenceless baby. She glanced down at Alice, who had slipped her small hand into her mother's and was standing quietly at her side.

What she'd said to Sam about Alexa was true. She'd never really known her mother, as she'd been a toddler when Alexandra had died, leaving just her and Billy. She loved her father and she knew he loved her, but she also knew she'd changed his life. Thrown a burden of responsibility on the young show-jumper that had altered the course of his future. Even now, when she was supposed to be all grown up, she still remembered those feelings she'd had as a teenager. She'd hated her mother, the woman she'd never known – truly hated her with a strength that had left her feeling sick and guilty – for leaving and turning their lives upside down.

Her only real memories came from photographs, of a laughing carefree girl, forever young. A girl who'd flitted away, abandoned her. They'd got by, but she dimly remembered the many heated arguments she'd overheard between Billy and Elizabeth, and the frequent occasions when a groom had picked her up from school. 'I wish I was a better dad,' he'd said when he rang her from yet another show-jumping event, apologetic that he'd missed a parents' evening, a sports day. But he *had* been a good dad, a good dad trying to be a mum as well. Struggling to be everything, when her mother should have been there. How could she even think about being a mother herself when she didn't know what one really was? She'd either be stupidly over-protective or resent the whole idea of motherhood and carry on as she always had.

'I do love this terrace.' Amanda ran a hand along the stone balustrade, trying to change the subject, glancing up at her through long eyelashes with a worried frown.

But there was no need. Sam had already been distracted.

'Bloody 'ell, look at that.' She was staring across the grass towards the dark figures of Rory and Mick, suddenly illuminated as a Catherine wheel sprang into life, sending them dashing for cover as it spat out an uneven shower of light in all directions, like water from a hosepipe with kinks in it. 'Girls, come here, quickly, Alice, Roxy, come on Davey.'

The fireworks had started with a bang, well, a splutter. Davey galloped up the steps, little Roxy clapping her hands in delight at the turn of speed, the giggles turning to a wail as a huge rocket exploded like a cannon, scattering an enormous shower of sparks into the black night sky. She burst into tears, while Alice clutched Amanda's hand tightly in both of her own and looked up at her aghast.

'They won't get you, darling, they're in the sky, like the stars.'

Alice's brow was creased in a frown as she listened to her mother earnestly, and Roxy stopped the noise while she considered the new revelation.

'If they're stars why do they disappear? Stars stay until I go to sleep.'

'Only a few more,' Lottie glanced at her watch, 'then it's midnight and there'll be one big bang and all over.'

'Friggin' hell.' The yell from Rory carried clearly across to the terrace. 'Run Mick, the whole bloody lot's about to go.' The two men started sprinting towards the house, still carrying their torches and their audience watched open-mouthed. 'Maybe not.' Rory ground to a halt and grinned up at them from the bottom of the steps. 'False alarm, folks.' But he'd spoken too soon, as with a terrific squeal the firework show started in disorganised earnest.

'You stupid eejit.' Mick was laughing as he doubled over, trying to get his breath back. 'I told you to put the lid on.'

'Lost it.' His words were drowned out by the noise as more fireworks lit the night sky.

Roxy had forgotten her tears. Hands on hips, she stood at her mother's side looking down at Rory, then she waved a finger. 'I'm,' bang, 'vewy' double explosion, 'disappointed. You've,' bang, 'wuined everything.' And with that she folded her arms and, marching to the back of the terrace, sat down.

Mick laughed. 'God knows why I agreed to help you, you idiot.'

'I think it's pretty spectacular, actually.' Rory rolled over and lay on the damp grass, staring up at the sky. 'Synchronised displays are for sissies.'

'Anybody for a glass of bubbly? Close enough to midnight, by my reckoning.' Dom popped the cork as the last of the fireworks fizzled out and Lottie passed the glasses round, saving Rory's to last.

'Happy New Year, darling.'

She stared into his eyes and what shone back was pure optimism, love of life, and love for her. It was going to be alright. This year would be fine. They'd sort something out, work out how to raise the money they needed to keep Tipping House going until the wedding business was back in full flow. They'd come up with a plan together, and he was happy with the time he spent with Roxy and Alice. No responsibility, just fun. 'Happy New Year, Rory.'

'Stop worrying.' His kissed the end of her nose and grinned. 'It's going to be a good year. I've got a feeling in my water.'

Lottie giggled. 'Hmm, that could be all the beer you drank when you were setting the fireworks up.'

'You could be right, but I think I deserve a New Year shag anyway, after providing such brilliant entertainment.'

'Shush.' Lottie put a hand over his mouth and glanced over at Roxy anxiously. The little girl had surprisingly good hearing and a habit of repeating new words at the worst possible time. Shag, she was sure, should not be part of a three-year-old's vocabulary.

'Sorry to break the party up, but we'd better go.' Amanda smiled and scooped up the yawning Alice. 'Past bedtime isn't it, poppet?' The little girl rested her head on her mother's shoulder and put her thumb in her mouth. 'Happy New Year, Lottie.' She kissed first Lottie, then Rory. 'Thank you for a lovely evening.'

'Me too.' Mick drained his glass. 'I better get a move on. I promised to call Niamh, she's not forgiven me yet for not making it back home to Ireland with her to see the New Year in. I need to earn some brownie points.' He winked at Lottie, then ruffled her hair. 'I think I'd better be checking the cheap flights out and keep her company for a few days. Happy New Year, treasure.' He shook Rory's hand. 'Cheers, mate. See you all tomorrow.'

* * *

'I can't believe it's so long since we last had a wedding here, can you?'

'Peaceful isn't it?' Rory pulled Lottie to him and nuzzled at her neck until she wriggled and tried to escape. 'Lovely, just us and the kids. No bossy mothers-of the-bride about. Maybe we should have one of our own?'

'Bossy mother? We've got Gran.'

'I meant a kid.' He smoothed his hand over her stomach and felt Lottie instinctively tighten her muscles.

'We've got Roxy and Alice.'

'One of our own would be nice, wouldn't it?'

'Nice when you can hand them back.' She smiled, but he didn't miss the tightness in her voice, or the little sigh of exasperation that he was sure she had tried to keep in. 'And anyway we're having enough trouble looking after ourselves and the horses.'

'You'll be able to start up the business again soon. Stop worrying.'

'But I do worry.'

Rory grimaced. He'd got worries of his own; worries that he'd rather hoped would have disappeared by now, before Lottie found out. But he knew that life for them would never be straightforward, they didn't live a nine-to-five existence and didn't want to. There would never be a good time to start a family, but people did it anyway, didn't they? 'Well there's plenty of time. I didn't mean we had to rush into it, but it's what everybody does, isn't it? I mean not even Dom and Amanda wasted time.'

She stared. 'We're not wasting time. Is that what you think? You're wasting your life?'

'Don't be daft, Lots. I only meant it's what people do, it's just normal.'

'But we don't have to be the same as everybody else, do we?'

'Well no, but . . . I mean, it's the next step, isn't it?'

'It doesn't have to be. I mean, aren't you happy with it just being the two of us?'

'Of course I am.'

'You're not getting bored?'

'How could I get bored of you?' He pulled her closer in to his side. 'But I thought it might be fun teaching our own kids how to do stuff. And Mum was saying how she'd love to be a grandma . . .'

'Oh, I'm sorry.' Lottie looked down. 'Look, I am sorry if that's what she wants, I just . . .'

'It's not a problem, honest. No rush, let's make them wait a bit, eh? Anyway,' he grinned, 'I know that one day you'll love having a tiny version of me to boss around.'

She didn't smile back. 'Maybe, but not yet.'

'You're not doing my ego much good here.'

'Your ego does fine on its own, Rory Steel.' The smile didn't quite reach her eyes. 'I just want things to be right between us first.'

'Right? But they are, aren't they? I thought you were happy. Is it you that's getting bored?'

'Don't be daft. I didn't mean between us in that way. I meant money-wise, this place. Nobody is making bookings for next year, they're all too worried it won't be fixed.'

'It'll be fixed.' He said it with the type of conviction he knew she needed to hear. 'Come on, gorgeous,' he pulled her to her feet and drew her in close so that he could look straight into the big green eyes he loved so much. She still looked the same old Lottie, his Lottie. The money thing was obviously worrying her more than she let on, that was the trouble – she was just too good at coping sometimes. 'Let's see the year in with some baby-making practice. You don't want me to forget how to do it, do you?' He winked. 'Just in case.'

Chapter 5

'What are *you* doing here, Andy? Up to no good, I bet.' Sam grinned at the slightly overweight middle-aged man, then transferred her attention to Lottie. 'Everything okay, babe?'

'You know each other?' Lottie raised an eyebrow. The man standing on her doorstep had just announced that he had an appointment with Lady Tipping, then had smiled reassuringly at her as though she was ten years old, although she probably did look like a kid in her scruffy breeches, old fleece, and spotty socks. A very big kid, though.

Quite honestly everything wasn't okay. She was fed up of fending off property developers and trying to be nice to insurance investigators. This one hadn't even bothered to do his homework properly. There was no such person as Lady Tipping (well, not to her knowledge, and certainly not in Tippermere). There was Lady Elizabeth Stanthorpe and there was her, Charlotte Steel.

'Course we do. We go way back.' Sam winked. 'This bugger ran a full-page spread about me and my Davey when he played in the World Cup, didn't you, darling? Called us girls *plastic fantastic.*'

'Spread? So he's a journalist?'

Andy ignored Lottie's interruption. 'Well to be fair, Sam . . .'

'There was nothing fair about that, babe.' She waved a stern finger. 'Martina was well pissed off with you telling everybody how much her nose job cost. She'd told her Frankie that it cost half that. Made him out to be a right dickhead, you did. And you know the boys don't like to look stupid in front of the rest of the team.'

Lottie, who had been trying to work out how to slam the front door in the stranger's face in a polite way, looked from Sam, who was a vision in skin-tight maroon leather trousers, matching jacket and brown thigh-high boots, to the guy and back again.

'And you said I'd been to that dodgy London geezer for my new boobs. Davey wasn't pleased at all when he'd arranged it all special for me. I mean, look at them.' She opened her leather jacket with a flourish and cupped her generous breasts in both hands. 'They're perfect. There's nothing cheap about my Dave. No way would he let just anybody mess with my body.' She jiggled them about. 'These are as real as fake ones get, you know. Look.' He was looking. 'And they're quite squeezy – not solid at all like those cheap ones.' She flexed her fingers. 'You have to look dead close to see the scar. Davey was really insulted when you said that.'

'Sorry, no er insult intended.'

He didn't look sorry, thought Lottie, more like transfixed.

'So you don't have an appointment?' She took the opportunity, while the pair of them were engrossed with Sam's boobs, to get a word in.

'You've made an *appointment*?' Sam let go of her boobs and said the word in such a tone of astonishment that Lottie giggled.

'Well not an actual appointment, more like an arrangement. Give her the first chance to comment on this.' He shoved a news-paper in Sam's direction, tapping a finger on the headline. 'Only fair to get her side of the story, isn't it? In the interests of fair play and all that.'

'Fair play?' Sam guffawed. 'You're a cheeky bugger, you are.'

She grabbed hold of the paper before Lottie could and took a swipe at the man's head with it. 'You don't want to look at that, babe, it's a real load of bollocks. That's why I came. They've not got it right at all, have they, babe?' She waved it in the air so that Lottie had to bob her head up and down to try and catch a glimpse, although she wasn't quite sure now if Sam was telling her she should or she shouldn't read it.

Lottie had never thought any of the headlines associated with the Tipping House Estate and her family could be called 'right', though.

The 'Billy-the-Bonk' headlines about her father (while she was still at school) had made her cringe, the more recent 'Flaming Family Pile' one had nearly made her cry, as had the 'Lady Elizabeth's Ashes', which was just plain cruel. Then there had been the 'Wizard of Oz' one, when her Australian ex-lover had arrived unexpectedly in the village, which had made her laugh and the 'Tippingly-Good Theme Park', which she'd actually torn up and was going to use as loo paper until Rory pointed out that the ink would leave her with a black bum.

But this one, flashing before her eyes as Sam waved it like a flag, brought a sharp pain to her chest. 'Upstairs Heiress Rips Off Down-town Bride.' She opened her mouth to object and got a warning look.

'Don't you say anything while he's here listening, Lottie,' Sam glanced at the journalist, 'cos he'll write it down, won't you?'

'Well that is my job.' He looked affronted. 'Some of us have got to earn a living, we can't all be lords and ladies, you know.'

'I'm surprised at you, Andy, I really am.'

For a brief moment Sam sounded just like her daughter Roxy, Lottie thought.

'Not my headline, darling, I'm just here for a quote. So you're Lady Lottie?' He raised an eyebrow and gave Lottie a once-over from head to toe.

'I'm not a Lady.' She said it automatically and folded her arms, trying her best to look like a somewhat affronted Lady rather than an angry kid. 'That's why you came round, Sam?'

'Come on, let's get inside, babe. And you,' she blew a kiss at the journalist, who looked like he was intent on following them inside Tipping House, 'can bugger off back to Fleet Street or wherever it is you come from.' The man looked unsure whether to make a bolt for the door with them, but Sam waggled a very long (which Lottie thought probably qualified as a lethal weapon) glittery-bronze fingernail at him.

'So, it's no comment then?' He had one hand raised, as though to ward off the inevitable.

'You can write the truth about my boobs instead. Move your fingers, babe, you don't want them getting squashed, do you?' And with that Lottie found herself pushed firmly back into Tipping House and the door slammed behind them.

Lottie glanced worriedly at her watch. She really had to muck out the horses before Rory got back from the gallops, and she'd had a summons from her gran, Elizabeth, which she really couldn't afford to ignore or her life wouldn't be worth living. 'You came to show me the latest headlines, then?'

'And my new extensions, babe. What do you think?' Sam flicked her hair back over her shoulder. 'Do you think they look natural?'

'Well,' Lottie paused, how natural could that particular shade of bleached blond look?

'Never thought I'd need them, but my hair has been a right state since I had Roxy. I mean, at first it was really thick, you know?' Lottie didn't. 'I mean that happens when you're preggers, doesn't it?' She didn't pause for an answer. 'But then it started coming out in handfuls. I mean, we're going to have loads more kids, so I suppose it will get thick again,' she looked doubtfully down at her handful of hair, 'but I can't wait, can I, babe? I mean, it has to look right for Davey every day, doesn't it?'

'It's lovely,' said Lottie truthfully. It was. Sam always had a full head of perfectly tamed hair, even if the colour wasn't always a shade that nature intended. Unlike her own hair, which tended to resemble something a bird would make a nest in, and was a kind of very natural brownish shade. Like bark. The same colour and not far off the texture when she got out of bed in the mornings.

'Aww thank you, babe. I know you always say it as it is. Mandy said it suited my personality, isn't she the sweetest?'

'Very. Er, where's Roxy?'

'She's in the car, babe. Scruffy is looking after her.'

'He's a dog.'

'I know that, but he's dead protective, wouldn't let anybody harm a hair on her head.'

Lottie, who had been worrying more about what Roxy might be doing to the dog and the car (she had what Sam called an 'inquisitive nature') let it go.

'Don't worry, babe, I've got the key this time.' Sam waved it in the air; leaving it in the ignition one time had led to the roof being put down, which was quite handy seeing as Roxy had managed to lock all the doors and was howling as she'd then shoved the keys down the back of the seat and got her fingers trapped trying to get them out again. Heaven only knew, Lottie thought, what she'd be like by the time she was four years old. 'She was good as gold when I left her, promised to stay in her seat with the seatbelt done up and everything, bless her.'

'That's, er, good.'

Sam beamed, totally confident in her role as mother. 'Well, it was little Aggie told me.'

'Aggie?'

'My new au-pair. She arrived the other day and she's such a sweetie. That other one decided to stay in Croatia, said me having little Roxy had reminded her how important family is and she was homesick. Isn't that sweet?'

Lottie had a feeling that generous and lovely as Sam and her family were, trying to cope with them would remind anybody how much they treasured their own.

'So, anyway, Aggie said had I seen the paper? She never stops reading stuff, was asking where my library was the other day.' Sam giggled. 'She's a right card. I gave her a pile of mags, but she seems to prefer to go and get her own from the village, says it's no trouble and she wouldn't dream of taking mine. Anyhow, she brought this back.' Sam opened the newspaper out. 'Makes you out to be a right cow, and we all know you're not. You didn't do that though, babe, did you?' She frowned. 'Says here that you wouldn't give this poor girl any money back or let her have her special day here and she's skint, can't afford to get married at all now.'

Lottie sighed and sank down into a chair next to the Aga as she studied the picture of the distraught bride-to-be. 'I never said she couldn't get married here.' The problem was there had been so many cancellations lately she was struggling to remember exactly what she'd said to this one. 'But, I wouldn't have given her a deposit back, cos you don't do you? That's the point of a deposit, isn't it?' She chewed the side of her thumb.

'Well, yes,' Sam looked doubtful, 'but if she can't have her wedding here, then it's only fair to give it back, isn't it? I mean, it's not her fault the place burned down, is it? Haven't you got insurance for that type of thing, you know Acts of God, or whatever.'

'It wasn't God, it was the act of a drunken toe rag.' It was rather unfair that this article was all about how evil she was and barely mentioned the inebriated groom, who had nearly toasted his family and friends as well as her own. 'But I haven't cancelled her wedding. It's not until next year and the house should be fine by then, so she can still have it here. That's why I haven't given her a deposit back.' She skimmed over the article again. 'In fact it's right at the end of next summer, I remember her now.' And she did. It had only been yesterday and one of the shortest conversations of the lot. In fact it consisted of 'I want to cancel and can I have all my money back?' followed by the dial tone before Lottie had even had time to discuss reduced rates or extra flowers (which was her latest tactic in the effort to stop the rush of cancellations). 'She says here I've ruined her fairy tale, wrecked her dreams, and it has to be perfect or her whole life will be destroyed 'cos his family will think she's cheap.' Lottie pulled at Harry's ears absentmindedly and he wriggled, trying to lick her hand. 'And she didn't say any of that to me.'

'What about this one, babe? Here's another one.' Sam pointed to a paragraph further down the column. 'I think this is the *Downton* bit, where she says *I just wanted to be like Lady Charlotte.*'

'And I'm not bloody Lady Charlotte,' sighed Lottie, knowing she was sounding a right grump.

'Look here, she says *I was promised I'd be treated like a lady of the manor on my special day and now they won't give me my money back or give me my dream wedding, they just think they can do what they want to normal people like us, it's a disgrace.*'

Lottie peered at the photograph, this time the bride-to-be had actually gone to the trouble of putting on a wedding dress. 'Isn't it bad luck to let your groom see the dress beforehand?'

'Probably not hers, hun. I bet the press lent it her.'

'I remember her.' Lottie jabbed at the picture. 'We bloody did offer her some money back. I gave her a cut price and offered them a marquee.' She hugged Harry to her. 'The thing is they're not the only ones. They're all pulling out. It's like somebody has told them to. None of them will discuss it. The moment I ask they just slam the phone down.'

'Like who, babe? Who would tell them to cancel? I mean that Andy that was just here. He's a bit naughty but he wouldn't do anything like that, not on purpose.'

'I don't think it's the papers,' she paused, 'I keep getting these other phone calls all the time, as well as the cancellation ones.' In fact the phone rang almost non-stop and Lottie always leapt on it in case it was good news. But it never was. 'There's this bloke who says bungee jumping is the answer to all my problems, then there's the boot-camp lot who want to do squats on the front lawn, and this hyper weirdo who says we need an adventure park, not forgetting the loony who said we need lions because they are so going to be the in-thing next year.'

Sam giggled.

'Then there's the luxury hotel chain who want to offer spa breaks.' Lottie frowned, but Sam clapped her hands.

'Ooh a spa sounds exciting, that would be amazing.'

'But I don't want somebody running a spa here. It's my home, Sam, but it's just like there's a load of vultures circling; you know, waiting for us to cave in and accept an offer. Do you think one of them is behind this?' She sighed. 'I can't really afford to pay back all the deposits for next year. We actually are pretty broke, you know.'

Sam shrugged, but looked far more serious. 'I don't know, babe, but it's quite a lot of work to find out who all these people are, isn't it? I mean how would anybody do that, get their names and phone numbers and everything?'

'Oh I don't know. Am I just imagining it all? And then there's the insurance people. They keep asking so many questions, it's as though they don't believe a word we've said.' She opened the paper out fully. 'They asked just how hard up we are, and even though I told the last one how well the business had all been going and asked why on earth I'd set fire to my own home, he still gave me a look over the top of his specs and then made a harrumph noise, muttered something like *not for me to say* and wrote something down.'

'Isn't it scandalous or libellous or something, what she's saying here? About you not being honest about everything?'

The problem was, Lottie thought, she had every intention of being up and running again by next spring, but what if she wasn't? What if the insurance company still hadn't paid out and she really did have to start paying the remaining deposits back? Not that there were many, but it would leave their bank balance in rather a dire state. She'd be back to square one, just as she'd been when she agreed to take on the responsibility of the Tipping House Estate and try and save it from rack and ruin.

'Aww don't look so sad,' Sam gave her a hug, 'it will all work out. Tell you what, I'll work my charms on Andy and find out who put that girl up to this. I'll give him some goss.' She grinned. 'He's a real pushover, if you know what I mean. Oh no, look at the time. I'm going to have to go soon. Me and little Roxy are going to the Botox clinic.'

Lottie looked at her horrified. 'You can't . . .'

'Oh don't be daft, babe, she's coming with me not having it done.' She giggled. 'You're a hoot, babe.'

'Oh shit, I didn't realise it was that time either. I said I'd go and talk to Gran, and you know she hates me being late. Oh God, I hope she hasn't seen this.'

'She probably has, babe. She doesn't miss much. Amazing isn't she?'

Amazing was one word, thought Lottie, but there were many others. She did love her gran, but sometimes wished she didn't interfere quite so much. It just made her feel worse, as though she really was totally incompetent and not up to the job.

'I'll leave you to it, then, shall I, hun? I hope Roxy hasn't tried to plait Scruffy's tail again or got stuck under the seat. She's the spitting image of me at her age, you know. My mum says I used to hide all the time and the other day she was stuck under the car seat. Like a cork in a bottle she was, with her bottom in the air.'

'Maybe you shouldn't leave her on her own?'

'Aww you're so sensible, Lottie. I suppose it's having all these horses and stuff. You know, my Roxy can't wait to ride her little horse again. She might grow up just like you. You can give her lessons if you like.'

Lottie tried her best to look thrilled at the honour and headed for the front door, half expecting to discover Roxy had somehow managed to drive the car off. She hadn't.

'Bless, look how pleased little Scruffy is to see me.' Sam waved in the direction of her convertible and Lottie was fairly sure that the poor dog was desperately trying to dig his way out of the car, rather than enthusiastically greet his owner.

Chapter 6

'Oh good, you're here.' Elizabeth checked the clock. 'And on time. Sit down. Now, I think it is time you met an acquaintance of mine, Charlotte.'

Lottie looked at her grandmother and wondered what she was up to. Elizabeth Stanthorpe liked to meddle. Despite handing over the day-to-day running of the Tipping House Estate to Lottie, she had the distinct feeling that when decisions were made, her gran was often behind them. And now she was pretty sure that the old woman had something up her sleeve. She didn't indulge in idle chit chat, there was always an agenda. Even Bertie managed to look guilty as he lay at her feet, raising his eyebrows alternately and giving an occasional lazy wag of his tail.

'Now, don't look like that. I think this person may be able to help you, dear.'

Lottie raised an eyebrow.

'You are doing splendidly, but if anything, matters seem to be getting more difficult. This problem isn't going to be resolved overnight, is it, Charlotte?'

'No.' Every last hint of hope had disappeared from the long, drawn-out syllable.

At first Lottie had thought it was a case of putting the flames out, getting the cleaners in and carrying on as normal. Instead, the room had been declared out of bounds (there had even been a strip of red and white tape at one point that made it look like the scene of a murder) and there was a lot of poking about by firemen, none of whom matched her mental image of a muscled-up firefighter stripped to the waist and smeared in soot.

It was a good job, thought Lottie, that she'd not seen the Hunky Heroes calendar in the village shop before the fire, or she'd have been sorely disappointed.

The heroes that had clambered out of the fire engine bore no resemblance to the hose-wielding hunks who were raising money for charity: no nudity (covered by helmets or otherwise), no cheeky grins, no offers of a fireman's lift. In fact, totally covered up they looked more like her dad than Mr January, February, or March.

The first lot had very efficiently put the blaze out and the second lot had poked around, grimaced, and written notes.

She would never look at a firework or bonfire in the same way again.

'Are you listening, Charlotte? I do sometimes wonder how you get anything done with your head in the clouds.' Elizabeth tapped her stick impatiently against the table leg.

'It's not in the clouds.' Lottie, brought back to the present abruptly, decided to change the subject. 'Why did you really buy Alice a pony?'

'The girl needs to get in the saddle – nothing wrong with a bit of responsibility.'

'It's cold, wouldn't it have been better to wait until the weather warmed up?'

'No point in putting things off, and ponies are too easily ignored when they're turned out to grass.'

Lottie sighed and wondered if it was too early to crack open a bottle of wine. 'She's only three years old, Gran.' Although she was three going on thirty, but that was irrelevant.

'Nearly four, by my reckoning, so she's got long enough legs. And you can stop raising your eyebrows, young lady, she's tall enough to sit astride. No good these little podgy toddlers, roll straight off a pony.'

'Did you ask Amanda first?'

'I think it's time for a G&T, don't you? Then I can tell you all about this nice young man I've invited for you to meet. Ah,' she paused, 'that must be him now, his name is James and I want you to be nice to him. I told him to come straight up. I do like punctuality.' She gave Lottie, who usually raced in at the very last minute, a pointed look.

Lottie wanted to do more than raise her eyebrows; she wanted to lie on the floor and scream. 'How come you can hear somebody coming in and you don't hear a word I say when I'm explaining why you can't afford to bet on the horses? And,' she paused, wondering if it was worth wasting her breath, but decided to crack on anyway, 'buy the girls ponies.'

'I look at it as speculating, Charlotte. And I didn't hear him, I saw Bertie cock his ears.'

Lottie glanced down at the fat Labrador, who was flat out at Elizabeth's feet, his paws twitching as he ran after rabbits in his sleep, little snuffles of excitement ruffling his lips every now and then. 'Of course you did, Gran.'

From the moment he walked into the room, Lottie realised that it was going to be hard *not* to like James, with his willing-to-please but slightly awkward air. He was lanky, with a lopsided verging-on-cheeky grin and slightly too-long hair (in fact to Lottie's eye he had a definite forelock). His jeans, which no doubt should have been skinny, had plenty of room in them (and looked like he'd rolled down a hill), his hoody hung off his frame and the outfit was finished off with Converses that were green-smudged.

If he had been a horse she would have had to wrap her arms around his neck, kiss his nose and tell him what a clever boy he was, and assure him that everybody would love him once she'd fed him up. As it was, kissing noses might have been misinterpreted.

Elizabeth was frowning at her – no doubt she'd read her mind again. Lottie frowned back trying to convey the message that she really, really wasn't about to kiss anybody's nose.

James hadn't noticed; he was staring at the floor. God, the poor man; here she was trying to weigh him up with her best imitation of Elizabeth's shrewd look (although Rory always asked her if she'd got something in her eye when she tried it on him) and he no doubt thought she was some haughty lady of the manor. She'd never get to grips with the whole aristocratic thing, which Gran and Uncle Dom did so well, she'd rather hug people.

'Love the stars and stripes.'

Okay, he didn't think she was haughty. Failed on that front, again. He was staring at her socks not the woodworm-riddled floorboards. 'Clever to avoid convention and split them up.'

'I never wear matching socks. Stars and stripes should be kept apart.'

'Stars and stripes? You are not an American are you?' Elizabeth peered at him more closely. 'So hard to tell these days, you youngsters all sound the same. Nobody enunciates, even when one has been to a decent school.'

'Gran!' But Lottie knew it was useless trying to stop Elizabeth's tendency towards Prince Philip-isms.

Elizabeth gave her a look, intended to silence her, and then cleared her throat. 'James, this is Charlotte, who is in charge of our fundraising.'

Lottie loved the way that in one sentence her gran had managed to lower her status to that of occasional help.

'It isn't going too well at present, for obvious reasons.' Incapable, occasional help. 'She's also my granddaughter and runs the estate.' Better. 'And will one day inherit it.' She'd put a slightly unnecessary emphasis on the 'one day' Lottie thought (she could well sympathise with Prince Charles), but she grinned. Whatever Gran was plotting, it at least did have her in the position of heiress-in-waiting and not the home help. 'Although, of course, she won't inherit the title. This, Charlotte, is James Shilling. I found him in a rhododendron bush and he says I don't know his mother.' Elizabeth considered it her duty to know everybody within a twenty-mile radius, and everything about them.

'Trilling.'

Lottie stared at him. What a peculiar thing to say.

'It's Jamie Trilling, not Shilling.' He grinned sheepishly. 'And it's Jamie. Everybody calls me Jamie not James.'

'Well, why didn't you say so, young man? Speak up, no use mumbling.'

He sighed, he obviously had said it before, but Elizabeth only heard what suited her. Lottie tried not to smile, more likely she'd done it on purpose not misheard him. Reducing him to loose change, and old currency at that.

'That explains it, no Trillings round here.' She frowned. 'So where *do* you come from, young man?'

Jamie suddenly looked worried and Lottie could sympathise. Elizabeth knew just how to make somebody feel that their dream deal was inches away, that she valued their opinion, only to dash it with one carefully worded statement and then look at them like they were an alien life form. 'Well, I . . .'

'We'll discuss that later. Now, tell Charlotte why you're here. Speak up, now, we can't sit around here all day.' She waved an imperious finger and waited expectantly for him to perform.

* * *

Jamie looked from Elizabeth to Lottie and back again and felt like he was in front of a firing squad. This was worse than any interview he had ever had, not that he'd had many. She changed tack more often than a boat heading into the wind; Lady Elizabeth was unlike any old woman, well any woman, any*body*, he'd ever met before.

He'd spent several hours on the internet after meeting her, desperately trying to find out more about the Stanthorpes and the Tipping House Estate, but had largely drawn a blank. In fact, he'd discovered more when he'd popped into the Tippermere village shop to buy a newspaper on the way over.

The woman in there had been quite chatty and had insisted on filling him in on the history of the church and local pub, as well as some rather colourful tales about Rory (that's Lottie's husband, such a naughty one he is), Billy (and that's her father, the tales he could tell, won a gold medal at the Olympics, he did), a guy called Mick (he really had a soft spot for our Lottie, he did, but I reckon they're more like brother and sister) and an Australian called Todd (you should have seen him, rode up like a knight on a charger, he did, and we all thought he was about to sweep little Lottie off her feet, but then, would you credit it, he whisked Pip off to Australia, a right character he was. Mind you, I'm not sure Elizabeth was happy, she misses that girl). In fact, by the time he'd paid for the newspaper, he felt quite dizzy, but not much the wiser about Tipping House.

Not that he was any expert at digging for facts, he was more visual, which was why he loved the job he was doing.

'I'm a location scout,' he told Lottie.

'Found him loitering in the grounds in the middle of the night, didn't we, Bertie?'

Lottie raised an eyebrow and Bertie gave a single thump of his tail. 'What were you doing out in the middle of the night?'

'She was in her nightie. I thought she was a ghost.' He leapt on the opportunity to deflect attention.

'Gran!'

'I was quite alright, dear, had Bertie with me, couldn't sleep.'

'But . . . but . . . you met him, anything could have . . .'

'Oh, he's harmless.' She waved a dismissive hand.

'And she had a shotgun.' Jamie didn't want to get side-tracked onto the rights and wrongs of old ladies wandering out in their nightwear on a winter's night.

'Gran, you promised not to go out shooting.'

'I wasn't shooting, Charlotte.'

'You had a gun.'

'Nonsense, carrying a gun and going out shooting are two totally different things. You, of all people, should know that. I went out prepared. And Bertie doesn't sleep properly these days, now he hasn't got Holmes, he gets restless, poor chap. Now stop fussing and let this young man explain.'

Jamie opened his mouth and there was a loud whine. 'That wasn't me.'

Lottie giggled. The noise came again, along with a sound like scrabbling rats. 'It's Harry, he's found me.' There was a loud bark as the dog heard his mistress's voice, followed by more frenzied scrabbling at the door interspersed with snuffles and whimpers.

Elizabeth pursed her lips and frowned.

'Shall I?' Jamie moved towards the door.

'I wouldn't—'

It was too late, he'd thrown it open and been swept off his feet by an ecstatic spaniel and a whirlwind of brown and white fur. After trampling over the visitor's body in his rush to see Lottie, Harry went back, his back end wagging to apologise. Followed by the terriers, who, rather than apologising, treated the boy as an obstacle to run over and round. Harry then set off again, his nose to the ground, the pack following in his wake.

'He's good at sniffing things out.' Lottie shrugged apologetically as Jamie sat up, rubbing a bruised elbow. 'He doesn't like me leaving him.'

'Seb is never going to believe this place.'

'Seb?' Lottie passed him a gin and tonic, which he rather felt he needed, and started to prepare a new one for Elizabeth.

'He's my boss, Seb Drakelow. I check out places to film for him, well, really I'm just an intern, which is another word for dogsbody.' He stayed where he was, sat on the floor. It felt the safest place to be. 'He needs a location for this drama he's making with his wife.'

'His wife?'

'She's an actress.' One who can't get any parts because she's such a bitch, he thought, but didn't say so aloud. Talk about 'fake it until you make it', she'd got it down to a fine art. He was pretty sure that the only part she had nailed was that of 'prima donna'. But she'd always treated him okay, and if it hadn't been for her help he might never have spotted the potential of Tipping House, so he really shouldn't have any gripe with her. She just made it so difficult to like her though. 'Pandora Drakelow.'

Lottie was looking at him blankly. 'I'm sorry, I don't really watch much television.'

'She's quite, er, well known.' Or she had been very briefly, but that was some years in the past. In fact, he reckoned he'd probably been at school when Pandora was in the one production that had achieved popular acclaim, and now she was struggling to reach those lofty heights again.

But she had tried to help him this time – he had to give her credit for that. And if he delivered on this one he had a proper job in the bag, plus Pandora's appreciation, which was always useful. 'The setting is a country estate.'

'Oh, so it's like *Downton Abbey*?'

He didn't like to say no, because she was actually looking like she might be mildly interested. But he had no choice. 'Well, no, not really. I mean I don't know all the details, but it's like modern-day stuff. It's about a rock star and his wife, who buy a country pile,' he glanced from Elizabeth to Lottie, who didn't seem offended, 'you know, escape to the country and all that, and she's kind of bored with nothing to do, then decides to learn to play polo.' Lottie was staring at him with a blank expression. 'Well, she falls for this polo player and persuades him to teach her because she thinks it's all glamour and thrills. That's where you come in.'

* * *

Lottie suddenly realised that they were both staring at her expectantly. 'But we don't play polo here. We haven't got a ground.' She looked from Jamie to Elizabeth in confusion. 'I'm not quite sure what this had to do with us, and it really isn't the right time of year in this country, I mean the season doesn't start for ages.'

'He wants somewhere majestic,' Jamie was clearly warming to the subject, 'but warm, you know, that centuries-old lived-in thing.'

Lottie nodded, but wasn't sure she did know.

'It kind of glows, this place, if you know what I mean?'

She did get that bit. In fact, as they all knew, it had glowed literally not so very long ago, which wasn't something she wanted to dwell on. It left a hollow feeling of dread in her stomach.

'I saw this place in the papers, you know, after the fire and knew it would be totally amazing. Polo on your front, er, lawn. So cool, you know?' She half-expected him to add 'wicked' or 'awesome' on the end, like Tab would have done. And he was, she thought, around the same age as their part-time groom. 'So I, er, decided to come and have a look, and met . . .' he glanced at Elizabeth.

'Very fortuitous. They will pay, Charlotte, which is sadly more than your business is doing at the moment. Look on it as a temporary measure. It will fill a gap until you can start to take bookings again.'

'But I thought you didn't want people here, Gran? And they will,' she didn't want to offend Jamie, but she had to say it, 'be traipsing everywhere. You said that no way would you let me open the place to the public.' Not that she wanted to.

'James?'

'We'll only work outside. We just want the grounds for shooting. The rest is all sorted.' Jamie didn't look offended.

'But there will be people and catering vans . . . burgers!' Lottie finished triumphantly, knowing her gran abhorred everything fast-food related.

'I'm sure there wouldn't be food in wrappers, would there?'

'No, definitely no, I mean not. We have a very good catering van, with, er, plates and forks and everything.' His voice tailed off as he looked from Elizabeth back to Lottie, then back again. 'Proper forks. No plastic and lots of bins. And people to tidy up.'

'There.' Elizabeth tapped her stick on the floor, which was usually followed by a 'that's settled'.

'But we need money now, not when the polo season starts, Gran.'

'We'd want to shoot now – well soon. You know, all the setting-up shots. It's not just polo. And,' he paused, 'you'd get some kind of payment as soon as the contract's signed.'

'You can't gallop horses flat out this time of year, you'll ruin the grounds and their legs.'

'It's not all about the game. Well, I don't think it is much at all, to be honest. It's about one player, mainly. There's only a tiny bit of actual polo. The horses are just a kind of backdrop really. But, I mean, you still do stuff when you're not in the show-jumping season, don't you?'

'Three-day eventing.' Lottie tried not to scowl. 'We event. It's Dad that does the show-jumping.' She liked the weddings because they were, well, contained. Usually. Apart from when they had the fire.

The bloody fire. She sighed and tried to keep her attention on Jamie and the closest thing to a survival plan that they'd got. 'So there isn't actually any polo?'

'Well, yes, there is some.' Jamie frowned. 'But not much. It's not a film about polo, more a love story.'

'Do you really know?'

'Well, not in detail.' He shrugged and pulled the type of comical face one of the horses did when he could smell perfume, but minus the curled lip, which would have been very strange. 'I am just the advance party. You'd get told loads more before you had to sign the contract, you know. All your questions answered. But Seb and Pandora have both seen pictures and they're really mad about this place. Honest.' He looked so sincere that Lottie felt guilty about not jumping in and shouting yes. 'They'll be gutted if you say no.' She tried not to feel even worse. 'And initially we'll shoot the other stuff, without the horses, well, without the riding. The story is a kind of love-triangle thing. You know, the rock star wants a hideaway and his wife isn't keen at first because she doesn't want to be stuck in the sticks, but then she falls in love with the glamorous house. She gets a bit carried away, wants to do the whole ladyship thing, and then meets the real deal – a guy who's old money, posh, not like her husband. He's the polo-player. I think at first he comes to see if they can carry on playing polo here and they have an affair, but it all goes wrong. She realises she doesn't belong here and goes back to the city. Or something like that.'

Lottie frowned. 'With her rock star?'

'Yeah, I guess so.'

'So they aren't actual polo-players, just actors?' Lottie couldn't put her finger on exactly why she didn't like the idea, but it made her uneasy. In fact, it sounded worse now he'd told her more. It spoke of upheaval. And the fact that Elizabeth was all for it just made her even more suspicious.

Elizabeth would rather be penniless and have battles with the bank than let riff-raff into her beloved home. They'd been dodging the march of progress for years; it had been a major triumph when she'd finally got decent broadband installed and it didn't take three days to download an eventing entry form. But the pipes were still gurgling, the moth-eaten rugs still lay on the woodworm-riddled floor, and she'd threatened the last property developer who'd suggested a theme park and open days with a shotgun. Which made the idea of her welcoming a film crew all very strange.

'Well, there is one player. He advises and sorts everything.'

'One?'

'Actual polo-player. He'll be advising on all the horse stuff, the rest are actors. It's all going to be done properly.'

'And you won't be straying around the estate, or coming inside the house, or—'

'Setting it on fire? Was that really a disgruntled groom, like the paper said?'

'Well *he* said it actually, on his Facebook page. Said we were a load of stuck-up toffs who deserved what we got.' Lottie frowned. 'If you don't mind, I'm getting rather fed up of discussing it.'

'Sure. I guess the bit in today's papers hasn't helped?'

'That's one way of putting it.' She really had to stop thinking about the past and move on to the solution. She glanced at Elizabeth, who hadn't actually directly mentioned the latest reports, and wondered if she'd read them. She probably had. As Sam had said, very little got past her eagle eyes. 'Well, I suppose this could be a good idea, as a one-off, of course.'

'Splendid,' Elizabeth pursed her lips as though she'd decided it was time to have the final say. 'I knew you'd come round to my way of thinking, dear.'

'So, it won't be until Spring, I suppose, when the weather picks up?'

'Oh no, dear. James came to me before Christmas, not long after we'd been in the papers with the fire. This Sebastian chap would like a meeting as soon as possible. I suggest that you invite him here next week and sort all the paperwork. Haven't spoken to him myself. Thought I'd leave all that to you, seeing as you're in charge, but I'm sure he's a splendid chap. Seems keen to get a move on from what young James said.'

'Next week?' Lottie, who'd been feeling comforted by the 'you're in charge' comment, sat down abruptly and took a large gulp of gin and tonic.

'No use in dilly-dallying. We've had long enough with no income, and we are still no further forward, are we?'

Lottie wondered if that was the royal 'we', as in 'her', or if they were in this together. She opened her mouth, thought better about asking, and shut it again.

'We really do need some more money coming in,' Elizabeth paused and peered at Lottie, 'before it starts going out.'

Ah, so that answered one question. Her grandmother did know about all the cancellations and demands for deposits to be returned.

'Right, splendid. I think this warrants a toast. Do pour us all another drink, James.'

Jamie scrabbled up from his position on the floor and took Lottie's empty glass from her frozen fingers.

Next week. She watched as he capably poured the drinks. Yes, it made sense. He hadn't been awkward, he felt at home, he'd been here before (lots of times, no doubt) without her knowing. He'd just been embarrassed about the fact she didn't know. Elizabeth had been planning this for weeks and biding her time to announce it.

'I thought I was running the estate, Gran?'

'You are, dear.'

'But, you can't just barge in and make new arrangements like that. You're, you're . . .'

'Interfering? If you'd have had any real objection, then we would have stopped it. But,' her tone softened, 'we can't wait any longer, can we? And this is just a short-term measure. What else can we do, Charlotte? You've done a splendid job with your business and, believe me, I would not even consider a project like this if we had an alternative. But we don't, do we my dear? And I really think that newspaper article this morning proves that we're not going to get any new bookings until we're in a position to prove we can honour them, are we, dear?'

Lottie sighed. 'Give me until tomorrow, I'll talk to Rory.' She doubted very much that her fun-loving husband would be able to magic another solution out of thin air. But who knew?

Chapter 7

Rory Steel stared into the stable, which reflected the emptiness he felt inside perfectly. He couldn't put it off any longer. He had to come clean with his wife.

They'd hit lows before and struggled through them together, but this time he had a horrible feeling they were well and truly sinking. Adding to the burden of responsibility that Lottie shouldered so stoically hadn't been part of his plan at all.

Rory had always been known in Tippermere, and throughout the three-day eventing community, for his sense of fun, and, it had to be said, a certain irresponsibility. But, since he had taken the blind leap into matrimony he'd been surprised to realise just how important his wife was to him. He wanted to love and care for her, but it was more than that. He wanted to protect her, to share the responsibility of looking after the inherited estate that he'd grown to love.

Rory admired and loved his scatty wife, and he wanted to provide for her. To fill the house with children and to help put food on the table, so that she no longer felt the need to take a spreadsheet, calculator, and frown to bed on a regular basis.

Now he looked gloomily into the echoingly empty stable and knew that one particular gift horse had bolted.

With his easy manner and dashing good looks people always assumed that Rory had it easy, but he'd worked his way up the hard way. He had an eye for a good horse, and the type of natural riding ability that meant that he was prepared to take a risk – buy a difficult horse cheap and turn it into a winner. Sometimes all the bruises and scrapes were worth it and it worked; sometimes the best he could hope for was to break even and sell the animal on as a slightly safer ride, but one that was never going to survive in the demanding world of eventing. But he always bounced back onto his feet with a grin on his face and a joke at his own expense.

Six foot tall, with the toned thighs of an athlete, roguish grin, and a wicked sense of humour, the easy-going Rory had always been a hit with the girls. But now, in his early thirties, he was at his peak, both physically and mentally. Rory had always been one of the lads, as comfortable with a pint in his hand as he was with a good malt whisky, and he'd had a female following since his first televised outing, where he'd had a disastrous encounter with a lake.

After the type of ducking that should have left him gasping, he'd very carefully removed his hat and body-protector, run a hand through his sopping curls, then strode out of the lake in full-on Mr Darcy mode, but with a cheeky grin rather than brooding intent. The resultant photographs that were splashed (as he liked to recall) over many a Sunday newspaper won him an adoring fan club and a sponsorship deal that had finally meant he had a reliable horsebox and a horse that wasn't intent on killing both of them. Over the years he'd come to count his sponsor as a friend. Until today.

Closing the stable door with a heavy clunk, Rory shoved his hands into his jacket pockets then glanced down at the terrier that was seldom far from his feet. 'We'd better wave goodbye and then go and break the bad news, hadn't we, Tilly?' The dog cocked her head on one side, as though she understood every word, then she spun round and made a run towards the archway that divided the stable yard from the main part of the Tipping House Estate.

* * *

Lottie stared at the horsebox as it trundled its way down the long driveway away from Tipping House and wondered if she'd forgotten something important.

As it was winter it was unlikely Rory was competing, and even if he was going to an indoor show-jumping competition with one of the youngsters she was absolutely sure he would have texted her before he set off. It was also highly unlikely he'd just pop out anywhere without telling her, unless he'd discovered a bargain horse that he couldn't resist and daren't tell her? She frowned. No, surely he wouldn't? Not when they were in such dire straits, and even *he* didn't often buy horses at this time of year unless they were real bargains, as it just meant months of feeding another mouth. There was the slight possibility he was taking one of the young horses out for a run in the lorry, so that they could add 'travels well' to its CV, but she was sure he'd have mentioned it, even if he was only going round the block.

A slight movement down by the yard caught her eye and she was surprised to see Rory standing in the archway, Tilly in his arms, staring after the horsebox in much the same way she was. Which was totally confusing. If Rory was still on the yard, who the hell was driving off with their horsebox?

With a sense of foreboding, Lottie flew down the stairs two at a time, Harry the spaniel at her heels. She shoved her feet into the nearest pair of wellingtons and flung the door open just in time to see her husband disappearing back into the stable yard.

It wasn't hard to spot Rory when Lottie dashed through the archway into the small circular yard. He was sitting on the edge of the fountain, with Tilly the terrier perched on his knee, looking as sad as she'd ever seen him. Dejected, she decided, was the word.

'I just saw the horsebox. What's happened? Rory?' He put the dog down and stared at her wordlessly. 'Is one of the horses ill?'

'Worse. I'm afraid,' he glanced towards one of the stables, 'I've got some bad news, darling.' He groaned and put his head in his hands. 'Shit. I was really hoping I would be able to sort something out before I had to tell you.' His voice was muffled. 'I'm sorry.' The sigh came from somewhere deep inside him and Lottie felt a twinge of alarm. Rory might not be reliable, but he never gave up, he always saw the positive side of things.

She looked around the yard, from stable to stable.

'Simon. Where's Simon? He's not . . .' For a horrible moment the word 'dead' hung in the air between them, but that was impossible. 'He's not in his stable.' The handsome grey liked to know what was going on, his head was the first to appear at his stable door whenever he heard voices on the yard. He'd nicker a welcome and then wait for the polo mint that he knew he deserved.

'He's gone. Oh Christ, I am so sorry.'

Rory repeatedly saying sorry was nearly as alarming as the missing horse. Lottie strode across the yard and peered over the stable door, not because she didn't believe Rory, but because it didn't seem possible.

'Gone, but how can he be gone? You can't just sell him, Rory, he's not ours . . .'

'Exactly. He's not ours to sell. David sent somebody over to collect him,' Rory looked up, tawny eyes sorrowful, 'he's pulled out, he's not going to sponsor me any longer.'

'But I saw our—'

'Horsebox? It's his horsebox, remember, darling. He's taken his bloody lorry and his horses.' Rory stood up abruptly. 'Shit.' Simon wasn't just any horse, he was the best horse he'd ever had the opportunity to compete. Maybe not the best he'd ever sat on, but a brilliant, talented horse and a top-class eventer were two different things. Simon was as honest and big-hearted as they came and he knew his job.

The second horse that David had provided was a talented youngster who hadn't been with them long, but Rory had already bonded with the animal and was convinced he had a brilliant future ahead.

'But why?' Lottie stared at him in disbelief. Rory and Simon had gelled from day one, and over the last twelve months had started to look like serious contenders. 'Why on earth would he do that?'

'Divorce. He's getting frigging divorced.'

Lottie looked at him blankly, wondering what that had to do with them. 'But Simon was going so well for you, and David knew that. I thought he liked us.'

'He did like us.' Rory sighed. 'We're not the issue. Well, it isn't actually him that's got a problem, it's his wife. He told me a while ago that she's taking him to the cleaners, wants half of everything and that includes the horses. He was talking about shipping them out of the country, all of them, including Simon, until after the court case, but she beat him to it. It's her that sent somebody over.'

'Her? But it's David who sponsors you. How can she? Couldn't you stop them?'

'It's her name on the papers too, for tax reasons, no doubt.' Rory rolled his eyes. 'I couldn't stop her, believe me I tried to, but she's got as much right . . .'

'Did you tell David?'

'I rang him, he went ape-shit, but there's not a lot he could do apart from rant.'

Lottie cringed. David on a rant wasn't a pretty sight.

'I can understand her leaving him, I suppose. He could be pretty nasty. To be honest, I'm surprised she didn't go earlier. They didn't exactly get on, did they? They were always having a go at each other. He could be so rude and bossy.'

'Well, I suppose he wanted a glamorous wife, and she wanted a rich husband who took her to places.' Rory shrugged. 'There's lot of people like that, even these days.'

'But why did she have to go after the horses? She hates horses. The only thing she liked about them was being able to dress up and boast when you were competing.'

'Exactly.' His tone was dry. 'She liked being an owner but she knew he liked it even more. I don't think she's exactly planning on keeping them to ride herself.'

'So couldn't we offer to buy them? You know, put down a deposit?'

'And where would we get that from?' His voice was soft and he grabbed hold of Lottie's hand and pulled her towards him. 'He's a top-class horse. We'd never get our hands on that kind of money even if things were going well. Besides, as far as the horses go she doesn't give a shit about the money, she's just having a go at him. She'll probably hide them away for a bit then give them away. It's spite. She wants to wind him up and I reckon she's succeeded. She knows how much Simon's success means to him. From what he said, I reckon he's been stingy over the settlement, so the gloves are off. Come here, you're cold.'

'I'm fine, honest.' Lottie, who hadn't thought to grab a coat, wrapped her arms around herself and concentrated on stopping her teeth chattering. 'So no more sponsorship money.'

'Nope. He's not going to pay me if I'm not riding his horses, is he?'

'You don't think he'll buy you another one? You know, that she doesn't know about?' She was clutching at straws; she knew she was.

'He's busy trying to look as poor as possible; going out buying horses isn't going to work in his favour when it comes to agreeing a divorce settlement, is it? I was rather hoping they'd reach some kind of agreement and it wouldn't get to this. Oh shit, I am so sorry this had to happen right now, Lots.'

Lottie sighed. 'It's not your fault, darling.' Then she looked up, determined to see the bright side. 'At least we didn't sell Minty to him.'

After a couple of years' battling with Lottie's very temperamental mare, Black Gold, Rory and Lottie had realised that despite her huge potential she was never going to be suited to competition. She was just too inconsistent. And Rory was afraid that one day she'd fall too hard, or spook in the wrong place and put Lottie in hospital. Or worse.

So they'd put her in foal, hoping that it might settle her, and if they were lucky produce an eventer that had talent and temperament to match. And it looked like they'd hit the jackpot.

Her filly foal, Araminta, had been a hit from the moment she'd struggled to her feet on impossibly long, wobbly legs. She didn't bite or kick and she moved like an angel – eating up the ground effortlessly with the type of movement and natural carriage that made her stand out. David had wanted to buy her, promising that he'd guarantee Rory the ride, but something had stopped Lottie and Rory from signing on the dotted line. She was the first homebred horse they'd had with that elusive star quality, and despite their seriously diminished bank balance they'd been loath to let her go.

'True, thank God for that. But she's only two; we'll be destitute by the time she starts to compete, and I really need to attract another backer now.' He gave a rueful smile and ruffled Lottie's hair. 'And we need a new horsebox or we'll be hacking to events.'

'So we really haven't got any choice at all now, have we? Gran was right, we have to let the film crew in or the money will run out long before we get back on our feet.'

'Much as I hate to admit that the old dragon has won again,' he shrugged and held her tighter, 'what else can we do? It is pretty quiet round here right now, though, so I can keep an eye on them and we've had the contract checked through – it all seems straightforward enough.'

'I don't like it.'

'Me neither, if I'm honest, but do we have any choice?'

'Not really.'

'Let's go for it, gorgeous, and come next season I'll have a new loaded sponsor, and we'll have a new USP for the wedding business.'

'USP?' Lottie looked at him blankly.

'Well before, people just wanted to come so they could imagine they were gentry for the day, but after this they'll be able to boast they've been on the film set. USP, unique selling point.' He shrugged and grinned. 'Maybe old Lizzie has done us a massive favour. How bad can it be?'

* * *

'What is it with fucking scriptwriters who think they're directors?' Sebastian Drakelow jabbed irritably at his laptop, adding, no doubt, a sarcastic comment, then ran long, slim fingers through his ash-blond hair before resting thumb and forefinger on the bridge of his nose. 'For God's sake, will somebody answer that bloody phone?'

'It's your bloody phone, you answer it, darling.' Pandora's tone was mild and faintly bored, the voice of a disinterested mother talking to a toddler. She crossed one long, elegant leg over the other and stared at her husband as she took a sip from the champagne flute, and then shifted her gaze so that she could watch the bubbles slowly rise to the top. 'What did your last servant die of?'

Seb looked up, cold, grey eyes narrowed, and scowled. 'Where's Jamie?'

'It's Sunday, darling. The terms "intern" and "interned" have different meanings.'

'Ha, bloody, ha. Who's ringing on a Sunday anyway?'

'Why don't you answer it if you want to find out? It's probably your mother demanding you go over and change a light bulb for her.'

Seb looked at his wife and wondered, not for the first time, how he'd managed to marry somebody who was even more selfish than he was. She was beautiful, in a thin, slightly brittle, contained kind of way, and she was smart. A lethal combination, he'd discovered. What Pandora wanted, Pandora got. She possessed more manipulative instinct in her little finger than most people thought existed, and she used every wile at her disposal in pursuit of her desires. The fact that she had such a striking appearance, with her flame-red hair and feline, green eyes certainly didn't hamper her. Seb might not always like his wife, but he admired her; he'd always found it impossible to resist pure, unadulterated passion and ambition.

Pandora might not be an intellectual but she was as streetwise as they came and she was quick. A born improviser. She was also, he deduced, pissed off with him for some reason – or curiosity would have forced her to answer his goddamn phone.

'She has a little man to do that for her these days. A home help.'

Pandora raised one beautifully arched eyebrow and he laughed.

'Oh I do love you, you miserable cow. What have I done now?'

'I'm bored. We need a change of scene.'

'We'll be filming again soon.'

'A proper change of scene. This place is so,' she waved a dismissive hand that took in the luxurious penthouse suite in one gesture, 'so crass. It has no class, darling. I want class. I want to be somebody.'

'You are somebody.' He leant back and rested one ankle on his knee, wondering where this was going.

'I want to be in *Tatler*, not *Heat*. I need a challenge, Seb. Oh, what's the point, you will never understand. Answer that fucking phone, it's giving me a headache.'

'No, you're right, I don't understand. Why on earth would you want to be in *Tatler*? Country life involves tramping about in the countryside and wearing tweed.' With a sigh Seb folded down the lid of his laptop and started to rifle through the papers that were strewn across the large desk. The fact that whoever was trying to talk to him was being so persistent was mildly intriguing. He finally spotted his mobile on the chair across from his wife.

'Yes?' Seb sank down into the ornate reproduction armchair and put his feet up on the glass-topped table, winning a disapproving glare from Pandora that brought a grin to his face.

His habits annoyed her, she frustrated the hell out of him, but in a strange way the relationship worked.

'You'll leave marks on the glass.'

'You'll get frown lines. Sorry? No, I wasn't talking to you, I was talking to my wife. Who did you say you were?' He straightened up at the response and put his feet firmly back on the floor. 'Lady Elizabeth?'

Pandora stopped glaring, and froze, her glass of bubbly inches away from her parted lips.

'You're not Lady Elizabeth? Well who the f— . . . oh, her granddaughter, I see. Next week? You are kidding? We either get on with this or the deal is off. We'll make it tomorrow . . . yes, sorry there's no leeway, no point in delaying. I've got a schedule to work to. I'll be there mid-morning, before the light fades so that I can see what I'm paying for . . . That's fine . . . right . . . no, the solicitors deal with contractual questions. We'll see you tomorrow, then. Any issues, deal with Jamie before I arrive.'

Seb very deliberately placed the phone face-down on the table, then he slowly lifted his gaze to meet Pandora's and fought the triumphant smile that was threatening to split his serious features.

'Well? You look like the cat that got the cream. Tell me.'

'I think you might yet get to be in *Tatler*, darling. I've just done a deal on the most amazing location for our shoot.'

Pandora gently put her glass down. 'Really?'

'Really. You might even have heard of the place, the Tipping

House Estate. There's some photos lying about the place some-where.' He waved a dismissive hand. 'Shame it's out in the fucking sticks, though, but you can't have everything. Knew we'd wear the old trout down in the end. Looks like Jamie is finally earning his money.'

'You don't pay him, darling.' She was as restrained as ever, but he could tell by the tight edge to her voice that she was interested.

Seb ignored the comment. 'I'm going over tomorrow before she gets chance to change her mind. They think they own the country, people like that. All the bloody same, need pinning down.'

She smiled, or rather her mouth did, the rest of her face remained rigidly Botoxed into position. 'It sounds wonderful, Seb. If you're impressed by it, it must be fabulous. Worth a toast?' Oh yes, she'd heard of it. She raised her own half-empty glass and wiggled it in invitation. 'And then, maybe I will let you do some pinning down of me.'

Seb, shocked by the suggestion of sex with his wife, who really hated any messiness, forgot his golden rule of keeping her away from all business arrangements. 'I don't suppose you want to tag along, do you? Meet these Stanthrops, Stanhopes, whatever they're fucking called, for yourself.'

She did, but she wasn't going to. 'I'll leave it in your capable hands, darling. I trust your judgement totally. There will be plenty of time for me to meet them when they've signed the contract,' her eyes narrowed, 'I'm sure it will be as watertight as ever. You know I hate disappointment.'

'You won't be disappointed, darling.' He breathed normally again. 'Once they've signed there will be no turning back. It will be, as they say, in the can.'

'How wonderful.' Her tone lifted. 'Do bring the bottle to the bedroom, darling, and we'll celebrate by putting that cute little cock of yours in my capable hands.'

Seb allowed himself a smile. He had been about to warn her off the Botox, get some expression back in her face before she went in front of the camera, but he knew that in life timing was everything.

Directions could wait, which was more than his body, fired up with the excitement of success was prepared to do.

Chapter 8

Seb was tired. If he had his way he would never set foot north of Birmingham, well Stratford-upon-Avon, if he was honest. Life 'up north' depressed him. The skies were permanently grey, the people mumbled and there were far too many terriers, whippets, and too much scratchy tweed for his liking.

He had never forgiven his father for sending him to school in Scotland to make a man of him. The place had been fucking freezing, the food awful, and the boys had been either landed gentry who looked down their aristocratic noses at him, or locals who were unintelligible. It was an experience he'd never discussed with his wife, and never intended to, and one that meant he would never ever be prepared to move out of the city as she currently seemed obsessed with doing.

Seb had no desire to be in *Tatler*. He was more than happy to let Pandora act out her fantasies on a film set, but by the time they shot the final scene he fully expected her to have got the silly idea out of her system and be content to return to civilisation. It was an infatuation he would be relieved to see the back of.

He hated 'the gentry', he hated fresh air, he hated animals, and he hated the shambolic disorder that often accompanied all three.

But he was very fond of his wife and trusted his market research, which told him that this particular project could be a winner. Even if it did sound like his worst nightmare.

It niggled him that he hadn't been able to find the perfect location in Oxfordshire, or at least nearer to home, but Jamie had found this place and he had to admit it did look perfect. And it was cheap, well, relatively cheap.

Seb suspected that Pandora, in common with many people, was under the illusion that country manors were still symbols of power and affluence, with a butler in every corner and villagers who doffed their caps in a show of subservience. He had a feeling that she was about to be sadly disillusioned by the reality, but no doubt his polished on-screen version would soften the blow. She would be portrayed as a rich, happy bitch wallowing in perfect surroundings. She could live the dream and then they could have a wrap party and return to their immaculate penthouse apartment overlooking the Thames and plan the next project. Hopefully one that did not involve livestock and the accompanying outdoorsy crap.

After spending an interminable amount of time on the M6 motorway he had actually been relieved when he'd emerged into the relatively green countryside that was Cheshire. The uniform hedges, level fields, and neat villages had soothed his nerves, until the main roads had petered out and he hit the winding lanes that announced Tippermere, and he got lost. How could it be so frigging difficult to find a stonking big country estate?

Xander Rossi, it appeared, had encountered no such difficulty. His four-wheel drive was parked just inside the imposing gateposts when Seb swung his own, far sleeker and more highly polished, Mercedes between them. Seb would have liked to have hated the suave, independent man. He was far too self-confident and with a tendency to overrule Seb's decisions 'for the animals' sake', which pissed him off no end. But he knew he needed the man.

One, he needed some kind of horse expert on the shoot, as he'd seen first-hand the havoc the beasts could cause in uneducated hands. If he had the choice he'd never have an animal of any shape or size on set, but he recognised market forces. Cute and cuddly drew in the crowds, so he'd incorporate the beasts if it killed him. Though he'd rather it didn't, which was why he employed people like Xander. And two (perhaps more importantly) he needed somebody to step in when Pandora upset the natives. Which she was guaranteed to. The man might be taciturn and aloof at times, but he had a certain charm and people, for some unknown reason, seemed to warm to him. His apologies carried far more weight than Seb's offers of compensation and Pandora's grudging apologies ever did, and the fact that he was Pandora's brother didn't hurt one bit. If Pandora got abusive, the man barely flinched. He was used to her acidic tongue.

As long as Xander didn't make Seb look like a dick he was willing to make allowances. The benefits outweighed the disadvantages big time.

Xander wound down the window of his vehicle and his dog stuck its nose out. 'Get lost?'

'Fuck off, and why did you have to bring that thing?'

Xander laughed. He was used to fractious horses and treated Seb and his tantrums in much the same way he'd treat a temperamental mare. Unlike most of Seb's minions he didn't rely on an income from the man, so he always had the option to walk away. Which Seb was well aware of and it niggled him no end. He expected to be treated with respect and if he said 'jump', people were supposed to frigging leap off the floor not ask why.

'She likes an outing, don't you, Ella?' Xander stroked her head, thinking how much more pleasant a dog's company was than most humans. The little wire-haired dachshund might be quite strong-willed, but she took most things in her stride and never failed to make life a little bit better, however hard a day he'd had. 'I can see you don't.'

'How sitting on a motorway for hours surrounded by morons is supposed to put me in a good mood, God only knows.' Seb glared at the dog, which he considered scruffy, noisy, and smelly. Why the hell did some people have to be accompanied by an animal everywhere they went?

'You didn't have to come. You could have sent somebody else to get the contract signed.'

'I need to know this is done properly. These people think they run the bloody country, give them an inch and they'll take a mile.'

'They do, don't they?' Xander was amused. 'Run the bloody country? House of Lords and all that stuff. It's a different way of living out here, Seb. You can earn as much as you want, but if you've not got the breeding . . .'

'Bloody archaic crap.'

'Are you sure you want to make this film?'

'Pandora does and we can make a killing with it. It ticks every box right now. Anyhow, it's not about gentry, it's about real people.'

'You call rock stars real?'

Seb ignored him. 'And it's about a wife who soon discovers what a load of crap this country living is and practically begs to go back to the city.'

'Ahh.' Xander raised an eyebrow, genuinely amused at the power games his half-sister and brother-in-law played with each other. 'Have you told Pandora the ending?'

Seb, for the first time since he'd set off on his trip, smiled. 'She'll get it. It makes sense. After a few months' shooting in the back of beyond she'll be dying to get back to normality. She will recognise the truth in the fiction.'

Xander shook his head slowly. Normality to Pandora was a weekly manicure, a monthly massage, and her adoring fans camped on the doorstep. Camping out here would be literal.

They'd need a tent and thermal underwear and he wasn't convinced her fans were quite that besotted.

'Come on, I need to get this contract signed before I change my mind and shoot it all on green screen. Where's this frigging house?'

'Just round the corner.' Xander swung his car door open and stepped out. 'We'll walk. Some fresh air might improve your mood.'

Five minutes later Seb allowed himself a full-on smile, a rare occurrence that Pandora had once told him lifted his sour features into haughty good looks. The 'frigging house' was worth the long drive. Although it did serve as a reminder that in the great United Kingdom there were certainly the haves and the have-nots.

This project had been Pandora's idea, although he was well aware that she wanted him to think it was his, but he wasn't as daft or as easily manipulated as she thought. At the moment he still wasn't sure if it was because she wanted to sleep with the scriptwriter, saw real potential in it, or just wanted a change of pace. But it was irrelevant.

Their relationship very much worked on a need-to-know basis. She turned a blind eye to his OCD; he never commented on the money she spent on Botox and shoes. He knew that in her head she was faithful to him and that the other men meant nothing. Pandora needed to have her ego massaged: on the outside she was an ice queen but on the inside she was like a small child with a desperate need of reassurance.

Despite her conniving though, he'd recognised this project as a stroke of genius. Or he wouldn't have been here.

'Remind me to let Jamie have a day off.'

'Surprised you didn't get him to look for somewhere closer to home.'

'I did, didn't Pandora tell you? It fell through, which is why we need to get a move on and make sure this place can't.' Tipping

House had been top of the list when he'd seen Jamie's pictures, which, shot in the moonlight, had lent an otherworldliness to the place that was hard to resist, but the owners had stalled, been unwilling to commit, so he'd abandoned the idea. With the decisiveness that had made him the success he was, he had moved on to the next location on the list. It was their loss not his, except now he was beginning to feel rather pleased at the way events had turned out. He wouldn't say it was down to fate or fortune. Seb made his own luck, defined his own future. 'Right, you go and check out the stables and see where we can set up the temporary block. It's arriving tomorrow. Any problems, get them sorted. They're expecting you, so let's start as we mean to go on. I'll go and set out some ground rules with this woman and make sure they don't think they can stick their noses in. God, how I hate dealing with these aristocratic twats.'

* * *

'Hi.'

Tabatha Strachan, who had been shovelling muck in time to a very heavy rock track, didn't hear the voice, but she did feel the tap on her shoulder. She wheeled round, an angry retort on her lips, then forgot everything as her jaw dropped, along with the pitchfork, which hit the ground with a clatter.

At twenty-four years old, Tab had enjoyed an uncommunicative Goth phase, struggled through a hormone-and-embarrassment-ridden early twenties, and was now at the smart-talking, take-no-shit stage. Today was the first time in months that she'd been dumbstruck.

'Woah!' The man responsible held his hands up in surrender, then stuck one out in greeting. 'Sorry if I made you jump. I'm Xander. Thought I better introduce myself before we get started.'

Tab hastily tugged her glove off and wiped her own, rather sweatier, palm, down the back of her jodhpurs before grabbing hold of the offered hand and hanging on in much the same way she'd hang on to a horse that was trying to bolt with her.

Working for Rory came with one big drawback (little if no pay) and two main benefits. One, she got close to Rory, who she had idolised for, well, like ever (even if he only seemed to lust after his wife and was getting worse from what she could tell, which was pretty yuk), and two she got to ride some pretty good horses. Being ordered to stick her bum out less, her heels down more, and stop waving her elbows about like flags in the wind could get pretty boring, but she had to admit her riding had improved no end since she'd come to Tippermere with her ex-model father Tom.

Now she had to add a third benefit. This man was ab-so-lutely fucking gorgeous. Lots of the eventers that Rory and Lottie knew were fairly sexy, but this guy was off the scale.

She suddenly realised he was trying to extricate his hand and dropped it like a hot coal.

Wow. Just wow. Amazing. 'Tab, I mean Tabatha, well Tab to friends. I work here, well I help out. I ride and er . . .'

Xander tucked his reclaimed hand safely away in his pocket, a faint crinkle of amusement around his eyes. 'Muck out? Nice yard, Tabatha.'

'Er, yes.' Tab's mind was more on 'nice arse', which the stranger definitely displayed when he swung around to take in the view. Along with nice broad shoulders, washboard stomach, amazingly gorgeous thick, dark hair and startlingly blue eyes that contrasted with his tanned skin in a way that made her want to stare like a loony. 'Before you get started?' His first words had finally filtered through to her brain.

'I've got a feeling Seb will be moving quite quick once he's sorted the paperwork. There aren't any stables free in here, are there? Most of the ponies will be fine in the temporary stables we're setting up, but a couple of them would settle better where it's a bit quieter, if you can squeeze them in.'

'Would they?' Maybe it was a dream. She definitely felt light-headed. In fact if she wasn't careful she'd start purring like a cat any second now, and possibly rubbing her head against his leg . . .

'Away from all the noise.'

She cleared her throat. 'Noise? What noise? It's pretty quiet round here.'

'When the rest of the crew arrive.'

'Crew?' Tab stopped watching his sexy lips moving abruptly. She hadn't got a clue what he was on about and had the distinct feeling she was about to make herself look a complete twat.

'Film crew? You don't mean, you . . .'

No way was she going to admit that he wasn't making any sense at all, that nobody around here told her a frigging thing. She really was going to give Rory a mouthful when he got back to the yard. How could he not tell her that he was expecting a film crew? What was it, a documentary on what a star-in-the-making he was, or just some other Tipping House promotion? And they had more than enough horses already. They'd better not be expecting her to muck out even more stables. 'Well, there are a couple of boxes free, the horses Rory lost, but I'm not sure if he's got other plans for them. I mean it isn't really up to me, if you haven't already agreed it with him. You need to check with him, really.'

'Rory?'

'It's his yard.'

'Oh.' Xander frowned. 'I thought it was part of the estate?'

'It is.' It was her turn to feel confused now.

'Which is run by Lady Elizabeth Stanthorpe?'

'Oh no, it's Lottie and Rory, her husband, that do all this. Elizabeth's quite old. She doesn't have anything to do with the yard.'

'Lottie?'

'Lottie's her granddaughter. Lottie Brinkley, I mean Steel.'

'Brinkley? Charlotte Brinkley?'

'That's what I said, isn't it?'

'The daughter of that show-jumper?'

This would be funny if it wasn't so confusing, Tab decided. And if he wasn't so hot. In fact, if he hadn't been so good-looking she'd have chased him out of the yard with the pitchfork by now. Tilly the terrier was ace at chasing idiots off the premises – she was unbeatable when it came to ankle-nipping. 'Yeah, she's Billy's daughter. Why, do you know her?'

'I might.'

'Elizabeth's like her gran on her mother's side, but her mum died years ago.' Tab shrugged. 'Which is why she gets the place. And she's Steel now,' she could have sworn there was a flicker of irritation across those beautiful features. And despite the fact that she shouldn't enjoy being the bearer of bad news (if that's what it was), she was actually quite pleased, 'since she married Rory.' She'd scream if he was just here because he was after Lottie. She thought about adding, '*Who she loves very dearly*' but decided that might be over the top.

'Ahh. I had better go and find this Rory, then, I suppose. Any hints?'

'He's out teaching, but Lottie's in. She's up at the house.' Tab waved vaguely in the direction of the yard entrance.

'I suppose I better go and ask her, then.'

He didn't look too enthusiastic, thought Tab. 'She's very nice, but you already know that, don't you? I'm sure she'll say yes. I mean I would.' *Oh God, I would, I would.* 'I can take you there if you want.'

He raised an eyebrow. 'I'm sure I'll find it.'

Which anybody but an idiot would, thought Tab. Who could miss a bloody big mansion that was literally yards away?

'Catch you later. Thanks for the help.'

'Any time.' She was talking to his back as he strode off, but she didn't care. She didn't have a clue who he was, why on earth

101

he'd want to stable his horses here, or why he seemed so reluctant to talk to Lottie. But it didn't matter. He said he'd catch her later, which meant she'd see him again.

Chapter 9

'Are you expecting somebody, babe? We're not in your way are we?' Sam, who had been busy filling Lottie in on just how many children she intended presenting her darling husband with, paused mid-sentence at the sound of the doorbell.

'Not that I know of.' Lottie frowned up, from where she was crouched on all-fours on the floor pretending to be a horse. 'Unless it's somebody with an offer for the house that I just can't refuse, but I can.' She sighed. 'Why do people think that everybody has a price?'

'Cos they usually do, hun. It's okay, don't you worry about it, I'll get it. You carry on playing with Roxy. You're so much better at it than I am, isn't she princess?' Roxy giggled, and Lottie heaved a sigh of relief.

Thinking about developers trying to buy the Tipping House Estate was bad enough, but she'd really started to wonder if all this baby talk was just Sam being Sam, or if she was in cahoots with Rory in a bid to persuade her that being pregnant was all she wanted to do with her life.

'I bet it's just one of them tenant farmers of yours. Some of them are really dishy, aren't they? I'll sort him out for you and if it's anybody else I'll tell them where to stick their offers.'

Sam winked as she waltzed out of the room on her bare feet, her bracelets jangling. The pause for breath hadn't lasted long and she was in full flow again, but at least it was nothing to do with swollen boobs, morning sickness, or dribble. 'My mam still can't believe this place, babe, she says she's going to read that Lady Chatterley-thingy book and find out what you really get up to.'

Lottie's groan was drowned out by the sound of the large front oak door being opened and then rather rapidly closed again. 'Hang on, don't go away.'

It didn't sound like she was about to tell anybody where to stick anything. 'What's up, Sam? It's not reporters again, is it?'

'Oh my God no, babe.' Sam was in the room, had grabbed her high heels from the corner, and was heading back into the hallway as she spoke, hopping on one foot as she tried to get a shoe on. 'But it's not one of your hunks in wellies either. I need to get me heels back on. Does my hair look okay? I can't talk to somebody that looks like that when I look a state. I'd never forgive myself. Oh my God, babe, if he's gay I want him as my new best friend.'

Lottie stared after Sam. She knew her friend was very happily married, but there was a definite husky catch to the normally bubbly, and quite loud, tone of her voice, which meant whoever was at the door had made some kind of impact.

She frowned. She wasn't expecting anybody else now that she'd got her perfunctory meeting with Seb Drakelow over and done with. Gosh that man had been rude, most unpleasant. And she couldn't think of a single man she knew that Sam hadn't already met.

Sam, she knew, had never thought being happy should prevent her from admiring the scenery. A lot of men, in her opinion, qualified as cute, or fit, or smouldering, and worth a second look. And she liked to look her best, though no one would ever compete with her Davey.

Lottie rather hoped people would just take her how they found her, but Sam always wanted to make the right impression. Which was why, she supposed, she always looked a complete mess in photographs and Sam looked like a model.

There was the sound of the door being flung open again. 'Sorry, babe, you caught me on the hop. Come in, hun, whoever you are.'

'Charlotte?' There was a slight edge to the deep, and very masculine, voice and Lottie decided that whoever he was he wasn't gay. She didn't even need to see him.

'Can you say that again, babe? You have the most amazing voice,' Sam giggled, 'oh God, Lottie has got to hear you say her name, it is just so sexy. Did you hear that, Lottie? Actually can you say mine? It's Samantha. I'm Sam, by the way, Sam Simcock. My Davey is a goalkeeper. Wow I am so pleased to meet you. This will cheer Lottie up no end, what with all her problems at the moment. Nothing like a new face. Come in.' Sam finally paused. 'Hang on, you're nothing to do with them insurance people are you? Or the police or newspapers? Not that you look the type.'

'No, I erm, am not the type.' He sounded amused. 'But I'm not sure having me here is going to make Charlotte feel any better, to be honest, whatever the problem is. In fact, I could be part of it. Is she in?'

'Oh.' Sam stopped, suddenly wondering if she'd misjudged. 'Why do you say that, babe? You weren't one of that wedding party were you?'

'What wedding party? Look, I'm just with the film crew, and I know people don't always want film crews invading their front gardens, do they? But, to be honest, I only came about the hors—'

'Film crews? Oh my God.' Sam squealed and let go of him so she could clap her hands, then clamp one over her open mouth. 'Oh my God you're a film star. I knew it, I knew with a body like that.' And she was clip clopping across the hallway as fast as she could in her five-inch heels. 'Lottie, Lots.' She might be used to mixing with premiership footballers on a daily basis, but Sam was as star-struck as the next girl when it came to actors, and this one just had to be famous. 'Lottie you will never guess who's here. It's,' she stopped short in the doorway and turned round. 'Sorry, babe, who did you say you were?'

'I don't think I did. I'm—'

'Sam, what on earth is going on?' Lottie, who had been busy crawling across the floor with Roxy on her back stopped in the doorway and trying to listen to as much as she could, glanced up.

Her gaze travelled over a pair of what even she could tell were handmade leather shoes, and up a pair of long legs, which were clad in brown-belted chinos that gave him a definite foreign appearance. His broad chest was hugged by a pale-blue open-necked shirt, which showed just enough of his tanned throat. The higher she went the hotter she felt. Her face was positively burning as her gaze lingered on the dark hair, which licked the collar of his perfectly cut jacket (which had to be a designer label, even though she was far from expert). She only stopped when her gaze locked with his, and she really wished that she'd been standing up like a normal person when he'd walked in, and not been caught giving him a once-over from the bottom up.

Suddenly that deep, rich voice that had sent a rash of goose bumps popping up all over her body, like a load of meerkats on full alert, made sense.

It couldn't be him. No way. Not here in Tippermere. If there was one person in the whole world that she never thought she would see again it was this man, who was stood in her doorway.

'I'm Xander Rossi, but I'm not a famous actor. I'm just helping . . .' He finished, his words tailing off as he took her in.

She'd been totally besotted with Rory throughout her teenage years, but Xander Rossi had still made a lasting impression. It all might have been a long time ago, but the man was completely, and embarrassingly, recognisable. If anything, he was even more of an unmissable force. He'd filled out and muscled up (so had she, but not in a good way). The brooding boy had turned into a smouldering man.

Xander Rossi had been impossible to ignore at school. Despite only attending for two terms, he had been the pin-up of nearly every girl in her class. And in that short time he'd broken many a hormone-ridden teenage heart – and he'd seemed entirely oblivious. She hadn't been one of that group – for her it had been worse. He'd hated her. That startlingly blue gaze had turned black when he'd seen her, and he'd seemed to do everything in his power to make her feel uncomfortable and stupid. But now he was smiling.

'Xander.' Shock that he was there and relief that he wasn't glaring, so he must have forgotten their uncomfortable past, made the word come out far more breathy and flustered than it should have. Good heavens she was a very happily married woman with self-confidence and responsibilities. She didn't care what he thought.

'Charlotte, so it really is you. I wondered if I'd got it wrong.'

Lottie deposited Roxy on the floor, staggered to her feet, and tried again. 'Xander, what on earth are you doing back in Tippermere?'

'Oh my God, so you do really know each other?' Sam squealed again. 'Wow, that's awesome, babe.'

'Why have you stopped being my horsey?' Roxy planted herself, hands on hips, at the side of Lottie and tugged on her polo shirt. 'It's not fair, he's only a man. You can play with him later.'

'Oh he's not just any man, hun,' Sam giggled, 'and I'm not sure Auntie Lottie should be playing with him at all. Come here, I'll be horsey.'

'I'm not playing with him.' Lottie tried not to scowl.

'But Lottie is the best horsey. She goes faster and makes all the wight noises and bumps me up and down. I do need to pwactise, you know, if I'm going to Lympia.'

'Pure chance that I'm here, if I'm honest, it's as much a surprise to me as it is to you, actually.' Xander shrugged. 'I didn't quite believe it could be you when your groom told me. But you've not changed one bit, Charlie.'

'She's not called Charlie, she's Lottie.' Roxy had decided the best way to regain attention was to position herself between Xander and Lottie and concentrate on the stranger. She tugged at the bottom of his jacket. 'If she's not allowed to play with you, I will. Do you want to see my horse? I've got a weal one, not just Lottie. I only used her to pwactise on.'

'I'd love to see your horse.' Xander put out a hand and Roxy instinctively slipped hers in it. 'I didn't realise you were Lady of the Manor now. You were the daughter of a famous show-jumper when we were at school.' He smiled at Lottie gently. 'Always in the papers.'

'Oh I'm not.' Lottie rubbed her knees, trotting across bare floorboards was not a good idea, especially with Roxy energetically bouncing on her back in an over-enthusiastic attempt at rising trot. 'A lady, that is. I am still the daughter of a famous show-jumper, although he's not that famous these days. It is still Gran's place, really, but we kind of run it. Well we try, when she lets us, me and Rory, that is.'

'So Lady Elizabeth Stanthorpe really is your grandmother?'

'Didn't you know?'

'Well no. Who'd have thought it? You kept that quiet. And Rory?'

'Is my husband.' Lottie blushed and wasn't sure why. 'Er, you probably remember him, well he was at school, in the year above us, but you weren't there long, were you?' Twenty-four weeks and two days, she could have added, but that was only because her best friend had kept count, and for years after he'd gone had lamented the one hundred and seventy days of lost opportunity.

'Oh, that Rory. Yeah, I remember him. No, you're right, we weren't in Cheshire long, but how could I forget the boy you were mad about? Guess not much has changed, then. You certainly haven't.'

'Oh my goodness, I have. We were only fifteen. I'm fatter and I've got grey hair now, look.'

'Sixteen, and you haven't. I'd know you anywhere. Even trotting across the room on your hands and knees.'

Lottie, feeling more embarrassed by the second, groped around for a change of subject. 'What on earth are you doing here? Did you say something about the film crew? I never knew you acted. It's not just me that's kept things quiet.'

'Oh Christ no, I don't act, it's not my thing at all. I am with Seb, though. I'm advising on all the horse stuff for the film.' His expression looked more frustration than pleasure. 'Heaven only knows why he needs me, but I suppose I've not got much else to do. I got roped in, more because he's my brother-in-law than anything else.' He shrugged, then smiled. 'It is lovely seeing you again. You haven't any idea where Seb is, have you?'

Lovely wasn't quite the word Lottie would have used. 'He's gone.' She couldn't keep the note of relief out of her voice. Xander might be behaving much more nicely than he had as a teenager, but Seb really hadn't been a character she'd warmed to. He'd gazed around their cluttered living room with an air of disbelief and stared in distaste at the chairs (which admittedly did have a good layer of dog hair on them). He'd shied away from Harry's rather exuberant welcome and she could have sworn he wiped his shoes on the way out. In fact, he was altogether very rude and if she'd felt she had a choice she would have ripped his contract in half and told him where he could stick it. But that would have been stupid.

It hadn't been a very promising start, though. Even Xander was a much more welcome sight.

'Wow, this is a coincidence, though. I really can't believe it's you.'

'It's me, though I have to admit, I never thought I'd see

Tippermere again and, to be honest, it never occurred to me you might still be here.' He grinned disarmingly. 'Though it's great that you are, but I never in a million years guessed this place was yours.' Xander gazed around as though he was assessing her as well as her home, and Lottie wasn't sure if he was just surprised or thought she didn't belong there. 'I guess you and Seb didn't hit it off, then? I know he can come across as rude, but it might be worth cutting him a bit of slack, at least at first? He's out of his comfort zone, hates the countryside. He'd shoot everything in a studio if he could, but at the same time he's a perfectionist. Likes gritty reality,' he laughed, 'so he takes it out on everybody else. But he's okay, really. He might grow on you – and the rest of them are fine. Honest.'

'He was just so rude and bossy. Worse than Gran. How on earth did you get involved with him? Oh sorry,' Lottie put her hand over her mouth, 'that sounds terrible.'

'He's good at his job,' his smile held a hint of apology, 'no excuses for his behaviour, but he mellows a bit when he knows you, and, like I said, it's hard to say no when it's family.'

'Oh I do understand that bit.'

'Look sorry to barge in and out like this, but I will have to get a move on. I've got to sort the horses and your groom said you might have a couple of boxes free on the yard?'

'Groom?' Lottie had spent so long doing her own horses that she found it hard to adjust to the idea of staff, and, she had to admit, she thought of Tab as more of a friend helping out than a hired hand. 'Oh, Tab.'

'A couple of the ponies would settle better up here, if you had room, that is? She said something about some of yours had gone?'

'A couple of ponies? How many are there?'

'Enough for a game, of course.'

'Oh.' The enormity of it all started to hit home, to the extent that Lottie had a sudden overwhelming desire to tell Xander to go away, that it had all been a massive mistake. Instead she took a deep breath. This would be a success. It would. Even with the rather uncomfortable reminder of a past she'd rather forget, a cocky, control freak of a director, and a herd of horses, sorry polo ponies, galloping across the front lawn. 'Well, I suppose so, but you'll have to pay extra. Livery fees.'

'Of course.' There was a quirk to his mouth and Lottie was sure he was amused by it all.

'We're broke. It's pretty dire right now, if I'm honest,' she really did have to make that quite clear, 'or you wouldn't be here.' He might actually be quite a hunk now, and doing his best to be pleasant, but, quite honestly, a picture of him stuck in the tack room for any passing girl to drool over would be a far better alternative to having him and a film crew here.

'Sure.' It was almost like he'd read her mind. Though she knew she had an expressive face, Rory always told her she'd never make a poker-player. 'How about we get together some time and I'll explain how I got involved in this and what it's all about? It's a long story.'

'Ooh I love stories.' Lottie had forgotten all about Sam, who was staring appreciatively at Xander. 'This is just so exciting, it's amazing you two knowing each other and we're going to be famous, we're all going to be film stars, what do you think about that Roxy? Would you like to be famous? My mum always used to tell me about that Elizabeth Taylor, you know. She was in that film with a horse in it, wasn't she? Mum does love those glamorous film stars, I mean she does like my Dave, but I'm sure she'd have preferred me to marry George Clooney. He's a bit old for me, though, isn't he?'

Roxy looked from Xander, to Lottie, to her mother. 'He's making Lottie cwoss so I don't think I want to be a filming star, I'd wather be a pwincess, and he wants to see my horse so we're going to the stable. Come on Xander. I will see you later, Mummy.'

* * *

111

'I hope he's paying extra to use these stables.' The pony nodded its head enthusiastically, as though agreeing with Rory, and Lottie linked her hand through his arm.

'He is. Thank goodness he's gone.'

'Come on, I was just about to do a final check of them all and lock up for the night.' Rory led her across the cobbles towards the first loose box in the circular yard. 'He'll be back tomorrow, though. They'll all be here soon, so I suppose we need to get used to it. When are we expecting the full monty? March?'

Lottie nodded her head glumly. It would all be low key for a few weeks, the horses settling in, a small crew shooting a few scenes that didn't involve the actors. Then, as Rory put it, the full monty.

'Chin up, darling, we'll be fine. Anyway I thought you liked him when we were at school? He seemed okay to me.'

'He's fine,' *he just didn't like me, then I made it ten times worse,* 'it's just the whole things is weird, and so rushed.'

'Fine?' Rory raised an eyebrow. 'I thought you fancied the pants off him. All the girls did.'

'I fancied the pants off you.' And she had done. Rory had always been her man, even before he'd realised it. 'Don't you think it's weird, it being somebody we know?'

'It's a small world, and anyhow it isn't his film is it? He's just helping with the horses.'

'But Seb is his brother-in-law, he told me, that's why he agreed to help out, and he never even used to like horses.'

'Brother-in-law? I thought he only had the one sister, you know that scrawny girl who was always scowling.' Rory frowned.

'Sarah, she was called Sarah wasn't she? I can't really see her being married to that Seb, and I'm sure somebody said that his wife is the star of the show.'

'Really?'

'Yes, it was that Jamie, you know the one that came and saw Gran, I'm sure it was. She had some film-star name.'

'He must have another kid sister, then.' Rory shrugged. 'That Sarah was just a half-sister wasn't she? He lived with his mum and dad in one house, then she lived with her mum a few doors up. That's why she got teased so much.'

'Did she? I never really knew her. That's not very nice, though, is it? It wasn't her fault.'

'No, but she was spooky. She used to just sit and watch us all the time, then flounce off if anybody took the piss. Weird girl, so I wonder what this other sister of Xander's is like? Might be another Sam?' Rory laughed at the expression on Lottie's face.

'Oh God, can you imagine? Although she could be. I know, I remember now, he said her name was Pandora. What if she turns her nose up at everything like Seb did?'

'Stop worrying, it'll be easy money.'

'Things are going to work out, aren't they?' Lottie bit her bottom lip. 'Xander really hated me at school, you know.' It had all been so long ago, they'd been kids, and they were all grown up now. Water under the bridge, she hoped.

'Of course they're going to work out, and nobody hates you, darling, you're imagining it.' Rory kissed the top of her head. 'Look, we carry on with life as normal, no extra work, no hassle, just a great big dollop of cash in the bank and then at the end of the year when they've all buggered off you pick up the wedding business again, and I find another nice rich backer to buy me some new horses, a flashy box, and to keep this lot in shoes and hay.'

'So you really don't mind having them here?'

'Me?' He gave a rueful smile. 'You know me, I'm always up for a party, the more the merrier.'

'But it's not exactly a party, and what if they make a mess? What if they get in our way?'

'Oh, I'm sure they'll make a mess. God only knows why Lizzie likes the idea of horses galloping across the lawns and a bunch of strangers being here day in day out. She's going to have a fit

113

if some lovey-dovey director starts chopping her topiary.'

'Are they really like that, you know, lovey-dovey?' She frowned. 'That Seb bloke didn't seem to be. He seemed a bit of a cold fish, to be honest, and very rude, but Xander reckons he's okay.'

'Then he'll be okay. They're probably not loveys at all these days. Maybe they're all like Guy Ritchie with a shotgun, flat cap, and a best friend that's more Vinnie Jones than Eddie Izzard.'

'Crumbs, I'd never thought of that.' She stroked Black Gold's long nose and the horse tugged at her shirt with none-too-gentle teeth. 'Maybe Xander's sister is more of a Madonna?'

'Now that would give Lizzie a heart attack.' Rory chuckled.

'Don't keep calling her Lizzie,' Lottie thumped his arm play-fully and giggled, feeling slightly happier. The thought of a Madonna look-alike at Tipping House Estate was far more outra-geous than anything she'd imagined would result from allowing a film crew in. 'Gran would just look down her nose at her and tell her she'll catch her death if she doesn't put some more clothes on. I heard her not long ago telling Sam that she really should take advantage of her husband earning a good salary and buy something warm and a decent length before she died of pneu-monia and left him on his own, which would be most unsporting.'

She rested her forearm on the door of the next box and watched the bay filly, Black Gold's daughter, tugging at her hay-net uncon-cerned. 'Do you think we should put Gold in foal again? Minty is just so adorable.'

'All babies are adorable according to you.' Rory grinned. 'Do you think it might make you broody?'

'Sod off.' Lottie swatted him away playfully, trying to ignore the hard lump in her throat. She didn't want the 'baby talk' again, not now. But she knew she couldn't avoid it for ever. Her eggs would be hard-boiled, as Sam had helpfully pointed out. 'I'm not sure I'm the broody type, apart from with foals.'

He caught her hand in both of his, his face suddenly serious. 'You won't know until you try it, Lots.'

'Do we have to talk about this now?' She pulled away, trying to ignore his hurt look. Feeling suddenly exposed, alone, when he just stared back at her and didn't try to pull her closer to him.

'We're getting older.' His voice was soft, but it trickled along her spine, a warning that made her suddenly feel defensive.

'So Sam said.' She knew she sounded sullen, but she couldn't help it.

'Sam?'

'I wish you wouldn't talk to other people about this. It's not fair.'

Rory sighed. 'I've not talked to anybody else, why would I? I can't even talk to *you* about it. Lottie, is there something going on here that I don't get?'

'No.' She clutched the stable door, the flaking paint rough beneath her fingertips, and stared in at the horse, so that she didn't have to look at his face.

'I don't get why this is an issue, I only thought . . .'

'It's not an issue.' Except everyone but her was making it into one.

'Fine.'

'I'm not some brood mare.'

'That's not fair, Lottie, I never said . . .'

'But everybody else just expects it. What about what I want? What if I just don't fancy the idea?'

'Then,' his voice was so scarily gentle that she felt a sudden lurch of fear in the base of her stomach. What if he left her? What if he decided he wanted more than they already had, if just having each other wasn't good enough for him? 'Then I think we need to talk about it properly, don't you?'

Black Gold suddenly stuck her head out of the door and gave an ear-splitting whinny, and Rory grimaced. 'Whenever you want to, that is. God, your dad knew what he was doing when he offloaded this mad horse on to us, didn't he?'

Lottie tried to smile back at him, but her face was struggling against muscles that had tightened into a mask. She could cave in, get pregnant, do the easy thing, like they all wanted – and then what?

'Stop worrying. We'll be fine.' He kissed the end of her nose, was back by her side where she'd always wanted him to be. Life without Rory was unthinkable. Her fingers trembled just at the thought of him not being there to hold them. So she shoved her hand under his elbow, knitted her fingers into his coat. 'Let's forget it for now, shall we?' His breath warmed her as he rested his chin on her head. 'You're right, darling, we've got plenty of time and it's nothing to do with anybody else.'

'We'll talk, I promise, when everything is sorted. I'm sorry, Rory, really. I know I'm being a pain, being daft.'

'Shh. You're not being daft. This film business is the important thing right now.'

She'd think about it when all this was over. Definitely. She owed it to him, to tell him exactly how she felt. Right now though, changing the subject was easier. 'I really don't get why Gran suggested the filming. She didn't even like us having the weddings here at first. Do you think she's up to something, or,' and this was what worried her more, 'does she think we really are in such a mess that this is the only way out?'

'Well, I hate to say it, but we aren't far off. This could be the best offer we're going to get, and even if I manage to get another sponsor next week we're not going to make it through to next year are we?'

'If only the bloody insurance people would pay up, but all they keep doing is sending letters and men in suits to ask more questions. I never knew a fire could be so complicated.' She sighed. It had all been going so well.

'Never trust a man who spends all his day in an office staring at a spreadsheet, that's what I say.'

'But I should trust a man who spends all day mucking around with horses?'

'I don't muck around, woman, this is serious man stuff. Apologise or I might have to spank you.'

'Sod off.' Lottie squealed and made a run for it, hoping that he still really wanted to catch her.

Chapter 10

Pandora did her best to suppress a contented sigh. It was perfect, and well worth the wait, as she'd known it would be.

Since Seb had returned with the signed contract, she'd been itching to get to Tippermere and see the Tipping House Estate with her own eyes. But she'd realised the importance of patience. She couldn't appear over-eager, her husband had to feel in control if this was to work. He had to think it was his idea, his discovery.

Learning lines and shooting scenes in the studio had kept her occupied, and Pandora had satisfied herself with leafing through the newspaper reports that she had secretly cut out and saved after the fire at Tipping House. In the evenings, with Seb often absent, she had searched the internet for images of the wonderful setting. She could have stared at it all day.

Pandora didn't believe in fate, but she did believe that some kind of justice had been served the morning Seb had lifted his daily newspaper and Lottie had stared out from the front page straight at her.

She hadn't even had to do a double-take. Pandora had instantly recognised Lottie, who was pictured the morning after her beloved ancestral home had been torched; the girl who had effortlessly commanded attention when they were still teen-agers, despite being completely disorganised and ungroomed. Who could forget the time she'd arrived at school in her filthy breeches and stinky boots crowing about her father winning a gold medal?

She gave a small shudder. How her half-brother Xander could have been so besotted with the creature had been beyond her comprehension. But then, who understood men? Or why such a tasteless class system still survived, where the women hee-hawed like donkeys and dressed in the most unflattering garments. Everything about them was hairy, from their houses to their clothes and bodies. None of them seemed to have heard of waxing and, as for the smell, it was either horse or nothing more sophis-ticated than lavender perfume.

But by the time she'd finished her black coffee she didn't care. She had a plan. Her time had come and Xander was actually going to prove of some use for once in his life. After all, if it hadn't been for Lottie, Xander would have given *her* the attention she deserved all those years ago, and so it was right that he now make amends. And, if it hadn't been for Lottie and her family things would have been so very different. Their father, Michael Rossi, would have been happy, and when he was happy he was nice. He would never have sent her and her mother away, never exploded in that fit of rage, saying things that he couldn't possibly mean. He would have loved her, been proud.

He was going to be proud now. He would want to tell the whole world she was his daughter, instead of trying to hide her away.

It was quite incredible how all of a sudden things had fallen so perfectly into place. Xander had come back into her life at exactly the right time, and now she was back in the place where things had all started to go so horribly wrong. But this time she was the one in control.

Pandora shifted her focus back to the present and the building in front of her. She was actually here, gazing at the stately home that would change their fortunes.

* * *

'What do you think, Pandora?' Seb wasn't sure whether his wife's silence was a good or bad thing. She was staring out of the car window, an expression of boredom etched across her perfect, unblemished features.

'It looks fine, I'm sure it will do, darling.' She shrugged her slim shoulders, then patted his arm before swinging the door open and making her normal graceful exit. 'You always know best, but do you think those flowers look cheap and nasty?' She gestured back down the driveway at the swathe of bright daffodils. 'Yellow is just so, well, obvious.' She gave a small shudder of distaste.

Seb sighed. 'They're daffodils, they're always yellow. Wordsworth didn't have a problem with them. Okay, fine, don't give me that look. We'll shoot so you can't see them, but they'll all be dead soon anyway.'

'Whatever you say, darling. But I really think you should have a word with your scriptwriter.'

'Really, darling?' Seb steeled himself, there was always a 'but'. He followed her example and walked around the car bonnet to join her.

'I've started to feel that my character is far too wet. She needs to be more forward about her needs. I mean if her rock-star husband is playing away then she'd be more demanding with these men that come into her life, don't you think? Polo is a contact sport, after all, and I know just what kind of contact she'd be after. She isn't the doormat type. She'd be taking what she wants and standing up to him as well. Challenging him, not just,' she waved a dismissing hand, 'shagging the locals. I like to think she'd be laying down some ground rules.'

120

'Let's try it this way first, shall we? Just see how the characters develop?'

'I need to know her, feel her emotions, and how can I do that if we don't share the same vision?' Pandora pouted. 'I'll talk to him.'

'No,' it came out more sharply than Seb had intended, and earned him a steely look. '*I* will be the one to talk to him, darling. The decisions have to come from me or things get confused.'

'He'll listen to me, Seb.'

'Pillow talk, Pandora?' He hated the fact that he'd let a sour note creep into his voice, but there were times when Pandora needed reminding who was supposed to be in charge.

'There's no need to get nasty.'

Seb knew that it was an argument best avoided. 'I'm the producer, he'll listen to *me*.'

'Sure.'

He clamped his mouth shut, suspicious of the sudden back-down, which was unprecedented, then noticed that Pandora's attention had been diverted.

A tall girl was standing at the top of the stone steps, a spaniel pressed close to her side, watching them. 'Oh. I'd better introduce you, that's—'

'Shush.'

'Sorry?'

'Be quiet a moment, darling. I know damned well who that is.' And she was off, stalking across the lawn; she ground to a halt at the bottom of the steps, arms folded. 'Well, well, if it isn't little Lottie Brinkley. You haven't changed a bit, well apart from getting bigger. All round.' The short bark of a laugh was humourless. 'You always were well built, weren't you, honey?'

'You know each other?' Seb, who had hastened after his wife, wary of her intentions, looked from one woman to the other in genuine surprise. The contrast could hardly be more striking. Pandora groomed to within an inch of her life, not a shiny hair out of place, and Lottie, the woman with everything, except it seemed a decent wardrobe or hair-straighteners. How on earth could they know each other? Pandora had never been to Tippermere, and the woman he knew as Lottie Steel had almost certainly never graced a film set.

'Oh, only vaguely. Didn't I mention it, darling?' Pandora didn't even glance his way, her attention was fixed on the other woman, like a fox eyeing up a chicken. 'We were at school together. Briefly.' He watched as her assessing gaze scoured Lottie from head to toe. 'Although Lottie is, of course, much older than I am. You're the same age as Xander, aren't you?'

* * *

Lottie stared at the glamorous woman standing next to Seb Drakelow and wondered if she needed new contact lenses. 'Crumbs.' She peered. 'It is Sarah, isn't it? It is, oh my God, you look so different. I wouldn't have recognised you if I hadn't heard your voice, and if Xander wasn't here.' And she wouldn't.

The girl Lottie had known as Xander's sister (the girl she and Rory had dismissed as definitely not having film-star potential, and so not in a million years likely to be Seb Drakelow's wife) had looked nothing like this. She'd had a brace on her teeth, been unbelievably skinny and the corners of her mouth had been on a permanent downturn, unless she was pouting. All things that the generous-hearted Lottie would never be unkind enough to voice. This new version was so incredibly different, though, it was hard not to be gushy. 'Oh gosh, you look amazing, Sarah. And you're working on the set as well? Xander never said.'

She stopped short. They'd never been friends back then, and from the glare she was receiving things weren't going to be any different now. Sarah might have changed on the outside, but it looked like the transformation hadn't altered her view of life, or of Lottie.

Lottie had spent the last twenty-four hours convincing herself that the whole filming process was going to be much more fun than she anticipated, that nothing was going to go wrong, and that the boost to their finances would more than compensate for any inconvenience. Now, in a few short seconds, under the disapproving scrutiny of an unfriendly Sarah, the feeling of doom returned. She took a deep breath and fought to keep the smile pasted to her face. 'Sorry, er, are you looking for him? Xander? I'm not sure where—'

'I prefer to be called Pandora now.' She waved a dismissive hand. 'Sarah disappeared a long time ago. Nobody calls me by that name.'

'Pandora? *You* are Pandora?' Lottie looked at her in shock. So this was the star of the show. 'Crikey, you're really the star of this thing? *You're* Seb's wife?'

'Yes.' Pandora glared and huffed, her joy at shocking Lottie being remarkably short-lived now that she felt wrong-footed by her. 'Why, is there a problem?'

'But you hated the countryside. You hated Tippermere.' And me, Lottie could have added.

Pandora gazed at Lottie's filthy boots for a moment. 'I'm an actress now, darling. I'm paid to pretend.' Then, with barely disguised distaste, she shied away as Harry bounded down the steps.

The dog didn't stop though. Veering around her he headed towards the archway that led into the stable yard and they all turned to watch as he bounded straight up to the much more dog-friendly form of Xander.

Hearing the unmistakeable voice that announced Pandora's arrival, Xander had reluctantly left the safety of the courtyard, where his ponies were stabled, and went out to greet her, his wire-haired dachshund, Ella, close behind.

The second that the little dog spotted Harry, Lottie's spaniel, her whole body started to quiver with excitement. Her strange twittering noise of greeting reached a higher and higher pitch as she squirmed around on the grass in response to Harry's excited welcome.

'Can't you shut that animal up? Why on earth does she have to squeak like that? She's giving me a migraine,' Pandora's hand went up to her temple theatrically.

Tab, who was hot on Xander's heels, stooped to pick up the little dog, who she had already fallen in love with nearly as much as his master. 'Leave her alone, she's sweet, aren't you my little cutie pie?' She kissed her on the nose and was rewarded with a sloppy kiss.

Shooting Tab a withering look, Pandora swept over, being careful to sidestep Harry, and wrapping her arms round Xander she kissed him on the cheek. 'I am so pleased to see you, darling.'

'Oh, my God, I'm going to puke,' muttered Tab into Ella's fur. Xander could not, definitely not, be involved with this creature, whoever she was.

'Oh wow!' They all turned at the squeal of excitement to see Sam, in even higher heels than Pandora's, her blonde extension-enhanced hair cascading over her shoulders and her wonderful body encased in the type of designer outfit you normally only saw on the catwalk, emerge from Tipping House. 'You're here, babe. It is you, isn't it?' She clapped her hands together and then wrapped a confused Lottie in a hug. 'She's here. How awesome is that?'

Pandora smirked, her ego restored now that at least one person in the back of beyond obviously knew who she was. Ella wriggled and Tab shot an anguished look at Lottie and Sam, silently pleading with them to tell her this couldn't be true.

She could accept the newly arrived sex god gazing after Lottie with a thinly disguised look of unrequited love (because, after all, it was unrequited and quite a few other men seemed to be in the same boat), but to even imagine him with this brittle, dog-hating mannequin was a step too far. And the normally wonderful Sam looked pleased to see the two of them reunited, which was even more horrifying.

Sam winked, then chuckled, an unrestrained sound that stopped them all in their tracks. If anybody had hijacked centre stage it was Sam, not Pandora. 'Oh my God, you look just how I imagined. You're Xander's sister, aren't you, babe? Wow, I love the Louboutins by the way, much better than this season's shades, aren't they?'

'You've got to be kidding.' Tab suddenly felt better.

'Oh no, I never joke about shoes, Tab. Davey bought me a pair of the new ones as soon as they came out.' She smiled warmly at Pandora. 'But that colour is much nicer, babe.'

Pandora scowled, and Tab was pretty sure that Seb was fighting a smile.

'Not the shoes.' Tab groaned. 'I meant the other bit. She's his *sister*?' Which was a million miles better than being his girlfriend, but pretty unlikely, looking at the two of them.

Sam grinned and waved a copy of *Hello* in the air. 'I was sure I'd seen gorgeous Xander somewhere before. I never forget a hunky man,' she giggled, 'so I dug out my mags last night, and they're both in here. I was just having a gander when you arrived.' She started to make her way down the steps towards Tab, who was looking more than a little relieved. 'Here you are, hun, have a look. Pandora is looking really glam, aren't you babe? Shall we call you Pand? You'll have to tell me who does your brows. They look so kind of natural. I'm Sam, by the way, Sam Simcock.'

She held out the picture for Tab, who stared at it, then looked from Xander to Pandora with suspicion. 'You don't look like you're related.'

Pandora rolled her eyes. 'I'm his half-sister, actually, and it's an old picture.' She stared coldly at Sam, her tone to match. 'And no, you shall not call me Pand.'

'She is.' Lottie confirmed, displaying rather less enthusiasm than Sam. 'She's his sister. She went to the same school as us for a few months.'

Seb, who by now was getting exceedingly bored with the conversation, and the presence of so many excited animals (and females), decided it was time to move on and get some answers of his own.

'So sorry to break up the reunion.' He gave Pandora a pointed look. 'But we have work to do. Come along, darling, we need to talk about the script. Our trailer is over there.'

* * *

Pandora knew that the moment he got her in the trailer, the inquisition would begin, which was frustrating but inevitable. Seb didn't say a word as they made their way across the lawns to where the crew had set up, but the moment they got there it started, before the door was even shut.

'You've been to this place before, then?' He'd put his reading glasses on and was peering over the top of them, no doubt thinking she would take his authority more seriously. It was something he did with crew members and actors just before giving them a bollocking. Along with the steepled-fingers thing, which gave him an intimidating stillness. Pandora was sure he studied body language and method acting online when she wasn't about.

'No.' She sank down onto the nearest seat and kicked her shoes off. She would never, ever, wear them out again in public. How could that cow do that to her? Last season, my arse. 'No I have not been here before, and who on earth was that hysterical blond?'

Lottie and her horse-faced friends she could handle, but Sam was an unexpected addition. Hadn't she got better things to do, like get a boob reduction? Those tits were so unfashionable. Nobody looked like that today unless they were married to a footballer or wanted to be on *I'm a Celebrity*. Who the hell did the woman think she was? The name sounded very vaguely familiar, but if she'd been in the business Pandora would have remembered.

'No? So how come—'

She pushed Sam out of her mind and concentrated on her husband, the one person she was bothered about. 'I have never been to Tipping House before, darling,' she gave an exaggerated sigh, 'but we did live in the area for a while, though, if that's what you're getting at. We met that Lottie girl at school, but she didn't live here then, she lived at some horse place with her father. If you don't believe me, ask Xander.'

Xander, who had followed them in and was sprawled on the uncomfortable bench seat with his arms folded nodded, knowing that Pandora had dragged him along to back up her story. Which, for once, was true. 'We were only here for a few months.'

'You both lived here, in the same place? Together?' Seb looked from one to the other with a raised eyebrow.

'Oh don't be ridiculous, darling.' Pandora pursed her lips. 'Xander lived with Father at one end of the village.' She wasn't even going to mention that woman, his pathetic mother. 'Mother and I lived in our own home because she wanted,' she glared at Xander, who didn't react, 'me to grow up close to my father. To get to know him better. Not that he was ever here.'

'So you all lived in Tippermere. How cosy.'

'Oh honestly, Seb, you've got no idea what it was like.' Pandora retreated, folding her arms protectively and letting the hurt feelings chase across her features, knowing that it made her husband uncomfortable. He didn't deal in emotions, just facts.

'We weren't exactly in the middle of Tippermere. We were on the outskirts, actually, practically in the next village.' Xander glanced from Pandora to Seb and she knew he hated to be piggy in the middle of their relationship. He didn't understand the way it worked. 'But all the local kids went to the same school we did, which is how we knew Charlie, I mean Lottie. Her dad's a well-known show-jumping hero, so you couldn't not know her if you lived round here. They lived in the equestrian centre up the road, and I have to admit I was pretty surprised to find her at Tipping House. I never even realised she was related to Lady Stanthorpe. She was pretty down to earth at school.' He shrugged. 'They're related on her mum's side, apparently, and her mum died when she was a baby. Look, do you really need me? I do have things to do.'

They both ignored him.

'Quite a coincidence, then?' Seb's eyebrow still hadn't dropped to its normal position.

'It is, isn't it, darling?' Pandora tapped the script with a long nail. 'I thought we didn't have time for small talk. Anyway I can't see that it matters that we know the woman, it's hardly relevant. Honestly you make such a fuss over such trivial things.'

'So how come she lives here now?'

'She moved in when she found out she's due to inherit it when her grandmother dies.' Xander tried to deflect Seb with common sense, not because he felt any desire to protect Pandora, but just to stop the pointless discussion. Then he could get the hell out and talk to his far more sensible horses. 'Apparently she wasn't told until a few years ago.'

'And you know this because?'

'Because, Seb,' Xander listened to Ella, who was whining on the other side of the door and knew exactly how she felt, 'I asked her when we came to set up the temporary stables. Like I said, she used to live with her father up the road. But this place seems to be her responsibility now. It was her business that went up in flames, the wedding business. And she's Lottie Steel now, not Brinkley.'

'Steel?' The skin tightened, almost imperceptibly, along Pandora's brow – which, despite Seb's ban on Botox, was still plumped up and tightened to a degree that made movement practically impossible.

'She's married to Rory Steel.' Xander raised an eyebrow. 'I'd have thought you'd remember him.'

'Rory Steel? Oh, that terrible horsey boy.' Her green eyes narrowed to slits. She remembered Rory well. In fact she'd had an embarrassing crush on the clown until he had inadvertently made a fool of her when a prank had gone horribly wrong. A balloon full of water intended for the headmaster's secretary (who everybody hated, as she had such an inflated sense of self-importance, which any self-respecting teenager had an instant urge to pop) had hit her fair and square on the head.

The village idiots had all thought it hilarious, and so she had felt forced to join in with the laughter. At least Rory had noticed her then, but it was too late for Pandora to use it to her advantage; she'd just discovered her family were on the move again. 'Shouldn't you be shovelling shit or something, Xander?'

Xander, realising he had served his purpose, gratefully took the hint and opened the trailer door to a chorus of twitters from Ella, who was so delighted to see him her tail wagged wildly until her whole body squirmed and her yelps turned hoarse.

Pandora grimaced and looked pointedly at the open door, until Seb took the cue and slammed it shut.

Her tone softened. 'Honestly, darling, you do make mountains out of molehills at times.'

'I just had no idea you used to live here. Why the subterfuge?'

'It's not a secret, but you never asked, did you? And it was only for a few months. We were always on the move. There are lots of things you don't know about me, but a bit of mystery is good for a relationship, isn't that what they say?' Taking hold of his belt she pulled him closer and ran one talon like fingernail up his thigh, stopping just short of his crotch.

'Sex is not the answer to everything, Pandora.'

'Oh really?' She pouted and leaned back. 'Anyway, I hardly remember the place. Most of the people were ghastly. Come here,

129

darling.' She patted the seat next to her. 'Let's talk about the script, eh? Forgive me?'

* * *

Seb sighed, flicked some imaginary dirt off the seat, and sat down. At least he now held a trump card when it came to deciding which way the script would go. The balance of power swung from one to the other of them with the regularity of a pendulum, and it was now on the upswing in his favour.

'You won't need to be here much, darling. A few key shots and then it can all be pulled together at the studio.' He was, in fact, hoping the whole thing could be done and dusted in as quick a time as possible. Provided the weather held, the sodding dogs behaved, and nobody fell off a horse. He hated the variables as well as the dirt.

'I'll be here as long as you need me, Seb. I know you hate the countryside, so I'll support you.' Which seemed unusually generous for his wife, but then she was keen to ensure that this venture succeeded. 'And I can ride, you know. I thought it would be much more authentic if I did some of the shots on horseback, galloping after the ball with one of those sticks. I was quite good at hockey, darling. I'm sure it can't be that difficult to get some good action shots.'

'I thought we agreed to a stunt double.' He saw the start of a defiant gleam in her eye. 'For your safety, of course. We can't risk you getting hurt,' the look softened slightly. 'I'd never forgive myself if anything happened. Those animals are dangerous things.'

The thought of Pandora having a theatrical moment atop an unruly horse whilst waving a mallet between its ears made Seb break out in a cold sweat. The camera loved his wife and there were moments of pure magic, but they were interspersed with temper tantrums and demands for other actors to be removed, lines to be changed, and camera angles refined. He could cope with her outbursts on the ground, but he wasn't sure what the outcome would be if he was left chasing even the most docile beast.

'Oh you're so sweet, Seb, but you do need at least one or two shots of me in the saddle. All the close-ups will need doing and I'm sure I'll be fine. Xander will be at hand.'

'You don't need to be on an actual horse. We can do that later.'

'While we're here we might as well go for as much realism as we can,' she stroked his hand, 'but the main thing is for me to feel part of the place, live the part. Isn't it?'

'I agree. So it's just for close-ups, any mounted parts are when the animal is stationary?'

'If you insist, Seb, but don't say I didn't offer.'

Seb suspected that Pandora had never actually had any intention of galloping across the park on a horse. She'd backed down far too quickly. It still worried him how adamant she was about 'living the part', and he had a horrible feeling that if she marched into Tipping House declaring a need to be lady of the house for a day, Lady Stanthorpe and her Amazonian granddaughter might throw them off the estate. Contract or no contract.

'I won't. Now all we have to hope is that these aristocratic twits stay out of our way and let us get on with the job.'

'I'm sure if they don't,' Pandora smiled sweetly, 'they'll get everything that's coming to them. They should be extremely grateful that you've offered them this opportunity. Some people just never know when they should admit defeat. Honestly they've let this place go to rack and ruin, and it's no wonder with their disgraceful high-handed attitude. But you're going to insist everything is done your way, aren't you?'

'I am.' And he was. Handling this lot would be a piece of cake compared to keeping his wife under control.

Chapter 11

'It's not that I don't want you to make money, love, but there are limits.' Billy Brinkley lifted his pint and took a gulp before peering over the top of it at his daughter and her husband.

Billy was known throughout Tippermere, and considerably beyond, thanks to the TV coverage he had garnered over the years for his exploits in and out of the saddle – for his direct manner. He was blunt to the point of rudeness as far as some were concerned, which was why some of the villagers thought he was the best person to pass on their concerns to Lottie.

'I'm not going to beat about the bush. Some twat parked a bloody big truck across our driveway in the middle of the night, love, and I had a right performance getting the horses past it this morning. It didn't help when some stupid idiot jumped out of the hedge with a camera either. Bloody stallion nearly landed on top of the Very Reverend Waterson, who was sneaking past on his bicycle. Why the hell can't the man get a car like everybody else?'

'Sneaking?'

'Well he used to ring his bell as he went past, until one of the dogs took a fancy to his bicycle clips, think the sun was glinting off them, went arse over tit into the ditch a couple of times, he did, and that soon put a stop to his bloody tinkling.' Billy grinned. 'Had his frock on the second time, was on duty.'

'And it isn't just that, Charlotte.' Dominic, Lottie's uncle, sat down next to Billy and looked across the table sternly. He shared a driveway with Billy – his leading up to Folly Lake Manor, which lay just beyond Folly Lake Equestrian Centre, home to the Brinkleys. 'Have you seen the state of the lanes? They're churning up the verges and spreading mud on the roads, not to mention the amount of rubbish they're leaving.'

'But,' she looked from one man to the other, unsure which was easiest to mollify, 'it isn't the film crew that's doing that, is it? It's reporters and people who want to watch.'

'That is immaterial.' Dom tapped his glass. 'If they weren't here we wouldn't have half the county climbing the trees trying to catch a glimpse of them. Is it really worth the upheaval, Charlotte? They've only been here a short time, so things are bound to get worse not better. Heaven only know what Mother thinks.'

'Well, actually, it was Gran who suggested it to me.'

Billy chuckled. 'Wonder what the crafty old bird is up to this time?' He had a grudging respect for Lady Elizabeth Stanthorpe. He was well aware of the fact that she would have rather her daughter, Alexa, had married somebody more suitable than him, but after Alexa's death she had done her best to support Billy and Lottie. At first the two adults had nearly come to blows, but once they had realised that they both had Lottie's best interests at heart they had decided to work together. True, at times it had been a difficult relationship, but just as Billy admired Elizabeth, so she too respected him.

'Dad!'

'Aww come on, love.' He ploughed on despite Lottie's outburst and Dom's raised eyebrow. 'We all know she's always plotting something. You mark my words, if she suggested this shower invade the bloody estate then there's a reason behind it.' He tapped the side of his nose.

'True.' Dom nodded in acknowledgement. 'But you are still responsible for this, Charlotte. How much is it going to cost to repair the hedges and fences? And it isn't just the expense, it's about goodwill. The estate has always respected the wishes of the rest of the village. Poor Mrs Jones looked out of her window yesterday straight into a telephoto lens, and,' he frowned sternly, 'my groom was deposited onto the road yesterday when some fool jumped out of the hedgerow, shoved a notebook under the mare's nose and asked if she was a famous rider or celebrity. I cannot afford to have staff injured. Amanda is feeling unwell, Alice is neglected, and I have a string of horses to exercise. Speaking of which,' he glanced at his watch, at the end of what was really quite a long speech for him, 'I really do need to get back and check that Amanda isn't doing too much. Pregnancy really doesn't suit her at all. But,' he stood up and looked down his long, aristocratic nose at his niece, 'you have to remember that you have a duty to the village as well as this estate.'

'I know that, Uncle Dom.' Lottie frowned, wishing she could be more like her uncle, who rarely, if ever, made a mess of anything. He must really think she was making a pig's ear of it if she deserved a lecture of that length. He was so much better at this duty thing than she was.

'I am trying, but we really do need the money and Gran is sure it will pay off in the end and make the wedding business even more profitable.'

'She is, is she?'

'And it isn't for long. I mean, I don't feel we've got any other option, to be honest. Unless you've got any ideas?'

Dom shook his head in exasperation. 'I'll leave it with you. It is your call at the end of the day, but your gran is an old lady, Charlotte. You are the one who has to make the decisions now. We don't want to cause upset, do we? Amanda was quite shocked when she caught somebody trying to climb onto our roof to get a better view.'

'Oh God, you're kidding me?' But Dominic seldom joked. 'I'll try, I'll talk to Seb, and maybe Xander can help too. I just never expected all this fuss.'

'I'm sure you'll do your best. Right I'm off.'

'Give my love to Amanda, won't you? Is she okay? I did mean to pop over and see her, but there's been so much going on in the last few days.'

'I'm sure she will be fine. It's no worse than last time, but I honestly think two children will be our limit, I'm not sure we can go through this again.'

Lottie smiled at Dom's weary expression. She had never seen him as the paternal, or even demonstrative, type until he'd met Amanda and she'd given birth to beautiful little Alice. He worshipped the ground they walked on. He also liked to be in control, to know where he stood, with as little fuss and chaos as possible. Dominic Stanthorpe most definitely didn't like change and disruption.

Amanda's illness at the start of her pregnancy, coupled with an influx of visitors to the village and a film crew invading the estate, just had to be his worst nightmare. He was probably more worried about the effect on his wife than himself, and he had always been more than encouraging when Lottie came up with her 'save the estate' schemes, so she knew that she shouldn't take his words too much to heart.

'You know we can look after Alice any time, if it helps.'

'Oh yes.' He smiled, and the tired look dissipated. 'She loves spending time with her naughty Uncle Rory – heaven only knows why.'

In Dom's view, Rory took life far too lightly – both with his horses and in general terms – but once his own strict regime had been abandoned to family life he'd started to appreciate the other man's stance to a certain degree. 'I dread to think what type of hooligans your kids will be. Goodnight all.'

'Maybe,' he wasn't even at the door before Billy spoke up again, 'you should just let the buggers in.'

'Sorry?' Lottie, who had dreaded the 'your kids' conversation, which she was sure her dad or husband would pick up on, was totally confused by the comment.

'Let the idiots in, you know onto the estate and charge them for the privilege of watching. It'll stop them littering up the lanes and climbing over the walls.'

'But Dad, Seb said he needed peace and quiet to shoot.'

'Nothing in the contract to stop you, is there? You can stick up an electric fence to stop them getting too close to the action. In fact, if I was you I'd pen them in and hitch it up to the mains. Five quid a head and you'll be laughing, love. Keep the village happy and make some more dosh.'

'That's not a bad idea, actually, Billy.' Rory, who had been listening with mild disinterest, suddenly perked up. 'I'm not sure about the legalities of the electric fence, but why can't we charge them?'

'As long as you stick a high-voltage sign up nobody can sue, can they?' Billy chortled.

Lottie had a sudden vision of her father rounding up all the fans and journalists and corralling them like sheep, then chasing them all off the estate at the end of the day on horseback. Well, those that hadn't already been electrocuted. 'Well, I'm really not sure . . .'

'If you ask me, if you're not going to do that, love, you'll have to do what Lizzie would do and get the shotguns out.' One of the things Billy did appreciate about Lady Elizabeth was her direct approach; he thoroughly approved of that.

Lottie sighed, thinking that this was getting out of hand, as a lot of discussions that took place in the pub tended to. 'They, er, asked if you'd be an extra actually, Dad. So I suppose that's a no?'

'An extra bloody what?'

'You know, be in it. I think they just want you to ride past.'

'Ride past?'

She tried to dismiss the thought of him galloping past, Western-style, with a lasso, after an escaped newspaper man. 'Well pop over some jumps in the background, not many of the extras can do that without falling off. The ones I've seen all seem a bit hopeless, actually.'

'So, I'd be getting paid for wasting my time cavorting for the cameras?' Billy was as canny as they came and as careful with his money as a farmer. '*You don't get owt for nowt*' was a saying Lottie grew up with, even though Billy hadn't been back to Yorkshire since he was a child.

'Well,' Lottie looked at him doubtfully, 'I hadn't thought about being paid, to be honest, I just thought it was nice to be asked.'

'Nice to be asked? You're doing them a bloody favour, love, I sometimes wonder about you, girl.' He shook his head and downed the rest of his drink. 'Another one, Rory? Lottie? Nice to be asked, my arse.'

'I'm sure they'll cough up, Billy. We got them to pay extra for stabling their horses on the yard. Mine's a pint, please.' Rory finished his own drink and pushed his empty glass across the table. 'Didn't they say they wanted him to yell at somebody to get out of the way, Lottie?'

'Well, yes, something like that,' said Lottie, worried about exactly what her father might shout.

Rory chuckled. 'So it's more of a cameo than an acting role, then. Just be yourself, Bill.'

'Guess that'll cost them extra then, eh?' Billy winked and waved the empty glasses at the barman. Despite being more than a little annoyed at finding the lanes blocked with reporters' cars and bystanders who were trying to get a glimpse of the stars, he could more than hold his own. And the thought of making some money out of it all had cheered him up no end. 'Joking aside though, love, you know I'm not one to make a fuss about nothing, but I do have to say, old Dom has a point. There's one or two in the village that are a bit worried this thing is going to take over.'

'Push up a bit Billy, love.' Tiggy, Billy's eccentric but very loveable wife, squeezed her way onto the seat next to him, her ample figure taking up well over half of the seat, despite Billy's portly frame. 'If you ask me,' she leant forward conspiratorially, displaying a fair amount of cleavage despite the cold weather, 'they're just jealous. You should have heard the vicar and Mrs Jones moaning about why it all had to be on the estate and why they couldn't benefit too. It's all a load of hot air about nothing, love, don't you worry about it. They just don't like the fact that it's nothing to do with them. Nosey lot.' She patted Lottie's hand. 'Anyway, what's all this about a sexy polo player? Do you think he'd pose for me? I'm really thinking I need to get back to doing some portraits.' She kissed Billy on the cheek. 'That fireman calendar you got hasn't half inspired me, but there's nothing like a real body, is there? It's always so hard to get your hands on a good life model, though.' Her voice drifted off wistfully.

'There's nothing like getting my hands on your body, love.' Billy kissed her back and wrapped his arms round her in a show of affection, and Lottie studied her drink intently.

Lottie's mother had been the love of Billy's life and her death had left him devastated. For years he'd struggled to come to terms with the event and with caring for his young daughter, but throughout it all Tiggy had been there in the background. Quietly supporting him, loving him in the same way her devoted spaniel loved her, and expecting nothing in return except his happiness. His gruff exterior shielded his emotions from most people, but Tiggy saw right through it.

When Billy had finally realised he was in love and had proposed, the whole village had been amazed that 'tatty Tiggy' had made an honest, and slightly less grumpy, man out of him. They'd also been more than a little bit shocked that Billy was willing and able to cope with such a scatty wife. She would constantly get distracted mid-task and forget what she was doing, which resulted in horses being put into the wrong fields and water buckets overflowing. If Tiggy had been a groom, Billy would have sacked her several times over (especially when she turned his stallion out with his mares). But she wasn't and he couldn't. In fact, Billy couldn't imagine life without her.

Tiggy guffawed, her whole body quivering with laughter and then she planted a big kiss on Billy's lips. 'And it's all yours when we get home, my darling. Now, tell us all about this man, Lottie. I'm coming over tomorrow to see him with my own eyes.'

* * *

The man in question, Xander Rossi, was leaning over a stable door, his dog cradled in his arms.

He'd had mixed feelings about returning to Tippermere, but they always said you could only feel one source of pain at a time, didn't they? He was a grown man now, not some hormone-ridden kid with a chip on his shoulder, so the half-forgotten discomfort that Lottie had caused him in the past had to pale into insignificance alongside the mountain of problems that he'd been trying his damnedest to block out more recently.

Alcohol and feeling sorry for himself hadn't helped one bit when his career had train-wrecked, he'd hit the newspaper headlines for all the wrong reasons, the hate mail had started and Miranda, his ex, had done a runner. But wallowing in self-pity wasn't really his style anyway, and he'd soon had to snap out of it when the one real constant in his life, his mother, had started to disintegrate before his eyes.

Xander ran his fingers through his hair agitatedly. Pandora had come back into his life at just the right moment. He'd needed to get away until the journalists lost interest and he was yesterday's news – and a few weeks on location where nobody knew who he was had seemed ideal. Well, it was either that or hiking in the Himalayas. A grin twitched at the corner of his mouth, the weather was supposed to be okay there at this time of year, a damned sight less variable than Pandora anyway.

He reached into his pocket and found the ever-present mints, then fed one to each of his two ponies that were stabled in the courtyard. It was so damned peaceful here, away from the hustle and bustle, away from the strident voice of his sister and the barking commands of her husband. With just the tinkling sound of water in the fountain to accompany the whinnies and nickers of the horses.

It had been a stroke of luck that there were looseboxes free, as he knew he'd get no peace in the temporary stable block that had been set up for the rest of the horses to be used in the production. Here he could hide from the crowds and the questions he didn't want to answer.

It was strange to feel almost at home. As a teenager he'd been the oik, the outsider, and he'd hated the lot of them, and resented what they had, but right now this place was actually taking the edge off things. He could breathe properly for the first time in months. Maybe that's what you got if you had enough money, a protective barrier against the rest of the world.

Or maybe it was just him who had grown up. That teenage version of him had probably been a pain in the arse, blowing imagined slights out of all proportion, like kids do. Now that he was older, more jaded, he supposed the little things didn't matter as much. And, he guessed, he'd found his place in life. What he wanted to do. Play polo. Well, he had thought so, until recent events had shaken him more than he liked to admit.

Some elements of the press were still out to get him – egged on by his ex – keen to paint him as the cruel sportsman. He had to face it, his polo-playing days were over; he couldn't win now as far as the sport he loved was concerned. If he announced his retirement he'd be hailed as a coward who couldn't cope with the pressure; if he returned to the field he'd be the heartless bastard who'd been responsible for the death of a pony but carried on regardless.

And if he did go back, what kind of player would he be anyway?

He'd lost his nerve, lost the killer instinct that would let him gallop up a line, ride off a player recklessly, spin so fast he risked going down in a tangle of tack and legs. It wasn't about protecting himself; it was about the horses. The accident had been his wake-up call, the red flag that announced his competitive spirit had taken him over that invisible line.

The pony nudged his hand and Xander stroked the velvet-soft nose. 'You're going to be bored stiff working on a film set, aren't you?' She blew sweet hay-scented air down her nose. 'Even an old girl like you.'

He'd had to sell his best ponies, so getting back to the top of the game was a hopeless dream anyway. All he had left were the steadier ones, the troupers that had been with him longer than he dared remember.

He'd had no choice – raising funds had been his priority – and all he could hope was that the money lasted until some kind of settlement had been agreed. Throwing himself into a legal battle with his father was as good as burning fifty-pound notes, but he had no choice. He couldn't abandon his mother. If he didn't stand up for her against the selfish bastard, nobody else would.

Pandora had known he was in some kind of mess. His sharp-eyed and sharper-tongued half-sister had spotted the weakness and taken advantage. She'd swooped in, a vulture thinly disguised as a guardian angel, as the hate campaign against him had peaked, and she'd offered her condolences when Miranda had shown her true colours and as good as sworn allegiance to the tabloids. But he was sure Pandora had still got no idea about the family battle lines that were being drawn up.

Yes, the production did need somebody to work with the horses and advise, but they could have employed any number of people. There had to be another angle, another reason she'd been determined that he be involved. And it wasn't a gesture of goodwill, to help him. Pandora didn't help anybody unless she benefitted. But he hadn't, as yet, worked out what her end-game was.

All he knew was that it was one hell of a coincidence that they'd ended up here, at Tipping House. Just as there were scores of horsemen who could have taken his role, so there were scores of stately homes that could have fit the bill. But somehow they were here, back in Tippermere. Back at the scene of teenage angst and the feeling of not belonging.

It made him uneasy.

Ella licked his chin, as though she understood, and he ruffled the wiry hair on the top of her head. 'What the hell is Pandora's game, eh?' The little dog waggled her eyebrows and Xander smiled. 'Let's hope it doesn't end in tears. I've got a horrible feeling that Lottie is going to wish she'd never set eyes on us again.'

He had never been particularly close to his half-sister. If anything he preferred the coldly detached Seb, who had looked decidedly irritated when he'd discovered that Pandora had been to Tippermere before. Seb liked to be in control, to know everything. Unfortunately Pandora liked to scheme, and keep secrets. In her book, knowledge was power, and despite her show of surprise, Xander suspected that finding Lottie here was not totally unexpected. She was up to something, and he felt like he'd played right into her hands, that she wanted him here for some reason.

And what did he get out of it? A place to hide until the fuss died down, a distraction, a wage that wasn't much more than loose change?

There were a lot of things in his life right now that he had no control over, and there were some things he wanted to hide from. But the truth wasn't one of them.

He should carry on what Seb had started. Talk to Pandora. Find out what they were really doing here. Then work out if the Himalayas was a better option after all.

Xander glanced at his watch. It was too late now. His half-sister and her husband would be ensconced in their hotel room. Together. And this was a conversation he wanted to keep between him and Pandora. For now.

Some things were better kept quiet. Like his own secret. If his devious sister ever found out the actual cause of all his pain, the person he was really up against – their father – then she might not be quite so keen to drag him into her own little plan. Things were already nasty enough, and Pandora, he was sure, was more than capable of making them ten times worse.

Chapter 12

Seb pulled the scarf tighter around his neck and shrugged himself further into his jacket. The sun might be out, but there was an icy wind blowing across the open expanse of parkland that sat at the front of Tipping House. The daffodils were no longer jaunty, but instead looked decidedly dejected, and the horses were tossing their heads and dancing about in a way that unnerved him, and it appeared, some of the extras.

He looked up at the sky. They had to get this scene done and dusted before the light started to go and so far the day had been a disaster. Who knew that horses could act so bloody stupid when there was a bit of a breeze?

'All I fucking want is for them to do it one bloody time, to get it right one bloody time. Is that too much to ask?' He glared at Xander, who looked back like he didn't give a shit. He didn't know what was more annoying, having to deal with the animals or his brother-in-law.

'They aren't animations, they're horses, and it was you who employed the extras, not me. Why didn't you get people who could ride? Or do it in a studio with CGI.'

'Oh save your sanctimonious sermons, Xander. They're bloody horses. One shot, one bloody realistic shot towards the camera, where they're all going in the right direction and the sun is fucking shining. Is that too much to ask?'

Xander raised an eyebrow, determined to ignore the sarcasm and not let Seb bait him. Although he was very tempted to just thump him.

'We can add the ball afterwards. Just get them to fucking gallop towards the marker. I want the real thing – can't you get that into your head? The drama, the light. Christ, you really haven't got an artistic streak at all, have you?'

'And you really haven't got a human side, have you?' Xander shook his head and headed back towards the horses.

Seb gritted his teeth, wishing he could return to civilisation. His clean and tidy penthouse in London would be perfect, soothing, but even the hotel in Kitterly Heath would be welcome after today's shoot. He longed for a good glass of wine and some decent food. All this hearty-fayre crap was playing hell with his digestive system; it was no wonder they all felt the urge to run around with dogs and horses, to work the pounds off.

He shook his head to try and dismiss the unsavoury thoughts, then put a hand up instinctively to his stiff neck. Right now he'd kill for a proper bed, with decent pillows.

'Okay, are we ready to go again? What the hell is the matter now?' He glared at the runner, whose name escaped him, who had slid to a halt in front of him.

'Er, we have an, er, problem, Mr Drakelow, sir.'

'Don't *sir* me, and *we* don't have a fucking problem, you do. I pay you to make sure everybody is ready when I say go.'

'One of the horses stood on Jake's foot and he's supposed to be in this shot.'

'Well he doesn't need his bloody foot to ride a horse, does he? Give me strength.'

The man backed off nervously. 'He's in agony, he . . .'

'What the fuck is wrong with you all? Do I have to throw him in the bloody saddle myself?'

'Can I help?' Under the pretence of concern, Pandora has sent Jamie to defuse the situation, but they both knew that really she was being nosey – she wanted to know what was causing the delay.

The man shot Jamie a look of relief and scurried away before anybody got a chance to sack him. He'd already been dismissed three times since shooting began: twice by Seb and once by Pandora.

'Can you fucking ride?' Seb glared at his intern, not expecting an answer. 'I thought not, so how the fuck can you help? Jesus, this film is going to kill me, I need a drink and civilisation.'

'He can't, but I can.' Tab, who had followed in Jamie's wake, refused to shrink under Seb's withering gaze. Instead she folded her arms defiantly.

'Really?' The sarcastic tone came easily to Seb, and never more so than when he felt under pressure.

Tab had spent as much of her spare time watching the filming as she could, not because she had any interest whatsoever in the production, but because it gave her a chance to ogle Xander, who was surprisingly elusive when she searched him out in the yard. It had got boring, though – he seemed to spend most of his time either hiding in the stables, a trailer, or surrounded by admirers – and she'd been rather relieved when Jamie had sidled over each day for a chat. Jamie was nice as well, easy to talk to. He was also full of good ideas.

'Honest, it's my job. I can ride more or less any horse. Try me.'

'And I can get you a drink, Seb.' Jamie looked from Tab to Seb, awaiting a verdict.

Seb looked the girl up and down. 'I suppose you're tall and stringy enough to pass for that youth,' he paused, 'and flat-chested enough. You've got two minutes to get changed. Well, go on then, move. I haven't got all fucking day.'

Jamie grabbed Tab's hand and the pair bolted towards the

costume trailer before he had a chance to change his mind.

'What are you two grinning about? You look like simpletons.' Pandora, who was expecting an update from Jamie on what had upset Seb now, looked pointedly at their joined hands.

But Tab couldn't care less whether Pandora, or indeed the whole world (apart from Xander), thought she looked like a simpleton. She was going to ride on set. She was an extra. Which meant two things: she was going to be famous and she was going to have the opportunity to get closer to Xander.

* * *

Xander was standing by the pony line, Jake's helmet and mallet in his hand, his dog watching proceedings closely when Tab arrived, slightly out of breath.

The polo whites that she'd been given to wear (Jake's, complete with stains – for continuity reasons) were several sizes too large around the waist, and decidedly short in the leg, and in the generous polo shirt she felt like she'd been dressed by a jealous aunt who wanted her to resemble a sack of potatoes. But with some judicious belt-tightening and tucking in she almost felt the part.

'Not that anybody will be able to see you, duck.' The girl in the wardrobe trailer had said as she'd tightened the knee pads. 'The speed you're going, at that distance you could be anybody. Here,' she pulled Tab's long hair into a band and shoved it into her collar, 'that'll do. Now don't you go falling off, he's in a right mood already and at this rate none of us will be getting any supper.'

Which all meant that by the time she'd staggered down the steps, she wasn't feeling quite as chipper any more.

Jamie was waiting for her, a massive grin splashed across his friendly face. 'Wow, you look the part.'

'Really?' Used to wearing tight jodhpurs and even tighter t-shirts, Tab certainly didn't feel the part. In fact, if Xander fancied her in this get-up he'd have to be deranged.

'Really. The sexiest extra on the pitch.' He kissed her cheek, then blushed. 'Come on, Xander's waiting.'

'You don't look anything like Jake.' Xander's tone was dry. 'Hopefully you won't ride anything like him, either.'

Tab grinned, feeling slightly more confident once she had a foot in the stirrup iron. The polo pony looked remarkably laid back to her and she really couldn't see what all the fuss was about.

'Here.' Xander passed Tab the mallet, then lifted an eyebrow. 'I take it you've never played polo from the way you're holding that.'

'I've never even watched a match, to be honest.' Tab glanced over at Jamie, who gave the thumbs-up.

'Not a problem for this shot. Right, stick up.' He put one hand over hers, the other steadying her elbow, and Tab, who wasn't one bit flustered about the riding came over all jittery. She'd never managed to get this close to him before, and now his flat, warm stomach was pressed against her thigh. She forgot all about Jamie and how to breathe as well. 'All you need to do is canter down that line towards the camera. You're not supposed to be in a game, just galloping over. Okay?' He was giving her a quizzical look.

'Fine.' God, he smelled good. 'Towards the camera?'

'Straight at it, at a reasonable pace. This little mare knows her job. If you stay straight, she will. But she's very sensitive to your body weight. If you start shifting around in the saddle you could end up anywhere.'

'Okay.' It certainly didn't sound difficult at all, even if holding the mallet felt decidedly strange. She shifted her foot more firmly into the stirrup iron and Xander drew his breath in. Christ, jabbing him in the balls with a spur wasn't going to help her case.

'Straight. Now wait on that line until you get the signal, walk to that marker, then go into canter. Have a quick canter round here to get the feel of her and, remember, these ponies are used to going fast. Don't use your legs too hard. She doesn't need a jab in the ribs any more than you do. She's used to light aids – it's all about weight.'

Tab was just about to take his advice when one of the crew rushed up. 'Seb says can you stop arsing about,' he looked apologetic, 'his words not mine, and get lined up before the light goes. The message was, you only have to ride in a fucking straight line.'

'Well you can tell him—'

'It's alright, Xander. I'll go. I get it.'

'These are my horses and I'm not having that jerk—'

Before Xander could say anything else, Tab had walked down to the line and was watching for the signal.

'Christ, he was right.' At the lightest touch from her legs, the little mare sped off, eating up the ground with alarming speed and reaching Seb and his cameraman within seconds. Seb glared as she sat back a few yards short and the pony obediently slowed to a walk.

'Fantastic.' The sarcastic tone carried clearly. 'You didn't fall off. Now do it again, and this time come straight at the camera, stop wandering about like you're drunk and don't slow down until I say, got it? I thought you said you could fucking ride.'

Tab swore under her breath and nodded, not trusting herself to speak.

'And for fuck's sake keep that stick still, it's waving around like a bloody flag. It's not the charge of the fucking light brigade.'

She rode back slightly despondent, to find Xander and Jamie side by side.

'You can ride.'

It was a compliment! Whatever happened now, it didn't matter. Xander had noticed her; Xander had said she could ride. Fuck Seb and his rants.

'Stay light in the saddle and focus more so you don't drift,' he patted the mare's neck and gave her a mint, 'she's used to somebody riding with one hundred per cent attention on where they want to go. Concentrate.' The corner of his mouth quirked. 'Imagine Seb's head is the ball and head straight for it.'

Tab went for it. She'd never sat on such a responsive horse, never felt such acceleration as they shot across the park, and with the wind cold against her cheeks she felt like whooping. But she didn't, she headed straight as a die towards Seb, who was standing next to the camera, clutching the mallet as firmly as she could and wishing she could take a swipe at the imaginary ball when she got there.

As she got closer the cameraman twitched, holding his ground as long as he dared, then with a grunt tried to drag his equipment out of the way. Seb was made of sterner stuff, or he was more confident that Tab would bottle first.

'No way, you twat.' Muttering through gritted teeth, trying not to smile, Tab refused to rein in. She was close enough to see the scowl on his face, to see the stony expression in those cold grey eyes, before Seb finally shouted 'cut'. Then he leapt for safety as she put the brakes on and veered off to one side, inches from where he'd been standing.

'Cripes, it really is you!' Lottie, who had finished feeding the horses and been unable to find her groom anywhere, had wandered out to watch the last shots of the day. After several years of riding out with Tab and giving her riding lessons, she was convinced she'd recognise her riding anywhere. But she must have got it wrong. Tab wasn't in the film and she certainly didn't play polo. But, as she got closer to the crew she saw quite clearly that it was indeed an elated Tabatha who was stood up in her stirrups, waving her mallet in the air jubilantly as she came to a halt.

'This horse is ace. I want to play polo.' She patted the horse's neck enthusiastically and grinned down at Lottie. 'It's awesome.'

'What the hell do you think you're doing? You haven't got time to chat.'

She turned to look in surprise at Seb. Surely that had been what he'd wanted?

'You veered off the line, out there.' He gestured back in the direction she'd come from.

'I never did.' Tab glared, and Seb met the look head on.

'Well from here I say you did.' His features were set, dead-fish eyes expressionless. She hated him. 'Just ride in a straight bloody line at the camera. Even an idiot should be able to understand that. Can't you?'

Tab lost the look and smiled sweetly.

Sweet meant trouble, thought Lottie, and shrank further into her coat.

'One more time before we wrap up, to be sure. And,' he gave his cameraman an assessing look, 'don't you dare duck out.'

'I'd got the shot.'

'And get the Segway to follow her down.'

'Why on earth do we have to do it again?' Grumbled Tab to a grinning Jamie when she returned to the start position. 'Just ride in a straight bloody line.' She mimicked Seb's tone perfectly.

'It's always like this, sometimes there's like a dozen takes. These film sets are pretty boring, to be honest. It's much more interesting going out finding locations.'

Xander, who had been checking the horse over, straightened up. 'I've never seen Seb actually move out of the way before.' There was a hint of humour lurking in his eyes, which made him seem much more human to Tab than he had before. True, he was amazingly dishy, but he was detached, he had that distant 'don't touch me' air about him. 'Don't worry, this will be the last take, the one before was good enough, he's just stamping his authority.'

Tab scowled, swung her mallet in a circle and then held it in position and walked the mare to the starting point.

'What do you think she's going to do?' Jamie's voice was low.

Xander grinned as he watched her gather the horse up. 'Mow him down if we're lucky. Atta girl.'

At the signal, Tab, now feeling like a seasoned pro, nudged the mare forward. The wind had eased off so that the tired daffodils were nodding gently in front of Tipping House, which was bathed in the last of the spring sunshine.

As the dark bay mare moved effortlessly onwards, the lush, young grass cushioning each footfall, Tab let her run. For a moment she shut her eyes, heard the galloping horses on both sides, the whoosh of sticks swinging through the air, the clunk as the ball was hit. She was there, the crowd was cheering.

Except it wasn't cheering, it was excited barks.

She didn't mean to slow down, but the super-sensitive horse read her body language. Tab glanced off to the side. Across the grass sped a blur of brown and white spaniel, his nose to the ground, his tail wagging furiously.

Lottie had left Harry locked in one of the loose boxes when she'd gone in search of Tab, but now he was out and intent on tracking his mistress down, Tilly and the other two terriers in his wake. The terriers fanned out and Tab, sensing disaster, sped up, heading straight for Seb. If she could only get there first he'd have his take.

She might have made it, if Sam hadn't chosen just that moment to drive through the gateway, the soft top of the sports car down, radio blaring out a happy tune, with Roxy and Scruffy in the back. Seeing the horse and rider speeding towards them, she stopped the car, flicking up her sunglasses to take a closer look, and her dog, seeing the pack approaching, gave an excited bark and made a bid for freedom.

Scruffy leapt over Roxy, who clapped her hands with excitement, and he was out of the convertible before Sam had even pulled the handbrake on.

'Oh my God how amazing, look at that Roxy. They're filming

on the—oh no, oh Scruffy darling, don't babe. Come here.' Flinging the door open, she took chase after the dog, who was fast approaching the cameraman, Lottie, and Seb from the rear.

'Oh sugar. Scruffy pet, Scruffy.' Kicking off her high heels she got a glimpse of Seb as he spun round, his mouth open, face aghast, and knew this called for urgent measures. Throwing all her energy into a last sprint, Sam realised that Scruffy was almost within reach and, trying not to think about grass stains, she dived for him, arms outstretched.

'Woohoo, girl.' There was a shout from the watching crowd – safely contained behind a tape (not electrified, rather to Billy and Rory's disappointment) – before they burst into a mix of spontaneous applause, catcalls, and laughter, with shouts of 'she should be in the film' and 'loving them knickers'.

Sam giggled and straightened up, her hand still on the dog's collar, but she was no longer the centre of attention.

Seb was glaring outraged at the recaptured Scruffy when the sound of barking alerted him to a new danger. He spun back round to see the pack of dogs headed straight towards him. Or rather towards Lottie, who was only a few feet away.

'Oh no, Harry.' At the sound of his mistress's voice, Harry barked and put a new burst of speed on, and Tilly yapped in excitement, which set off the other terriers.

'Christ.' There was a yell from the cameraman on the Segway as Ella, spotting Harry, who she was besotted with, streaked in front of him, intent on joining in the fun.

He veered off course, to the delight of the crowd, who had now realised that their five pounds had been well spent.

Seb was so busy shouting, he didn't even hear the pounding of hooves that announced Tab's arrival. There was no 'cut', so with a 'that'll teach him' curse under her breath, she just kept going, galloping through the narrow gap between Seb and Lottie so that Seb staggered to one side, dropping his clipboard and launching into a new tirade of expletives that Tab was sure she'd never heard before.

Tab didn't stop. On she galloped towards the onlookers, who were reaching for pad and paper, convinced that she had to be a star with an autograph worth getting.

'And what the fuck are rent-a-crowd doing here?' By now, Seb had lost it, his blond hair on end he lurched towards Lottie, arms waving about wildly, face puce with rage.

'I told you.' Lottie emerged from under the pile of dogs and Tilly ran circles round her barking. 'We charged them to come in and watch, to save the lanes getting blocked, and' she finished reasonably, 'they've been very quiet and well behaved.'

'Unlike these bloody, fucking animals.' His arms dropped down by his sides, fists clenched and his tone turned scarily robotic. 'Well you can tell them to all fuck off home. I've paid for exclusive use—'

'Well, no, you haven't actually, we looked—'

'And the insurance doesn't cover us for accidents. You'd better not be filming this.'

The cameraman, who had been watching intently, shook his head, clamped his mouth shut and tried not to laugh.

'Oh wow, isn't that fab, babe.' Sam staggered over, still bent double so she could hang on to Scruffy's collar as he leapt about, determined to get to the other dogs. She grinned disarmingly at Seb. 'You must be so clever to think of all this,' and waved an expansive hand.

Seb was used to his wife's ways and his cold look would have sent Lottie running, but Sam seemed oblivious.

'I didn't write the script.'

'Aww sorry, I thought you were somebody important, seeing as you were stood over here.' She did a double-take and laughed. 'Oh, you joker, it is you, isn't it Seb? You saying you're not clever, and we all know you are. Oh my God,' she caught sight of Tab, who was heading back their way, 'it's Tab.' And stopping to clap her hands, she forgot about her dog again, who sensing freedom jumped over Harry and then set off back across the lawn, the other dogs in pursuit.

'Jesus Christ will somebody get rid of all these fucking animals.' Seb covered his eyes briefly with his fists, then straightening up he took a sobering deep breath before bellowing into his walkie-talkie. 'Jamie get your arse over here with my car. I need to get out of this dump and get a fucking drink.'

Chapter 13

'Who rattled his cage?'

Lottie glanced up with relief at the sound of Rory's voice, just in time to see him being rudely shouldered out of the way by a very irate Seb. 'Sorry I let Harry out.' He grinned, not looking one tiny bit sorry, and sat down on the grass next to his wife. 'I didn't realise you'd put them all in that loosebox. I opened the door and he shot out and Tilly followed him. Where's she gone now?' Hearing her master's voice, Tilly was on her way back, with Harry behind and Ella determinedly tagging along.

Sam joined them on the grass. 'He's a bit of a one isn't he, that Seb? Do you think he'll calm down soon? He'll give himself a heart attack if he carries on like that. There was this football manager that Davey used to have and he was just the same, effing and jeffing all over the place. He threw a boot at Davey's head once,' she giggled, 'but he missed cos he was only little and you know how tall my Davey is when he stands up. Well, he retired, like, and he still went to all the matches and was jumping up and down one day like he was still on the touchline, and you know what? He dropped dead, he did.' She stood up. 'Dead as a dodo in the middle of a big game. Caused a right kerfuffle, what with the ambulance and everything.'

The cameraman finished packing his things away as they watched Seb get into his car. 'He'll be fine when he's had a drink. More of a prima donna than the actresses, that one is, sacks us all on a weekly basis then has forgotten all about it next day, though you'll never get an apology out of him.' He peered more closely at Sam, then stuck his hand out. 'You're married to that goalkeeper, David Simcock, aren't you? Pleased to meet you. Damned good tackle you did back there.' He winked.

Sam ignored the hand and gave him a kiss on the cheek. 'Lovely to meet you too, babe. I hope we didn't upset him too much, what with Scruffy and everything. He's probably the artistic type, and he does have that Pandora to put up with, doesn't he? Bless. Ah well, I'd better get off and find Scruffy. He's probably in the catering trailer, if I know him. Can you keep an eye on Roxy, please?'

'Sure.' Rory glanced over at the car and waved at the little girl, who was doing her best to undo the child-proof buckle of her car-seat.

'Aww, you're a gem, Rory. Make a lovely father, you will. Won't be long, I just need to find my shoes. See you in a bit, babe.'

'A lovely father.' Rory winked and squeezed Lottie's thigh as Sam waltzed off. 'How about it? I know we said we'd wait, but I think we should just get on with it.'

'No!' Lottie was shocked at how loudly the word had exploded from her.

Rory's eyes opened wide and he moved his hand. 'Oh. That's telling me.'

'Sorry, I didn't mean to say it like that. I just, oh Rory, we can't, I don't want to.'

He sighed. 'Then tell me why.'

'But I can't . . .' She didn't know how to put it into words, this dread that filled her every time the conversation came up. Lottie pressed her fists into her eyes.

'I thought we trusted each other, talked about everything.'

'We do.'

'Then talk to me. Let's plan for the future, Lottie.'

'You never wanted to plan before, we just got on with things.'

'Maybe I've grown up.'

His lopsided grin forced a lump into her throat. She loved him, and she wanted to make him happy, but she wanted to be honest with him too. 'What if I couldn't have kids?'

'Oh, darling.' He'd moved back closer. 'Don't worry about stuff like that. We could adopt, people do it, or get help. You daftie, why would you think that?'

'No, I mean, if I didn't want them, couldn't be . . .' *A mother* was what she wanted to say, and couldn't. She glanced up over her knuckles to see the look of confusion, mixed with what she was sure was disbelief. His body had stiffened. How could she do this to him? 'I just don't want a baby, Rory.' The empty feeling at the pit of her stomach seemed to expand. She'd said it. She wanted to add 'ever', but it froze in her throat.

He looked harder, then laughed, relaxed and hugged her. 'You are daft at times. Oh Lottie, it's scary. I get that. Yeah, I suppose adoption isn't for everybody, but we'll be fine. I think you're over thinking this.'

'I know you want children, Rory, but—'

'I never seriously thought about it before, but I actually do. I'd love a kid of our own like Roxy.' He kissed the tip of her nose. 'Well, maybe not quite like Roxy. I love you, darling, but I get it if you're not ready. It is scary, but everybody does it.' He shrugged. 'Can't be worse than jumping a four-foot hedge.'

It was more than scary, but he'd obviously decided she couldn't possibly be serious about not wanting children. Everybody did it. He just took it for granted that they would too. And she couldn't. But the thought of losing him was far worse than jumping any hedge. 'I'd rather put Black Gold in foal again.' She knew her grin was weak as she tried her normal diversionary tactics, but this time Rory didn't bite straight away.

'Not quite the same, is it? Don't you ever get fed up of just having the animals to cuddle?'

'I've got you.' She glanced up and he was looking at her so earnestly that she had to look down again quickly.

'It would be nice to have a family of our own.'

'But we're so busy, Rory, and we're totally broke.'

'Lots of people are broke and still have children.'

'And I'm not sure I'd be a good mum.'

'Bollocks, you'd be a great mum. Come on, don't look like that.' He put an arm round her. 'Look if there was a problem and we couldn't have kids, then that would be fine, but there won't be.'

'I don't think we can't have them, I just really don't want . . .' Her words were drowned out by the bellow of frustration that came from Sam's car.

Rory sighed. 'I better go and rescue Roxy before she takes the car to pieces. We'll chat about this later, okay?'

* * *

The look on Xander's face was enough to tell Tab she was in trouble when she finally made her way back over to him. One thing was for sure, it wasn't the look of love. That appeared to be reserved purely for his little dog.

It was at this point that Tab remembered she was supposed to be looking after Ella. It had been one of her tactics to get him interested in her. Surely if she looked after the dog the man would follow? Well, that had been her reasoning, but now it looked like it could be her downfall. I mean, how was she supposed to know that Harry would get loose? She was well aware that Ella looked on the springer spaniel as a big brother, and would happily follow him anywhere. But the last time she'd seen him he'd been with Lottie, following her around while she skipped out stables and exercised horses.

'What the hell are you playing at? You were supposed to do that shot then ride straight back.'

'But I—'

'This isn't the pony club, have you any idea how valuable that animal you've been galloping around on is?'

'So this is about money?' Her self-defence mechanism kicked in and she fought back.

'I wasn't talking about money, it's about animal welfare.' His eyes were steely. 'And what about Ella?' He pointed behind him towards the little dog, who was now curled up on her blanket, and raised an apologetic eyebrow. 'Did you forget all about her?'

'But you knew I was riding. You can't blame me for not keeping an eye on her. She was curled up on her blanket when I went. She's your dog. What were *you* doing?'

'Okay.' He held up his hand, then ran his fingers through his hair. 'I'm sorry. Sorry. I'm overreacting. I admit I should have noticed when she took off, but I was too busy watching you. Give me the horse and then go and get changed.'

Jamie, who had been hovering on the sidelines, nodded his head in the direction of the trailer. 'Come on, I'll wait while you get changed.' He had her by the hand and was dragging her off before she had a chance to retaliate. 'Don't mind him, you were brilliant. He was actually laughing when you flattened Seb.'

'What the hell has got into him?' Tab didn't wait for a response. 'I don't know why he has to be that grumpy.' It seemed so unfair to Tab. What had seemed like so much fun at the beginning had turned into a disaster of a day. Xander thought she was an irresponsible idiot, and Seb would probably pack up and leave the very next day.

'He's just a bit overprotective about his horses.' Jamie shrugged, then pushed her up the steps into the trailer. 'Ignore it, he's better with animals than people these days, and he's probably worried about the mood Pandora will be in. I reckon we should get a move on before either Seb or Pandora comes and gives us an earful.'

'Too late, I'd say. Seb's gone back to the hotel, but look who hasn't.' Tab leaned down from her vantage point, took Jamie by the shoulders, and swivelled him around so that he could see Pandora heading their way. 'Uh-oh, she looks cross.'

'You, yes, you. Jamie. Why did you fetch Seb's car? Where was he going?'

'Back to Kitterly Heath, I think.' Jamie shrugged. 'He'd had enough of all the, er, animals.' He glanced up at Tab, who was doing her best not to giggle.

'Oh, for heaven's sake. How I am supposed to get back? He never thinks about me, does he?' She looked Jamie up and down. 'And where has Xander got to now? That man is never about when I need him. *You* will have to drive me.'

'You know I haven't got a car. One of the crew . . .'

'He'll do.' Without another word Pandora veered off. Jamie and Tab looked in the direction she was taking. She was not heading for either her brother or one of the crew, but straight towards Lottie and Rory.

'That'll go down well.' Tab frowned. 'Lottie and her don't get on well at all. Maybe you should get somebody to head her off while I get changed?'

Jamie grinned. 'I was actually hoping I could help you get changed.'

'Sod off.'

He laughed. 'Okay, hurry up, I'll persuade her to go back with one of the crew, or Xander.'

Tab found that 'hurrying up' was easier said than done. The girl in the wardrobe trailer, who had expertly dressed her, was nowhere to be seen.

She'd wobbled about for quite some time trying to undo the knee pads, before giving up and sitting on the floor, which made the job slightly easier. She was still a bit out of puff, and was in her underwear, peering under chairs, when Jamie got back. Tab had a problem, quite a serious one.

'Aren't you done yet?'

'Hang on.' The wardrobe mistress obviously liked to keep things tidy. 'I can't find my stuff.'

'You sure you don't want a hand?'

'No I don't. Stay out there.'

'I can close my eyes.'

'It's your hands I'm bothered about not your eyes.'

Deciding that it really couldn't be that difficult to find her clobber in such a small space, Tab started a methodical search – and finally found a box in the far corner of the room.

'Ha! Found them.'

'Oh.' In just one syllable Jamie managed to express enough disappointment to make Tab laugh.

By the time she'd put her own clothes on and felt more like her normal self, Tab had completely got over her Seb-and-Xander-induced bad mood. 'You got rid of old Panda, then?'

'I did. Somebody agreed to chauffeur her, she likes the idea of a chauffeur and they liked the idea of not having to talk to her.'

Tab giggled. 'They're a weird lot, aren't they? Why do you work for them?'

'I like my job.' Jamie paused. 'And I like it here.' He gave her a sidelong look, which she chose to ignore.

'Seb seems to hate the countryside. I really don't get why he's doing a film like this. He hates us, hates the place, and he really hates the animals.'

'Well I wouldn't say "hates".' Jamie fell into step with her. 'He's just uncomfortable, he likes to be in control, and it doesn't always work that way here, does it?'

'You can say that again.'

'Seb's life is clean and tidy, it's all organised, not dirt and chaos.'

'Dom can be a bit like that, but he's not such a complete arsehole.'

'He seems okay to me.'

'He's a lot better since they had Alice, not as snooty. So why is Seb shooting this film at all?'

'Pandora's idea.'

'Really? Wow, he always does what she wants? She's just an actress.'

Jamie laughed. 'Pandora isn't *just* anything. But he doesn't always do what she wants, well not really, she tries to make him think things are his idea, but he's not daft. He likes to keep her onside, and he says she's actually got a good eye for trends, things that will be a hit. He's good at his job though.'

'So why can't he use those green screens, you know special effects? He doesn't need to use horses at all, does he?'

'He's a bit of a perfectionist. He likes to do stuff for real. I don't mind Seb that much, he's okay. He can be a bit of a prick, but he's not always scheming like Pandora is.'

'You reckon she's scheming?'

'Well she always knows what she wants and she makes sure she gets it. To be honest, she has helped me a bit recently, but I don't trust her.'

'So she's determined, but not very nice.'

'And she doesn't care who she hurts along the way.'

'Oh. And where's Xander gone?'

'To do the horses. Look, do we have to talk about everybody else? I know you fancy the pants off him, but . . .'

'I don't!'

'You do.' He laughed. 'I get it. Everybody does Sam, Lottie, even Tiggy.'

'Bollocks. Are you jealous?' She grinned, but his normal playful smile was absent. 'Oh come on, Lottie doesn't fancy him, she's got Rory.'

Jamie raised an eyebrow and didn't comment.

'She doesn't. Does she? You do know,' she slipped an arm through his, 'you're catching the Xander grumps.'

'You're obsessed with him.'

Tab was just trying to come up with a suitable response when an unmistakable authoritarian voice stopped her in her tracks.

'Ah, there you are.' It was Elizabeth, standing on the stone steps that led to the entrance door of Tipping House. 'Whatever have you been doing?'

'I couldn't find my clothes.'

'Oh really.' She gave Jamie a stern look. 'I've been watching from upstairs. What a carry on. You two can come with me. Come along, I want to talk to you. Quickly, before that dreadful man appears and starts shouting again.'

'He's gone back to Kitterly Heath to recover.' Tab giggled.

'The man should stay there. He is such an unpleasant individual, so uncouth.' She gestured for them to follow and went inside, heading for her sitting room. 'Sit down both of you.' They shared a glance, like naughty school children, then sat side by side on the Chesterfield, knees touching. 'Now James, I seem to remember when you first came here that you were telling me all about the cause of our fire.'

'Was I?' He looked surprised at the sudden line of questioning.

'You were. About that man – the bridegroom from that wedding. Speak up, don't mumble.'

'I don't think I was telling you anything.' He frowned. 'I just asked if it was true, what I'd read in the papers, and online.'

'Online. Exactly. I seem to recall hearing Samantha say something similar about this chap talking on, what was it? Face something or other?'

'Facebook?' Supplied Tab, wondering what this was all about.

'That's the one. Right, young James, you can make yourself useful. Pour me a gin and tonic, and you, Tabatha, can show me this Facebook thing. You can use my machine.'

'Machine?' Tab looked in astonishment at the tablet that was on the table in front of Elizabeth.

'Philippa purchased it for me, so that I could talk to her on that sky system, you know where one can look and talk. I've told you about this once, James, haven't I?'

'Skype.' He filled in, for Tab's benefit.

'That's what I said. Think she wanted to keep an eye on me. Although it isn't the same as being with somebody, is it?' She looked, thought Tab, rather sad. Everybody knew that she missed Pip, who had been as naughty as she was. Together they had livened up Tippermere no end with their mischief-making, the staunch lady of the manor and the freelance journalist, who was always on the lookout for a story heavily laced with scandal and gossip. Elizabeth was determined to age as disgracefully as possible, and although she had encouraged Pip to follow her lover back to Australia, it had obviously left a gaping hole in her life.

'Come along, girl. I really would like to find out what all the fuss is about, and then you can help me with a little investigation. These new-fangled ideas really aren't my thing at all.'

Chapter 14

As Lottie rode out through the archway she realised how quickly she'd got used to the presence of the film crew. She had steered well clear of Seb since the dog incident, though, and felt that the greater distance from Pandora she had the better.

Although Lottie had experienced many insecurities over the years – like was she really a good enough rider to compete, was she really good enough for Rory, and would she ever be a worthy heiress as far as the Tipping House Estate went – she'd never felt that anybody had hated her. Until now.

She couldn't put her finger on exactly why; as far as she could remember she'd never even spoken to Sarah, or should she say Pandora, when they were at school, and she barely remembered her. It was all very strange, but there again Pandora didn't seem particularly fond of anybody except herself, and maybe her husband.

After the disastrous scene with Tab word had spread, and much to Seb's fury, there had been twice as many people paying the entrance fee the next day, many carrying cameras with very long lenses.

Lottie really did find him rather intimidating with his cold, grey, lizard eyes, which seemed to be constantly assessing everything and finding it wanting. Even when he was in a good mood. Which he clearly wasn't today.

He'd been practically frozen with rage when he'd arrived on set to see them all neatly lined up behind the rope, and Rory and Lottie had been unlucky enough to be within hearing distance.

'You, yes you two, come here.'

Rory grinned at Lottie, then leaned over from his horse and whispered in her ear. 'This could be a laugh, come on, gorgeous.' And he'd kicked his horse into a spanking trot and headed straight for the prickly producer, who'd flinched, but resolutely held his ground. Lottie had to hand it to him, despite his obvious distaste, and possibly fear, of horses, he was determined not to let anything get in the way of the film.

'I thought I said that they,' he pointed, his mouth tightening with disapproval, 'had to go.'

'You probably did, mate, but it's not really up to you, is it?'

'Get them out of here, and what is that old bag doing on the driveway? She's not even behind the bloody rope. Somebody get her out of here. Jamie!'

Rory chuckled. 'Rather you than me.'

Jamie, who had run over, waving at the 'old bag' on his way, awaited instructions. 'Yes, Seb?'

'Sort her out.' He waved a dismissive hand. 'We're nearly ready to roll.'

'Her?' Jamie looked around, confused.

'That!' Seb pointed. 'Oh, for fuck's sake, do I need to do everything myself?'

'Er, that's Lady Elizabeth, Seb. Haven't you met her yet?'

Seb, who had sorted all the contractual obligations out with Lottie, had certainly not met Lady Elizabeth Stanthorpe. He glared at Jamie. 'Well,' his tone as coldly controlled as ever, 'ask her and that hound to move, or I won't be shooting a film and she won't be getting paid.'

Jamie had done as bid (couching it more diplomatically), and

Elizabeth had told him with a smile that of course she'd move. In her own time. And wasn't it a beautiful morning? And how was he getting on with Facebook? So the two had edged slowly back towards the house, Elizabeth using her stick as theatrically as possible, while Seb had ground his teeth with impatience and wondered if he'd have any left by the time they left this goddamned awful place.

Two weeks on and the crowd, Lottie noted, had depleted. They'd grown fed up with the monotonous retakes and the absence of any real stars. After all, they could see galloping ponies any day of the week.

Mrs Jones, from the village shop, had told her they'd all be back when they knew there was going to be some beefcake on show, and then she'd winked in a rather alarming way and said she was relying on Lottie to keep her updated.

Lottie slowed her pace as she heard hoof steps not far behind and Badger, her horse, tried to turn so that he could see who it was.

'Mind if I join you? I need some exercise to stretch the kinks out of my spine. I'm getting too old for sleeping in horseboxes. Even luxury ones.'

She'd expected Tab or Rory, not Xander.

Xander looked sideways at Lottie as his horse fell into step with hers, and wondered if he'd been wise to come back to Tippermere, or more precisely to her. Maybe he should have followed his instincts and left as soon as he'd realised that the girl he'd been besotted with was still in Tippermere, and the heir to the Tipping House Estate.

At first he'd kidded himself that with the passing of time his feelings for her would have changed, then he'd convinced himself that the only time he'd be on the estate was when they were filming and so the chances of him seeing her were practically

168

zero. Then it had become such a headache getting past the press that he'd been forced to move into his horsebox parked on the estate, and avoiding her had become impossible.

But he could cope. Even if she was as gorgeous as ever. She was a married woman now. All he had to do was keep his distance – so what the hell was he doing following her around like a sheepdog?

'Is the hotel in Kitterly Heath really so bad?' She was looking at him quizzically.

'The hotel's fine,' he grimaced, 'especially the bed, but it wasn't much fun eating breakfast with a telephoto lens trained on the muesli.'

'They had muesli?' She grinned. 'Gone upmarket in that place these days, then.'

He returned the smile, but it hadn't been amusing at all. The real nightmare had been getting to his car. There were more press cars in the hotel car park than there were visitors. They weren't there to see him, they were there to see Pandora and the actor playing her 'rock star' husband, but he didn't want to get caught in the crossfire. To get asked questions.

'I didn't know you were famous.'

'I'm not. They're not there for me. Look,' he could see the questions that were going to follow on, 'I'm not exactly famous, but I did get pretty well known when I was playing polo. These guys aren't sports photographers, they chase celebs, but if my picture appears in the papers . . .' He shrugged. He'd not spoken to anybody about exactly why he was so keen to keep a low profile. 'There are reasons why I agreed to do this for Pandora.'

Lottie raised a questioning eyebrow and he smiled in response.

'I could just tell you I needed the money.'

She grinned. 'Really?'

'Well I do, but I wanted a hideaway as well.'

Her big green eyes opened wider. 'Carry on, you can't stop now.'

'Well I had some bad publicity.'

'You don't need to tell me what that's like. Dad used to get some terrible headlines but they're a bit kinder now. What did you do? Shag somebody you shouldn't?'

He paused. Wondering why he felt a sudden urge to explain.

'Shag two people you shouldn't, at the same time?' Her voice dropped to a new husky level that sent a shiver between his shoulder blades. 'Kill somebody?' He must have looked horrified rather than trying to resist feelings of lust because she held up a hand. 'It's okay, you don't need to tell me. I was kidding, honest.'

He shook his head, the reality bringing him back down to earth with a bump. 'I was riding in a pretty tough match and lost a horse.'

'Lost? You mean . . .' Those green eyes looked straight at his with a compassion that made it harder. 'Oh gosh, how horrible.'

'It was, she was a brilliant mare, the newspapers had a field day about how the ponies are mistreated.'

'I meant for you.' The tone of her voice gave him an unexpected jolt. 'Although of course it was horrid for the horse, but I'm sure you'd never do anything to harm one of your animals. It must have been so upsetting.'

'That's not how the press saw it. I was the heartless bastard who'd flogged it to death. I actually hit the tabloids,' he shrugged trying to rebuff the painful memories, ignore the knot of guilt that had settled low in his stomach, 'front page and back, which is unheard of for a polo player. I'm just a bit bothered that if anybody recognises me it'll all kick off again. I'd rather not give them the ammunition.'

'So you're not playing now?'

'Nope. I needed a break, and to be honest I'm not sure my heart's in the game like it was.' It was a good enough explanation, and true, even if it wasn't the whole story. But, if a journalist did recognise him and started digging into what he'd been doing for the last few months, then he didn't know where it would end.

The shit would really hit the fan if the state of his mother became public knowledge. '*Horse killer's mother in suicide attempt*' was not a headline he wanted to see, and if they moved on to trying to interview his father . . . Shit, it didn't bear thinking about. The fewer people that knew the full story, the better. 'So I let Seb and Pandora sign me up, but I never realised that there would be a media circus. I thought we'd all be safe and sound hidden away in some remote corner of Cheshire.'

'You're kidding?' Lottie laughed. 'There are too many juicy stories around here, the footballer wife stuff over in Kitterly Heath, stately homes going up in flames here.' Her eyes were smiling at him, even though he knew it wasn't a laughing matter. Lottie's fighting spirit, that life force that had drawn him to her years before, was shining. The bright moon that pulled the restless tide close, then tossed it away. He was close to her now, closer than he'd ever been and if he'd been the shit the newspapers insisted on saying he was he'd grab her, before he lost the chance, was pushed away. Instead he settled for staring at her full mouth.

'How come you call her Pandora, not Sarah? She's your sister.'

His horse danced sideways, bumping hers, and Xander patted the animal in apology and relaxed the thigh muscles he hadn't realised had tensed. 'Half-sister.' He pushed his horse over with his inside leg to a safer distance. Thigh-to-thigh contact was the last thing he could cope with right now. He glanced back up. 'Don't look at me like that. It's a fact. Her name wasn't exactly spoken at the dinner table. Even Dad was furious that her mother followed us here to Tippermere, but I felt sorry for Pandora. She was an angry kid, like I was. Look, I know you're not that keen on her . . .'

'Me? She hates me.'

'Pandora hates everybody and, believe me, my life would be hell if I called her Sarah. Anyhow, I don't really care what she's called. She offered me a distraction, I needed one, and so I'm here. It suits me.' And it suits her, he thought, but didn't voice the words. Was she so sadistic that she just wanted him there so she could watch him squirm in Lottie's presence, or was there something more?

'You hated me too.' Lottie didn't give him a chance to respond. 'If we cut across this field we can get onto Dad's land without being seen and have a pipe-opener, if you fancy it?'

'Sounds good to me.' It sounded bloody good. It might distract him from thoughts of dragging her out of the saddle. He paused. 'And I didn't hate you.' Oh no, he hadn't hated her. She'd been the most vivacious girl he'd ever known, quiet but with an inner confidence that said she knew she could do anything if she tried hard enough. But she'd been 'one of them' – and he hadn't. The horsey set, the rich, the ones who had lived here for generations, and had the type of sense of self that money couldn't buy. Unlike him. He'd watched her chasing Rory resolutely, and she'd never even noticed him until he'd pushed himself forward and made a complete fool of himself.

'You ride a lot better now than you did then.' There was mischief in her eyes, and the stab to his gut was as unexpected as it was raw. Which wasn't the way it was supposed to be at all. So much for being grown up.

'I'll race you to the next gate.' Without waiting, he kicked on, needing a rush of adrenalin to bring him back down to earth. His little mare, displaying her thoroughbred breeding, surged forward.

'Cheat.' Lottie's shout, and laughter filled his ears as she urged her larger, but much heavier, horse on beside him. Badger had been bred and trained as an eventer, and he was used to galloping across uneven ground. On the flat, the polo pony would have been at a distinct advantage, but here, as they pushed on up the hill, over undulating ground, the gelding was in his element. He was a nose ahead as they reached the crest of the hill, winning by a length as they started to pick their way down the steep fall on the other side. But as their hooves pounded over the flat field he lost ground to the nimble pony, and the two were neck and neck as they galloped over the expanse of open land towards the finishing post.

Xander's pony spun to a stop and he laughed as Badger slowed ponderously.

'You're lucky to live in a place like this.' They were both out of breath and when he managed to tear his gaze away from the rise and fall of her chest, it was to meet the gleam in her eyes. Which was worse. Better to concentrate on talking and stare across the field, seeing nothing.

'I know.' She patted Badger and let him have a long rein. 'I never forget how lucky I am.' They both stared down at the fields spread out below, a pale-green quilt broken only by the dark copses of trees, symmetry of fences and the meandering muddy brown stream. 'I still don't get why you came back, though, you never seemed to like it much here. I mean, it's fine if you don't want to say. You hardly know me, honestly.'

'I wasn't happy before, you're right. But I was a kid. Teenage boys are supposed to be stroppy, aren't they?' He tried to grin as casually as he could. 'All that testosterone. But,' he shrugged, 'it was just coincidence that Seb decided to shoot here.' He hoped. 'I've not got anything against the place, it was just a bad time and we weren't here long enough to get to know people.'

'And some people didn't make life easy?'

There was a smile playing at the corner of her generous lips, the breeze tugged playfully at her hair, and a sudden pang of loss swept over him. It was a waste of time dreaming, though; she couldn't be his, she never had been. Never would.

'No, you didn't make it easy, did you Charlie?' His tone came out lighter than he thought it would.

'Sorry, I was a bitch. Nobody calls me Charlie now.'

'So I gather, about the Charlie bit, not the bitch. We were kids, kids are cruel, and to be honest you did me a favour.'

'I did?'

'When you put me on that evil pony of yours you set me a challenge, I had to learn how to ride after that humiliation.' He grinned. 'I never was a good loser.' It had been quite a kick in the teeth, being shown up by a girl. Especially one he'd fancied the pants off.

'Oh God, I'm so sorry, I never meant to be that mean. You could have been hurt.'

'I don't hurt that easily.'

'But you'd never ever been on a horse, and I knew that, and she was a right cow too.'

'Forget it, you only dented my pride and ego. Well, more than dented, you blew a bloody big hole in it.'

The look on her face stopped him short. 'Honest, it was just a joke, I get that.' *At my expense.* 'But I learned to ride after we left Tippermere and I fell in love,' he paused, 'with horses. I discovered a whole new life.'

Xander rested one hand on the pommel of the saddle. Life could change in an instance. You thought you knew the answers, then the roulette wheel spun and suddenly you questioned everything. What you were doing, who you loved, why you were here. It had happened to him back then, and it had happened after his polo pony had collapsed beneath him on the field. 'Have you ever felt completely alone? Like nobody else understands?'

She frowned at the sudden change of conversation. 'Well, er, no not really. I mean I suppose when I was a teenager I went through that stage when I told myself nobody understood me, and if I'd had a mum she would. But she'd stupidly gone and died.'

He winced at the catch in her voice. 'Sorry, I didn't mean to bring back memories like that.' He knew all about Lottie's mother. Who didn't? Everybody in school knew the Brinkleys' story, knew that Lottie had been brought up by the Olympic medal-winning Billy, that she'd lost her mother in a riding accident when she was only a toddler.

Billy couldn't do any wrong, he was the toast of the county, the hero who had brought his daughter up single-handed and still gone for gold.

She seemed to read his mind. 'It wasn't always that easy, not having a mum.'

'No, I suppose . . .'

'Dad hated it at first, hated having to look after me. He used to work all day and drink all night until Gran told him that if he didn't get his act together she'd take me away.'

'Your gran seems to be a force to be reckoned with.'

'She is. But I'm not saying it was all bad. I mean he did try and he was fine after that.'

Loveable Lottie, always being completely fair.

'I'm sure he was. Maybe it was losing your mum that he hated, not the looking after you bit.'

She shrugged, plaiting her fingers through Badger's mane. 'So, what about you? Have you ever felt completely alone?'

'For a while.' It came out a bit bleak. Harsh. But for a while he had. 'Maybe that's why I went along with Pandora's plan. Not that we're close. Sometimes I think she cares, sometimes,' he smiled, 'I'm not so sure.' Maybe agreeing to come back here was to find answers to questions he didn't even know he had. A person, a place. Or maybe he was just testing himself, proving he'd moved on. Either way, he hadn't expected to find Lottie still here, or his answer might have been different.

'Oh, I'm sure she does really. Deep down. She can't be that bad, I mean you've always hung out, haven't you?'

'Not really. When we were kids, yeah. But then after we left here her and her mother moved, and I didn't see her for years. She got in touch; during my lonely patch.' He gave a wry smile. 'I'd lost my favourite horse, things weren't going well with my girlfriend, Miranda.' *Not going well* being the understatement of the century. 'She decided she needed a break from me, not that I could blame her. The trolls were out in force.' Troll being the word, although he'd have preferred to have met with the old-fashioned club-wielding cave-dwelling variety. At least then he'd have been able to see them face to face, and they might have shown more humanity than the faceless kind that inhabited cyberspace. He'd been cut up enough about losing the horse, without having the whole world and his dog rubbing it in. 'I probably deserved some of it, but Miranda's only crime was knowing me. Anyhow, Pandora's offer meant I could be out of the limelight and hopefully off the radar, as long as nobody catches on.'

'They'll soon get bored, and, I mean, you're not exactly doing anything that's exciting, are you?' She suddenly grinned. 'Unless there's some scandal we don't know about?'

'Nope, sadly not. Unless you fancy starting something?' He really shouldn't have said that. 'Joke.'

She laughed, blushed. He really had to change the direction this conversation was taking. 'My parents went their separate ways none too amicably as well a few months ago.'

'Oh no, your mum seemed lovely. I mean I didn't know her that well but she always seemed so . . . bubbly.'

But she wasn't so bubbly now. 'She is lovely. It kind of pulled the carpet out from under my feet. I guess I'm not very good at handling change, so that probably made me even harder to live with. I'm surprised Miranda hung around as long as she did.'

'Crikey, that's a heck of lot for anybody to handle.'

'Mum had a breakdown. Guess she wasn't very good at handling it either. And,' he paused for breath, wondering why he was babbling on like the village idiot, 'that's partly why I need to stay away from the press. I don't want her dragged into it. So I reckoned if I found a focus, did something different . . .'

'That's horrid, is she okay?'

The million-dollar question. 'She will be, but I need to support her until things are sorted. I need a job because there's no one else she can rely on. So I suppose that's what made me feel a bit isolated. Miserable bastard, aren't I?'

'I know the feeling.' She looked sideways at him through long eyelashes and grinned. 'Not that I'm a miserable bastard.'

He stared back. How could she know the feeling? A girl like her, with everything. His feelings for Lottie had always been pretty mixed up: lust tumbled together with envy that at times had verged on hate. 'But you're not alone, you've got family, this place.' He'd watched her the other day, her and her husband sitting on the grass together, and that teenage ache that he should have lost years ago had been back with a vengeance. The girl he'd fancied, always out of reach. She wasn't just on some slightly out-of-reach pedestal, she was up there on another planet.

'I have, but we could lose this place to the bank any day if I don't make enough money.'

'You've still got Rory, and you'll have a family of your own soon as well, no doubt, won't you?'

Her fingers stilled on the reins and Badger faltered, before she urged him on again. 'Actually, you know when I do feel lonely? When people go on about having kids. Then I feel like I'm the only person in the world who isn't sure. Rory wants them, Gran's waiting, even Uncle Dom is all broody and as for Dad . . .'

'Nobody is making you.'

'Yes, they are. Don't you see? People expect. Like people expect me to somehow find a way to keep this place going. I love this place, but it's hard. And I love Rory so, so much, but what if I can't do it? What if I really can't have the family he wants? That's what makes me feel lonely.'

'Have you told him, Lottie?'

'Told him what? That I think I'd make a rubbish mother? That I could hurt our baby the way my mother hurt me? I hated her for years, really, absolutely hated her for dying like that. She just abandoned me. I couldn't do that to somebody else, and I couldn't do it to Rory.' There were pink points of anger and frustration on her cheeks. 'My dad hated the responsibility, it changed his life completely, what if I did that to Rory?'

'You don't know he hated it, though, do you? Why didn't he just let you live with Elizabeth if it was that bad for him?'

'Well he wasn't going to admit it, was he?' She glared. 'Men don't.'

'You're funny.' He shook his head. 'You've said yourself he made sure you stayed with him.'

'I'm not saying he didn't love me, just that it changed his life.'

'Kids change everybody's lives. I'm sure life would have been easier for my mum if I hadn't been around, but she told me all she'd ever wanted was a baby to call her own. People, parents, make mistakes but everybody survives.'

'But it's not fair to get it wrong, is it? If you have a baby then you can't make mistakes and ruin their lives, you're all they've got.'

'Everybody is allowed to make mistakes; as long as you put them right, do your best. Children are pretty forgiving, Lottie. You forgave your mother in the end, didn't you?'

She sighed, then swung angrily away, every inch of her body telling him to sod off. 'I'd like to say yes, but I'm honestly not sure. Which is very selfish, isn't it? Oh hell, I sound horrible, but I don't really know anything about her.' She studied her hands, the horse, anything but him. 'I sometimes look at Rory and Dad and just think history will repeat itself.'

'You just do your best, that's all you can do. I can't blame my mother for having a breakdown, and I guess, at the end of the day, I don't blame my father for going off and giving me a sister like Pandora. Well I do, but shit happens, as they say.'

She glanced his way, gave a wry smile. 'Your dad came back. My mum didn't. Oh God, I just wish I'd known her.'

'I know.' It took every bit of self control he had to resist reaching over, hugging her, and telling her he really did understand. But he couldn't. 'Babies do change lives, Lottie. Rory would be responsible whether you were here or not. Don't you think you should just talk to him about how you feel? It's not just your decision.'

'I suppose so. Sorry I shouldn't go on. I don't know why I'm telling you all this. I think I just need to talk to someone who isn't family. And I'm sorry about your mum.'

'So am I. She's a nice lady.'

'And your girlfriend.'

'I don't think she liked sharing me with the horses. Anyway, she was a bit too high maintenance to fit in with my lifestyle.' Miranda was the least of his worries, it wasn't losing her that kept him awake at nights.

'You could play polo again? It might make you feel better.'

'Not an option. I had to sell my best horses to raise money for Mum. I'm back to square one.'

'Teach. I've been watching you on set. You are so patient with those goons.'

'Have you any idea how much competition there is down where I live?'

'Oh.' Lottie frowned. 'Well do it here.'

'Yeah, sure. Hang around in scandalous Cheshire.' He did his best to grin. 'Come on, that's enough worrying about the future. It's a beautiful day. We shouldn't be talking like this. Anyhow, who knows why I let my bossy little sister persuade me to come back.'

She laughed, a wonderful light tinkle of a laugh that left him feeling sad and empty. 'You started it.'

'I know, sorry.'

'A friend of mine told me a few years ago that my feet would always take me back to where my heart was.'

Xander raised an eyebrow. 'Yeah, right. Bit of a dippy hippy was she?'

'Don't look at me like that. And it was a he, not a she. He meant that deep down I knew where I belonged, what and who I loved. I came back here because I couldn't not, if that makes sense. Maybe it's the same with you. You just need to let yourself find the right place.'

179

'Fine. That makes me feel tons better.' Great, yeah, he'd come back because once Pandora had mentioned the place, he couldn't not. He wanted to see how time had distorted the memories. And he wanted to check if Lottie was still in the village, even though he'd never in a million years thought she'd be at the Tipping House Estate. 'This is getting a bit too deep for me. Race you back? I need to restore honour for the male of the species.'

Chapter 15

Rory put down the pitchfork as the clatter of hooves announced Lottie's return. He watched as the two horses, their coats shiny with a light lather, picked their way over the cobbles.

'You look happy.'

'I am.' She slipped down from the saddle, landed at his feet, then twisted round to look up at him. Her green eyes bright emeralds, a soft-pink blush on her cheeks as she leant closer and planted a kiss on his lips. 'Xander said Seb wants me to be an extra.' She grinned, then turned to look at the other man. 'I'll get paid, won't I?'

Xander nodded. 'You will. Despite the chaos and the fact she tried to kill him, he was actually impressed with Tab the other day. He said he wants some shots of people who look like they can actually ride. I think he's sacked half the extras he took on.'

'Doesn't Pandora mind? I'm not exactly her favourite person.'

'Doesn't seem to, it might even have been her suggestion.' His words were muffled as he dismounted from his own horse, ran up the stirrups and loosened the girth.

'Well as long as you've got time, darling.' Rory picked up the fork again and nodded towards an empty wheelbarrow. 'Come on, get stuck in, my little diva.'

'I'll get this horse rubbed down and get out of your hair, then.'

But Rory didn't hear Xander, or notice him moving off. He was watching his wife untack her horse, giving him cuddles and mints. He didn't really know what had got into him lately, but the feeling that he wanted a family had crept up on him and wouldn't go away. And it was turning into something of an obsession.

He grimaced, he knew he was ultra-competitive in everything he did – from riding to drinking and a lot in between – but Lottie would make a wonderful mother, and for some reason she was always dodging the issue. Not that he wanted to force her if she didn't want kids, but deep down he'd been sure she felt the same way he did.

As he'd waited for her to get back from her ride, though, he'd begun to have doubts. Each time he'd tried to talk to her about it she'd got more defensive, which wasn't like the open and happy-go-lucky girl he loved. They'd fought together to make the estate a going concern, cried together as they'd watched the firefighters quench the hungry flames, and vowed together that they wouldn't let it beat them.

But now they weren't joking together and fighting together – they seemed to be fighting against each other. There'd been a subtle change from the 'let's wait until we've got the business going again', to 'I want things to be right between us first.' What the hell was that supposed to mean? He'd thought things *were* right. True, he'd been a dick at times, and might not always be the most attentive husband. He didn't do romantic gestures, and they didn't have much time to do stuff together. But they never had.

She'd even thrown in the comment that she didn't want kids the other day, but everybody did, surely. It was just natural, unless you couldn't.

He'd checked his watch each time he'd emptied the wheelbarrow, and she still wasn't back. And each time he'd felt more wound up, more like he needed to grab her and ask what was going wrong with them.

Then, on the one day he'd offered to hack out with her and she'd said she quite fancied a ride out on her own, she'd come back with *him* and looked the happiest he'd seen her in a long time. Which made him decidedly tetchy, especially after what he'd read in the morning newspaper. She was flushed and happy, which was more than she was most of the time she was with him these days.

He swept the shavings back at the doorway to the stable and could hear her singing to Badger in the out-of-tune way that they'd always joked about, except now it was Xander that was hollering at her to shut up before she set the dogs off howling.

After skipping out three more stables and preparing hay nets, he was actually feeling even more frustrated. Rory was naturally cheerful, he always saw the bright side of life, so being unable to shake the uneasy feeling was dragging him down alarmingly. Slamming the final door shut he decided he needed a brew.

'Are you okay, darling?' Lottie's big eyes were filled with concern as she plonked herself down in the tack room and picked up the cup of coffee he'd made.

'Not really.' He tried to smile, thinking it probably looked more like a leer. 'Here.' He fished the newspaper out of the feed bin and dropped it in her lap.

The shot was slightly out of focus, a snatched shot taken with a telephoto lens, but it was obvious who it was. Lottie was in the saddle and you could tell she was laughing, and standing at her side was Xander, his hand on her knee.

'*Childhood lovers reconciled on film set*'

'Bloody hell.' Lottie held the paper at arm's length. 'Can't we do anything without it getting in the paper? And that is *so* untrue.'

Rory raised an eyebrow. He had to admit it niggled him a bit. He'd always trusted Lottie completely, but as he'd read the article it had hit him just how involved she had become in the filming, and why?

He'd said he'd keep an eye on things so that she could carry on as normal, but instead she'd been dragged in – or perhaps even dived in. More than one time, as he'd ridden out he'd seen her and Xander sharing a joke, their dark heads close together.

'Which bit?'

'What?'

'Which bit isn't true?'

'Oh, Rory, all of it. We were never lovers. He was only at our school for a few weeks, don't you remember? And I hardly knew him, to be honest him and his sister both hated me.'

'He seems keen enough now.'

'Rory!' She giggled, taking it as a joke, and then saw the serious look on his face. 'Don't talk rubbish.'

He shrugged. 'Just my view.' He hardly remembered Pandora and Xander from their time in Tippermere.

Rory had been busy growing up, having fun, chasing girls, and riding horses. Pandora, or Sarah as they'd known her, had been skinny, intense, and no fun at all. Girls who couldn't take a joke hadn't been on his radar at all, though he had registered the sneer and her sarcastic tone if the football ever went near her on the yard. Some of the others had made fun of her, trying to take her down a peg or two, but Rory hadn't been interested.

It seemed to him now that she hadn't changed at all, she was still too thin, still sarcastic, and as aloof as ever. Which was a trait her brother, Xander, shared. Why Lottie was even smiling in his presence was a mystery. The only thing Rory really remembered about Xander was the way he stood on the sidelines, watching. He was always there looking on, and Rory had put it down to jealousy, to wanting to join in with him and his gang. But maybe it wasn't, maybe he'd been watching Lottie. He was certainly keeping an eye on her now.

'He's lonely, that's all.'

'Is he?' he muttered grimly.

'His parents have split up, after his mum had a breakdown, and I think he really misses her, then his girlfriend left him. He just wants somebody to chat to.'

'Don't you think you're getting too involved? I mean why's he telling you all this stuff? To make you feel sorry for him?'

Her eyes opened wider.

'I just think it's a bit weird, that's all. How would you feel if I spent all my free time with Pandora?'

'But we were just riding out.'

'And it's everything, not just Xander, who never struck me as the chatty type anyway. He never bloody spoke to anyone at school. I mean, why do you have to get stuck into the filming, playing the star, the lot? Doing this?' He waved the newspaper.

'I was only helping get the horses ready, and I'd exercised all of ours. You were out at the gallops.'

'You could come with me, do things together. I asked if you wanted to ride out with me.'

'But we said somebody should keep an eye on things. You didn't object when Tab asked for time off to join in with the filming.'

Rory sighed. 'That's Tab, darling, she's just the bloody groom.' He fought the urge to shout. Did a mental countdown to hold in his temper. 'It's just, maybe we should keep our distance, you know a professional distance? Or is doing all that more exciting than being with me?'

'Oh don't be daft.'

'Well, every time I try and talk to you there's something more important to do and you dash off.'

Lottie bit the inside of her cheek and looked at him like a dog expecting a beating. 'He asked if I could be an extra.'

'I know.' He softened his tone. He was acting like some spoiled kid. Shit, he'd be telling her not to talk to other men soon and acting the complete chauvinist twat. What harm could it do?

They were already knee-deep in this and it was extra money. 'Just don't get too involved, eh?' He nodded at the paper. 'We could do without this type of speculation, couldn't we?'

What was he supposed to say? You're my wife, come and make babies with me and stop talking to other men? He'd never been the jealous type. In fact, Lottie had always had plenty of male friends and admirers, but now he felt like he was out of his depth. He didn't understand the rules of the game.

* * *

The first person Xander saw when he made his way back to the temporary stable block was Pandora. Which ruined what had, so far, been an okay type of day. He always enjoyed riding out on his own, but when he'd seen Lottie leaving the yard he hadn't been able to resist catching up with her.

She'd not mentioned the incidents at school – apart from her jokey comment about his riding ability – it was history. They'd started again and he liked the woman she'd become. As he'd known he would.

Lottie was easy going and giving, not at all the aristocratic lady he'd feared she might be. Which had loosened his tongue. But some instinct had told him that Lottie wouldn't judge, and she hadn't. What *had* surprised him was that she'd opened up a little, too, expressed some of her own fears and frustrations. Who'd have thought that life hadn't been quite that perfect for her as a teenager? All he'd seen was the popular rich girl with the famous father, sailing through life without a care, oblivious to people like him.

Now all he had to do was get over his urge to tell her she'd married the wrong man and things would be hunky dory.

'Have you seen this?' Pandora was waving a newspaper in the air, nearly whacking one of the horses in the face. Despite its even temperament, it shied away. It was such a good job that she wasn't keen on 'the smelly creatures' despite her insistence on riding in some of the shots. It made the stables a bit of a safe haven. Usually.

'When would I have time to read the newspapers?'

'I thought you had a girl to help with those animals?'

Xander sighed. Tab had been happy to fit in some work for him around her duties for Lottie and Rory, but he was still doing the majority of the work. He might trust somebody else to muck out the stables, but he wanted to exercise and groom the horses himself, to check them over properly each day. 'What do you want, Pandora?'

'Read it.'

'When I've finished what I'm doing.'

'Oh, for heaven's sake.' She flung the pages open and pointed. 'Look.' She jabbed at a picture with a red talon. 'You and that woman have made the headlines. What on earth are you playing at?'

Xander side-stepped her, pushing the newspaper out of his face. From the stormy look Rory had given him, he already had a good idea who '*that woman*' was. 'If my memory serves me right, it was Seb who found this place, and you that insisted I come along. What are *you* playing at?'

Pandora huffed.

'I don't trust you, little sis.'

'Don't call me that. I'm not—'

'Keep out of my way until I've finished checking the horses. Go on, wait in the trailer and I'll come and read whatever it is, I need to talk to you anyway.' She glared and he purposefully turned away and willed his blood pressure down to a level where he didn't think he was going to explode if she said another word.

Xander's mood didn't improve when he got to the trailer to find her standing in the doorway still swishing the paper about like a red flag.

'You are always up to something aren't you, Pandora?' Her eyes narrowed in response. 'Well if this article has messed up your plans, then tough. But what do you expect me to do? Ignore her? In case you've forgotten, we're only shooting here because Lottie and Rory have agreed to it.'

'I think you'll find it is Lady Elizabeth who makes the decisions.' Pandora scowled. 'Not that useless lump. Well if you're going to be obnoxious, I'm going to go. I have to get ready to shoot anyway. Honestly, Xander, for somebody who wants to keep a low profile you haven't a clue, have you? Following your heart like you always did. You really should keep away from that woman.'

'You nasty . . .' If he carried on he was going to say something he'd regret. She shouldered her way past him and was halfway down the steps before he could react. 'Come here, I said I wanted to talk to you.' He was round her, blocking her exit, and her nostrils flared as she literally stamped one foot.

'Move out of my way, Xander.'

Christ, she was like some uncut colt that needed teaching some manners. 'Get back in there.'

'No.' She folded her arms.

'This headline is your doing. You knew damned well that Lottie was in charge of this place before we got here, didn't you?'

'Oh keep your voice down.'

'I bloody won't. You knew, didn't you?'

'Go back to your horses, Xander.'

'If you want to have this argument here then that's fine, I'm not going anywhere.' As she made a move to sidestep him, he reached out to take her arm.

'Let go of me.' The snarl wasn't sisterly at all as she pulled away.

'Well, get back in that trailer.'

'I'm not one of your animals that you can boss around.'

'Well thank fuck for that, because I'd have to have you shot.'

This time she flounced in and he slammed the door behind them. She flinched. Stepped back.

He should have had this out with her before. Like on the day they arrived, as soon as he'd seen her reaction to Lottie. Up until now he'd kept his temper, brushed his suspicions away, but it was him that was going to be affected by this, and she'd caused the problem. If things blew up again in the press he'd never forgive the selfish cow.

'You knew Lottie and Rory lived here and you just left me to find out.'

'So?'

'So? So I'm not doing this. You can stuff your job, Pandora, I'm not one of your bloody pawns. Find somebody else to do your dirty work.'

'You signed a contract.'

'Sue me.'

'You're being ridiculous.' The confidence was creeping back into her voice. Nothing scared Pandora for long. 'She's just some stupid girl, so what if I did know she lived here? We're here for the location, even if,' she gave him a withering look, 'you want to do more than admire the rather rustic scenery. Now move out of the way and stop acting like a caveman.'

He didn't shift. 'I want to know what you're up to. You hated her, the whole lot of them, when we were at school, so why come back?'

'Jamie found the place, you can't blame me.'

'Did he?'

'Yes he did.' Her look challenged him. The same look his belligerent father always had before he walked into a board meeting. 'Seb thought it was perfect, so who was I to argue? Oh grow up big brother and stop letting your cock make the decisions.'

'I'd be very careful what you say next.' He paused. 'Why haven't you told Seb?'

'It's irrelevant.'

'Tell him, or I will.'

There was a knock on the door, a shout of 'make-up'.

'Get out of my way, I need to work.' This time he did step away from the door. She sniffed, threw the paper at him, and then, pulling the door open wide, stomped down the steps.

Xander watched the pages separate, flutter to the floor. He really shouldn't let her get to him like this. Life was too short. He unclenched his fists and forced the air in and out of his lungs in a long, slow breath, then bent to pick a page up.

His gaze drifted over the words, then settled on the photo. Pandora might know, but how on earth had the press found out that they'd been here before? That he knew Lottie years ago? There was very little substance in the story, but enough to bother him. If this brought the press down on his shoulders and they started to dig up the dirt he'd kill Pandora.

He marched down the steps of the trailer and slammed the door behind him, hoping his darling half-sister was nowhere to be seen or he'd be tempted to strangle her. But it wasn't Pandora he saw but Jamie, who was staring at him. His mouth was open, lips moving, as though he was asking him something, but Xander didn't hear. He wasn't in the mood. 'Not now.' He needed peace and quiet.

So far he'd ignored all the offers of a game in Argentina, but they were starting to look more inviting by the day. Except he couldn't leave his mother. Not yet.

* * *

Pandora stared at her reflection in the mirror, hardly noticing the girl who was touching up her make-up. Men could be so stupid. It was hard to believe at times that she shared a gene pool with Xander.

She was much more like Seb: calm, detached. Determined.

And Xander was so like his mother, far too over-emotional. She hadn't been surprised at the stupid woman's breakdown – just astounded it had taken so long.

Their father had been driven, but Pandora's own mother had been even more determined to make it. Just like Pandora. The fact that her parents had never married, that her father would never agree to leave his stupid, melodramatic wife, who had threatened suicide, never ceased to amaze her. How could people be like that?

Together her parents would have been unbeatable. They would have really made something of their lives. But it was of little consequence now. She allowed herself a small smile. This film was going to change everything.

'So, dear brother of mine, you think you can lay down the rules, do you?' Her voice was soft. 'Well, let's see about that.' She stared at her reflection. Nobody told her what to do, least of all him. She was going to talk to his darling Lottie and ruffle some feathers.

'That's fine, go.' She waved the make-up girl away irritably as she dabbed at her cheek for the umpteenth time. 'I said go away.' Picking up her mobile phone, she tapped her newly painted fingernails on the desk as she waited for the call to be answered.

'Lottie? This isn't a social call, but it's rather delicate . . . Of course it's me, Pandora, who do you think it is? . . .Your indiscretion is causing Seb all kinds of problems, and I don't mind telling you that Xander is most distressed . . . no, just listen . . . no, it is your fault. If you hadn't invited all those stupid people in to watch the filming then this wouldn't have happened would it? . . . Yes, I do blame you, we all do. All publicity is not good, this is so inappropriate . . . I do want to avoid nastiness, this isn't personal, but I rather think Seb is on the verge of moving elsewhere . . . yes, you heard me right . . . of course he'd be suing for the loss you've caused him . . . no, it might not specifically be in the contract. Look, let's not blow this out of proportion . . . Sorry what did you say? . . .

I'm only trying to help, there is absolutely no need to be like that . . . I just suggest you remove them, yes remove them, stop them coming in . . . Oh, it's up to you, of course. I must go, sorry. I'm needed on set . . . no don't discuss this with Seb, just take it as a friendly suggestion from an old school friend.' She raised an eyebrow at the muttered expletive as she finished the call. Honestly that girl was insufferable, she really did need taking down a peg or two.

Chapter 16

'I think Xander should be the star, don't you, babe? He is gorgeous.' Sam stared across at the film crew, who were gathered at the front of Tipping House preparing for a shot. 'He's much nicer than that guy they've got playing the rock star, isn't he?'

'But that guy is much more like a real rock star, isn't he?' Said Lottie reasonably. The man in question was stood to one side, smoking and looking remarkably bored and star-like. Leather trousers clung to his thin legs like wrinkled cling film, giving up the attempt when they reached his stomach, which was hanging over with the abandon of a well-risen Yorkshire pudding.

'I suppose.' Sam was doubtful. 'Looks a bit seedy, though, doesn't he?'

'I think he's supposed to be a bit over the hill, that's why he's retiring to the country.' His black t-shirt was stretched to its limits, and the black leather waistcoat did little to hide the fact that the aged star was well past his prime.

'What's seedy?' Roxy, who was perched on top of the pony that Lottie was leading, piped up. 'Seedy, weedy, squishy cheesy.'

'Shh.' Sam giggled. 'When do we get to see the other man? You know the one that she falls for. Xander could play that part instead. I mean he used to play polo, didn't he?'

'Well, yes, he can ride.'

'I bet he can, babe.' She winked. 'And he knows everything about horses and stuff.'

Lottie groaned and wondered if everybody had seen that picture of them in the paper. 'But he's not an actor, he's just helping, you know advising. To be honest, I don't think he wants to be noticed.' Xander, Lottie thought, just had to be the most camera-shy person on the whole set. He took it to a whole new level; moving out of a nice hotel and into a horsebox seemed a bit extreme even to her just because he didn't want to be recognised. And it hadn't worked anyway.

'Maybe they'll get that bloke who played Poldark instead. He can ride horses. I saw him galloping across Cornwall on the TV. I'd go for him rather than a rock star any day, wouldn't you, babe?' She wriggled her skirt down and patted her stomach. 'You don't think I look preggers, do you? It's either that or I need a tummy tuck.'

'I don't think you look pregnant, no.' Lottie stared. 'Why – have you been trying?'

'We're always trying, babe. Practice makes perfect.' Sam giggled. 'Look if I pull the bottom down my boobs nearly pop out of the top of this dress, do you think it's a sign? They were enormous when I had little Roxy and sensitive as hell.' She prodded them as though to test out her new theory. 'I tell you, babe, if anybody touches your boobs when they've filled up like mine did, you really know about it. Rock hard they were, but I was randy as hell. Davey didn't know what had hit him.'

Lottie tried not to look too alarmed by the news, and wished Amanda was there to add some wise words about childbearing.

'By the way, where have all the crowds gone? It was a right laugh having them here, made me feel like a film star when I drove in. I promised I'd bring Davey in one day to sign some autographs and kick a ball about.'

Lottie smiled, glad that the topic of conversation had changed.

Billy's idea of charging an entry fee had worked like a dream for the first few days. Even Dom had commented on how traffic free the grass verges were, and how life had almost reverted to normal, but then she'd begun to wonder if it was worth it. Seb hated having them there, and she was beginning to think it was actually making things worse.

After the dog incident there had been a flurry of reports in the local newspapers, and accompanying video footage on YouTube, Twitter, and Facebook, which she was sure was feeding speculation. The crowd had grown, Xander had been forced out of the local hotel (though she still wasn't sure why he was so keen to keep a low profile), and then there had been that photo of her with him in the paper, which had been the last straw for Rory.

He'd been uncharacteristically upset (she still hadn't got to the bottom of that one). If he'd had his way the whole thing would have been cancelled and they would have been able to return to their normal, quiet life.

But Lottie knew they hadn't got a choice. They needed this income desperately.

'Pandora rang and gave me a telling off.'

'Telling off?' Sam was indignant.

'She more or less threatened that they'd stop the filming if we carried on letting people watch. I mean I don't know if they can, really, because we haven't done anything wrong, but we do need the money and if they sued us we'd be totally knackered.'

'Sued you? Can they do that, babe? I know a really good lawyer if you need one. She's a gem, worked for loads of my friends.'

'It's okay, I don't think they can, but it won't come to that. She more or less said all the bad publicity was my fault. So, I talked to Gran and we thought it was better not to do it.' She sighed. Elizabeth had also said that she suspected that Pandora was jealous of the attention Sam was getting from the spectators. After all, she'd added, there was no such thing as bad publicity if you were a celebrity. But, Pandora was the star, and she wanted all the adoration, not to share it. 'It wasn't really worth the hassle. They made such a mess, it took hours to clear up after them and Rory was really cross about that picture in the paper. I'm just hoping they all get fed up.' She really couldn't win. If they snarled up the village again she'd be in trouble with her dad, and if she let them in the grounds she'd be in trouble with everybody else.

'I bet he was cross, babe. I mean, even my Davey would be put out if I was caught snogging that Xander.'

'I wasn't snogging him!'

Sam winked. 'You were nice and close, though. It's hard, isn't it, when you see your first love again. Aww, so sweet isn't it? After all this time. Your first one.' Her voice had a dreamy edge.

'Sam! Honestly, he wasn't my first anything. I can't believe you just said that. I hardly spoke a word to him at school, him and Pandora hated me, and they were both so miserable all the time.' She paused. 'And competitive, they were always making out they were better than everybody else. She scowled and he used to glare.'

'I think the correct term is smoulder, my dear, or glower.'

They both jumped at the sound of Elizabeth's voice, and Roxy bounced up and down in the saddle giggling. 'I saw you, Lizbet, I saw you.'

'I know you did, clever little girl.' Elizabeth winked and put a finger to her lips. 'I remember Alexander's mother, such an attractive girl, quite stunning, if I remember rightly, but slightly unstable. Flighty type. They weren't here long, but she so wanted to stay. That man was having none of it, though. Domineering type. That poor boy didn't know where he was supposed to fit in, and the disgrace of having Pandora here as well made it that much worse.' She sighed. 'It was quite a scandal at the time, having such a dysfunctional family in the area. I hear the poor woman has gone completely doolally now, so her husband has finally left her. For Alexander's sake, I do hope it isn't genetic, poor child.'

'What scandal, Your Ladyship?'

Lottie cringed. Sam insisted on treating Elizabeth like royalty and it had taken her over a year to convince her friend that there was no need to curtsey. She still hadn't managed to persuade her that no title was necessary.

'That girl, of course.' She waved her stick in the direction of Pandora. 'It was no secret. Michael Rossi, Alexander's father, had an affair, and quite honestly one can't really blame him, that dippy girl he'd married really was away with the fairies at times. But to have a child from the union and then parade her so publicly was quite outrageous, unforgivable. One does not wash one's dirty laundry in public. But Pandora's mother was just like she is; what she wanted she got, and her child had to have what Alexander had. Where he and his parents went she followed, dragging her daughter with her. So sad. Alexander was rather stoic about it, for a child so young, but I gather his father would rather they had not associated. There was quite a rumpus just before they left Tippermere. I do believe Michael made a substantial settlement and attempted to cease contact with Pandora and her mother.'

'Oh, I didn't realise.' Lottie couldn't really remember much at all about Xander or his mother, and she certainly couldn't remember his father.

'You were children, far too busy having fun, but I really wouldn't have said the boy glared. He just has that dark look about him.'

Lottie wasn't convinced. He'd certainly glared the one time she had really noticed him, but he seemed much nicer now. In fact, she'd got quite used to having him around.

'Well, you'd have thought Xander wouldn't do what his sister wanted, wouldn't you, babe? Your ladyship? I mean, he doesn't look like he'd let somebody push him around.'

'We all need somebody, Samantha. I'm sure he has his reasons.' She peered at Lottie, who shrugged and looked down at her feet, hoping she wasn't as pink-faced as she felt. 'Well, I suspect Pandora is here for a reason other than fame and fortune. You need to be careful of that girl, Charlotte. Rory is right to be concerned.'

'Has Rory told you that?' Lottie looked at her gran in surprise. 'He's worried?'

'Oh no, he doesn't need to say a word, child.'

'So you think we should stop it? The filming?'

'Oh no, good heavens, no. The money will be a godsend, but you should keep a very close eye on Pandora. And do try and keep out of the newspapers, dear. All publicity might be good for this film, but it is not good for our reputation in my eyes. I do also rather suspect that Alexander would prefer to keep himself to himself as well, given past events.'

'What do you mean?'

'You'll see. Well, I do believe he has turned into quite the horseman.' Lottie was sure there was a naughty glint in her grandmother's eye as she changed tack. 'Despite the bad start.'

'Gran!' She was definitely beetroot-red now, and she couldn't do a thing about it. 'You read my diary.'

'I did no such thing, young lady. I use these.' She pointed to her eyes, 'and these,' then indicated her ears. 'Just like little Roxanne does. Well, girls, if that Poldark man, Aidan Turner, isn't going to make an appearance, I rather think it's time for a G&T.' She turned to go, then stopped. 'Oh, and Charlotte dear, do tell Pandora to stop snooping around inside the house. They haven't paid to use our facilities, just the grounds. Oh, and if you see young Tabatha and James, tell them to come and see me. I have a little job that needs taking care of.'

Lottie groaned as Elizabeth marched off, Bertie at her heels. 'What on earth is she up to now, and why does she need Tab?'

'She's a right card, isn't she, your gran? I wish I had a gran like that. What did you mean about your diary?'

Lottie shook her head. 'It's nothing, really. I'll tell you later.'

'Well come on, babe, let's go and tell Pandora what she said about the snooping. I want to talk to her anyway. She's got loads of stuff wrong.'

'But it's just a film, Sam.' Lottie, pony in tow, hurried after

Sam, who was already wobbling off on her heels in the direction of the house. Telling Pandora not to snoop was easier said than done. 'It isn't supposed to be real, and I'm not sure we should interrupt when they're busy. Maybe at the end of the day?'

'Look they've stopped for a cuppa. Come on, I want to talk to that Seb too. I mean everybody else is an extra, so I think my little Roxy should be. Look at her on her little pony, bless, she's a natural, aren't you poppet?' The poppet waved both hands.

It was, though, Lottie decided, better to just bite the bullet and get on with it. If Gran had said something needed doing, then she knew from past experience that it was wise to do it – before Elizabeth took matters into her own hands. In theory Lottie was in charge, but whilst her gran was around she'd always have a say, either directly or by her own slightly more devious means. Some people called it interfering, but Lottie also knew that she was a wise old woman. She was seldom proved wrong.

* * *

'Oh God, here come the cavalry.' Pandora rolled her eyes as the trio approached, giving Lottie a disdainful once-over then narrowing her eyes more shrewdly at Sam. She didn't know whether it was wiser to ignore the woman or try and get her on side. The child she regarded much as she would a dog, annoying, far too time-consuming and best ignored. Why anybody would want to waste such a large part of their lives on looking after another being escaped her.

'Just try and be nice to the natives for once, darling.' Seb didn't bother looking up from the script, which he was red-inking with abandon. 'Or they might take your country house away.'

'Look I hope you don't mind me saying this, babe. Maybe I shouldn't, but—' Sam gave Pandora the benefit of her full, disarming smile.

199

'Well, don't then.' Muttered Pandora under her breath, unimpressed, and earned a severe look from Seb. 'Please do.' She smiled, sweetness personified. 'I'm all ears.'

'Well we were watching you earlier, and I've got to say you've got some of it wrong.'

'You haven't got to say that, actually.'

Sam ignored the mutter. 'I mean if you've got this money, like I have, then you've got to do everything the right way, haven't you? It was just the same when me and my Davey moved here, we were like moving to the country.'

'If I hear one more word about my Davey . . .' She was only talking loud enough for Seb to hear, or so she thought, until Roxy piped up.

'That's Daddy, my daddy is Davey.'

Pandora scowled and Seb hissed at her to keep her mouth shut.

'Well I wanted to do stuff, you know, and fit in, like you're doing in this film. Well not the horse stuff for me personally, but anyway if the girl you're playing wanted to fit in and ride horses, she wouldn't just put anything on to do it, would she now?'

Pandora looked at her blankly.

'Look at my Roxy.' Sam beamed at her daughter. 'She's got everything, dressed the part she is. I mean, you've got to be authentic.' Pandora straightened at the sound of the word 'authentic', and stopped sniping. 'Even Mandy got all kitted out when she had a lesson with you, didn't she, Lots? She looked just like one of them pictures in *Horse and Hound* or *Tatler*. You know she did it proper, babe, the right gear and everything, and you just aren't, are you? And if I was going to put one of those riding helmet things on I'd get my hairdresser to style my hair so it didn't go all flat afterwards. I mean what if you didn't and then some photographer took a snap and made you look a real flat-head?'

'She's after a shag from a polo-player, darling, not to ride the Grand National.'

'Exactly.' Sam nodded sagely.

'Sorry?'

'A shag, not a slag. He'd just think you were after his money or something, not that you were loaded.'

'But I own this frigging place.' Pandora waved wildly at the house. 'Why would he think that, you stupid woman?'

'Because,' Sam wasn't fazed, 'women like you are good at pretending, aren't you, babe?' She studied Pandora for a second too long. 'For all he knows you could be some gold digger and you've just borrowed the place. I don't like to be nasty, babe, but you've not convinced me. I'd be right suspicious. If I was that polo-player I'd think you might be a right slapper.'

'But my husband's a rock star.'

'An ex-rock star. Look at some of them, babe. They're broke, spent it all on getting bladdered, and looking at the one you've got . . .' She shook her head. 'If you were a proper rock chick then you'd put some effort in, wouldn't you, even if he was old and fat? Or he'd have dumped you a long time ago and got off with one of them groupies. Plenty of kids out there that are after a sugar daddy. None of us girls would turn up half done, even if we were only going to the gym.'

'I'm not,' Pandora spoke through gritted teeth, 'a footballer's wife.'

'No, you're not, babe, are you? He'd see straight through you. In the countryside you're only allowed to be poor if you're a lady, like Lottie. What do they call it, impoverated?'

'Impoverished,' corrected Lottie.

'She's got the breeding and everything.' She turned back to Pandora. 'And you haven't, have you, babe? You've got to buy your way in.' Pandora spluttered and Seb dropped his red pen. 'Oh and I nearly forgot the message from her ladyship with all the excitement. She said, could you stop snooping in the house, you've only paid to use the grounds not the, what did she say? Oh, yes, facilities. That was it, wasn't it, Lottie? I think by facilities she meant the loo didn't she, babe?' She didn't stop for a response. 'You don't want me to give you the number of my stylist do you? She's ace. Got me some amazing clothes since I've been here. I mean, they're different in the country than in the city, aren't they? I had some lovely stuff when me and Davey lived down south, but it just doesn't look right here.'

'Thank you.' Pandora was tight-lipped, and Seb looked like he was smirking. 'But I'm fine. Wardrobe are responsible for what I wear on set.'

'No, babe, I was talking about your stuff, you know the stuff you wear the rest of the time. If you think it's getting a bit, you know, stale then just let me know. I could even take you into the Kitterly Heath boutiques if you like? I never thought there would be any good shops here, but they're amazing.'

'So kind. But we aren't going to be here long, are we, Seb?'

'Not at all.' His tone was brisk. 'Well, ladies, nice to chat, but we must crack on while the light's good.'

'There was something else, actually. Me and Davey were talking about it, and we're happy for you to use Roxy as an extra. I mean, obviously she has to go to nursery sometimes, but we're here quite a lot, aren't we, poppet? Now we've got the pony it gives me a good excuse to come and see Lottie.'

Seb paled. He was having enough problems coping with the livestock, let alone adding children into the mix. 'No need for any more extras at the moment, but you'll be the first to know if that changes. And you can reassure Lady Elizabeth that we will not be snooping anywhere, will we, darling?'

Pandora scowled. 'I wasn't actually using the *facilities*. Ours are more than adequate, thank you. All I was doing was having a quick look at where the fire was. I mean it *was* in all the newspapers wasn't it, so what's the harm in looking? Honestly, I don't know why you're all so precious about the place.' She glared at Lottie. 'You really haven't changed at all, have you? When you were at school it was all so secretive, like, like a private club. You and your friends talking about ponies and what Mummy said all the time.'

Lottie stilled. 'That is so untrue, we talked about ponies because that was what we did after school, and,' her voice dropped, 'I didn't have a mummy.'

'Oh well, Daddy, then. Or in your case, Gran.'

'You didn't even know she was my gran.'

'Oh whatever.' Pandora waved a dismissive hand. 'It's not like I committed an offence is it?'

'This is our home, Pandora. It's private. I wouldn't go wandering around yours without asking, would I?'

'Oh do stop splitting hairs.'

'And there's nothing to see anyway.' Lottie, who hated conflict, tried to soften the blow. 'Honestly, it was just a fire, and it still stinks, so it isn't very nice.'

'The newspapers said it did extensive damage. Not that I'm that interested, of course.'

'Well it did make a mess, but it was all the curtains and stuff like that more than anything, and the panelling is burned, and the ceiling.'

Pandora, who had seemed to briefly soften her attitude, went back to being sniffy. 'Well I'm surprised you haven't sorted it out more quickly, then, if you're so,' she paused, 'impoverished and your business relies on it.'

'We're having to wait for the go-ahead from the insurance company, and it's a very big room and it all has to be done properly of course. Even the window frames . . .' Lottie stopped talking when it became obvious that Pandora had lost interest and was gazing past her at Rupert.

'Well that's settled then, darling.' Seb put a hand on his wife's shoulder and was shrugged off. 'We don't need to go into the house, do we?'

'Why on earth would anybody want to do that?' Pandora sniffed. 'It's a good job we've got a better location for the interior, the smell of smoke gets everywhere. And it looks all dark and musty, I'm not surprised nobody wants to come and get married here. You are going to clear up that pile of mess that pony has just made, I suppose?'

Seb raised an eyebrow and the corner of his mouth lifted, which Lottie supposed was the nearest he got to apologising. Although it must be terribly hard working, or living, with Pandora, one must constantly feel one had to apologise for her.

'We'll leave you to, er, crack on, then.'

'Cheerio, catch you later.' Sam grinned. 'And if you want them boobs sorting, I know just the man, these country types like something to grab hold of, if you know what I mean.' She winked and Pandora visibly paled.

They were halfway back to the stables, and the sound of Pandora and Seb's raised voices were fading, when Sam linked her arm through Lottie's. 'She's not very nice is she, babe?'

'She never was.' Lottie sighed. 'I thought she might have changed.'

'You know what, hun? People like that never change. Oh look, Tab and Jamie are here, do you think there's something going on with them?' She grinned.

'Oh heck, Gran wanted to see them and I completely forgot.'

'Here, Tab, can you put Roxy's little horse in the field for me, babe? And Lady Elizabeth says she wants to see you.' She winked at Jamie. 'And you as well, babe, have you two been up to no good?'

Tab looked at Lottie for confirmation. 'She did ask. I don't know why. Is she up to something?'

Tab shrugged and looked, Lottie thought, as guilty as Harry when he'd stolen the last biscuit. 'She asked us to find some stuff out.'

Sam clapped her hands, then swung her daughter down from the saddle. 'We can all go and see her, and watch the filming with her.'

'Gran watches the filming?'

Sam giggled. 'She's been watching all of it. I've seen her peeking from upstairs. Doesn't miss a thing, does she? Bless. Come on, babe, we'll tell her you're on your way, Tab.'

* * *

'You don't fancy going out for a drink do you?'

'What, with you?'

'Yes, with me.' Jamie had been working up to asking Tab out for a drink for over a week. When she wasn't mucking out stables, Xander's dog seemed to be a permanent fixture under her arm, and she was always obediently following the dog's master with a look of hero-worship on her face, but it didn't stop him fancying her. And she hadn't looked cross at Sam's innuendos, which had to be a promising sign.

He wasn't quite sure why, he'd never been out with a girl who smelled of horses, and had every inch of her body toned from hours of riding them, and a dry sense of humour had never really appealed. But Tab had it all, and he definitely fancied the pants off her.

She was model-tall, but unlike any model he'd ever seen. Her long black hair framed her pale face like curtains, with a bang fringe that came down to her eyebrows, and the gimlet stare had been trained on him more times than he dared to mention. Humdrum bored her, but Xander and the filming excited her, and she'd lit up from inside when they'd ask her to ride in the scene that had ended so disastrously.

At that moment, as she'd ridden back, standing high in the stirrups and whooping as she waved her stick, Jamie had wanted her more than he'd ever wanted anybody. Every feeling he'd had up until then suddenly faded into nothing more than schoolboy lust. He felt like he was teetering on the edge of living, that Tab could take him somewhere he'd only dreamt of. He wanted to kiss her, taste her, and touch her. He wanted to shag her. And he was rather shocked by the realisation. He'd tossed and turned for several nights before he'd decided he really had to do something about it, because the threat of being turned down couldn't be any worse than never knowing. He hoped.

'As in a drink, or a date?' She looked suspicious.

'Whatever.' He shrugged. 'We could talk about what Lady Elizabeth wants us to do.'

'We could do that here.'

'You're not going to make this easy, are you?'

'Nope.' She grinned. 'My dad said if a guy can get a girl into bed before he's been made to suffer then she's a slag, a model, a groupie, or a sex addict.'

'Really?'

'One of the few things he's ever said that stuck in my mind. I think he was high on something at the time, and anyway he's a bit past it, old fashioned and jaded.'

'Oh.'

'So where are you taking me?'

'Really? Wow, well if you want to.'

'I'd hurry up and say before I change my mind.'

'I wasn't actually suggesting we sleep together.'

'You're losing points here.' She saw the look on his face and grinned. 'I'm teasing, but you had actually thought about it, hadn't you? I can see it in your eyes.' She leant forward. 'Smell it.'

'You're scaring me.'

'Stop being a wuss. If you can handle Pandora you can cope with me.'

'Believe me, nobody can handle Pandora.'

'I think,' she slipped her hand through his arm, 'you can tell me all about the hold she has over you and Xander. I reckon I could learn some useful tricks from that woman.'

'Don't you dare try and learn anything from Pandora. I did actually quite like her at first. Well not really like, but I thought she was okay. She got me this job. It was her,' he leant in conspiratorially and Tab shivered as his warm breath bathed her neck, 'who suggested I come out and take photos of Tipping House.'

'Wow, was it? I thought Seb picked it.'

'He thinks I found it, and I did in a way, and I came to check it out. But, it was Pandora who made sure I came. I'd kind of convinced myself it was all my doing, but the more I think about it the more it kind of hits me that she steered me into choosing it.'

'So you're saying coming here, actually to Tippermere, was her idea all along?'

'She saw the photos in the paper, after the fire and thought it had potential.'

'You know what? I think we do need to go and chat to Lady E before we go for that drink.'

Jamie groaned. 'Me and my big mouth. Can't it wait?'

'No, we'll forget, and anyway.' She turned her head so that her black gaze met his head on. They were practically nose to nose and he suddenly felt like it didn't matter what he had to do to get there, they were going out. 'A big mouth can be very useful sometimes.'

Chapter 17

Sam stood in the archway that led through to the stable yard and couldn't help but smile. Moving to the country had been amazing. When Dave, her husband, had first mentioned a move to Cheshire she'd been horrified. Her family were in the South, the best clubs were, the best designers, everything. The north contributed rain and some pretty scenery in the Lake District. And two high-profile football clubs.

She couldn't say no, could she? No way would Davey pass up on the transfer of a lifetime, to play in goal for one of his dream clubs. If she'd said no then she'd be stuck where she was, and he'd be living away from home for the most part. She'd seen what that had done to some of the other girls. They might have looked happy enough, spending their husband's money and partying, but she knew all about the gnawing doubts that hit during those long nights home-alone. The desperate need to make it perfect for when he got home, so he'd always think it was worth coming back. The hours at the gym to ensure that the perfect body would be the memory he left with, before the groupies sidled up in nightclubs and bars.

That kind of life wasn't for her; she simply wanted to be with her Davey. It wasn't exactly the lifestyle she'd bought into – their first date had been a pint followed by a kebab, and then a bus ride home – but the day he'd rushed in, swept her off her feet, and told her their time had come she'd known that although everything on the outside was about to change, the stuff on the inside, the stuff that really mattered, had to stay the same. They were Sam and Davey, wherever they were, however much money they had to spend.

She loved her husband and she'd fallen for him long before the big clubs had talent-spotted him. They'd married in secret in the days when his agent had told him to concentrate on his career and not get tied down, which Sam translated as 'stay single, I don't want anybody else influencing your decisions'. Then they'd renewed their vows in public, in a ceremony that had included all the bling Sam loved.

Moving to Kitterly Heath had been the cherry on the cake for Sam. She had a glamorous house, the most perfect designer shops to wander round, the king of Botox on her doorstep, and a hair-stylist who understood that the day a newspaper reporter managed to catch her having a bad-hair day would be the day she'd fall out of favour.

And she'd now got her gorgeous daughter and the best friends she could imagine. Sam was as down to earth as they came, and in Lottie she'd met somebody just as warm-hearted and generous, if a little more scatty and less appearance-aware. She had her own beautiful home and Tippermere was just a few minutes away.

The fact that Lady Elizabeth was a real lady was amazing, and the lovely Tipping House was awesome. And now it was the setting for a film. Which was beyond exciting. It was like living in a fairy tale, a dream world – but better than anything she had ever imagined.

If her friend Tracey had been here now she'd be blown away, but she'd never believed in dreams or bettering yourself. They'd been the best of friends until Trace had told her to dump Davey, told her he was a boring fart who loved his football more than her, and that you had to live in the moment. Go out with some-body who had a proper job, had managed to buy a second-hand car and would treat you to cocktails and a curry on a Saturday night, Trace had said.

Years on she'd tried to make it up with her friend, but Tracey, stuck with four kids and a boyfriend who spent his evenings out on the razz with his mates, had shut the door in her face. 'Come to gloat, have you? Stuck up cow. Bet you think you're too good for people like us now.'

She'd not really thought about Trace for years, until the other day when she'd been watching Pandora and something had struck a chord, lifted a memory until it hovered just out of reach but wouldn't go away. Pandora reminded her of Trace. She wanted to grab what was there and she didn't care about loyalty or love, and Sam couldn't shake the bad feeling off.

'I'm going to show Worwy my new hair bobbles.' Roxy tugged on her hand and brought Sam back to the present.

'I bet he'll be impressed with those, babe. We'll have to get some for Rupert, won't we?'

'Woopert is a boy horse, Mummy. He doesn't wear pink.'

'How about we get him blue ones?'

But the little girl had spotted Rory and was running across as fast as her chubby legs would take her. He swung her up in his arms and waved to Sam. He was a natural with kids, thought Sam as she headed over to the tack room, where she knew she'd find her friend. If Lottie would join the baby club life would be pretty much perfect.

'Everything okay, babe?'

Lottie was throwing horse nuts into buckets so hard they were bouncing. She stopped and dropped the scoop into a bucket.

'Not really.' She sighed. 'You know that stuff in the newspapers when that reporter guy you knew was here?'

'You mean them brides, hun?' Lottie nodded. 'They wanted their money back, didn't they?'

'They did. They still do.' She looked up at Sam and her normally cheerful face was glum. 'They're threatening to take us to court now. They've even written to the solicitor and I can't even prove we'll be ready to re-open in time for their weddings.'

'Maybe you should just pay them back, then? Save all the hassle.'

'We're broke. We just haven't got the ready cash, Sam, and they want all these other costs for emotional distress and crap like that as well,' she paused, 'and interest on top. The solicitor has suggested we offer to pay it back in instalments, but then we'll have no spare money at all, and no bookings at all for when we re-open. If we ever do.'

'Aww don't be so down, babe, course you will.' She wrapped her arms round Lottie. 'What does Rory think? He'll help you sort it all out.'

'I really don't know, Sam. He's getting fed up of all the hassle, and of me too, I think.' She pulled away, picked up a handful of carrots and started chopping them with what Sam thought was unnecessary force.

'Of course he's not fed up of—'

'He just wants to be normal. He said maybe we should sell part of the estate. He didn't even want to talk about it.'

'You wouldn't would you, babe? Sell?'

'You've no idea how broke we are. We owe the feed merchants a fortune now Rory hasn't got a sponsor, and the money from the film just isn't enough. Have any idea how much it costs just to shoe these horses?'

Sam shook her head, deciding it was better to stay quiet and just listen.

'David, Rory's sponsor covered all those costs, and I think he feels guilty about that. But, to be honest, all the developers want the lot, including the house. Nobody just wants the fields, so I don't know how we *can* just sell part of it. And we need all the grazing land anyway.'

'Something will come up. You'll think of something, you always do.' Sam decided that the last thing she should do was mention her concerns about Pandora. Those were best kept to herself right now. Cheering Lottie up had to be the main priority. She looked totally out of sorts.

'Guess what Roxy called your Rory? She said he was her other daddy yesterday.' She giggled. 'Isn't she a gem? But he is gorge. If she says that out in public they'll think she's from a two-daddy family, won't they? And I'm just the nanny.'

'Nobody would think you were a nanny.' Rory appeared in the doorway, Roxy on his shoulders squealing. 'Well, nobody normal. Come to ogle the stars again, Sam?'

'More like ogle you, babe.' She kissed him affectionately on the cheek and gave him a squeeze. 'I was just saying to Lottie that you'd make a fab dad.'

'Were you?' Lottie looked up from her carrot-slicing duties.

'Another little playmate for Roxy, you'd love that wouldn't you, babe? It'd be like a little brother or sister.'

'We're going to fill the place one day, aren't we, darling?' Rory bounced on the spot and Roxy giggled. 'Put those child-bearing hips to good use.'

'Cheeky bugger, maybe one day.' She reached for another carrot. 'Roxy could babysit for us.'

'Oh you don't want to wait that long, babe. Think about your eggs going stale. My gyno said there's no time like the present, so me and Davey are going for it. Never stops practising when he's here.' She had a dreamy look on her face. 'He can go on for hours.'

'Sam!' Lottie looked from Sam to Roxy.

'Mummy is always playing with Daddy.' The little girl had an earnest look on her face. 'They play kiss chase. Come on Worwy, I want to go wide Woopert.'

'Down you go, then.' He lifted her effortlessly down and grabbed the small riding hat from a shelf just inside the tack-room, then jammed it on her head. 'Let's go widing and Mummy can find out why Auntie Lottie doesn't want babies, or' he gave a wry smile, 'if it's just me she doesn't want them with.'

Sam watched them go and then turned to Lottie, who hadn't cheered up at all. 'Is everything okay, babe? You know, with you two, not just the house stuff?'

Lottie shrugged. 'Maybe I'm not the woman he thought I was. Come on,' she dropped the knife, 'I need some fresh air.'

* * *

It wasn't that Rory was lazy, but he felt that horses should be fun and Roxy was far too young to be told what to do. As a child she had a naturally good posture in the saddle, perfect balance, and with her open mind was receptive to the pony's reactions in a way that an adult seldom was. So at every opportunity he would put her up on the untacked pony and lead her about.

He watched her run across the yard to the loosebox they kept Rupert in, laughing as she jumped up and down trying to undo the bolt. 'Here you go.' He grabbed Rupert's head collar, the brightest one on the yard, from where it hung on the top stable door. Neither Rory nor Lottie knew that it was possible to get blingy, diamante-studded stable wear for ponies until Sam had scoured the internet. It was purple, it was shiny and it matched his stable rug, which unfortunately was now covered in stains and shavings.

Two minutes later and Roxy was on the pony's wide back as Rory led them out to the field.

'Bless, chokes me up to see her, you know,' Sam said. 'I never thought I'd have kids with ponies. Come on, babe, let's watch that Pandora for a bit. It'll give you a change of scenery. You can see her from here, they're filming in front of your house. I hope Lady Elizabeth doesn't get cross, she told Tab she was going to throw a bucket of water over that Pandora if she went snooping around inside again.'

'Better than shooting at her.'

'She wouldn't?'

'She shot at Jamie when he first came.'

'She's a card isn't she? She didn't hurt him, though, did she? And he seems to like her. He's always chatting to Tab, then off they go to talk to her Ladyship. Do you think he's after her? Tab, I mean, not your gran.' Sam giggled and linked her arm through Lottie's. 'Come on, we can get right up close where we can hear everything.'

* * *

'This feels naughty.' Lottie settled down on the grass next to Sam and felt like she was truanting from school. It was a gorgeous sunny morning, the sun was reaching out for Tipping House, wrapping it in a warm golden glow of a hug, and it was amazingly peaceful. She felt the air of gloom that had been hanging around her lift slightly. If only every film day could be like this.

At the bottom of the sweep of stone steps, Pandora was having her make-up touched up and there was the soft buzz of people at work. She really hoped it wasn't the calm before the storm.

'Mind if I join you?' She glanced up, straight into the by-now familiar dark stare. Xander.

'Course we don't, babe.' Sam grinned and patted the patch of grass next to her. 'Park your bum here, hun. You can explain the plot.'

'I haven't got a clue. I'm just the sidekick. All I know is I've got a day off.'

'Aww you could never be just a sidekick.'

The three of them sat in silence as Seb shouted for the cameras to roll. The first swallows of spring swooped low over the ground, circling gracefully and as some soared high until they were faint spots of black against the azure blue of the sky, others headed into the courtyard like an acrobatic display team, darting and diving as they celebrated their return.

Lottie loved it when the swallows returned to Tippermere. It was confirmation of spring. As a little girl she'd competed with Billy to see who could spot the first one and she would scour the skies for days determined to win. As an adult she saw their return as an affirmation that anything was possible. If a small bird could be so resilient there was hope for her. There had to be a solution to their current problems and maybe Rory was right. Maybe amongst all the offers they had there was a solution, somebody who would just buy some of the grounds, or hunting rights, fishing rights – there had to be some way around the problem apart from giving up completely.

'Penny for them?'

She shook her head, aware that Xander was watching her, and he didn't press it. Just stretched out his long legs. 'It's beautiful here, you're lucky.'

'I know.'

'Oh my God, just look at her.' Sam's stage whisper carried clearly across the air and Jamie, who was standing only yards from the shoot, waved his arms in alarm. 'Sorry.' She shuffled closer to Lottie so that she could hiss in her ear. 'Isn't she fab? She's like a proper star.'

'She is.' Xander grinned, a crinkle of lines fanning out from his eyes, lifting his darkly handsome face from brooding to sexy. 'A proper star.'

Pandora reached out, touched her co-star, her fingers teasing at the button on his shirt. 'You could come in.'

'Won't your husband mind?'

'He's away.'

Lottie held her breath. She'd never heard Pandora sound breathy and seductive before. They'd only seen the real Pandora, the one with the sharp tongue and cutting retorts.

Pandora moved in closer and Lottie could swear that even from this distance she could see the actor's erection.

'He's always away.' She undid the button, slowly, deliberately. 'I get so lonely and bored.' She sucked one finger, slowly drawing it out of her mouth with a pop, and then traced a damp trail down his chest. He closed the distance between them, putting a hand on her slim waist. 'Oh, Michael, you are just so—'

'Cut.'

Lottie jumped, Pandora scowled.

'Where in the fucking script does it say you maul her?' Seb waved the script in the air.

'I was just impro—'

'Well don't. You're not Robert de fucking Niro. She's seducing you, get it? Jesus, have you no idea what she's like? She's a man-eater, working her way through the bloody countryside one shag at a time because she's so fucking bored of being stuck in the sticks. Understand?' Seb, who had been marching forward and pointing his finger to emphasise his point, suddenly spun round and headed back to his seat next to the camera. 'Again.' He paused. 'And remember you're only the frigging farmer delivering muck for the roses, you're target practice not the star.'

Sam giggled. 'He's quite hunky for target practice, isn't he?'

'Nothing like the farmers we normally get round here,' said Lottie wistfully. 'They're usually going bald, have baling twine holding up their trousers, holes in their socks, and cow shit in their hair.'

'Their hair?'

'From when they're putting the milking machines on. I don't think she'd be putting her hands down Tom Edlin's shirt, who knows what she'd find in there.'

'Oh look. They're starting again. He looks scared now.'

'I'd be scared if Pandora was seducing me,' Xander said lazily.

'She's got a good grip on his shirt. Oh my God, she's got a good grip on something else, his tackle will be all bruised,' Sam gasped.

Lottie giggled, she couldn't help it. And the more she looked at Sam the worse it got, until she had to clamp her hand over her mouth.

'Cut. For fuck's sake, man, don't stand there like a limp rag. Now's the bit when you take control.' Seb stabbed his finger at the script. 'You're supposed to pin her against the stone pillar. And, darling, look like you want to eat him, not like you're afraid he's going to rub your lipstick off.'

'He already has. You, yes you, come and touch up my make-up. And you,' she glared at her co-star, 'stop rubbing your dick against my leg, if you leave a stain we'll have to shoot the whole scene again.' She rolled her eyes and averted her face so that the make-up girl could repair the damage. 'And no tongues, or God help me, I will bite it off.'

It was amazing, Lottie thought, how Pandora transformed the instant the cameras started to roll. She melted into the man's embrace, stared at him with lovelorn eyes that meant his cock instantly stiffened despite the threats. Her voice was hoarse, laden with desire in a way that would have made Lottie sound like she'd got laryngitis, but Pandora pulled it off. As she grabbed the collar of his shirt, her co-star followed her meekly up the steps. A lamb to the slaughter.

'Cut.'

Pandora thrust the man to one side and flounced down the steps. 'I need a drink to get that nasty taste out of my mouth. Jamie, Jamie, where the hell have you got to?'

Jamie jumped to it.

After an hour of watching, Lottie was sure she was more exhausted than the crew. The 'farmer' had been shagged on the steps, a rather upright member of the Conservative party, canvassing for votes, had been wooed with whisky and the promise of a good spanking if he played his cards right, and a passing horseman looking for grazing had instead found himself with a rather willing rider, who had sat on his cock and called him a stallion. The scenes, Xander explained to an open-mouthed Sam, were not contiguous, but would be spread throughout the film.

'Be a bit much cramming all of that into one day, wouldn't it, babe? She wouldn't be able to walk next day.'

'Who wouldn't be able to walk?' Rory ambled up unnoticed and the Shetland pony dropped his nose to the grass, nearly sending Roxy over his head.

'Pandora, babe. Too much nookie.'

'Oh.' He looked over to where the film crew were taking a breather. 'I'm off to the gallops. Need to give Rio a bit of a pipe-opener.'

'I'll come back to the yard with you; I need to go and do some ground work with Minty.' Lottie stood up and stretched. It had been a bit of a revelation watching how the morning unfolded, far different from the chaotic scenes with horses and dogs.

'I don't want to tear you away.' Rory looked from Lottie to Xander and back.

'You're not. I want to come.' She took the lead rope from Rory and kissed him. She loved him, they'd sort this out. Everything. They had to. 'Sorry I've been a grump, I do love you, you know.'

He studied her silently for a minute, then finally, when she'd just started to think she really had blown things, he smiled. 'Good.' He kissed her back.

'Shall I take Rupert back for you and stick him in the outdoor school?'

'Aww, are you teaching him his A, B, C's now, Lots?' Sam giggled.

'I'm trying to teach him that big isn't best.' She stared at his round tummy, then gave a tug on the lead rope. He carried on mowing the grass with a dedication and thoroughness that had to be admired. 'I don't think Shetland ponies understand the concept of diet. Come on, podge.'

* * *

218

After Sam had dropped a protesting Roxy at pre-school, met up with her new (and very dishy) personal trainer for a work-out (well, if you have to suffer you might as well have pretty scenery, was her reasoning), called in at Amanda's to give her an update on the filming and discuss swollen boobs (or breasts, as Amanda insisted on calling them – she was such a doll, so proper) she decided she'd earned herself a spot of retail therapy.

She was just trying to work out if Davey would appreciate the heels, or a cleavage and thigh-showing dress, when she spotted a familiar figure across the road in her favourite wine bar.

'I thought it was you, babe. Shove up, me feet are killing me.' She perched herself on the edge of the bar stool, smiling when Seb's gaze dropped to boob level. 'Do you think they're swollen? I keep asking everybody if they think I'm preggers again. It would be lovely, wouldn't it? Another Roxy, or if it's a boy, I could call him something posh like Tarvin.'

'I presume you mean Tarquin?' He straightened the napkin holder.

'Oh no, Tarvin. It's a place near here. I mean all them Parises and Milans are a bit common now, aren't they? I think it's a lovely name.' She noticed Seb had averted his gaze. 'All alone are we?'

'We are. We needed a break.'

'It must be hard work, all that shouting at people all day.'

'It is.' He gave a wry smile. 'Very. We don't exactly fit in here, do we? I mean, no offence, there's nothing wrong with the place, it's just not my type of thing.'

'Well, you're a bit of a control freak, aren't you? No offence.' She patted his hand. 'But you can't control animals, you know.'

'Or children.'

Sam was intrigued by Seb. On set he was domineering to the point of rudeness, he was cocky, overbearing and, as far as she was concerned, as nasty as his wife. With a glass of wine in his hand he seemed almost human.

'Well, your Pandora seems to think it is her type of thing.'

'Oh yes, it's one of Pandora's projects.' He smiled, a thin smile. 'She gets a bee in her bonnet about things sometimes.'

'More like a swarm, hun. A right queen bee, isn't she?'

'She's okay. I know you probably won't understand that, but we're good for each other. I try to keep her happy.'

'I'm sure you do, babe. But she's not making anybody else happy, is she? She's got to try and fit in, be a bit nicer. I mean I was a right fish out of the pond when I came here, and look at me now.'

Seb looked. Sam knew she didn't look like she fitted in this particular pond at all, but she was happy, she loved where she was and who she was and people laughed with her, not at her.

'Pandora isn't a people-pleaser, and we'll be off soon, anyway, so what does it matter?'

'But she doesn't think that way, does she, babe?'

'Not yet. But it's in the script.' This time the smile almost reached the cool grey eyes. 'Want another one?'

Sam watched as he straightened the drink mats so that they were perfectly aligned, then brushed an imaginary speck of dust from his trousers. 'Aw, go on then, babe.' She almost felt sorry for this detached man and his wife. She just couldn't imagine not having lots of friends, trusting other people, sharing. 'Have you told her that's how it ends?'

'Not yet, it's not in the version she read, there have been changes.'

'Ahh. Are you positive that's how it ends, then?'

'Positive.'

Sam relaxed and settled herself more comfortably. She'd once read something about knowing your enemies, and it had stuck with her. Right now she wasn't sure about Seb, but she knew that Pandora spelled trouble.

She couldn't help Lottie out with her money worries because she knew they wouldn't let her, but she could watch her back when it came to the Drakelows. Sam valued her friends, and if anybody hurt them then they hurt her too. She smiled at Seb. 'Tell me about your script and all them men Pandora's dragged off to bed.' Seb frowned. 'In the film, babe. I'm not one for gossip, we'll leave that to the papers, shall we?' He signalled to the barman to refill the glasses. 'You don't look like the type to be dirty in the bedroom though, I must say,' she winked, 'my Davey says never judge a book by its cover. Cheers!'

Chapter 18

'They do look sweet together, don't they?'

Rory, who had returned from turning two of the horses out, was surprised when he turned round to find Pandora lurking in the shadow of the archway. She nodded her head in the direction of Lottie and Xander, who were hanging over a stable door, sharing a joke.

'He still has such a crush on her, which is so cute if you're into that kind of thing.' She pulled a face that suggested she wasn't. 'I saw them watching together when I was doing my scene earlier. I'm surprised they've both got so much spare time. Some of us are busy,' she leaned in, her breast rubbing against his arm, 'aren't we?'

Rory had found himself increasingly niggled by the amount of time Xander was spending on the yard with his wife. He trusted Lottie, but that didn't mean he trusted the other man or liked the situation. But he wasn't going to say that to Pandora. Or admit that she'd just confirmed his suspicions.

'Lottie works very hard to keep this place going, she's entitled to some time off.' He shrugged. 'And I'm not surprised he likes her. Everybody had a crush on Lottie at school – she's a nice person.'

'And a very wealthy woman, I'd imagine, looking at this place.'

'Well you'd imagine wrong. People don't like her because she's loaded, she's just popular. Not everybody is like you, you know.'

'Oh really? Sorry if I've hit a nerve. I'm sure she'd never even *look* at anybody else. You're more than enough for any woman. And I mean, big brother Xander might be broke but I'm sure he'd *never* chase a woman for her money, he's got far more basic instincts.' She laughed. 'And I'm sure he's nowhere near as interesting as you, she's probably bored to tears with him, but being polite. No doubt there will be the pattering of tiny feet here soon, and not the doggy type?'

Her attempt at lightening the mood didn't help. In fact, although she didn't even appear to be trying to be nasty, at that moment she'd hit more than a nerve, she was going for total destruction, Rory thought. For some reason babies were not on the horizon for Lottie, unless they had four little hooves attached.

He'd thought they were happy together, and he'd thought that starting a family was just the next step – but one that he'd be happy to skip. Except now it was an idea that was firmly lodged in his mind, and he really was worried there was some reason for her disinterest that had escaped him.

She only looked happy these days when she was with other people, like Xander. In fact, he seemed to have taken the place that Mick used to have in her life. Maybe that was the issue. She was looking for somebody more like that, somebody serious to spend the rest of her life with. Not some clown like him. Oh God, he really had to get a grip and face it if they had a problem with their marriage. But since the film crew had moved in, since Xander had arrived, they seemed to get further apart each day.

'Oh, let's go and see what they're laughing about, shall we? You look like you need cheering up. I guess you don't really like having us here filming?'

'It's fine. As long as you don't upset the horses I don't have a problem.'

'Oh you're so nice, Rory. You always were. It must be difficult though, for you in this situation.' He didn't ask what 'situation', so she carried on. 'I'm sure more of these people do marry out of their class now, but with you being the man . . . I suppose she makes all the decisions, because it is actually her home.'

'We both make the decisions, it's *our* home and Lottie works very hard to make sure we can keep it.'

'Isn't that wonderful.' She patted his arm. 'You must be very understanding though. There's not many men prepared to let a woman take the lead. Most men need to know they're in charge.'

The way she said it wasn't one hundred per cent sincere, but Rory let it pass without comment. It didn't really matter what Pandora did or said, he did actually feel like chasing her and her brother off the estate. But that, he'd been told quite firmly by Lottie, was not an option.

Pandora took Rory's silence as agreement and headed straight over to Xander and Lottie, leaving him little choice but to follow.

'Oh, that's what you're looking at.' She stuck a tentative hand out in Minty's direction, which the filly thought might be edible and proceeded to try and take a tentative bite out of. With a yelp, Pandora retreated rapidly, but did her best to hide her horror. 'You could ride this one in the film instead of one of Xander's, couldn't she?'

Xander shook his head.

'She's only a baby.' Lottie pulled at the filly's forelock, which was still threaded through with soft, brown baby fur.

'So you are riding in the film?' Rory hadn't missed Pandora's comment.

'Only if they need me, just to stand in for Pandora if she's not happy. Seb said we were a similar size.'

Pandora gave a sharp laugh. 'The same height, darling, I don't know about *size*. You, of course, are much bigger than I am. All this exercise and healthy appetite nonsense. And, besides, I'm sure we won't need you. Why Xander pushed the idea I don't know.'

'I didn't push anything.' Xander's voice was mild. He wasn't going to let his sister draw him as she always tried to. 'Seb asked if I could suggest anybody as a stand-in for you and Lottie is a much better match than Tab.'

'It's only the odd shot.' Lottie threw an apologetic look in Rory's direction, wishing he could look happier about it. 'And I'll get paid, won't I, Xander?'

'I wasn't thinking about the money, just whether you've got time, darling,' Rory said quietly.

'Oh well,' Pandora smiled brightly, 'there's no time to waste chatting. Some of us have got work to do. I will leave you all to have fun with your horses. Can you drag yourself away, Xander, and give me some tips about my scene tomorrow? Of course I can ride perfectly well, but it has been a while. Just a quick refresher to make sure my position is perfect. Or you could help me, Rory?' She gave him a dazzling smile that almost reached her eyes. 'You were always such a good rider, so much better than the rest of us. Then we can leave Xander and Lottie here to chat about old times.'

'Stop trying to cause trouble.' Xander took Pandora's elbow firmly. 'Let's get you on a horse.'

Rory and Lottie watched in silence as the two left the yard.

'She was flirting with you.'

'And what was he doing with you?'

'He wasn't flirting. We were just talking about the film. It's different.'

'Hmm. If you say so. You do know he fancied you at school?'

'No he didn't. Who said that?'

'Pandora. But I didn't need telling. He still does.'

'Rubbish.'

'And you like him, don't you? Go on admit it.'

'Well he's nice enough, yeah, I like to chat with him, but that's all.'

'You talk more to him than you do to me at the moment, Lottie.'

'That's not true.'

'It is. Now Mick's not around you've got Xander instead. Isn't my conversation sparkling enough for you?'

Lottie frowned. 'That's such a silly thing to say and it's not fair. It's you that wouldn't talk about what the solicitor said about paying back those brides.'

'And it's you who won't talk about starting a family. I'm not good enough to chat to, and not good enough to father your kids.'

'Now, that's not true. Look Rory,' she sighed, 'it's me, not you.'

Rory laughed. 'Ah the old, it's all me, all my fault, not yours.'

'Rory, why are we arguing about this? You're the only person I ever wanted. I just don't know that I want children, but if I did it would be with you, honest. This is Pandora, isn't it? What did she say? She's just trying to cause trouble. She hates me. I've told you that what they put in the newspaper about Xander and me was rubbish, we hardly spoke a word to each other at school until,' a flush of colour spread over Lottie's face.

'Until?'

'Until that stupid bet.'

'Bet?'

Lottie squirmed. It was one of those memories that every so often would surface. Niggle at her conscience and tell her she wasn't such a nice person after all.

She'd been nasty, showing off, which was something she seldom did. But Xander had made her so cross, he'd made such a horrible comment about Rory and then made fun of everything her family stood for.

'Go on, what bet?'

'It was just before him and Pandora left Tippermere. My friend Becky dared him to ride my pony.'

'So?'

'Well it was completely bonkers. All the ponies Dad used to get me were. He said it was character-building, but what he really meant was that he'd got them cheap and wanted to make some money on them.'

'Worse than Gold?'

'Oh yes, you know how crafty ponies can be, it had learnt every trick in the book.'

'Nothing wrong in letting him do it though. If he wanted to ride it, it was up to him.'

'But he couldn't ride, he didn't understand. That was the point, he'd never been on a horse before and he was just going on about us making such a thing about nothing, and how,' she gave him a look under her lashes, then jumped as Minty took a nibble of the end of her finger, 'ouch, how you thought you were so great and you weren't, you were just a show-off. He knew I fancied you. I told him it wasn't that easy and he didn't know anything. And, I don't know, it was all stupid kid stuff, I suppose, but he got me so mad, he was slagging Dad off as well. So Becky said if he was so clever he should prove it. I did tell him he didn't have to.'

'He was trying to get your attention, darling, he wasn't going to say no was he?'

'So the first time Xander ever got on a horse was to prove me wrong.'

'And got dumped.'

'Oh yeah, she was a really naughty pony. First she wouldn't move, and Becky laughed, so he kicked her. She bounced around like she was on springs. He must have had a really sore bum and when that didn't work she took off. She jumped the fence out of the paddock and went straight down to the lake, and didn't stop until her belly was wet and then she rolled.'

They looked at each other and Rory couldn't help but grin.

'Becky thought it was hilarious and Xander looked furious, he really did hate me then, even though I said sorry. He glared and stormed off and never spoke to me again.'

Rory laughed. 'You silly moo. You shouldn't feel bad about something like that. Me and the lads did far worse.'

'But you're a boy. Even Gran thinks I was mean.'

'You've told Lizzie about it?'

'Well no, but you know what she's like. She knows everything. She even made some comment the other day about how much his riding's improved. I'm sure she was having a go. I think she read my old diary.'

'You had a diary? Full of girly secrets? Was I in it?'

Lottie went scarlet. 'You might have got an odd mention, but I'm not telling you. A diary is secret. Anyway, Xander could have got really hurt.'

'Only his ego. I reckon he just wanted to get you to notice him. Boys are daft like that.'

'Gran more or less said the same thing.' Lottie said glumly. Rory raised a questioning eyebrow. 'She said he probably just wanted to fit in, that he was like an outsider and didn't know where he fitted.'

'I meant he wanted to get *you* to notice him, not anybody else.' Rory laughed. 'There's a lot of hormones whizzing about in a teenage boy's body, you know. All we ever think about is sex.'

'That's all you think about now.'

'When you're about it is.' Some of the tension in the back of his neck eased. Oh God, he really did love her, and they couldn't let money, babies, Xander, Pandora or anybody else come between them.

Lottie kissed him on the cheek. 'Don't you think it's a bit odd that Pandora came down here, you know, to the yard?' She frowned. 'She was always one of those riders who wanted everything done for her, then she just climbed on board. She doesn't actually like horses.'

'Pandora doesn't like anything but Pandora, especially four-legged furry things. But I do think it's all a bit odd. No need for her to stick her nose in, is there?' Rory put his arm around Lottie's shoulder. 'Oh God, I'll be so glad when they've gone and we can get things back to normal.'

'Me too.' Lottie stroked Minty's velvet nose. 'Maybe I should talk to Gran.'

'And what can Lizzie do?'

'I don't know. It's funny, isn't it, a few weeks ago all I had to worry about was the fire and insurance people. Now the film is taking up all the time.'

'Not had anybody poking round for a bit, have we? Maybe it's good news, if they've gone quiet it could mean it's all sorted and soon we'll have the go-ahead and a big fat cheque in the post and we won't have to worry about court cases.'

'That would be brill.'

Rory hugged Lottie to him, and let the warmth of her body seep into his. Seeing Lottie with Xander unsettled him. But maybe, at the end of the day, she just wasn't ready to settle down and start a family at all, and if he pushed she'd start looking for a fun time with other people. Having kids could be one step too far for both of them right now. They'd got enough worries as it was.

This was just a hiccup – letting Pandora get under his skin and setting his imagination off on a wild-goose chase was a mistake. If he started to believe that hairline cracks were trickling into their relationship he'd be lost. Lottie was a part of him, without her he didn't think he could function.

'It would be fantastic, wouldn't it?' He really would be glad when it was over.

* * *

'Just how hard can it be to look good on a horse?' Pandora scowled at Xander. 'It will take five minutes of your precious time and then you can go back to combing their tails or whatever it is you want to do.'

'I thought you were supposed to be shooting a scene by the house.'

'Well as I've got all the gear on right now, I might as well refresh my memory. I mean, it's like riding a bike, I'm sure. You don't forget, do you?'

Xander, who had been looking forward to some time with his dog and horses, away from Pandora and the rest of the crew, tried not to let his displeasure show. It just wasn't worth it, she'd be twice as bad if she sensed he was annoyed. As far as he could remember, though, she'd never actually ridden a bike, and the few times she'd been on a horse was when she was around ten years old, and that could have been a donkey.

'I am not letting Lottie upstage me. If she can do it then it can't be that difficult. And look at you.'

Xander grimaced. He knew all too well how appearances could be deceptive. 'Lottie was probably riding horses before you could walk. Believe me, in a ride-off you'd be well upstaged.'

'Well you didn't start until you were quite old and you've managed. I will ride that horse that Tab was on, it was very pretty.'

'No you won't.' If Pandora so much as broke a fingernail, Xander knew that Seb would blame him. Even if the man did know that it was impossible to divert Pandora once she had an idea in her head. 'Here.' He steered her away from the sensitive mare towards an older horse that would suffer flailing arms and flapping legs more kindly. 'Hang on while I get a step for you to mount from.'

'I'm not infirm. I'm quite capable of getting my leg over.'

'So I've heard. It's for the horse's benefit, though, not yours.' With a scowl Pandora clambered onto the step. 'Foot in the stirrup and spring up.'

Getting her 'leg over' wasn't quite as easy as Pandora antici-pated, and, whilst she would never admit it, she was very grateful she hadn't attempted to do it from the ground. The ponies looked quite dainty from a distance, but up close they were surprisingly large.

'Don't worry about the reins, I've got him.'

She hopped on one leg, hanging on to the saddle, wondering how the hell she was supposed to 'spring up' and muttering under her breath that she wasn't in the slightest bit worried about the reins.

'Do I have to come round that side and push you up?'

'You touch me and you're dead.' With a super-human effort Pandora heaved herself up and managed to throw her leg over the saddle. She had to admit that after many years of Pilates and Ashtanga yoga she had thought that getting on the damned animal was the least of her worries. But this was absolutely nothing like working out in a gym. 'Can't you stop the thing fidgeting so much, it's no wonder I can't get my balance.'

Xander decided it was safer not to comment. Instead he checked the girth. 'Sit up straight, relax.'

Pandora, who never relaxed if she could help it, scowled. 'I am sitting up, stop fussing. You're trying to make this such a mystery and it's not, it's only a bloody horse. People ride them all the time, including,' she paused, 'tiny children.'

'These aren't ploddy ponies, they're well-trained horses. And you're tipped back now.'

'Xander.' It was a warning.

'You need to sit up straight. If you lean back like that you'll fall off when he moves. Do you want me to help you or not?'

'Well, quite honestly I'd rather ask Rory. He really has matured hasn't he? He was such a naughty boy at school, but I can totally see the appeal now.'

'Leave him alone, Pandora. I don't know what your game is but forget it, concentrate on the film and then we can all go home.'

'Hear, hear.' Seb, who had been watching his wife and checking his watch, joined in.

'I don't have a game, Xander. Honestly you always need to look for ulterior motives. I just think he could help me. I mean, what he does isn't that different to polo, is it? It's all just riding horses. And Seb did say I should try and be nicer to them, didn't you darling?'

Seb rolled his eyes. 'I meant be civil, that's all. I'd rather they kept busy and out of my way. There really is no need for you to even sit on the animal, darling.'

'A few shots, we agreed.'

'Even the bloody so-called polo-player you've got the hots for isn't seen on a horse.'

Pandora pouted. 'He does get her on a horse once.'

'Only briefly, before he drags her off to the stables for a shag.'

'Well, it has to look right. Honestly, you're the one that demands perfection.'

If there was one thing worse than trying to teach his sister to sit on a horse, it was being in the middle of one of Seb and Pandora's tiffs, Xander decided. 'Let's walk, shall we, and see how it goes.'

'Give me a stick. I want to hold the stick thing.'

Reluctantly Xander handed her a mallet and started to head across the grass, the horse following obediently behind him.

'Oh, for heaven's sake, I'm not a child. Even that horrible brat of Sam's on that overgrown ginger guinea-pig does more than this. I have ridden before, you know.'

Pandora flapped her legs, but the horse, recognising a novice, resolutely ignored her and carried on following Xander, its head lowered, nose inches from his shoulder.

'Oy.' Pandora liked to be listened to. She yanked the reins and it ground to a halt, tossing its head. Pandora pitched forward, her hat tipping over her eyes and her foot coming out of the stirrup. Which all served to annoy her. It really couldn't be that difficult. Xander was just doing his best to make her look an idiot. 'Stupid animal, I thought these things were supposed to be trained properly. Do you really know what you're doing, Xander?'

Sorting herself out, with both feet stuck firmly in the irons and her hat pushed back, she gritted her teeth and kicked. The horse started to walk again at an annoyingly slow pace, which made her look like a complete and utter amateur, so she swung her feet forward then kicked back as hard as she could. Taken by surprise the gelding shot forwards, lurching straight past Xander, who caught off guard, did nothing at all to stop it.

'Oh God, what is this thing doing now.' As the horse started to trot, Pandora decided to abandon her stick. Flinging it to one side and narrowly missing Seb's head, she grabbed the reins in both hands and pulled. Nothing happened. She leaned back and yanked, the horse stuck its nose further in the air and sped up. Pandora bounced from side to side, her heels kicking the horse's side with each step. It responded, breaking into a canter. 'Stop, you stupid animal.' She lurched forward. Doubled up over its withers, clutching on to the reins with one hand and the pommel of the saddle with the other, Pandora clamped her heels to its sides like limpets to a rock and it started to gallop.

'Help me, Xander, this instant.' On each syllable the pitch rose. 'I can hear you, stop laughing.' He did when he realised the horse really wasn't going to stop. 'Xannnnnnder!'

'Sit up, for Christ's sake. Lean in, put your weight in one stirrup so he turns.'

But Pandora was either too far away to hear, or too frozen with fear to respond.

'Oh shit.' Seb, who had been watching with his normal detached air, recognised the note of panic in his wife's voice. He grabbed Xander's arm with a surprisingly firm grip. 'Do something, man. Have you any idea how much it will cost if she falls off and injures herself?' Then he did the unthinkable. Seb broke into a dignified jog.

Xander was just about to follow him when he spotted Rory

riding out from the courtyard and, realising just how futile it would be to run after a bolting horse, he headed that way instead.

Rory was surprised to see a horse galloping across the lawn with no sign of an accompanying crew or cameras. He was even more surprised to see Seb trotting after it, his blond hair flapping in all directions as he jumped over the divots with a certain style, and Xander heading his way, pointing. It was then he spotted the bright-red hair that could mean only one thing. It was Pandora.

For a moment he was very tempted to turn around and leave her to it. But he couldn't. Seb had already ground to a halt and was doubled over, his hands on his knees, gasping for breath, his pale face bright pink with effort.

With a sigh, Rory nudged his horse forward and started cantering after the runaway.

The polo pony Pandora was riding, he noticed as he got closer, had barely broken a sweat. As a horseman he had to admire the beautifully turned-out thoroughbred, which Xander had brought to the peak of its fitness. But thoroughbreds were born to run, and he was fairly sure that a fair number of Xander's were in fact ex-racehorses. Unless it got bored, or Pandora fell off, he might never catch up.

Luckily as his horse hit its stride and sped up, the pony did a flying change and Pandora lost her balance. With a scream she lurched to one side and lost a stirrup. The horse slowed and, doing as it was trained to do, it responded to the shift in weight by turning in a large arc.

Spotting his chance, Rory urged his own horse on to intercept it. Standing in his stirrups he leant forward onto his horse's neck and, reaching out, managed to grab a rein.

Pandora stared at him. Her green eyes were wide, her teeth clenched and her lips slightly open and then her whole body seemed to sigh with relief and relax. Within seconds she'd recovered, realising that the danger was over, and as the horses pulled up Rory didn't know whether to admire her nerve or be afraid of it. They slowed to a walk, stopped.

'What on earth happened?' He was out of the saddle, wanting to get a proper hold of the horse in case it decided to take off again. 'Did something spook it?'

'Oh Rory.' And then, with perfect grace, Pandora fell forward straight into his arms.

'She really does faint quite beautifully, doesn't she?' Elizabeth shook her head, her lips pursed disapprovingly, as she turned away from the window to look at Lottie, who she had invited in for a drink and chat.

'She's quite a good actress, actually. You should have seen her yesterday.'

'I did.' Elizabeth sat down, still shaking her head. 'She always was melodramatic when it suited her, even as a child.'

'To be fair, you don't really know her, Gran.'

'I saw enough. Her poor teachers had a constant battle with that young madam, not that her mother cared. And now she has added lust and passion to her repertoire.'

Lottie stroked Bertie, who had plonked his fat bottom on her feet and was refusing to move, with the result that she was getting cramp in her toes. 'Don't you think it's a bit of a strange coincidence, you know, it being Pandora and Xander involved in this film?'

'I do. Pour the tea, will you, dear? Young James tells me that it was Pandora who suggested he come and look at Tipping House.' She handed Bertie a biscuit and Lottie heaved a sigh of relief as he moved his bulk and settled down on the rug, splattering it with crumbs as he wolfed the treat down.

'Pandora? But I thought Seb was in charge.'

'He probably does too.' Elizabeth's tone was dry as she added sugar and stirred her tea. 'Yes, it was Pandora. She was quite insistent, apparently. Gave him cuttings from the newspaper and had a train ticket booked before the boy had a chance to object. That was why he arrived so late at night. Sebastian was already considering other locations and James thought it had all been settled. He did think at the time that it was slightly odd that she was being so helpful, but she flattered the poor boy. She told him that she wanted to help him get a permanent job with her husband, and that showing initiative would make the difference. It was to be all his own idea, she would never mention her part in it. Boys can be so stupid, so easily manipulated.'

'She's capable of manipulating anybody.' Lottie stared into her cup of tea glumly. There was only one reason she could think of for Pandora to come back to Tippermere – she was after Rory. It explained so much, like her little trip down to the stable yard to whisper in his ear. Her perfectly timed faint from the horse. In fact, Lottie wouldn't have put it past her to set the whole thing up, knowing that Rory rode out at that time. Although the horse bolting probably hadn't been part of the plan, her screams could have been heard in Kitterly Heath.

Their lives were, by and large, predictable. The yard was run like clockwork, with horses fed at a set time and skipped out. Their meal times were governed by what needed doing and when; everything was done to a set routine. Even when they went to events, the preparation and day out followed a pattern. It was the only way they could fit everything in, and it was what the animals thrived on. Pandora would have known exactly what time to get on her horse.

When they were at school, Pandora had been stand-offish in a nervous kind of way. Taking in everything and pouring scorn on everybody. She watched from the sidelines – a nervous filly that would take off if she was challenged. But she hadn't exploded or run away the day that Rory had been responsible for her soaking.

True, it had been a mistake. The water had been intended for a member of staff, but Pandora had done her best to laugh it off.

Not stalk off as she normally did if life was not going her way. They'd all been laughing and Pandora had taken a bow and then taken her place in the queue by the classroom door as though nothing had happened.

Pandora fancied Rory. She'd always fancied Rory. And now she was back for him.

She was building up to a crescendo, and after seeing her acting performance earlier Lottie had no doubts that she could convince anybody of anything.

'Not anybody, Charlotte.'

'Sorry?' She looked up from her cup of tea, which she'd been stirring with the kind of vigour likely to remove the pattern from the cup.

'That female is not capable of manipulating *everybody*. Some men are wiser than you think.' She studied her granddaughter with a frown and then continued. 'As are the majority of women, I may add.' She passed Bertie another biscuit. 'You should also be aware that she has been in contact with that awful man who started the fire.'

'Allegedly started the fire.' Lottie said the words automatically, then stopped and put her cup down. 'What do you mean, she's been in contact with him? Why would she do that?'

'Why indeed? Rather peculiar, one would have thought.'

'Are you sure?'

'He has been bragging on social media about meeting her.' Elizabeth sniffed. 'In much the same way as he professed to starting the fire. One rather wonders if these people take leave of their senses when they go on the computer. In my day it was alleged that some males kept their brains in their trousers, which one could comprehend, but now their closest relationships seem to be with a keyboard or a joystick.'

'But—'

'Oh honestly, Charlotte. Do stop looking at me as though I have lost my marbles. Ask young Tabatha or James if you need to check the facts. I asked them to do a little bit of checking for me. I really don't trust that woman.'

Lottie stared at the tea leaves in her cup and wondered if the splodges they made really did reflect her future. If so it looked like there was a three-legged horse and a black cloud ahead.

'I don't get why she'd be talking to him, unless she was trying to work out just how desperate we were for the money, or—' she stopped herself short, reluctant to voice the idea that had formed in her head. Maybe she was trying to work out just how solvent Rory was before she made her move to lure him into bed.

'Or?' Elizabeth was peering at her, no doubt trying to read her mind.

'Or, well, maybe she thought they should shoot some scenes inside? It could have been Seb's idea.' Though she rather doubted it. 'When I asked her not to snoop in the house she said she just wanted to see the damage that the fire had caused, not because she wanted to use the bathroom.' Yes, that could actually be the reason.

Pandora was hatching a plan to steal her husband and half of her non-existent fortune. Oh shit, Lottie put her teacup down, determined to ignore the splodges that actually now looked more like a money bag and Rory on a black horse galloping away. She probably was.

Chapter 19

By the time Pandora had recovered her good mood and proclaimed that she was ready to soldier on, despite the fact that she really thought she had dislocated her shoulder, the best of the day had gone, along with most of the cast.

'Do we really pay you to just stand and watch?'

The wardrobe girl leapt forward, blushing crimson, reaching out and then stopping, not quite sure what she was supposed to be helping with. She loved her job, most of the time, but 'stars' like Pandora could be quite obnoxious as they desperately tried to prove their importance.

Pandora had wriggled one arm out of her polo shirt and was now glaring at the girl. 'Well, don't just stand there like a dollop. Help me get this over my head. I can hardly move my shoulder.'

The girl tugged and Pandora screamed, stamping on her foot. 'Careful, you idiot. Oh, for Christ's sake, go and tidy your clothes rail or whatever it is you need to do. Then tell that girl in make-up I need her.'

With her shirt still over her head, Pandora's words were muffled. It sounded like she wanted make-up, which didn't make any sense at all, but the girl didn't care. She fled. Let somebody else sort the problem out – Pandora was hard enough work on a good day, but in this mood she was frankly terrifying.

Touched up, with her red hair falling in soft waves onto her shoulders, and the most seductive silk dress she could find draped over her body, Pandora opened the trailer door a crack. 'Seb? Darling?'

Seb was sitting in the furthest corner, stabbing at the screen of his tablet as he altered his precious spreadsheet. Pandora hated his meticulously prepared spreadsheets, they were the source of most of his bad moods, and if she ever had the opportunity she would be tempted to delete the lot of them. They detailed when, where, and how each scene was to be shot, and woe betide any person or incident that led to changes being necessary.

He was extremely annoyed at his timetable being disrupted, but when he looked up, thin lips pursed, he was obviously fighting his natural urge to be cold and distant. When Seb was cross, the barriers came down, and he treated her, at best, like a naughty child, and at worst like a nobody.

She winced theatrically as she made her way over, and hoped that the make-up artist hadn't overdone the bruise on her exposed upper arm.

Seb stared at it, shocked at the splash of colour that marred her pale skin.

'Oh it's nothing, really, and make-up have assured me they can cover it up, it's really hardly throbbing at all now. Well nothing that a few painkillers won't handle. Shall we go back to the hotel and I can give you a nice massage? You look stressed, darling.'

'I am.' He bit back a harsher response and hit *save* on his amended document. 'We've not lost much time. I just hope the weather doesn't change.' A massage sounded nice, and Pandora knew exactly what to do to hit the spot. She always had done. He supposed they knew how to smooth the kinks out of each other. 'You looked the part, darling, wonderful. I know you were just striving for perfection.'

'And don't you dare add, before I fell off.' She looked up from under her long, and decidedly false, eyelashes and although he knew that every move had been practised it didn't matter. Overblown gestures of romance were messy and unpredictable, this was an apology.

'I wouldn't dream of it.'

'I do try, darling. I want this film to be perfect for you; you deserve recognition.' She slid along the seat until their thighs touched. 'I know you hate working with all these dogs and horses, so I've ordered some nice treats for when we get back to the hotel.' She crossed her legs so that her dress inched up just enough to show the top of her stockings. 'Call it stress relief, darling.'

Despite his asexual outward appearance, Seb did possess a relatively high sex drive. It was, though, a purely biological thing, and not to be confused with desire. He had never, as far back as he could remember, lusted after a woman, being able to look at the succession of glamorous actresses that passed before him without the slightest urge.

When Seb had met Pandora he had admired her appearance, but it was actually her ambition, and more importantly her detachment, that he had fallen in love with. She was a perfect partner.

Seb engaged in sexual activity in much the same way as he ate, drank, and slept, but was not foolish enough to suppose that his wife would do the same. He was also aware that the longevity of their relationship relied on his ability to provide Pandora with something she wanted. Something that nobody else could provide. And that definitely wasn't sex. Sex would please Pandora in much the same way as presenting her with a new designer fashion accessory would, and today's fashion was tomorrow's tat.

Today, although it wasn't ordinarily a sex day, he recognised that he wasn't averse to playing along with Pandora's game. Whatever she was after she'd probably get anyway, so he might as well gain some benefit along the way.

He smiled and slipped the tablet into its case. 'If you're sure your shoulder is up to it?'

'Of course, darling, I know you won't be rough.'

* * *

The hotel suite that they had booked in nearby Kitterly Heath was the best available, which Pandora regarded as barely adequate. The service though, was just how she liked it: efficient, and close enough to ingratiating to make her feel respected and admired, without it slipping into the kind of fawning behaviour that was obviously intended to solicit massive tips.

The room service menu was sadly lacking though. So, seconds after her escapade with the runaway horse, she had summoned Jamie. Arming him with her credit card, she'd given him strict instructions to search every deli in the area until he found somewhere that could supply a suitable hamper of goodies.

'Are we celebrating something?'

Pandora smiled and handed him the bottle of champagne to uncork. Although things hadn't gone exactly to plan, she couldn't have wished for a better outcome. Rory had positioned himself perfectly, and the genuine concern in his eyes as he'd held her against his strong body more than compensated for the slight bruising.

'Do we need to have an occasion?'

The only passion Seb displayed was for his work, and he regarded physical displays of affection with something bordering on distaste. Even after several glasses of champagne and a massage that left his cock standing at full alert, there were going to be no messy bodily fluids, inappropriate noises (of the squelchy kind or any other), spontaneity, or sexual gymnastics.

Sex was an almost mechanical process that allowed him to be in control at all times. He was not selfish but rather detached in

242

the way he viewed the whole process and he had perfected a routine that would result in an orgasm apiece, followed by a swift exit to the bathroom, which he was pleased to see had a bidet.

It worked for Pandora. She knew what to expect and knew exactly what to say and how to wriggle when she wanted him to come. Even if he was under the illusion that *he* was the one setting the pace.

'That was nice, darling.' She kissed him on the cheek and headed for the bathroom, a wad of tissue trailing between her legs.

'Very.' He followed her in and switched the shower on full blast, waiting until the steam was rising before he stepped inside. She sat on the bidet and watched him as he washed himself meticulously, towelled himself down, and then had a long pee. A routine that never varied.

He smiled at his reflection in the mirror, peering close to check for laughter lines, then frowned and studied his brow. 'Do you think I need a Botox top-up?'

'Probably, darling. That Samantha woman recommended somebody.' It was Pandora's turn to frown. 'She gave me a bloody list, cheeky cow.'

'Handy to have some local knowledge, I suppose, and I'm sure she only gets the best. She does look like she's had a professional job done.'

'But do I look like I need anything?'

Seb, knowing it was pointless to comment, changed the subject. 'How about we leave the riding to the experts from now on, darling? You did look good today, excellent, but it's dangerous. You're far too precious to risk getting injured.'

'You mean it would mess up the filming.'

He laughed. 'Well that as well, but believe it or not I was thinking of you. You were lucky Rory was there.'

'Oh I'm sure the animal would have stopped eventually,' she said airily, 'I had managed to turn it around by the time he arrived.

243

I should go and thank him though, at some point, I suppose, seeing as he probably thinks he saved my life.'

'I sent somebody to thank him for you, and told Jamie to stand a round at the local pub.' Seb started to brush his teeth, staring at his reflection while he did it. 'He didn't seem exactly grateful.'

'Maybe the personal touch will mean more. You did tell me to be nice to them, darling. What were your exact words? Or they'd take my country house away?'

'It isn't his country house, though, is it?' Seb dried the handle of his toothbrush off carefully and placed it in the holder, wishing he'd never asked her to behave in the first place. She always managed to twist his words and use them for her own purposes.

'It is. It's her house and she's his wife, which means it's his. Besides, I rather like him, he's sweet.' Pandora waited for Seb to move back and then started to line up the pots of lotion and tubes of cream that constituted her nightly routine.

'Let's move on to the next scene in the morning, eh? Forget Rory, forget the riding.'

Pandora smiled. She'd achieved her aim and was actually quite relieved that he was in effect banning her from getting back in the saddle. 'Well, if you really don't want me to, I suppose you know best.'

'I do. Don't be long. I'll go and warm the sheets up.'

* * *

The day hadn't started well for Pandora. She'd forgotten all about her dramatic bruise and managed to wash most of it off in the shower, not even realising until Seb had congratulated her on her miraculous recovery. She decided to brazen it out.

'I've got very sensitive skin. I bruise easily but they never last long.'

244

'Handy.'

'It is, isn't it, darling.' She smiled as sweetly as her stiff face would allow. 'They still haven't got any granola. What the hell am I supposed to eat?'

'Toast, like the rest of us, or a full English?' Seb, after his sexual exertions the night before, found he had a hearty appetite. He patted his stomach. If he wasn't careful he'd end up looking like Billy bloody Brinkley and be a laughing stock when they returned to London.

'Full English?' Pandora shuddered, her stomach churning at the mere thought. 'Eurgh just look at the grease – and you know bread bloats me, darling.' She settled for a cup of black coffee and reluctantly took a slice of toast, which she pulled mouse-sized bites off one by one.

By the time Seb had polished off two rashers of bacon, two sausages, scrambled egg, tomato, mushroom, and two rounds of toast with marmalade, Pandora had eaten half a slice and decided she couldn't face any more.

She was actually quite relieved he was ready to go. At least she'd get some decent food when they reached Tipping House. The one thing she always insisted on when they were on location was decent catering.

'Fucking hell.' A doorman opened the hotel door as they neared it, and they were met with a gust of wind. Seb's carefully combed hair stood on end, then flopped over his forehead. 'That's all we frigging need. The schedule's already slipped.' That's two gusts of cold air, thought Pandora as his wave of disapproval hit her. 'And now this. I hate shooting on location.'

The morning didn't improve when Pandora arrived at wardrobe to find Sam rifling through the clothes and having a good gossip with the girl in charge.

'Hi, babe. Katie was just showing me your stuff.'

Pandora, who hadn't even known the girl's name, scowled at

the camaraderie and resisted the urge to grab all the clothes and bundle them away out of her reach.

'I suppose you're going to tell me they're all wrong?'

'Oh no, babe, they're gorge. And it's not for me to say, is it?'

'No, it isn't.' Hissed Pandora under her breath, whilst keeping the smile pinned to her face.

'But I wouldn't ditch the fab stuff and go all boring when you meet the vicar and stuff like that, I mean I wouldn't. Look.' She jangled her bracelets and flashed a ring that had a diamond in it at least three times the size of any Pandora had ever borrowed for a function.

She wasn't sure whether she should demand something bigger from Seb, or brand it vulgar.

'That's really old fashioned you know. Even Lady Elizabeth doesn't wear twinsets any more, and she,' she leant forward and smiled, 'is a real lady, isn't she? And you'd never see Lottie in something like this.' She waved a prim and proper blouse under Pandora's nose, who snatched it away.

'You never see Lottie in anything but tat, how she attracted a man like Rory is anybody's guess.'

'Well she's got a heart, hasn't she, babe? Men love that. If you ask my advice—'

'I haven't.'

'You need to carry on being a rock chick, you know, be yourself, babe. Don't think you can be anything you're not.'

Pandora hadn't a clue what 'being yourself' meant, but she did know who her character was.

'Oh, nearly forgot, I've got a brain like a sieve I have.' Sam dug into her very large, bright pink designer tote and pulled out a business card. 'They're doing an offer on colonic irrigation and a thing to get rid of cellulite.'

'I haven't got cellulite!'

'I do all these things, just to be on the safe side, and when I saw that I thought of you. Here take it, you never know.'

'How sweet.' Pandora held the card with the tips of her fingers and looked at it with distaste.

'Shame you're not going to be here much longer.'

'You'd be surprised.' Pandora's tone was dry.

'Really, babe? You think on,' she pointed at the card, 'I always like to help my friends get rid of the nasty stuff. Some just end up where they shouldn't, don't they? Need a good blast to get rid of them.'

'Sorry, I haven't a clue what you mean.' Pandora glanced at her watch. 'I really haven't got time to chat, though, we do have a film to make. Come on, Katie, we don't want to keep everybody waiting, do we?'

Sam had developed a new daily routine since Lady Elizabeth had presented Roxy with a pony. Very keen to instil a sense of responsibility in her daughter, she made a point of taking her down to visit Rupert the Shetland each morning. It also gave her the chance to chat to Lottie, who she had grown to love like a sister, over a cup of coffee in the tack room.

She then never missed the opportunity to observe some of the filming, with Lottie in tow if she could drag her away from the horses, before heading off for lunch with the girls in Kitterly Heath.

In the afternoons Roxy would attend nursery, whilst Sam and the glamorous ladies who lunched would have beauty treatments, interspersed with shopping and champagne breaks, or chats to their footballer husbands, depending on upcoming fixtures and training routines.

Right now, with Roxy brushing her pony under Rory's supervision, she decided Lottie still wasn't her normally bouncy self.

'Tell.'

'What?'

'There's something wrong, isn't there, babe? I can see it all over your face. It's not still that business about all them girls suing you is it? Everything's okay with the horses and Rory, isn't it? Oh, no there's nothing wrong with her ladyship, is there?'

'I'm beginning to think this is all a disastrous mistake.' Lottie glanced up at Sam glumly, who was shocked to see her green eyes clouded with what looked suspiciously like tears.

'Aww, babe. It can't be that bad. I'm sure if you get your solicitor to talk to—'

'It's not just that. Look,' she waved a letter, which Sam hadn't noticed, in her hand, in the air. 'It's a letter from the vicar, the actual vicar. He's never written to us before, and it's on his headed paper, and look, it's signed the Very Reverend Waterson. He says we're bringing the village into disrepute.'

'That's a bit pompous, babe. You don't want to take any notice of that.'

'But we are, and he mentions all these people who aren't happy. Apparently, we were on the agenda at the last village committee meeting. An actual item on the agenda, not even Any Other Business. But I can't stop now or we won't get any money at all, in fact we'll probably end up paying them.'

'Oh Lottie, it's just like Tiggy said, it's just the ones that are jealous that don't like it, cos they can't be involved.'

'And it gets worse. I've had three messages left on voicemail by reporters asking if the rumours are true about Rory and Pandora. They've got a picture of her falling into his arms.'

'Oh my God, you're kidding?' Sam knew all about the runaway horse incident from a mother at Roxy's nursery, who had heard it from Mrs Jones in the corner shop, who had been told by Tab, so it had to be right. She paused, wanting to verify facts, but not sure if she should when Lottie looked so upset. She lowered her voice. 'Is it true that he leaned over and dragged her off it, onto his own horse?' Lottie shook her head. 'It reared up and attacked Rory and his horse?'

'No.' Lottie sounded defeated. 'It just bolted, but he caught up and managed to grab a rein and stop it.'

'Oh. So that's all is it, babe?' Sam felt mildly let down. 'But how come she, er, ended up in his arms?' That bit had to be true.

'He was just stood there at the side of the horse asking if she was okay, and she fainted on him.'

'Really?' Sam was sceptical, but seeing Lottie's lip wobble gave her a hug. 'How did they get a piccy of that, hun? Nobody comes and watches now, do they? I thought you'd banned that.'

'Well they don't come in and pay, no, but they still climb the walls and hide behind bushes until the dogs sniff them out.'

'Aww, babe, that's terrible. But you know the stuff they're saying isn't true. Your Rory's not like that. I mean, it's like all that bollocks they printed about you and Xander, that wasn't true was it?' Lottie shook her head. 'Rory loves you to bits, you do know that? I hope you told them to stuff off.'

Lottie nodded, biting on her wobbly bottom lip to try and get a grip. She was overreacting, being stupid. But she was beginning to build up quite an impressive drawer of newspaper clippings. The fire, her and Xander, Rory and Pandora.

'He'd never go off with her, doll. She is such a cow, so full of shit,' Sam giggled, 'I gave her a card for a colonic irrigation offer. Not that it'll cure her.'

'Sam! You didn't?' Lottie had never heard Sam say a bad word about anybody, and she didn't know whether to laugh or cry.

'I did. I have to admit,' she leant forward conspiratorially, 'I don't like her.' She straightened up. 'I gave her a subtle warning not to mess with us, but she probably didn't get it. I mean, I like people who go after what they want, but she was all over Rory, completely out of order she was,' she cast Lottie a worried glance, 'and it's not right, is it?'

It's not right, no, thought Lottie. What if Rory had got fed up of her? All they did these days was argue, then they did make up, but she could tell he wasn't happy.

'Is there something you're not telling me?' Lottie had known

Sam for a few years now, and her reaction just seemed slightly over the top – even for her. Or she was being paranoid?

'Well, babe, I have to admit, I did know. Not about our vicar's letter, but somebody already told me that they had some photo. You know that Andy who came here? He's okay really, and I was so cross about it. You're my friend, and I stick up for my own. Not that you've got anything to worry about with Rory. He's a doll. I told Andy that, said to him I'd try and get him something juicy if he didn't put anything in the papers about Rory and Pandora, but he said it wasn't up to him. He said if he didn't run it and everybody else did then he'd look a dick. Anyhow I don't think he'll make a big thing about her being in his arms, he said he'd go on about Rory being a hero, you know, say that he saved the star of the show. I gave him some quotes and stuff.'

'Quotes?'

'Well yeah, the kind of stuff Rory and you would say. I didn't think you'd mind? Come on, let's go and keep an eye on the silly cow. If she thinks she can mess with me she's got another thing coming.'

'I suppose I've got half an hour to spare, then I need to straighten the muck heap.'

'Ooh you've got such a glamorous lifestyle.' Sam giggled.

'Just let me put Gold out, then I'll follow you up.'

'Okee doke, babe. I'm going to see if I can persuade Rory to come too and we can drape ourselves all over him and wind her up.'

Chapter 20

By the time Lottie left the yard and was heading towards the film crew, with straw in her hair and muck on her boots, it was the immaculately made-up Pandora who had draped herself over Rory.

'I wanted to say thank you, you saved my life, literally.' Her words, buffeted by the strong wind, carried clearly to Lottie. 'You're my hero.' Lottie knew she should rush over and leap between them, but she felt such a mess. How could she compete with that?

Pandora gave Rory a winning smile and moved in for a kiss. Unluckily for her, Sam got there first. Throwing her arms round the bemused Rory she gave him a smacker right on his lips and a bear hug that made Pandora cringe. 'You're everybody's hero, aren't you, Rory?'

Pandora's eyes narrowed as she stiffened and glared at Sam. 'Oh, we'll catch up later, darling, shall we? I've got to find some way of showing my gratitude.' And blowing him a kiss she stalked off towards the waiting crew, taking her bad temper out on the man she knew would always stand by her.

* * *

'This is ridiculous, Seb. I cannot shoot in this, it's ruining my hair.' Pandora batted one of the sound engineers, who had nearly taken her eye out with a wind-blown boom, out of the way.

'Nonsense. It's very Wuthering Heights, it'll heighten the atmosphere.' Seb, his mind busy with working out angle shots, blanked out her protests and concentrated on the job in hand.

He had originally envisaged this scene taking place on a beautiful, calm, sunny morning, but the change in the weather added a whole new element. White clouds were chasing each other across the glorious blue sky, but behind Tipping House a gloomy mass was building, creeping over the horizon – an advancing army full of murderous intent. Impending doom. It was perfect.

'Into your places everybody. I want to shoot this before the weather changes. If it brightens up or starts to piss it down then we're knackered. Where the fuck is Dan?'

Right on cue, Dan, the main love interest in the film, opened his trailer door and paused theatrically.

'Oh my God, look at him.' Sam forgot all about draping herself over Rory and grabbed Lottie's arm. 'It's him, look, Lottie,' she pointed wildly in the direction of the actor, who, aware that he now had an audience, was sauntering over towards Seb, the wind tugging at his dark curls so that his high cheekbones were shown off to perfection. 'It's him. Look, he's even more gorgeous in the flesh than on the telly.'

'Who?' Lottie squinted and wondered if she'd got her contact lenses in the wrong eyes again.

'It's that Poldark bloke.' Her voice dropped with disappointment. 'He's not quite as tall as I thought he'd be, though.'

'I thought he was dead.' Rory folded his arms and wondered what all the fuss was about. 'My mum used to watch him.'

'No.' Sam giggled. 'This is the new Poldark.'

'Oh. I've just got to run over to your dad's to borrow some electric tape, Lots, then I'm going down to the gallops after that. Fancy coming?'

'Oh yes.' Lottie smiled at him, the first genuine smile for days. She felt slightly better now that Sam had thwarted Pandora's snogging intentions, and assured her that the newspaper reports would be slanted towards '*hero*' not '*lover*'.

'Please.' As his lips met hers, Sam grabbed Lottie's arm.

'What's his name? You know. Ooh he is such a dish even if he's a bit different to what I expected.'

Lottie shook her head. 'I'm pretty sure Seb's budget doesn't run to hiring stars like Aidan Turner. Shame really, but there again, would he want to be in something like this?' She felt like adding '*and with Pandora*', but that would be mean, so she didn't.

'Oh, you're probably right, babe. His hair doesn't look quite right either, now you mention it. He does look a lot like him, though, doesn't he?'

'I won't be more than an hour at Billy's.' Rory wasn't interested in ogling the stars.

'I could come with you now?' Lottie had a sudden urge to start following her husband around like Tilly the terrier did.

He grinned. 'You stay and keep an eye on things, gorgeous. Check Pandora doesn't start snooping again.' He winked, then squeezed her bum. 'Won't be long.'

'Can I come, can I come Worwy?' Roxy, who had been sitting quietly on the grass trying to plait Scruffy's tail, jumped up at the first sign of movement.

'Sure. Is that okay, Sam? We won't be long.' And he had swung her up onto his shoulders and was galloping across the grass, Tilly at his heels barking, almost before Sam had answered.

'Somebody shut that fucking animal up, I need quiet.' Seb sat down in his seat, his ankle resting on his knee, fingers steepled in front of pursed lips, and waited for silence. His wife, her arms crossed, glared at him. 'Brilliant, Pandora. That's the perfect mood I wanted you to capture. Ready for an argument about being bored, and why you should join in with the country sports. We've got a brief love scene, then switch back to that, and let it all out when your husband rolls up. Should come naturally to you.'

Pandora's co-star, who she detested because he always did his best to steal the limelight, sauntered into position and peered over his dark glasses at her breasts.

Pandora, and at her insistence Seb, had followed Sam's advice and she was dressed in the most expensive polo gear money could buy. Next to her, the man who was supposed to be the genuine article wore a well-washed polo shirt, stained polo whites, and brown boots. He pushed his sunglasses back up his nose into place.

'Nice of you to join us, Dan,' Pandora said waspishly.

He grinned. 'Now I know I'm irresistible, but no tongues this time, eh?'

Lottie was just beginning to think she should head back to the stables when Seb called for quiet. Sam smiled and linked arms with her, then whispered. 'I wonder if he'll take his shirt off, like Poldark does?'

If Pandora disliked Dan, her love interest in the film, it was nothing compared to the distaste she felt towards her other leading man – the rock star.

Despite her pleading, Seb had not let her have any say in the casting of the other parts. The actor he'd chosen to play Pandora's husband was as down to earth as they came. He swore, drank copiously, smoked roll-ups continuously (and the sweet smell told Seb there were definitely added ingredients in the tobacco) and sported some vivid tattoos that spoke of a close affinity with the devil. And that was all before he got into character.

A heated argument with him required no acting at all on Pandora's part, although Seb just hoped she was professional enough to remember her lines and not slap him across the face, as she had done once in the studio.

'Action.'

Pandora looked up at Dan through her eyelashes, her hand resting on the horse's reins millimetres from his. 'Thanks for the lesson, it was incredible.'

'You're a natural rider.'

'It makes me feel alive again. I was so bored until I met you.'

'A woman like you needs a challenge.'

'Are you offering?'

'A few chukkas on a Friday afternoon?' He raised an eyebrow, his wicked grin suggesting a different kind of horseplay.

He reached out, took her other hand in his, and turned it slowly over.

Sam's grip on Lottie's arm tightened, despite the fact that this was the third take and she knew exactly what was coming next. The first time the horse had barged between them, the second time it had snorted at the critical moment, showering them with spittle, and this time Seb said if it didn't stand still it was going to be canned dogmeat and they'd manage without it.

With agonising deliberation Dan lifted her hand, dipped his head, and pressed his lips against the soft flesh, and it wasn't just Pandora that trembled.

Sam muffled her little squeal with her hand then hissed into Lottie's ear, 'Have you seen the way his buttocks tighten? They're like two rock cakes.' Which left Lottie fighting for control over a threatening fit of giggles.

Dan looked up, straight into Pandora's eyes.

'My God, have you seen his hard-on?'

'Shut up, Sam.' Lottie couldn't take much more. Any minute now she'd have to crawl away.

'I was thinking, maybe we could,' Pandora reached up, resting her hand lightly on his chest, 'have some private lessons.'

'One on one?'

'Something like that.'

'We could start right now.' His hand was on her buttock, and she'd been dragged against his startling erection before she had a chance to react. Lottie stifled a giggle, certain from the fleeting stiffening of Pandora's body that his actions hadn't been in the script. A second later and he was crushing her mouth with his, strong fingers entangled in her windblown hair, giving her no chance to object.

Sam and Lottie were looking at each other with barely contained glee, but being very careful not to make a sound, when the roar of an engine announced a new arrival on the scene.

At the sound of the approaching car Dan released his vice-like grip and Pandora drew back. She glanced at the black convertible that screeched to a halt just inches away from them, sending a flurry of gravel over the grass.

The rock star flung his door open and leapt out, muscles bulging so that the snake tattoo seemed to writhe in the sunlight. The horse took a nervous step backwards.

'I didn't think you were due back until tomorrow.' Pandora's voice had a distinct tremble, and the watching crowd were fairly sure it was a reaction to Dan's assault rather than spectacular acting.

'Thought I'd surprise you, and a bloody good job too. What are you doing? Making me look a twat?'

'I'm not—'

'I've heard all about you shagging your way through the fucking county.'

Pandora drew herself up. 'And what about you and those groupies? You shag your way round the whole bloody country let alone one county. What do they call you, "dicks on tour"?'

He gave a smug grin. 'I'm expected to behave like that, you're not, you slag. You're my wife and you better fucking remember it. Well I've decided, we're selling this place and going back where we belong. They're hammering a fucking for sale sign up at the bottom of the drive right now.'

Pandora glared. 'But that's not what we agreed.' Her voice went up a tone. 'I belong here. I'm not going anywhere.'

'No, you don't you stupid cow. You're not like this wanker.' He gestured at Dan. 'You said you were bored when we first came here. You were the one who said you wanted to go back.'

'I *was* bored, but I did something about it, didn't I? Like you told me to do. I made a life for myself, didn't I? Found some interests. What am I supposed to do? Sit on my arse twiddling my thumbs while you're bonking your way from Bristol to Barbados.'

'Interests, my arse. You're mine. You do as I say. Who the fuck do you think pays for all this?' He moved closer, leaning over menacingly as he jabbed at her chest, which Dan had wisely vacated. Sam and Lottie watched, transfixed.

Pandora's voice dropped to a wheedle. 'But I like it here now, Spike, please. I love this place. I've found things to do. I belong. I've never belonged anywhere before.' She tugged gently at his t-shirt.

'We can rent this place out, then, for now, buy somewhere else and then decide.'

'I don't want to rent it out.'

'Well I do and what I say goes.'

Pandora pulled back. 'Not any more. I want it. It's mine.'

'No it fucking ain't.'

'I'm going to have it with or without you. Can't you see, you numbskull, this is all I ever wanted? I'm a lady now, people respect me here.'

'Respect you?' He laughed, a loud, harsh sound. 'You think they fucking respect you? You're a whore. You don't belong here any more than I do.'

'I do. People like me. I've got friends.'

'Fuck buddies more like.' He laughed in Dan's face. 'He's only here cos you're paying him, aren't you, mate? You belong with me, and you're packing and coming on tour. Like old times. Stuff this living in the country. I thought it would be a laugh but it's like living in a graveyard. We might as well be dead.'

'Fuck you and your tour. The old times were shit. You're past it. Can't you see that? I want to move on, do something different and I've found what I want here. Look at him,' she gestured towards Dan, 'he's a proper man, he's not let himself go.'

'Bollocks. We're moving, whether you like it or not. You can either pack your case yourself or we'll go without it.'

'No.' Pandora folded her arms. Her near-hysterical shout dropped to a deadly quiet tone. 'I'm not coming, Spike. This is my dream place. I've discovered who I really want to be, and it's not some wife sitting on a tour bus. I love it here.' She looked at 'Spike' with a steady, clear stare. 'I want this place and I'm not going to let you take it away from me. It's mine. Do you hear me? It's mine.'

With a huff, the rock star wheeled around and got back in his car, revving up the engine before tearing down the drive.

Lottie, watching, felt a sudden shiver. Pandora meant it. She wasn't acting. There was a real conviction in her voice, her body language. Every pore screamed out her desire and determination. She didn't just want Rory, she wanted this place too. It was obviously no coincidence that they'd come here. It was all Pandora's doing.

But what had come first, her desire to have Tipping House or Rory Steel?

Elizabeth appeared at the top of the steps, her Labrador at her side. 'Very melodramatic. I do hope you're going to tidy the gravel off the front lawn. It plays havoc with the mower.'

The tension was broken and Seb shouted 'cut' irritably.

Everybody relaxed, apart from Lottie. And when she glanced at Pandora, the other girl stared straight back, the smallest of smiles curling her lip.

'I better go and find Rory. Are you coming, Sam?'

Chapter 21

Running an eventing yard meant that there was no such thing as a day off. The horses still needed feeding, mucking out, and exercising and it had never occurred to Lottie to want anything different.

Lottie had been brought up surrounded by horses. She had a father who was a successful show-jumper, her Uncle Dom competed in dressage, and, despite a brief break to 'find herself', working with horses had always been part and parcel of Lottie's life.

Today though, she was glad that Sundays had always, on non-competition days, been designated a lighter day.

She felt frazzled.

She had never expected that letting the film crew use Tipping House Estate would take up quite as much time, or emotional energy, as it had.

Lottie knew that it was partly her fault. Sam, who had been an occasional visitor, was now there nearly every day. Elizabeth had to take some of the blame for that. She'd bought little Roxy a pony and it was inevitable that it would be kept on the estate – after all, Sam's knowledge of horse care was roughly equivalent to Lottie's own knowledge of hair extensions and the latest must-have designer handbag. And she was more than happy to help her out.

She had to admit, though, she'd been less keen on Roxy when she'd been a baby. Babies cried and wriggled, and despite her utter confidence in handling new-born puppies or foals, the idea of taking care of a tiny, fragile human being that could easily be dropped and broken made her insides quake. She'd rather face jumping a six-foot hedge on a runaway horse. Now, though, Roxy was sturdier and mobile, and even Lottie had to admit she was rather fond of her – although little Alice was a thousand times easier to handle. Alice was calm water, Roxy was a hurricane. But a lovely hurricane, if a little destructive at times.

But it wasn't the pony care that ate into the time, it was the fact that she let Sam persuade her to go and watch the filming – when she'd normally grab half an hour and have some down time. She loved Sam, the bubbly girl never failed to see the bright side of any situation and Lottie had to admit that she was a bit of a life-saver on the days when she was convinced that Panda-gate would succeed and she'd be left homeless and husband-less, but she was still knackered.

And then there was Xander. He was often about, taking care of the two horses he had stabled on the yard, and she'd started to look forward to seeing him, and their little chats. Which meant that she'd then only have a fraction of the time she normally had to do all her other tasks, so Lottie was doing everything at a run to catch up.

Sam kept her spirits up, but Xander was calm, grounding, and reminded her more than a little bit of their old friend Mick.

She missed Mick. He'd always been there, and she hadn't realised how much she relied on him until he'd got back together with Niamh and more or less disappeared from their lives. He'd been her life-support system, there in the background in times of need.

It wasn't that Rory wasn't hugely supportive, he was. But he was constantly on the go and Lottie recognised that sometimes she needed a quiet, reassuring figure in the background. A big brother.

In an alarmingly short space of time, she'd moved into Tipping House, got married, her best friend Pip had moved to Australia, and Mick had set up home with the love of his life – and these days seemed to spend more time in Ireland than Cheshire.

All the bits of her life had been tossed in the air and fallen down in different places. Most of the time it was fine, but sometimes she felt like burying her head under the covers and telling the world to sod off.

They'd had three years of change, and now she couldn't imagine living any differently. She loved the estate and her husband with all her heart, but sometimes she felt like she wasn't doing either justice.

Rory had always been her dream man, and despite his initial reluctance to take on Tipping House, he'd stepped up to the challenge. And now she was letting him down. The one thing, only thing, he'd ever really asked of her (albeit in a very understated manner) she'd run away from.

He wanted to take that next step, he wanted to start a family, and Lottie was dodging the issue. She was petrified, but could she ever explain properly how she felt, when she barely understood it herself? But if she couldn't explain, then she was as good as pushing him into another woman's arms. And if it wasn't Pandora, there would always be somebody else waiting in the wings more than willing to have his babies.

Minty nudged her gently and snapped Lottie out of her daydreams. 'Sorry poppet.' She put the filly's head collar on and pushed the stable door open to find Rory standing there, holding two horses.

'Come on, slow coach, I'm starving. How about breakfast, then we go for a long hack? It's lovely and quiet now that lot have buggered off for the weekend.'

She grinned and felt the anxious churn in the pit of her stomach filter away. 'Sounds good to me. Crumbs, I'd forgotten just how nice and quiet it is to have the place to ourselves. Shame we can't just lock the gate and refuse to let them back in.'

'Not long to go now, according to Seb's spreadsheet. That man is worse than Dom when it comes to planning. He's a complete control freak.'

'I suppose you'd have to be, with people like Pandora around.'

They walked around to the paddock side by side, the horses following behind.

'That woman is a menace.' He said it with such feeling that Lottie glanced up at him.

'Sam texted earlier to let me know she was in the newspaper again,' and it had to be the dreaded swoon picture, 'and mentioned you. I bet they've twisted it into a *Runaway Bride* thing. I don't think I like Pandora.'

'Maybe she's misunderstood.' He laughed at the look on her face. 'Only kidding, honest, don't look at me like that.'

'Really?'

'Lottie I wouldn't go near that woman even if you paid me a fortune, I'm way too fond of my balls.' He grinned. 'And I've got you. Haven't I?'

'I just don't trust her.'

'I wouldn't trust her as far as I could throw her, Lots, but stop worrying, it'll be fine. What can she do?'

The idea of locking her out was sounding better by the second. 'I think it was her who arranged that stupid swooning picture Sam is talking about, which they rang me about.'

'What is the matter with her?' He unlatched the gate, then they released the horses and watched as they wheeled round, kicking their heels as they galloped to the far end of the paddock, before settling with their heads down to pick at the fresh grass.

Minty went down on her knees, then flopped to the side and rolled, rubbing her withers and rump into the soft green bed before getting to her feet and shaking the last of the shavings out of her coat.

'She fancies you.' He laughed, but she didn't. 'No, she really does. Maybe she's one of those people who thinks that if other people are saying it, then it'll come true. That's why she wanted it all over the papers.'

Rory draped one arm over her shoulders. 'She's potty.'

'What Pandora wants, Pandora gets. That's what somebody told me.' She shivered, a ghost walking over her grave.

'Well she's not getting me, is she?' He kissed the tip of her nose. 'I'm all yours, darling, whether you want me or not. Stop frowning.'

'I'm not frowning.'

'You are, you've gone all wrinkly. Come on,' he took her hand in his, 'we need a break from this place. Let's skip the hack, we'll go for a walk, have a pub lunch then slob out somewhere until feeding time. How does that sound? I'll get Tab to come and ride Rio, he's the only one that needs to go out today.'

'But it's her day off.' Another pang of guilt hit Lottie, not just the idea of asking Tab to work another day, but the fact that Rory only had one horse that needed to be exercised.

'She won't mind.'

'But it's not fair. She's been doing loads extra lately to help out, and it's my fault 'cos I've been spending too much time watching the filming.'

'Somebody's got to keep an eye on them.'

'They don't, not really.'

'They do, darling. We can't just ignore them and pretend they're not there. Somebody needs to stop the bolting horses,' Lottie tried not to cringe, 'and the snoopers. You're doing a great job.'

'You stopped the bolting horse.'

He squeezed her closer. 'I just happened to be there. You stopped the snooping.'

'But—'

'If it hadn't been for the fire, you'd be spending a lot of time on the weddings, wouldn't you?' He shrugged. 'So, it's the same thing. It's your business. Just don't spend all your time chatting to Xander. It's making Tab jealous and I need her to be happy.'

She glanced up.

'And it's making me jealous too.'

'There's nothing to be jealous of.'

'I know. Come on, last one back to the house makes the breakfast.'

'Rory.' She put out a hand to stop him racing off.

'Yep?'

'I had this letter yesterday from the solicitors.' She pulled it out of her pocket reluctantly. She'd rather have binned it, but Rory had to have a say. It was his future as well. 'After they rang about the court threats, I asked them to follow up some of the offers we'd had. I mean, not the developers. But—'

'You don't have to even consider this, Lottie.'

'We do. There's one offer still on the table,' she took a deep breath and handed the letter to him, 'this one. They won't consider just buying a part of the estate, they want it all, but they would consider letting us stay here on a long-term lease.'

'Oh, Lottie.' He took the letter. 'Let's give it a bit longer, we're not that desperate yet, are we?'

'Nearly.'

'Nearly isn't good enough.' He tore the sheet in half and smiled. 'Let's give it a few more weeks before we even consider that route, eh? Something will turn up.'

'That's what Sam keeps saying. I'm sorry about you losing the horses and David as your sponsor.'

'Hey, stop looking so serious, Lottie. I know you are. I'm sorry too, but something *will* turn up. I've got a few ideas.'

'But I should be helping you.'

'Lottie, you're here, you are helping me. You're my wife. That's all I need.' His lips met hers, a light touch that lingered for a moment, then he was off, shouting over his shoulder. 'Time for that later, gorgeous.'

Lottie and Rory had walked around half the estate, got caught in a spring shower that sent them giggling for cover under the trees and were just drying out as they sauntered down the road towards the Bull's Head when Rory's phone rang.

He ignored it.

Lottie had never understood how anybody could do that. If her phone so much as gave a little beep she wanted to know why. Rory, though, seemed oblivious to the jangling and vibrating in his pockets.

It stopped ringing. Then it started again. Then it stopped and started again.

'Who's that?'

'I don't know.' He rubbed his hands together in anticipation. 'Don't know about you but I'm dying for a pint. I've worked up quite a thirst. If your dad's in there remind me to ask if I can borrow the leveller, the school's looking like the big dipper.'

'He said he's not lending you anything else until you give something back.'

'Like what?'

'Dunno. I'm sure he's got a list. Are you really not going to answer that phone?'

'Really.'

'What if it's important?'

'You're the only person I want to talk to, grumpy.'

'I'm not grumpy.' Unable to fight her nosiness any longer, Lottie shoved a hand into Rory's pocket and fished out the mobile phone.

'Who's Robert Lyons?'

'Lyons? Are you sure?' Rory grabbed the phone. 'You know Rob, he sponsors Toby.'

Lottie's eyes widened. 'Roaring Rob? Wow, you don't think . . .'

'I'm not going to even think. I'll play it cool. Let's grab a pint then I'll ring him back.'

'Are you sure?' Lottie bit her bottom lip. If Rob Lyons was thinking about sponsoring Rory it would solve all their problems. Well, the horse-related ones. A stay of execution. 'Don't you think you should call him straight back?'

'And look desperate? No.' Rory was firm. 'If he wants me, then he'll be happy to wait half an hour.'

The trouble was, although Rory was determined to play it cool, he obviously wasn't as laid back about the whole thing as he pretended. They sat in the corner, staring at his mobile.

There were no more calls, no texts, just a stifling silence that left Lottie wriggling about in her seat.

'You need to call.' After ten minutes, Lottie couldn't stand it any longer. She really wasn't enjoying her drink and nor was Rory. They just kept glancing at each other like a pair of naughty kids, then back at the phone. She prodded it. 'He rang three times.'

'I'll call him in a minute.'

'What if he's ringing somebody else now, and that's why he's not sent a message or anything. Have you checked your voicemail?'

Rory had. But he checked again. 'I'll call him.' He paused. 'Shall I?'

'I think you should.'

'You two playing hooky?' Billy, still in his jodhpurs, boots, and spurs plonked himself down next to Lottie. 'That bloody mare will be the death of me. I need this. Cheers!'

'Cheers,' said Rory half-heartedly, still looking at the phone, undecided. He picked it up, then put it down again. He didn't want to appear over-keen, but if there was a chance, even the remotest chance, of a sponsorship then he didn't want to miss it.

'You expecting that thing to ring or explode, son?'

'Roaring Rob rang.'

'And we missed his call,' added Lottie.

'Bloody hell, that's quick work.' Billy bent down, undid his spurs, and dumped them on the table with a clatter.

'What do you mean, Dad?'

'Haven't you heard, love?' He looked from Lottie to Rory, then took a long swig of his beer while Lottie edged forward until she was perilously close to the edge of her seat. 'Toby had a tumble on the gallops. Horse went arse over tit and used him as a cushion to land on.'

'Really?' Lottie decided the way she'd said it sounded far too cheerful. Trading on another rider's fall wasn't nice at all, so she tried again. 'How awful, is he okay?'

'I'm sure he's been better, but he'll survive. Just a broken arm and bruises, as far as I know. Screwed up this season, though, the silly bugger.' He picked up the phone and tossed it at Rory. 'Phone him before somebody else does.'

'Back in a sec.' He kissed Lottie on the head and squeezed past, heading for the door.

Two minutes later he was back.

Lottie braced herself. 'He didn't answer? He's already . . .'

'You know Rob.'

Lottie did. Rob was a man who knew his own mind. He made decisions on the run, there was no messing around. He trusted his instincts. The Roaring Rob nickname had, of course, come partly from his surname, Lyons, but it suited him. He could be lovable, he could be explosive, and when he wanted something he went in for the kill with unerring accuracy.

'Oh well, never mind. There'll be others, darling.'

Rory couldn't keep a straight face any longer. He grinned then wrapped her in a bear hug. 'I need to get over there now and prove that I get on with the horse. If I do, then the ride's mine. He'll move him here tomorrow.'

'I'll give you a lift home if you want.' Billy had downed his drink and was on his feet. He knew how much this meant to Rory and Lottie.

* * *

'Sorry, darling.' Halfway into his breeches, Rory hopped around the bedroom and gave Lottie a hug. 'I know I promised you a day to ourselves.'

'Don't be daft.'

'You could have come with me, but I don't know what time I'll be back. It's a good hour each way and the horses need sorting.'

'I know.' She pulled him back closer and straightened the collar of his polo shirt. 'Ring me straight after, won't you? Before you head back.'

'Promise.'

Lottie waved him off, then headed back to the kitchen and sitting at the large oak table with a cup of coffee she grabbed the newspaper.

She couldn't miss the article that Sam had texted her about. 'Fifty Shades of Downton' screamed the headline, under which sat a photograph of Pandora looking beseechingly up at Rory, who appeared to be leaning in for a kiss. It was great that your husband looked dashing, but less brilliant when he appeared to be gazing longingly into another woman's eyes.

She couldn't help it. She had to read on. Apparently things were hotting up on the latest Seb Drakelow production, with his wife winning the hearts and bodies of the villagers as well as her leading men.

Lottie stared, tracing a finger around the image of her husband's face. Her finger started to tremble and that familiar lump of panic rose in her throat. This was what it was about. History repeating itself.

Billy had cast a large shadow over her teenage years as he rode for his country at the Olympics and came back triumphant with a medal. He'd been a joker, loved to party. Just like Rory did. And so he'd partied, and the reports had filled the newspapers.

He'd been a father who was never at home, but a laughing picture of him in the daily newspaper goaded her at breakfast every day. Sometimes he was on a horse, but more often he had a girl, or two, draped around him.

Gran had told her that he'd always been faithful to Alexa, her mum, and he'd always behaved after her death. He'd never played away. It was just how it was reported. Lottie believed her, Elizabeth never lied. But now it was Rory who was in the papers, and if that part of her life was on repeat, what if the other side was as well? If she had a baby, she could well do what her mother had done – abandon it. She wanted to be there for Rory, she wanted to give him the one thing he'd asked her for. But . . .

'Very dramatic.' Elizabeth had crept into the room and was peering over her shoulder at the picture. With a start Lottie curled her fingers into a ball. 'Come along, child, let us walk. It clears the head as well as the lungs. Bertie.' The black Labrador wagged his tail so that it whipped against Lottie's leg, then reluctantly followed Elizabeth out into the hall, his nails clicking on the wooden floor.

They were down the steps and halfway across the lawn before she linked her hand through Lottie's arm. 'I think we need to talk, don't you?'

'About Pandora and Rory?'

'Rory? Whatever has Rory got to do with this? I rather think you are following red herrings. I am talking about that young woman.'

'You were watching them film yesterday, weren't you?'

'I was.'

Lottie was feeling more miserable by the second. Her earlier elation about Rory's phone call was almost forgotten. Her balloon of hope had been pricked by the newspaper report, and then thoroughly deflated by the realisation that Gran had picked up the same message she had.

'She wasn't acting, was she? She really wants Tipping House.'

'It would seem that way, wouldn't it? There was a certain passion and determination in her words that I think exceeded her acting capability. Although how she intends to achieve that aim escapes me at present.'

Rory, thought Lottie. 'She wants to take Rory from me and then grab the estate when I can't manage without him.'

'You're being melodramatic, dear.' Elizabeth peered at her. 'Most out of character.' She sniffed. 'Even if young Rory was susceptible to her wiles, which I can assure you he isn't,' she looked down her nose at Lottie disapprovingly, 'you would be more than capable of carrying on.'

Lottie wasn't so sure, but knew that arguing the point was a waste of time. 'Gran, why did you say be careful of her the other day? Did you know she was after the house?'

'I don't know anything, Charlotte. Pure supposition.'

'And you said she'd been talking to that man who started the fire.'

'Allegedly started the fire,' Elizabeth smiled, throwing her words back at her from the last time they'd discussed it.

'You don't think? Oh my God she wouldn't try and burn the place down?'

'Don't be melodramatic, dear. I think no such thing, I was simply exploring avenues of thought that she may have been taking advantage of the situation.' She ground to a halt and patted Lottie's hand. 'Those children never really belonged anywhere, so sad. Maybe she saw you and thought if she had the same things you did, she'd be happy.'

'But you don't take somebody else's belongings like that, that's like children stealing toys.'

'And from what I remember, young Pandora wasn't above such behaviour.'

Lottie threw the stick that Bertie had dropped at her feet while she thought about it. If Pandora wanted this place as badly as she appeared to, and she was behind the decision to use it as a location, then maybe they couldn't put it past her. Maybe she'd had something to do with the fire.

'Am I being stupid, just getting carried away because I don't like her and . . .?'

'And?'

'She can't keep her hands off Rory.'

'That is purely play-acting, Charlotte. If you heed my advice, you will rise above it and ignore her. Nobody likes a show-off.' She sniffed. 'Most unbecoming in a young lady, behaviour like that.'

'But you don't think I'm mad? She *has* been talking to that groom from the wedding?' Lottie started walking again. It was always easier to think when she was on the move. 'Oh gosh, you don't think that's why we've had trouble with the insurance claim, do you? All that talk about arson, you don't think she gave them the idea that we'd do such a thing?'

'Well I wouldn't put it past her to use anything she could, but you are straying from the facts, Charlotte. Young Tabatha and James are trying to talk to this chap and,' she paused, 'his associates, to establish the connection. But I rather think he has been brainwashed into thinking she is something of a celebrity.' She tutted. 'Celebrity, my foot. But you, young lady,' she flicked at the grass with her stick, 'must be very careful about what you say. I think we have hit the headlines quite enough for now, don't you?'

Lottie frowned. She knew better than to accuse Pandora of anything in public, but Elizabeth thought there was something going on, she was suddenly sure of it.

'Maybe she's come back to finish the job and ruin us for good. Do you think she hates us that much?'

'Envies, not hates, Charlotte. Although the two emotions run

271

perilously closely together in some people. I think we should turn around and head back now, dear.'

Lottie looked at Elizabeth guiltily; she'd been walking faster and faster, too busy talking and not even thinking about her grandmother. Sometimes she forgot just how old her gran was. Her mind was as sharp as ever, but these days she moved more slowly. 'Sorry, shall we go slower?'

'I'm not an invalid, dear.' She looked at her granddaughter sharply. 'I rather think it is time for a G&T, though. Come along, you can pour me one while we are waiting for young Rory to come back. And no, I do not think she has come back to start another fire. Why would she do that if she desires Tipping House for herself?'

'So why talk to that man?'

'That is what you need to find out, Charlotte. But it would appear to me that Pandora is something of a collector. She collects affection and adulation in the same way that others collect stamps or medals – it affirms her belief that she is important, has achieved something worthwhile. She flattered young James, our Facebook friend, and of course your husband, dear. And maybe,' she gazed over at her home, Tipping House, 'she also wishes to collect property.'

'Well collecting other people's husbands really isn't on.'

'I agree.' She patted Lottie's hand. 'But I don't think that is her intention at all.'

'But you saw that report in the paper and the picture of her and Rory.'

She sighed. 'I rather think you are letting other worries about your relationship,' she stared pointedly, 'cloud your vision. You really should buy a better quality newspaper, Charlotte. Now do come along and stop moping.'

Chapter 22

Rory turned down the driveway that led to Folly Lake Equestrian Centre, home to his father-in-law, and found he couldn't wipe the grin off his face. Five minutes after shaking hands with Rob Lyons, he'd parked up in the nearest lay-by and rung Lottie.

'Get the bubbly in the fridge, darling.'

'Really? Really? Really?'

He laughed as Lottie repeated herself, each repetition of the word reaching a higher pitch until she squealed. 'You've done it? Really?' He could hear the dogs barking, which meant she was probably running around or jumping up and down.

'Really.' He laughed. 'That horse is amazing, so bloody clever. You should have seen him over the jumps. Used to a strong rider on the flat, or he takes the piss, but over the sticks he's a dream.'

'Oh Rory, that's fab, you're so clever. What about Toby?'

He did love how his wife could go from sheer delight to worrying about somebody else. It was Lottie all over. 'He's cool about it. He knows the score. The horse is too good to be stood in a stable all season.'

'So we've got him all season?'

'Well, between you and me, Rob said he seemed to go better for me, so if all goes well . . .'

'Oh wow, oh I can't believe it. Oh gosh, poor Toby, he'll be devastated, oh I hope he isn't too upset.'

'Probably as upset as I was when David boxed Simple Simon up,' Rory said drily. 'But that's what this game is like, isn't it? And,' he paused.

'Yes? What?' Lottie sounded even more impatient than normal.

'There might be another ride in the offing.'

'And a horsebox?'

Rory chuckled. 'Now who's being greedy? Of course there is. He can't have his horse turn up and not trumpet the fact to the world, can he? I reckon he'll interfere more than David, but he already likes you, so you can have the job of talking him round, darling.'

'He's a bit scary when he's cross.'

'And very nice when he's not. It'll be worth it, Lots.'

'I know.'

'Only one problem, the stables are full because of the polo ponies and he's sending the horse over tomorrow. I was trying to work out if a couple of ours can be turned out for the summer.'

'Well Rio doesn't like the flies and he gets bored, and Flash will just keep breaking fences, and Gold will eat non-stop and look like she's in foal even though she isn't.'

'I know.' He drummed his fingers on the steering wheel.

'I know! Go and talk to Dad. I'm sure he's got some room. And Uncle Dom turned a couple of his away this year so he had more time to look after Amanda.'

'Brilliant, oh you're so clever, Lottie, I do love you. I'll call in there on my way back, won't be long.'

Tiggy opened the door dressed in an outfit that made her look like a deranged gypsy. Her hair, a mass of auburn curls speckled with grey, was wilder than ever – despite having a red scarf (which clashed horribly) tied around it – and she had a splash of black paint on her nose. Her white smocked top was cut low enough to show her ample bosom, which already had a good dusting of sun-enhanced freckles dancing across it, and was spattered with blue paint, and it was hard to tell whether the flowing multi-coloured skirt had started off that way or not.

Her hazel eyes widened at the sight of Rory.

'Oh my, we weren't expecting you, love. I was just in the middle of touching up his biceps. Wasn't I, love?' She shouted behind her to, Rory hoped, Billy. 'I've really got into my painting again. Come in, come in, I'll get the kettle on. Oh heavens, there isn't anything wrong is there? It's not one of the animals? Or Lottie?'

'No, no, no problem, well not really. Is Billy in?' Rory half expected him to emerge semi-naked, having been posing for one of his wife's artistic endeavours. But he was sitting at the kitchen table, well covered up by his riding gear.

'I take it Lyons was in a good mood, lad?'

'I've got the ride.'

'But?'

'We're short on looseboxes, because of the filming. I let Xander have the spare boxes. I could ask him to move his ponies, but . . .'

'Don't worry about that, easily sorted. Right, I reckon that calls for a celebration. Sit yourself down.'

'Oh isn't that lovely?' Tiggy gave Rory a hug. 'I'll get back to my naked man if that's alright with you, boys?'

Billy roared at the look on Rory's face. 'She's not got a man in the back room, have you, love?' He winked and she giggled.

'In my dreams, Billy boy, in my dreams.'

'Useful type of animal that.' Billy, without asking, poured Rory a generous measure of whisky. 'That big bay isn't it? Cheers.'

'Yep, Joker. He can certainly jump, and he's clever with it. To be honest, I would have been relieved to get any old nag, but he's amazing.'

'No good getting a bad 'un if it's got a keen owner, believe me. They're on your back all the time, and it's all down to you when they don't win. Expect bloody miracles some of them do. Only bonus is if they've got a soft wife who'll take your side. If they've not then the horse is either off to the hunt,' he gave a cut-throat gesture, 'or shifted to somebody else and the poor sod never gets to settle.' He topped up their glasses. 'Toby had a reasonable season with him last year, so they'll be expecting big things.'

'So am I.' Rory grinned. 'Toby has certainly got him fit – he doesn't half motor when you put your foot down.' He'd been impressed the moment they'd walked Joker out. He was a big rangy bay who'd looked a lightweight last year, but he'd filled out, matured, and he was dancing, as light as ballerina, the second his hooves hit the grass.

Built like a racing thoroughbred, it was his head that showed his mixed breeding. Kind, brown eyes, floppy lips and big ears, along with a broad, off-centre splash of white down the middle of his face that gave him an almost comical appearance. Joker was a horse to love and, Rory was convinced, he was just about to have a very good eventing season.

'Given Lottie the good news?'

'I rang her as soon as I left the yard. It seemed to cheer her up a bit,' he grinned, 'she's been a bit fed up – all this stress about the filming.'

'It's a lot to take on.'

'I just want to be able to take care of her.'

'I know, lad.' Billy sloshed some more whisky into the glasses and put his feet up on a spare chair. 'For better or worse, and all that.'

Rory, who hadn't planned to have a heart-to-heart with Billy suddenly found he needed to. Whisky on an empty stomach had the dangerous side effect of loosening his tongue. 'If I can get some money coming in, then she can stop worrying so much, and once the repair works are done to the house she can start up her business again.'

'It's bloody difficult when you've got horses, but all we can do is our best for them.'

'We can settle down then and start a family.'

'Best thing me and Alexa ever did.' Billy stared across the room into the empty fireplace. 'She was a lovely little thing, our Lottie. Alexa would do anything for her.' He sighed.

'Was she keen to have a family?'

'Alexa?' Billy shook his head. 'No, we were having far too much fun, wild she was. Beautiful, but wild. We were only kids ourselves, really, when we had Lottie and it didn't half turn our life on its head. We were having a ball here, at Folly Lake. I had some useful horses and was starting to do okay and we worked together. She made it all a game, right giggler she was, always playing pranks. I never thought anything would change, never expected something like her getting pregnant. We both had a shock.'

'It was a mistake?'

'Hang on, don't put words in my mouth. I've never said Lottie was a mistake, let's just say she was a bit ahead of schedule shall we?'

'And you stopped doing stuff together, you and her mum?' Rory hadn't thought about it like that before, and now imagining a life without Lottie by his side made him think twice. Maybe it would change her, maybe she was right and they'd got plenty of time before they made the leap into parenthood.

'No, no, it wasn't like that. It was Elizabeth. As soon as the old dragon found out Alexa was expecting, it changed everything. She was in there like a bloody terrier. Couldn't shake her off, we couldn't.'

'You reckon she'd bother us? Although, to be honest, she's always got an eye on us anyway, she'd probably know before we did if Lottie *did* get pregnant.'

Billy chuckled. 'You're not wrong there, lad, and she'd have it announced in the papers.' He waved a hand at an imaginary headline. 'Rory Steel finally proves his manhood.'

'Don't joke, I wouldn't put it past her.'

'Who's joking? No, it's different with you. She just wanted us moved up to Tipping House, where she could keep an eye on us, make sure any baby was raised in a manner befitting a Stanthorpe. She wasn't too keen on me back then. I wasn't quite what she had in mind as a suitor, but we get on fine now. We've had our ups and downs, but doesn't everybody?'

'But Alexa didn't mind it when she had Lottie? She loved her?'

'Did she 'eck as mind. She loved that baby from the moment she was born. I can never forget how she was, gazing down at the bundle in her arms when I walked in.'

'You weren't there when she had her, then?'

'Missed it. Bloody traffic. I was out competing when I found out. Dropped everything, left the groom to sort the horses and headed home. That's horses for you. Elizabeth had rung a couple of hours earlier, hopping mad she was that I wasn't there, but nobody had told me because they didn't want me to cock up my round, silly bastards, then what with the M6 being like it is, by the time I got there it was all over.'

'I don't think Lottie's that keen on having kids of our own.'

'You can't blame her, can you? She never was one to play with dolls.' He laughed. 'The other kids were feeding babies and Lottie was feeding foals and puppies. Whole bedroom was filled with cuddly stuff. If you'd not known us you'd never have guessed that we had plenty of the real thing right outside the door.'

'Maybe she'll never want them. It wasn't exactly something we discussed before we got married. It never occurred to me.' It was Rory this time who stared out of the window, unseeing. 'And now she doesn't think it's the right time, with all the work, the horses, and money stuff.'

'There's never a right time, and I'm not the only one that will tell you that. And it alters your life, even if you're determined to carry on as before. No arguing the fact, a baby's one thing, but when they get moving . . .'

'Like Roxy.'

'She'll give them the right run-around when she gets older, that one.'

'I feel like I don't know what Lottie really thinks about having kids. I thought she loved being with Alice and Roxy.'

'Loving the little blighters is one thing, having one of your own's a bit different. Give her time, there's no way of working out what's in a woman's head, Rory.'

'I just, well lately, what with Xander back and everything going on, I wonder if maybe she's not convinced that things are good enough between us.'

'Bollocks, you're talking like a girl now. I know my Lottie and she wouldn't have walked up that aisle with you if she wasn't sure.'

'People can change.'

'That girl knows her own mind. If she doesn't want kids, then there's a reason, and I'm damned sure it isn't you. Childhood lovers, my arse, don't know what they were thinking when they printed that about her and Xander in the papers. I remember that lad and Lottie didn't have any time for him, only the once there was when she let him ride that mad pony of hers and she was bloody ashamed of herself afterwards. I would have grounded her but it wouldn't have served a purpose. Drink up, you're slacking.' The whisky bottle was poised and so Rory drained his glass and watched the amber liquid slosh in.

'She probably thinks kids will just tie her down. I mean, look at how she went off to Australia and then Spain.'

'And look how she came back. That was ages ago, Rory. She was a kid.'

'She was bored of being here, maybe she still is. She loves watching the film crew – damned sight more exciting than mucking out stables aren't they? They've even asked her to be in some scenes.'

'They asked me too.' Billy grinned, looking pleased with

himself. 'And not just that cameo, bloody ride-by nonsense. Obviously after a decent-looking man.' He guffawed.

'Oh Christ, not you too? Is everybody in this bloody film? Even my terrier got a run-on part. Oh bugger, I forgot all about Tilly.' Rory suddenly remembered he'd left his terrier in the car. He'd only expected to be dropping in for a five-minute chat with Billy, and if he'd let her join them she would have caused havoc with Tiggy's spaniels.

'She'll be fine. Hang on a minute, though, lad,' Billy leant forward, forearms on the table, 'they might be a pain in the arse, that film crew, but if we didn't have them you'd be in a right financial mess. You'd do well to think on that.'

'You don't think she'll run off to be a film star?' Rory was feeling more morose by the minute, his earlier exhilaration about his new sponsor a distant memory.

'Don't talk daft. She's as happy as I've ever seen her, but maybe she's got a bit too much on her plate at the moment.'

'So you think I should just drop it, not mention a family again?'

'I didn't say that. But it's not my decision is it, lad? Up to the pair of you. You'll know when the time's right and you won't be asking an old codger like me. Will he, love?' Tiggy had come into the room with even more splodges of paint than before on her face.

'What's that, darling?' Tiggy plonked herself on his knee and wrapped her arms around his neck.

'Him.' Billy nodded at Rory. 'Getting broody, the silly bugger.'

'That's nice, love.' She smiled as though babies were an everyday occurrence, which Rory supposed they were. Just not for him. 'Don't ask me to knit anything, though. I can't handle those needles. Drop more stitches than I knit and it makes me go all cross-eyed.'

'He says Lottie isn't keen. Can't blame her, can you?'

'Aww never mind, pet. She'll make her mind up one way or the other.' She patted his hand. 'You're looking a bit peaky, love.'

She stared at Rory, then at the half-empty bottle on the table, then at Billy. 'Oh dear, I think we'd better get you a sandwich before we call Lottie, don't you?' She was up and slathering a generous layer of butter on two slices of bread before he could object.

Rory nodded, then wished he hadn't when the whole room tipped. He closed his eyes and re-opened them. Billy was sitting, glass in hand, watching him.

'I think you better drop him off, Tigs.'

'No!' Rory, who had been feeling decidedly light-headed felt much better after only one bite of the sandwich. Even full of whisky, though, the thought of being in a car with Tiggy behind the steering wheel was alarming. 'I'll walk.'

'Oh nonsense, love. It's no bother and Lottie will be worried, won't she? Eat up, I've got a nice slice of cake you can have when you've finished that.'

Rory looked at her warily. Tiggy might be well meaning, but she was also very scatty. Most of her attempts at home baking ended up cremated, as she tended to wander off and forget all about them until smoke started pouring out of the oven. The remainder often had a strange aftertaste, due to her habit of shaking packets without really checking what was in them properly first (or their use-by date). Her other little trick was to substitute 'similar' items when she discovered that she hadn't got one of the ingredients. Carrot cake and parsnip cake were not the same thing at all, Billy had discovered. And nobody had ever worked out how gravy granules got into the scones. The only explanation that Tiggy could come up with was that they were next to the baking powder in the cupboard, and she had been rather engrossed in reading Jilly Cooper's *Riders* at the time on her Kindle. She blamed Rupert Campbell-Black. If she hadn't been preoccupied with his exploits things might have been different.

'It's all right, love, I got a lovely sponge from Waitrose.' She beamed, not at all bothered about her reputation for creating culinary disaster. 'I haven't got time for baking at the moment, what with all my painting.'

Billy winked at Rory. 'Good thing, eh?'

'Ooh you cheeky thing, Billy Brinkley. If I didn't have to take young Rory home I'd be sorting you out.'

'Promises, promises, love. The night is young.'

Tiggy patted Rory's hand. 'If you ask me, love, it all comes down to love and trust. You trusted her enough to fall in love with her. Now do you love her enough to trust everything she says is for a good reason?'

The words swam around in Rory's head like two goldfish chasing each other in a snow globe. He felt queasy. 'I think you'd better write that down.'

'Come on, pet, let's get you home.'

* * *

The cough of a vehicle approaching up the driveway had Lottie leaping to her feet in relief. She dashed out, only to see her father's old Landrover making its way laboriously towards her, with Tiggy crouched over the steering wheel, peering short-sightedly in her direction. There was a loud crunch and grating of gears as they rounded the final bend and they shuddered to a halt at the bottom of the steps, only to lurch forward when Tiggy forgot to take it out of gear.

'Oh my God, is everything all right?'

Rory was slumped in the front seat, sandwiched between Billy and Tiggy, looking extremely pale, with a green tinge.

'Nothing that a good night's sleep won't fix. It'll take more than that to sort out Tig's driving, though, won't it love?'

Tiggy giggled, clambered out of the car, and went round to the passenger seat to watch Billy try and unload Rory. Tilly tumbled out after him, yapping with delight at being home, and the other terriers came running down the steps with Harry following on behind. 'You all right, lovey?' She hugged Lottie. 'They've just had a bit of a celebration. Isn't it lovely news? I think Billy got a bit carried away. He's a right one your dad, isn't he?'

'Dad!'

'Don't look at me like that. He's a big boy now, perfectly capable of deciding how much he can drink. Aren't you, lad? I'll expect you at eight in the morning, shall I, with whatever horse you want to leave with us? Gives you plenty of time to get sorted, then, before Joker arrives. And make sure you bring one that doesn't break fences.' Billy propped Rory against the front door and kissed Lottie on the cheek.

'Thanks, Dad.'

'How can your dad drink so much?' Rory, who could normally keep up with the best, looked decidedly wobbly as he wandered inside. 'Probably a mistake to start on the hard stuff when I've not eaten all day.'

'You've not eaten at all?'

'Well, Tiggy just gave me a sandwich.'

'What was in it?' It was no wonder Rory looked queasy. Lottie had been the recipient of many of Tiggy's strange offerings.

'Hard to tell. Lots of butter and something pink.'

Lottie giggled. 'So it wasn't dog food this time?'

'I am never ever going to eat one of her tuna sandwiches again. Come here and give me a hug and tell me how wonderful I am.'

She wrapped her arms around him and nestled against the hard, broad chest, breathing in the familiar smell she loved so much, along with a fair few whisky fumes. 'You're wonderful, Rory Steel. I'm so pleased Rob liked you.'

'I'm pleased the horse liked me. It never put a foot wrong. Now all we need to do is get rid of insufferable Seb and posh Panda and everything will be fine again.' He nuzzled her hair and it sent a rush of goose bumps down her arms. 'Do you still love me, Lottie?'

'Course I do.' She looked up into his eyes. 'I think I love you a bit more every day, if that's possible.'

'If you get bored, you will tell me?'

'I'm not going to get bored.'

'But if you do.' He put a finger under her chin, made sure she was looking straight into his eyes and she was surprised to see just how earnest his gaze was. 'I need to know you'll tell me.'

'I promise, Rory. If I'm ever the teeniest bit bored I'll tell you. Will you do the same?'

'Course I will. I think I need to go to bed. I love to trust you, Lottie, or is that trust to love . . . dunno, must check.'

* * *

The sun was casting a soft glow when Lottie staggered out to the stables at 6am, still half asleep. The lawn, still damp, cushioned each step, flooding her senses with the scent of earth and new grass, and the cold-edged air made her shiver with anticipation.

She decided she'd take such a glorious spring morning as a good omen. Rory had a new sponsor, he absolutely did love her, and everything else just had to start going their way soon. Together they'd make sure it did. 'Together', that was the word she had to concentrate on because that, when Rory was rambling on in a drunken stupor about love and trust, was what it was all about.

'Morning, gorgeous.' Rory showed no signs of wear and tear from his afternoon drinking with Billy and already had the horses fed and turned out. With his sweatshirt tossed over the stable door he was grooming one of the youngsters that they'd recently started groundwork with in his short sleeves.

'You're taking Maddie over to Dad's, then?' Lottie patted the filly's neck and she turned round, nuzzling her pocket for treats.

'Thought she was probably the best one to move. It's just as easy for Tab to pop down there and work her as it is for her to do it here, and his school is better than ours.'

Lottie straightened the horse's forelock. She was a lovely horse, but not as sharp as most on the yard and was amenable to most things. In fact, Lottie would be shocked if she didn't prove as easy to back as she had to get working well on long reins. They seldom, if ever, took on horses to back for other people, but this was for a friend. He'd bought the horse for his daughter and wanted to be sure that whoever backed it did a thorough job and was honest enough to warn him if anything was wrong. So far, Maddie hadn't put a foot wrong and was the darling of the yard.

'True, and it'll be better for them to come and see her working down there as well.'

'I thought I'd walk her down. She's sensible enough and it's not far. Save getting the trailer out.'

'Can I come?'

'I was hoping you'd say that.' The grin he shot her made her insides wobble, and reminded her just how little time they spent together sometimes. 'Tab is going to finish off here, then she's off filming.' He rolled his eyes and Lottie laughed.

'Rather her than me. Ready?'

Tab came back from turning out one of the horses just as Rory untied the lead rope. She watched Rory and Lottie chatting, their heads together, dark curls intermingled, body language mirroring each other.

When she'd arrived in Tippermere as a grumpy goth teenager she'd alternated between hating Lottie and wanting to be her when she grew up. With Rory. Now she didn't exactly want to *be* her, but she did want the type of life she had.

She knew Lottie worked hard, but she always seemed happy. She had friends who wanted to help out, a gorgeous place, and wonderful horses. It was hard not to feel at least a tiny twinge of jealousy. Above all, she had a man who always stood by her. They were a team. And Tab had never felt part of a team.

Tab sighed. She'd had high hopes of getting somewhere with

Xander, but he just seemed to shut people out – everybody, including Lottie, most of the time. He was like a cat – he'd let people near only on his terms, when it suited him. And even then it was perfunctory. It wasn't that he wasn't nice, he just wasn't *there*.

'We won't be long, Tab. What time are you going over to the set?'

She shrugged. 'Dunno. Soon as I've finished here. Xander wants me to dog-sit, then I think I'm supposed to ride in a scene. If Pandora will let me.' She ended on a sarcastic note and Lottie giggled.

It wasn't that Tab minded looking after Ella for Xander, but she'd rather hoped that it would help form some kind of connection between them. So far, he'd just politely thanked her and told her how much Ella loved her. Much as she loved Ella back, she'd rather her owner felt some kind of attraction for her too. Puppy love was so overrated.

The little procession marched out through the archway, Lottie and Rory, the filly between them. The terriers streamed ahead, noses down, taking in the exciting morning scents. And Harry lolloped alongside, next to Lottie.

The filly paused and raised her head, nickering a goodbye to her friend Minty, and Rory let her settle before they walked on.

Minty, realising that her pal was actually leaving the yard for the first time since she'd arrived, started to kick her box door in protest. 'Hang on you daft thing, I'm coming,' and Tab headed back to reassure her with carrots and mints that the world wasn't about to end.

By the time she'd settled Minty, skipped out the remaining boxes and filled the hay nets for later, Tab was running late. She'd really hoped she'd have enough time to wash her hair and touch up her make-up, but even changing into her smartest jodhpurs took up precious minutes she didn't have.

'Bugger.'

Pandora would be immaculately made up and looking down her long snooty nose at her again. She scrubbed at the dirty mark on her cheek and searched through the drawers for a comb. Maybe she should grow her fringe another inch, then it would go over her eyes and all she'd have to worry about was lip gloss. Although she would look a bit like a mad yeti, so maybe not. Xander would normally have his pick of the posh groupies at polo matches, so yeti probably didn't cut it. Unless he wanted a change.

That was funny as well. Try as she might to strike up a conversation about his polo-playing days he refused to join in. If anything, he got even more monosyllabic. The only thing he would talk about was his dog and his horses. Which was fine, up to a point. But it didn't help her towards a meaningful relationship.

She pouted at her image in the mirror to see if it helped turn her into a seductress, but it just made her look like she'd got something in her eye. Catching sight of the clock reflected in the mirror she spun round to double-check what it said. 'Hell.' If she didn't get a move on, Xander would have let the wardrobe girl, who was always cooing over him, look after Ella instead.

Chapter 23

'Oh do stop mooning over that girl and do something useful.'

Jamie, who had been watching Tab, hadn't noticed Pandora creep up behind him. 'I'm not mooning.' She was hugging Ella to her and staring up at Xander like she wanted to eat him. She never looked at *him* like that.

'Yes you are. I've been watching you. You're like a love-sick puppy.'

'Rubbish.'

'You could roll over and ask her to tickle your tummy. Or,' she raised an eyebrow, 'have you already done that?'

He could tell her to sod off, but she'd realise she was getting to him then and be ten times worse.

'She is rather attractive,' Pandora tipped her head on one side and studied Tab more intently, 'if you like that type of thing. So getting her into bed didn't make her fall in love with you, didn't it? So painful, young love, or so I'm told.'

Jamie felt himself go the colour of a pickled beetroot. He still hadn't actually managed to even kiss Tab properly, let alone get her into bed, despite several nights out at the Bull's Head, and several evenings in with a laptop as per Elizabeth's orders. She flirted with him and seemed to enjoy his company, but bodily contact was practically zero. If he was honest, and he did try to be, she wasn't exactly the touchy-feely type. She hugged animals not humans. It was driving him nuts.

'You really do fancy her, don't you?' Pandora laughed, showing her teeth in an unattractive way, and stared at Jamie, which made it even worse. He decided he preferred her when she was being her normal miserable, bitchy self. 'Poor little lover boy.'

'I might as well be invisible.' He knew Pandora was the last person he should be saying it to, but he just needed to say something to somebody. Let it out of his system. Jamie was open and easy-going – he wasn't used to bottling things up.

'I'm sure if she gets frustrated enough by Xander she'll jump into your bed. Even girls get desperate for it.'

'Only you could say that.'

'Well it's true.'

'Thanks a lot.'

'Oh honestly, does it matter? I thought at your age men were supposed to be moral-free when it came to sex. Would you honestly say no if she fell into your bed because he didn't want her?' She obviously found it highly amusing.

Jamie had always known she was pretty heartless, but he'd thought the manipulative, scheming bitch label was a bit over the top. Until now.

'Anyway Xander has much bigger fish to fry, so don't worry about him. He won't look at her twice. You tell that girl to stop wasting her time on him. All he's interested in is somebody to look after that bloody dog of his. You don't think she'd like to keep it, do you?'

'What do you mean, bigger fish?'

'You're not telling me you haven't noticed the way he hangs around Lottie? He was always crazy about her, and I did put that down to sex when we were at school. She was so ungainly and a bit stupid.'

'Lottie isn't stupid, she's just a bit disorganised.'

'Oh honestly. Just look at how she's mismanaged this place.' She waved an arm to encompass the house and grounds. 'It's totally wasted on somebody like her. Everything inside is so tatty.'

'You're not supposed to go inside.'

'I just looked through the window. I'm sure that old witch can't have me arrested for that. She can't even afford to repair the damage. If we weren't here supporting her she'd be penniless. If you ask me, Lottie and Xander are actually quite well suited. They're both pathetic. I wouldn't blame Rory if he moved on.'

'She isn't pathetic – she's worked really hard to keep this place going.'

Pandora shrugged. 'If you say so.' She switched her focus from Lottie and her shortcomings back on to her brother Xander. 'Slightly obvious Xander insisting on stabling two horses on her yard, though, isn't it? I would have expected him to be cleverer than that. Men can be so unimaginative.'

'Lottie's married and Rory is really nice.'

'Oh I know he is.' There was the hint of a smile playing at the corners of Pandora's lips – she looked like she was scheming.

'They're happy together and I think they make a good team. Wasn't it rather obvious you fainting into his arms? You didn't exactly deny it in the papers.' Jamie wondered if he was overstepping the mark a bit and about to get sacked, but had he really got anything to lose? Pandora had used him, the same as she did everybody. When he outlived his usefulness she'd move on, whether he'd annoyed her or not.

All he could do once that happened was rely on the fact that he'd proved himself to Seb.

'Nonsense, it's all good publicity for the film.'

'So it's true what it said in the Sunday papers?'

'What exactly are we talking about now?'

'About you and Rory?'

Pandora gave a hollow laugh that didn't have one ounce of sincerity in it. 'They really do just jump on the obvious headline, don't they? What would I want with a grubby horse rider, however good a body he's got? He's obsessed with manure heaps and things that fart at one end and bite at the other. It's taken me years to establish what I want from Sebastian, why on earth would I start all over again?'

'Well Lottie won't take it if you are trying to cause trouble. They're happy together.' Jamie wasn't convinced by Pandora's protestations, in fact he wondered if even she could distinguish between when she was lying and when she was telling the truth. He'd heard rumours about the Drakelow's open marriage and he had no doubts that if she wanted an affair with another man, she'd have one.

'Of course they are. Just like that horsey girl is happy following Xander around with her tongue hanging out.'

'I better go and—'

'You are not going anywhere. Play hard to get for once. It seems to be working for Xander. Now run along and help somebody – that's what Seb pays you for.'

She really was evil, Jamie decided, as he stomped off to see what Seb's assistant wanted him to do next.

After an uneventful morning fetching coffee for the crew, interspersed with watching Tab and Ella hang on Xander's every word, Jamie had finally decided that the best course of action was to sit in the shade of one of the trailers and immerse himself in social networks – as instructed by Elizabeth.

He'd actually started to become quite fascinated by the lifestyles of his subjects when a sharp kick to his ankle brought him back to the more boring reality of his own.

Tab flopped onto the grass next to him. 'What are you doing?'

'Ouch, what did you do that for?'

'You were miles away.'

'I've been doing a bit of digging, like Elizabeth asked us to do. You seem too busy to do any.'

She grinned and kissed him on the cheek. 'Mr Grouch. I said I'd help Xander with the horses, and they want me to ride in the next scene. Isn't that brill?'

She looked so excited at the prospect he couldn't help but snap out of his mood (which was more Pandora's fault than Tab's) and join in. 'Amazing. Well done.'

'Found anything new out?' She pointed at the screen.

'Not really, maybe there isn't anything after all. I mean, I don't really get what she expects us to find.'

'Anything about Pandora, she said.' Tab shrugged and moved in a bit closer to see, which had a strange effect on his body – every muscle in his stomach and thighs tightened in anticipation. From this angle he could see straight down her top, to a flimsy scrap of lace. Oh God, he really shouldn't.

'He, er,' he swallowed to clear his throat and concentrated on the screen, 'is friends with her.'

'Well I know that. Doesn't he look a creep? Those tats are gross.'

'She is still talking to him, and he's been chatting to some of the other people that have booked weddings here.'

'I wouldn't call it chatting exactly. He only talks in words of one syllable.'

'Seems to get that wrong half the time as well.' He risked a glance at Tab, who grinned.

'He thinks they all fancy him – he's a right twat.'

'But they do seem to be forming a bit of a club.'

'True. Why won't Xander talk about polo?'

Jamie groaned. 'Do we have to talk about him again?'

'Don't be like that. I think it's strange, he never says anything, I don't feel like I know him at all.'

'He's a very private person.'

'He talks to Lottie. Everybody talks to Lottie.'

Tab looked so downcast that he gave her a hug. 'You talk to Xander when I'd rather you talk to me. I don't feel I know anything about you.'

With a grin she rolled onto her back. 'Ask away, then.'

'Why do we never see your dad around?'

'He's a very private person.' Her tone was dry, but there was a look of mischief lurking in her eyes. She turned onto her side and propped herself up on one arm. 'He's a bit like Xander.' Jamie cringed. Did his name have to come into every conversation? 'Trying to avoid the press.'

'Why?'

'He was a model. Him and mum were kind of minor celebs and he got fed up of it so he made us move to the country.'

'And your mum didn't?'

'Oh no, she's a bit like Pandora. She loves being the centre of attention. She ran off with Dad's manager and all his money. And now she's married to her Italian toy boy – it's really, really gross. He's nearer my age than hers, which is so disgusting. It's a good job they live in Milan – it would be so embarrassing if she was here. Okay, my turn, what about your family?'

'Just me and Mum. Dad died years ago. She a librarian – boring eh?'

'Does she tell you to shush all the time?' Tab giggled.

'She's always got her nose in some book, dreaming about true love, so she doesn't really notice what's going on. Have you ever been in love?'

'Only with Merlin. He's my horse.' She sat up. 'Horses listen and they never let you down. They don't think they're better than you and they don't scheme. Well, actually,' she was resting her chin on her knees. 'That's a bit of a lie. Merlin schemes, but not in a nasty way, mainly about food or how to dump me out of the saddle.'

'And that's not nasty?' He grinned.

'It's just being a horse and we have a kind of understanding. He wouldn't do it if I was upset or anything like that. He's not mean, just lazy.'

'Elizabeth told me you were keen on somebody.'

'Elizabeth talks too much.' She shrugged. 'But it's not a secret. He spent all his time talking to his posh friends about things I didn't understand. They were all at uni like him, not thick like me.'

'You're not thick.'

'Not exactly Einstein though, am I? Anyway I wasn't that keen on him. I hardly ever got chance to see him. You don't exactly get weekends off in this job and in the week he was busy, so it just kind of fizzled out. Show me more of what you've been looking at.'

Jamie, who knew a hint to shut up when he heard one, touched the screen of his tablet.

'Oh God, why is Pandora heading over here?' Tab muttered.

He glanced up, then with a sigh, switched his machine off. He didn't have an answer to that. He'd been hoping she'd leave him alone after her earlier relationship advice. She'd probably decided to go down the complete humiliation route.

'I don't know how you can work for her, she's such a miserable cow.'

'She's not so keen on you either, and anyway, I don't work for her.' Jamie stood up. 'I work for Seb.' He put a hand out, but she was already on her feet. They both watched as Pandora made her way towards them.

'Same thing. He does what she wants.'

'You'd be surprised, he's actually quite a control freak; Seb just pretends to let her have her own way. Come on, somebody has stopped her, let's disappear.' He grabbed Tab's hand and for once she let him. Scooping up Ella under her arm, they ran giggling like children until Jamie dragged her behind the temporary stable block.

'I think we're safe here – she's not keen on the horses.'

'Pandora's not keen on anything but Pandora. Anyway, why did you say she isn't keen on me?' Tab asked.

'Well, for a start you're younger than her, slimmer than her, happier than her.'

'It's not hard to be happier than her.'

'To be honest, I think you're messing up her plan. I think she's trying to throw Lottie and Xander together, and every time she tries you're standing there in the middle with Ella in your arms.' It made sense now he thought about it. Pandora hadn't been trying to help his relationship with Tab; she'd been trying to use him again. To remove the obstacle in her way.

'Really?' Tab pulled at Ella's long ears and frowned.

'Don't you think so?'

'But why would she do that? Lottie's perfectly happy with Rory and what does Pandora get out of it anyway?'

'I don't know,' Jamie shook his head, 'but that's what it looks like to me. She made Xander come here and help out, and he's never worked on a set before. They could have got somebody experienced. Don't you think that's a bit strange?'

'But he wasn't busy, and he knows about polo and horses.'

'It would have been really easy to hire somebody else to do it. Seb has to employ experts for all the films.'

'Maybe she's just doing it so that Lottie won't notice her creeping up on Rory.'

Jamie laughed. 'Won't notice? Well swooning into his arms then getting it in the paper wasn't exactly low key, was it?'

'But it wasn't her that got it in the paper. There's always reporters around.'

'I bet it was her that arranged it – it's the kind of thing she'd do. Most of the press have gone since Lottie gave up on her idea to let them in. There's only a few lurking about in the village and that was a really good shot.' Jamie still hadn't worked out who took the photograph – it just shouldn't have been possible. And if any of the crew had done it off their own bat they'd have been sacked. 'And she said it was good publicity for the film.'

'Her being thrown off a horse would have been good publicity. I'm beginning to quite like the idea of break a leg, and I don't mean that in a good-luck way.' Tab's dislike of Pandora was growing by the minute. It was probably her fault that Xander hardly spoke to her. 'You reckon Xander knows what she's up to?'

'I doubt it. He didn't want to sign up for this at all, and he blew his top when he found out that Lottie lived here. He didn't realise Lady Elizabeth was her gran. Seb's PA overheard him and Pandora arguing in the trailer just after she got here. Xander literally dragged her in and slammed the door. She was screaming and he was yelling back so loud that she shut up. I've never seen him look so angry. He stormed out, then kind of shut down and wouldn't talk to anybody for hours.'

'Really? You're sure? Why?'

'Yeah, of course I'm sure. He hardly ever loses his rag. Haven't got a clue why he did this time, though. Somebody said there was some issue when they all knew each other at school, but that was years ago, and they get on okay now, don't they?'

'Yeah, fine.' Tab kicked at a tuft of grass. 'More than fine. I'm going to ask him.'

'Do you think that's a good idea?'

'Well it can't do any harm, can it? He doesn't exactly like me now, so what have I got to lose?' And before Jamie could stop her she'd stalked off back towards the front of Tipping House, where they were filming.

Xander watched one of the extras galloping towards him, standing in the stirrups and hauling on the poor animal's mouth as he'd no doubt seen somebody do on the television.

If there was one thing worse than having to be here on a set with his half-sister, it was having to watch a load of amateurs ride. If they'd actually admit they couldn't ride and listened to some advice he wouldn't have minded as much, but they probably thought that would mean they'd be chucked off the set. So they steadfastly refused, in the face of all evidence to the contrary, to admit that they weren't experts.

He waited for Seb to shout 'cut', then remembered he wasn't

actually there. He'd announced at breakfast that he had urgent business in London to attend to and he'd be back early the next day. Which meant that with the nervous assistant producer in charge, and a much-reduced workload planned it had been a considerably more peaceful day than normal.

It was actually a relief to see Tab heading his way, with Ella trotting behind. At least she could ride. 'Here, give me the dog.' He smiled. 'Do you mind going and grabbing the grey? She's tacked up, but I really need to stay here or that idiot will keep on galloping into the next county.'

Ella squirmed a welcome, wriggling her solid little body and offering her whiskered face up for a kiss.

If he could avoid seeing Pandora for the next hour or so, today wouldn't have gone too badly at all.

Chapter 24

Rory unclipped the rope from Minty's head collar, offering her half a carrot so that she'd pause for a moment before wheeling round and trotting up the field.

It was a routine he adopted with all the youngsters, although it was hardly necessary with this one. She was a totally different character to her mother, Black Gold, who would take off the instant she was free.

Minty rubbed her head against him, demanding a last cuddle, and he scratched her withers, his gaze drawn to the horses in the top field. One after another they stopped grazing, lifted their heads, transmitting the message through the herd, until they were all poised, ready to flee. Then he heard it. The whirr of a distant helicopter.

Rory looked up, eastwards, squinting against the sun as the helicopter grew from a tiny insect into something recognisable.

Some bloody tycoon from Kitterly Heath showing off, was his first thought as he watched, expecting it to veer off. But it kept on its course.

Black Gold started to trot, a long floating stride that she rarely produced under saddle, and the other horses, following the herd instinct, fell in behind her. As the drone got louder they broke into a canter, circling the field.

It was almost overhead now. Throwing a dark beetle shadow on the ground that chased the fleeing horses, an undulating swirl of air building to a harsh sound that splintered the morning stillness.

Gold threw her head up and sent out a shrill whinny of panic as her canter turned to a gallop. She dropped her head, ears flattened, nostril flared as she powered on. Her only thought was to flee from the monster, and the rest of the herd went with her, jostling for the lead.

Rory's throat tightened as he stood helpless, his fingertips grating against the rough wood of the fence. The drum of hoof beats reverberated through the dry ground, and his normally slow heart beat responded, picking up pace. They had to slow down soon, had to.

He could see the flare of Gold's nostrils, smell the fear and sweat of the herd as they bolted, mindless to everything and everybody, only escape on their minds.

But they'd stop any second, realise that the threat was passing.

They were at the electric fence now, the first two cleared it. Rory winced as a youngster went through it, snapping the white tape. The ribbon flew upwards, floating, spiralling, caught in the breeze created by the helicopter, whirling, grabbing out at the horses that followed. They veered to left and right, half-rearing to avoid colliding, some ploughing on blindly.

The front-runners reached the post and rail fence, the large bay was over, pecking as he landed, struggling to regain his feet, the next took it cleanly. The third horse was a youngster, green and unaccustomed to jumps, white circles of panic around its dark eyes, flared nostrils red. It crashed on blindly, desperate to escape, cutting across in front of Gold.

'Christ.'

The young gelding barely paused, carried along by the herd, his heart pounding. He hardly lifted his feet as the fence loomed close – it was outside his field of vision now. He powered on.

The full force of his chest crashed into the top rail at one end as momentum carried him forward.

For a moment time seemed to stand still. Rory froze, aware of the sounds that didn't stop. Distorted, fragmented. The smack of flesh against timber. The harsh crack of splintering wood as the rail dislodged, the drum of thundering hooves.

Then time caught up, the young horse crashed through, the rail tore loose, lifted. It spun around an invisible axis, becoming a wooden spear that hung in the air for an instant in time. The same instant that Gold took off, launching her powerful body forward towards freedom.

It was too late for her to see danger, too late for her to turn away, much too late to stop her flight.

Rory watched, horrified, unable to look away. She took her final leap, her chest swallowing the impact of the wooden rail as her body rose from the ground. There was a scream, an answering whinny from another horse. His own shout echoed in his ears. The other horse landed, galloped on, a blur of colour as other horses sped past, but all he could see was the black mare.

Black Gold pitched forward as she landed. Staggered, her feet scrabbling to find the ground. She lurched to her knees. Fell to her side with a thud that shook Rory back to life.

'Shit.'

Rory hadn't heard Tab coming, her footsteps masked by the pounding of hooves and the echoing thwup of the helicopter blades.

'No, no.' Tab was already climbing over the gate.

'No.' Rory caught her shirt, dragged her down. 'Go and ring the vet, and for Christ's sake don't let Lottie see.' He clambered over the gate, sprinted over towards the mare, between the horses that had already slowed to a trot as the sound of the helicopter faded.

Rory knew the moment he reached her that there was nothing he could do, nothing anybody could do. Her dark body was a shadow on the grass, her legs forward, as though in motion. But she wasn't going to move again. A slick of darkening blood clung to the blade of grass that surrounded her, the stillness of death hung in the air.

'Don't, Lottie no.' Tab's yell split the silence.

He should have known that Tab wouldn't be able to stop her. 'Let me see.'

He tried to stop her, to block the sight. 'No. You don't need to, no.' He was pulling her against his chest, trying to hold her head against him, but Lottie fought her way out.

The tight band across his chest grew as she stood, staring, her hand still on his arm, where she'd pushed him away. He should say something. His throat wouldn't let him. He swallowed, feeling his mouth twist, the burning heat of tears behind his eyes. 'Lottie.'

'Gold.' With a wail she sank down to her knees at the mare's head. Looked at the soft dark eyes that were staring ahead life-lessly into a future they couldn't see.

Rory was dimly aware of Tab at his side, rocking, her dark hair damp with the tears that ran down her face, plastered like damp seaweed against her cheeks. 'Mike is coming, he was over at Dom's.' The tremble in her voice spread to her body, the cry of anguish muffled as she clamped her hands over her mouth then started to run away from the scene, back towards the gate and the safety of the stables.

Seeing the state of Tab and her garbled account of events, Mike, the vet, knew the equipment he had would be useless. He grabbed the nearest rug and jogged across the paddock to where Lottie was hunched over her horse, the beautiful proud head cradled in her lap. Rory crouched down behind, his arms wrapped around her protectively.

'It would have been instant.' He draped the rug gently over the lifeless body, hiding the horrific cause of death. 'She wouldn't have felt a thing, Lottie. I'm ninety-nine per cent sure. I'm so sorry.'

'What the hell—' at the sound of Xander's voice, they all looked up. 'Jamie came and got me.'

'It's your fault. All of this,' Rory stood up, 'you and him.' He waved wildly towards the set, where Seb's helicopter had landed like a giant cockroach on the green lawns. It was taking off again now, rising slowly, veering off away from the yard and fields. Its job done.

Rory took a swing and Xander dodged. 'Fight, you bastard.' He threw another punch.

'Hey.' It was Mike, bigger than Rory, who stepped between them. 'Not now. Rory, don't.'

'I'm going to kill Seb. You can tell him that. What the fuck does he think he's doing? Nobody said he could land a helicopter here. And once I've sorted him out you can all get the hell out of here.'

Xander didn't say anything. He looked from Rory over to the horse lying on the ground, to Lottie, who was as pale as the horse was dark. 'Shit, I am so sorry. Christ. Really. Is there nothing . . .' He took a step towards her.

'Don't you dare touch her.'

'Rory?' The vet put out a hand to stop him. 'Leave it. Look after your wife and I'll check that Tab is okay.'

'I'll go.' Xander's voice was soft as he glanced from Rory to Lottie, then back at the vet.

'Fuck off, the lot of you.'

Xander didn't. He was standing next to one of the stables, stroking his horse in the eerily quiet yard, when Rory returned. 'Look, I don't want to interfere.'

'Then don't.' Rory brushed past him, not trusting himself to say more.

It was as though the horses that had been stabled all morning knew that something terrible had happened. Even the dogs were silent, lying in the shade of the tack room, their ears flat to their heads as they listened and watched every move. Harry wagged his tail feebly, crept forward on his stomach, and whined as Rory approached, then at the harsh words slunk back to join the other dogs. 'What the fuck are you doing sneaking round here anyway? I should have flattened you while I had the chance.'

'Hit me if it makes you feel better. But I'm not the enemy.'

'Well I bloody know who is.'

Xander put a steadying hand on his arm. 'Just don't go rushing in, Rory. Think, mate, use your head.'

Rory pulled away angrily. 'Don't fucking *mate* me. Who the hell do you think you are? I'm going to kill him. It was him, wasn't it? Seb? He swans around here shouting out orders and acting like he owns the bloody place, well, he's gone too far this time.'

'It was him, but he didn't think.'

'He never fucking thinks.' Rory folded his arms, his feet wide in a fighting stance and glowered at the other man.

'Look I'm not defending him here, but what good will it do? I'm just saying give it an hour or so, then talk to him.'

'Did you see what he's done?' The anger inside Rory was building, fear and hate rocketing around the hard lump in his chest.

He'd lost horses before. He'd seen horrific falls during cross-country events, broken legs and the threat of the humane killer – he'd seen horses sweating, fear in their eyes as colic twisted their guts, and he'd seen old age take many a friend. But he'd never lost an animal in this totally pointless way, in a completely avoidable accident that should never have happened.

'Did you see that animal out there?' He waved an arm in anger. 'That lousy git never asked permission to come flying in, did he? Did you know he was about to pull a stunt like that?'

'No, I didn't. And I doubt he asked anybody. Look, Rory, I know how you feel, though, and if there's anything—'

'How can you possibly know?' They both turned at the small voice. Lottie stood a few feet away, her pale face tear-streaked and dirt smeared where she'd rubbed it with hands dirty from the mare's coat. Long strands of her hair damp and tangled.

With a yelp Harry crawled over to meet her, sat on her feet, and squirmed up so he could lean against her legs, begging for comfort.

'Oh, Lots, why aren't you in the house with Tab? I told you I'd come the second I could.' Rory's arms were around her. 'Come on.'

'I want to know how he thinks he can possibly understand.' She swayed as she stared at Xander.

'I told you I lost that horse last year,' his voice was flat, 'and that's why I don't play now.'

'That was different. Gold was in a field, she was scared to death, hounded so that—' Lottie gulped, bit down on her lip to stop it wobbling, to try and stem the tears.

'It is different, and you're right, mine wasn't hounded.' Xander didn't look away. 'I as good as rode it to its death. He was hit hard by a ball because I put him in the wrong place, and then we kept on playing and he collapsed under me. I'm sorry, I know it doesn't make this any better.'

Lottie shivered, despite the sun, despite the warmth of Rory's arms around her, and the spaniel pressing against her legs.

'She didn't stand a chance. She wasn't competing, she was in a bloody field, supposed to be eating grass.' Her voice rose on each syllable until it reached a strangled peak and died on a sob. 'She was supposed to be having fun.'

'I know.' Xander looked from Lottie to Rory and then back at his horse. 'I'm sorry. I know it's different. I'm not competing here. But I do understand. Believe me, I blamed myself.'

'Well I don't blame myself, I blame Seb.' There was a harsh edge to Rory's voice that Xander hadn't heard before.

'I do.' With a sob Lottie turned and pressed herself against Rory, burying her face in his chest. 'I blame myself. It's all my fault they're here.'

'It's not.' Rory stroked her hair and wondered where the hell they went from here. 'Shush, it's not your fault. Nobody knew he'd pull a stunt like that. But it's ending here.'

'You can't stop it now.' Xander's shook his head. 'You'd be mad.'

'Watch me. It's taking over our lives, and I've had enough of it. I'm sick of seeing the bloody newspaper reports, sick of watching everybody run around as extras, sick of running the gauntlet of reporters with their bloody cameras every time I ride off the estate, and sick of being accused of ruining the village.'

'Don't rush into this, please. Just think about it, Rory.'

'What do you care? You're one of them – Pandora's darling brother. How much did she pay you to come over and talk me out of flattening him?'

'Nothing. They don't know a thing about this. I'm not saying don't tell him—'

'You're damn right you're not.'

'And feel free to smack him if it makes you feel better. Nobody's going to stand in your way on that one. But think, man, what will it do to you? There'll be a cancellation fee on the contract – he's bound to have a clause in there. And how do you keep this place going, without their money?'

'Why are you really here, Xander?' Lottie's words were soft, but unmistakable. 'What do you care?'

'I like you both. I admire you. I always have and you deserve to keep this place going. Don't make it hard for yourselves. Believe me, I've been there, done that, and it didn't help at all.' He gave a humourless laugh.

'I don't mean that.' Lottie brushed her sleeve across her face. 'Why did you come back to Tippermere?'

'She's family, Lottie, and family counts for something.'

'You are kidding, aren't you?'

'Okay.' He took a deep breath. 'That's only part of it. Like I said before, I'd have done something stupid if I'd been left to my own devices and she knew it. I'm under no illusions she was trying to save me, but she knew I wasn't so daft or self-absorbed that I'd ignore a lifeline. Don't ask me why she came back here, because I honestly don't know or care. Face it though, you need the money, don't you? Just think about it, please, both of you, use your heads.'

'Rory's got a new sponsor.'

'And is that enough?'

'No.' Rory's tone was flat, defeated. 'He's right.' He wiped a tear from Lottie's cheek with his thumb and his voice softened. 'It's nowhere near enough.'

'But we'll get the insurance money soon – we can re-launch the business.' It was a wail that tugged at his heart.

'We will, but not soon enough, Lottie.'

'What the fuck is going on here? Where's Jamie?' Seb's strident tone rang across the yard and Xander froze.

'Shit.' He put a hand out to grab Rory, but it was too late.

Rory had the soft cotton fabric of Seb's shirt twisted into his fist before he was even really aware he'd raised a hand. Was staring into the lizard-cold eyes that were only inches from his face. He wanted to hit him, hit him so hard he'd feel the pain they just had, let him taste the sweet-iron tang of his own blood like Gold had. But he couldn't. Seb's eyes had widened, his pupils dark with fear, his skin pale. Frustrated, Rory tightened his grip, his fist shaking.

'Rory.' Lottie's warm hand was on his. He studied her nails, darkened with what could have been earth or blood.

'Fuck.' He let go, then raised his fist. He could hit him.

'No. I want to show him.'

Seb glanced between them, then looked to Xander for reassurance. Xander glanced down. This wasn't his decision, he couldn't make this call, couldn't assume he had any right to comment now he'd said his piece.

'You can't, Lottie. I'm not letting you—'

'As far as the gate.' The words wavered, but Rory knew she wouldn't back down. She was going to do this if it killed her. 'He's got to see, I want him to know what he's . . .'

Lottie stopped when they got to the gate, but Rory didn't. He might not be able to beat the man to a pulp, but he wanted him to . . . what? Suffer, be shocked? He didn't know.

He pushed him forward and Seb stumbled on the rutted earth, then strode on without comment until he was yards from the body.

'Lift the rug.'

Seb looked blankly at Rory and didn't move, but Xander did. Wordlessly he lifted the corner, then dropped it again.

'But I—'

Seb looked genuinely confused, and shocked.

'The helicopter.' Xander's voice was soft. 'You caused a stampede.'

'The fucking helicopter, Seb. Nobody said you could land it here, did they? Didn't you think to ask, you moron?' The words caught in Rory's throat, came out harsh and stilted.

He looked from Rory to Xander, then down at the horse's body and shuddered. 'I didn't think . . .'

'I should kill you.'

Seb took a step back, half-raised an arm in defence, but Xander knew that the initial anger had seeped from Rory. He wasn't going to kill anybody.

'Have you seen what you've done to my wife?' Rory grabbed hold of his shirt, dragged him back towards the gate, and probably for the first time in his life, Seb didn't object to being manhandled.

'I'm sorry.'

'Sorry, you're fucking sorry.' Rory laughed. 'He's sorry.' He did swing for him then. It took them all unawares, even Rory himself. He'd thought he couldn't hit him after all, but that pathetic '*sorry*' had flipped a switch. He felt helpless in the face of Lottie's distress, didn't know what he could do except hold her. He didn't know how to put things right again. He was frustrated. So he hit him.

They left him there, standing just inside the gate. Swaying, wordless. His hand on his throbbing cheek.

'You shouldn't have hit him.' Lottie's voice was small, almost lost.

Rory shrugged and put his arm around her shoulders as they walked back into the yard, then steered her towards the bench. 'I needed to.' He rubbed a hand over his knuckles and was glad it wasn't something he often felt the urge to do. It hurt, and his stomach was churning. Probably from the whole thing – the anger, the pain, the sadness, the massive feeling of helplessness. Or he was getting old.

'We will be okay,' he said it as much to convince himself as her, 'we will get the money we need and this whole nightmare will soon be over. But for now, it's time we did this on our terms, darling, or not at all. I'll go and talk to him properly tomorrow when I've calmed down.'

'Are you okay?' She looked up from where her head was resting on his shoulder.

'I'm fine.' He kissed the tip of her nose. 'You need to rest.'

'I'm fine, don't hit him again.'

He tried a grin, but knew it was a pathetic attempt. 'I won't.' He looked at Xander. 'If you want to help then clear out that stable.' He nodded towards Gold's loosebox, 'and tell the vet we'll be sorting a burial if he can tidy—'

He stopped, unable to finish the sentence. He didn't want to see Gold in the state she was in again, and he definitely didn't want Lottie or anybody else to see her like that. There'd be no sign of the horrific cause of death when he dug the hole and lowered her into it.

'Sure.'

Chapter 25

'So they're all saying we're ruining the village?' Lottie was wrapped up in a rug, with a mug of coffee in her hands, huddled on the sofa with Harry across her feet and she still felt cold. She hadn't been able to sleep, and after tossing and turning for what seemed like hours she'd gone downstairs to make a drink. The kettle hadn't even boiled when Rory had appeared in the doorway.

There were bigger issues on her mind, things she had to say, but that seemed the easiest right now.

'Sorry?'

'You said before, when we were . . . you said you were sick of the filming, and everybody saying we were ruining the village.'

'One or two have done.' Rory sounded reluctant to admit it, but he'd said it in the heat of the moment, and he wasn't going to lie. 'Some of them are star-struck, some think they can be in the film, but one or two are fed up of the upheaval. The vicar said he doesn't mind them all going to the church hall for the tea and cakes, but he puts his foot down when it comes to their mobiles ringing louder than the church bells.'

Lottie grimaced, the nearest she could get to a smile.

'He's making a fortune in his little café, but isn't up for the way half the congregation dive out whenever there's a shout that some star is driving past. He was in the middle of a sermon about humility, apparently, when there was a call saying there was a photographer outside and half the women got mirrors and make-up out.'

'I really hoped after that letter he sent us that things would calm down.'

'They haven't. He went up to see Dom yesterday and told him in no uncertain terms that he should speak to his mother, as we obviously weren't going to resolve the issue.'

'But we're doing our best – why can't he understand?'

'Dom told him, but you know what the vicar's like when he gets a bee in his bonnet. He's a bit of a self-important old woman.'

'Oh well, it's not going to matter soon.'

'No, once they're gone we can get back to normal.'

'I didn't mean that.' Lottie took a sip of scalding coffee and her eyes watered. 'When I came out earlier it was because the solicitor had called. I came to tell you and . . .' She'd never imagined as she ran out of the house to find Rory that things could get any worse, but they had. Bad enough to make her forget that they'd reached the end of the road. The air drained out of her lungs and she rubbed the back of her hand over her eyes. 'When I said we'd manage, we'd get things going again soon,' she shrugged, 'it wasn't true.' Her eyes were brim-full, but it wasn't hot coffee. 'We've got court dates,' she took a deep breath to try and steady her voice, 'and we'll have legal bills, and the solicitor said that they chased the insurance company and they still aren't in a position to settle.' She looked up. 'Nobody is going to bail us out, Rory. The money we get for the filming hardly makes a dent in things. It doesn't really matter if they stay or go, it's tiding us over, but at the end of the day the insurance company isn't going to pay out soon enough. If they ever do.'

'But . . .'

'I worked it out before I came out to the yard to talk to you. The money that we'd built up from the business before the fire is just about all gone now. I mean, we had the roof fixed and those guest rooms redone when the income looked really good, and I paid off quite a bit of the bank loan. And then there was the cost of the horses before Rob signed you, which I know wasn't for long, but there just isn't much left – barely enough to live on.' She tugged at a loose thread on the rug. 'The solicitor tried to avoid court by offering to pay the deposits back in instalments, but they wouldn't agree and that's why he said we had no choice. We can argue that the weddings can go ahead, but he doesn't know if it will help, seeing as we haven't a clue when we'll be able to start work. But at least this way if we can prove we can't afford it in one chunk the court will work out what they think we can pay. But I don't think we can even cover all the court costs, let alone pay back all the deposits. Oh Rory, it's such a bloody mess.' She put down her coffee and cupped her hands over her face, willing herself not to cry. 'We haven't got a choice. The bank isn't going to lend us any more money if we haven't got a business. You know that letter you tore up? The offer to buy the estate in its entirety, but let us stay?'

She looked up and he nodded.

'I told the solicitor to get in touch with them again – see if we can come to some kind of arrangement.'

'But Lottie, there must be something else we can do.'

'There isn't, but at least they can't all blame us for ruining the village then.'

'Oh Lottie, they don't really blame you – they just like moaning. They'd be devastated if you left this place. But we won't.'

'I think we will, Rory.'

'Lottie, this isn't like you. You don't give up.'

'I'm just being practical.' She shrugged.

'But we'll be here, even if we don't own the place. You said we could lease it.'

'For how long? Rory, it won't be ours.'

Rory pulled her closer to him and rested his chin on her head.

'I hate to do this, but if it's a bad news day . . . There's something else I found out.'

Lottie pulled the blanket up to her chin. She wasn't sure she could cope with anything else. Not today. Life was never going to be the same. It had been a sign, Black Gold dying. She was as good as knocked down herself. 'What?' She might as well hear it – get it all over with.

'The latest leak to the newspapers came from Pandora. She gave them that photo. I don't know about the other report with you and Xander. But that picture of her collapsing into my arms was her doing.'

'You're sure?' She didn't really need to ask. He was sure, or he wouldn't be telling her this, not right now.

'I asked Elizabeth to talk to Pip, I know they still chat a lot.'

Lottie frowned, then chewed the inside of her cheek. Pip had been a good friend when she was in Tippermere and Lottie still missed her. Oh God, she wished she was here now.

'She made a few calls and called in a few favours, and found out Pandora got a photographer in under the pretext of being an extra. Hard not to admire her, really, isn't it? She's orchestrating everything, and I'd never had her down as particularly clever.'

'But why would she do that?'

Rory shrugged. 'Good publicity?'

'She's after you.'

He laughed. 'What would she want with me? Anyway, I'm yours, darling. You're never going to get rid of me, you know that, don't you?'

'I think she wants the house too – not that she's going to get it now.'

'The house?' He looked at her, brow furrowed in confusion.

'This house, Tipping House. I'm sure she does. She did this scene where she and her on-screen husband were fighting about staying, and she said this was where she belonged.'

'But that was acting.'

'It wasn't. She's not that good, ask Gran.' She paused. 'I think that's why she came back.'

'But they're paying us, they're making it possible for us to keep going. Well, they have been until . . .'

'I know, but it gave her the perfect excuse to come back, didn't it? She can work her magic on you, work out just how to get rid of me.'

'Lottie that's rubbish. Nobody is ever going to get rid of you. Listen to me.'

But Lottie had her face buried in Harry's coat and all Rory could do was hang on to her and hope he could somehow make it all right. They had each other, they had his old cottage that was rented out, but would Lottie ever cope with losing her family home?

* * *

Rory was up early the next morning. He was at Billy's, collecting the digger he'd arranged to borrow by 5am and had dug a large hole in the upper paddock before anybody else had stirred. By 6am he, Lottie, and Tab were standing by the newly covered grave saying a last goodbye to Black Gold.

There was a shrill whinny from the direction of the yard. 'Minty will miss her.' Tab knelt down and smoothed out the soil.

'We'll all miss her.' Rory put an arm around each of the girls.

'She could be such a cow.' Lottie sniffed.

'She was a rum-un, I'll say that for her.' They hadn't heard Billy walking across towards them and now he ruffled Lottie's hair, patted Rory on the back, and nodded at Tab. 'Never thought when I got her that she'd be quite such a madam, but you never know with horses, do you? Come on, love.' He nodded back towards the yard. 'It's a cold, hard fact but where there's livestock there's always deadstock, as my old man used to say. Tiggy's cooked up breakfast for you lot. Come and tuck in and remember the good times. It'll take your mind off the grub – you know what her cooking's like. You too, young Tab.'

'But the horses . . .'

'I fed them while you were out here. Turn them out when you get back. Come on before the eggs are harder than cricket balls.'

* * *

There was something exhausting, Lottie decided, about grief. It drained you. Real grief – unlike falling out with a boyfriend, deciding you're overweight, or falling off a horse and breaking bits you'd rather not – dug a hole deep inside you and excavated the contents. At least, that's how it felt. Like a black hole. And real grief hurt more as you got older. She didn't like being grown up.

The only positive she could glean, if you could call it that, was that it took her mind off the fact that each day brought her nearer to the one when she'd lose Tipping House. It was just a case of waiting now, waiting for a response about the offer on the estate, waiting for a court date, waiting for the film crew to wrap up and leave. In the meantime she couldn't wallow, she had to give herself a kick up the backside and get on with life.

After a week of welling up every time she looked at Gold's empty stable, she knew she really had to do something. As her dad had pointed out, none too subtly, if you had animals then there were losses. She wasn't quite sure if it was the way Black Gold had died, or the fact that she had been such a character that had got to her so much.

Gold had been a 'coming home' gift from Billy, after she'd returned from Australia, via Barcelona, gaining and losing a boyfriend along the way.

Her father had eyed her up and down and said 'well if you're staying here you'd better do some work. I've got a youngster that I picked up the other week. You can sort her out. I think you'll get on fine – two of a kind.'

Lottie didn't think they were any such thing, but the mare had certainly stopped her moping about her two-timing, beach-bum ex. Day-dreaming was firmly off bounds when you were with Gold. If you were in the saddle and she thought you were distracted, then she'd deposit you somewhere uncomfortable, and if you were in the stable a sharp nip, or strategically placed hoof would remind you she was there.

In the end, Rory had suggested they put her in foal. He loved Lottie too much to watch her risk life and limb every time she exercised the horse, and having a baby might settle her (Gold not Lottie). It didn't really, so apart from the occasional hack out Gold was destined for life as a brood mare.

Her first foal, Minty, was as obliging as Gold was awkward, and they'd more or less decided that next year they'd put her in foal again. The thought brought a new lump of grief to Lottie's throat and her eyes filled. She blinked, then wiped her eyes with her sleeve. She couldn't forget the horse, but feeling washed out and hopeless wasn't any good either. Which was why she'd given Tab a well-earned day off and after shooing Rory out of the yard on Joker she'd set to and given the tack room a good clean out, and the yard a sweeping even Uncle Dominic would have found impressive.

She propped open the door of the one stable that hadn't needed mucking out. Rory had left it empty, but it was so silly having Tab trail over to Billy's every day to look after Maddie – they had more than enough work on the yard for the three of them.

Grabbing hold of the wheelbarrow, she set off towards the barn. It was rather trickier making her way back with a bale of shavings and a dog balanced on it. The small wheel bounced over the cobblestones, veering alarmingly towards the fountain that stood in the middle of the yard, and Tilly slid off the shiny plastic, gave a yelp of surprise, and then ran round and round the water feature as fast as she could with her head down and tail tucked under.

As Lottie came to a halt, the terrier was back on top of the barrow, barking excitedly before tearing off back to the barn at a gallop, with Harry and the other dogs trailing behind.

She tipped the bale of shavings into the middle of the box and was ripping it open when a clatter of hooves announced Rory's return.

Rushing to the door, the sun behind her shining straight through the back window, she was surrounded by a halo of dust particles, and a fair few shavings were stuck in her hair and on her top.

'I thought that stuff was supposed to be dust-free?' Rory's deep laugh made her smile. 'You're not supposed to be rolling in them, darling.' He did a double-take, realised which stable she was bedding down and his smile dimmed.

'It's okay. I need to see another horse in here. By the time you've washed Joker down I'll be finished and he can come in here – then we can go and get Maddie from Dad's. She can have her old stable back.'

Rory kissed her on the nose. 'If you're sure.'

'Positive. And then you've got to help me get stuff sorted for the village show.'

He groaned. 'Oh God, I thought we'd escaped that this year.'

'You can never escape the Tippermere Village Show.' She gave a wry smile. 'Well not unless you leave.'

'Lottie.' His tone held a warning note. Rory kept telling her they'd find a solution, but that was just on the outside. She could see when she looked in his eyes that on the inside he knew they were running out of options.

'Well, you're definitely not escaping this one. Seb was told quite firmly that any shooting schedule he might have was to be suspended this weekend. Gran made sure it was in the contract.'

She actually loved the village show, despite the mayhem it often caused. In fact, she loved all the village traditions and was determined that whatever happened to Tipping House, the village show, Boxing Day meet, and annual charity cricket match would never be surrendered to what some might call progress.

Lottie was actually slightly worried that soon she was going to start sounding like Gran and say things like 'it will be cancelled over my dead body' or 'in my day' then follow it up with a demand for a stiff G&T.

'You look happier.'

'I am.' She'd resolved to live one day at a time, to savour every second. 'Now hurry up and get Joker untacked.'

'Yes, Miss.' Rory grinned, relieved to see his old Lottie back. Then he laughed as she ripped the bag, tipped the rest of the shavings out and was engulfed in a cloud of dust and fine particles, sending a waft of woody smells into the yard. 'I'll turn him out for a bit and let that settle.'

Chapter 26

Lottie had a love-hate relationship with the early morning, particularly since moving into the old and creaky Tipping House. The house might look welcoming, but it swallowed all trace of heat, despite the softly glowing oak-panelled walls, which tricked you into thinking the summer warmth had found a way in.

The part Lottie hated most was the actual getting out of bed, which meant cold feet whatever the time of year, followed by a shower that switched abruptly from freezing to red hot just as you were about to give up. But once she got outside it was different.

She loved the peace and quiet of the early hours, before the rest of the world awoke. It didn't matter what time of year it was, whether there was an eerie mist hovering over the lawns and distant coppice of trees, a crisp layer of white on the grass, or the sun rising on a beautiful morning. It was always glorious and made her realise just how lucky she was. Even with the agony of opening the bills that spilled from the groaning in-box, and gurgling pipes threatening to spill their contents that kept them awake at night, she had never been more certain that Tipping House was the only place she wanted to be. She'd do anything to stay here. Six months ago she would have laughed at the prospect of selling Tipping House, but now she knew she had to be practical. She gave a wry smile. The bank, for one, wouldn't give them any choice.

Selling to a developer was definitely a case of, as Elizabeth would put it, '*over my dead body*', but the solicitors had managed to make progress with other prospective purchasers. At first Lottie had been thrown back into a state of despondency when one after another of the offers had been withdrawn, for various – often incomprehensible – reasons. She'd swung between elation that maybe it was not to be, to despair that there really wasn't any other way out. But there was still one buyer wanting to talk terms – and willing to let Lottie and Rory stay on as tenants and run their business – when they finally got it up and running again.

The thought of somebody else actually having the final say in what happened to the Stanthorpe's ancestral home brought a dull pain to her chest, but she was trying to be realistic. Billy was only a tenant in his home – lots of people were in that position – and at least this would be a real person who she could hopefully get on with, negotiate with, not some nameless, faceless board from a company or a trust that would need to run the place strictly by their own rules.

Whatever happened, the negotiations and legalities would take time, and she had given herself a strict talking to. In the meantime she must *not* waste her life, she had to carry on as normal, live in the moment. And once she'd reached that decision it had made things easier.

Lottie glanced up at the sky, which had a smattering of innocent white puffs of cloud. The weather forecast hadn't been too bad. To be honest, she hadn't exactly been concentrating that hard on it so might have missed some bits, but she got the gist. The forecaster had definitely mentioned the words 'sun', 'dry' and 'cloud'. There had been no mention of rain or thunder, which was fine by her. The month of May was always a bit unpredictable, but by the looks of things the village show was going to be umbrella-free.

Today there was an expectant air, as though the place was on pins, waiting for the explosion of activity that would come later in the day. And it would be an explosion.

Despite wracking her brain for days, she had been totally unable to come up with a diplomatic reason for banning the village band from making an appearance. When the drummer had broken his wrist (she'd been informed it was from over-enthusiastic beating – which she hoped only involved a drum), the butcher had been drafted in and Lottie could have sworn he was deaf and had no sense of rhythm. The euphonium player had aspirations of soloist fame and seemed to play an arrange-ment of his own making, and two of the teenage cornet players competed to see who could wear the most revealing outfit and get the most wolf whistles. This successfully distracted from their variable playing, and drew a crowd, but had led to a fight in the refreshment tent last year when the father of one had taken umbrage and taken a couple of the more enthusiastic observers to task.

It was also practically impossible to stop the band once they got started. They took the heckling as a sign of approval and would continue to march around, restarting their programme of music and invariably clashing with the Morris dancers, who would jingle their bells and clash their sticks ever louder.

Not that the Morris dancers were much better. One year Brian the joiner had got so carried away his clog had flown off and hit the vicar on the side of the head. He'd had to attend church for six months before his wife had considered he'd repented suffi-ciently. And then there was the time that one of the terriers had taken a liking to the sashes they wore dangling from their waists, and had nearly deprived two of Tippermere's finest of their manhood.

Then, of course, there would be the barking dogs, keen to

impress in the agility competition, which would upset the rabbits and chickens, and there was bound to be at least one outburst of hysterical tears from a child whose pony had failed to win the best fancy-dress award. All in all though, she did love everything about the afternoon apart from the need to award prizes. Despite having the head teacher from the village school support her in a bid for a non-competitive spirit, the rest of the village pooh-poohed it; some of them (like Billy) very loudly declaring that a bit of competition never hurt anybody. She wasn't convinced. There would be tears, she was sure of it.

Along with half the village they'd worked late into the evening putting up bunting and marquees, setting out tables, and marking out a centre ring for the various competitions, and an area for the pony races.

She slipped her mobile phone out of her pocket to check the time. They'd probably got a couple of hours before the committee members arrived to put the finishing touches to everything, and then it would be all go. Which gave her just enough time for breakfast and to put some icing on the top of her carrot cake. She would kill whoever had come up with the idea of a Bake-off style show-stopper competition – whatever was wrong with a good old Victoria sponge with jam in it?

Which reminded her, she really did have to impress upon whoever was in charge of the cake tent that no food should be left unsupervised for even a minute. She still hadn't got over the time one of Elizabeth's Labradors had eaten half the food at the charity cricket match before they'd even broken for tea.

* * *

Lottie stared at the array of cakes crammed onto the table and wondered if 'accidentally' dropping hers on to Harry's head was a better idea than admitting it was an entry for the *Tippermere Village Show country pursuits themed cake competition*.

'Well you *are* brave, love.' Tiggy gave her an admiring smile, then reached out and snatched the cake before she had the chance to sabotage it. 'There's a tiny gap here for it. I didn't dare bring one of my attempts. Your dad says he'll never get over my beetroot cake. They really didn't make it clear in the recipe, though, that you couldn't use the pickled ones. Here we are,' she squeezed the cake in next to a perfect reproduction of the Hickstead Bank, complete with horse and rider sliding down the slope. 'Aren't you clever? A carrot cake shaped like a carrot. It is carrot cake, isn't it love? I thought those orangey bits . . .' She tugged an orange strand out and popped it in her mouth.

'It is carrot.' If she was lucky Tiggy might eat it before the show opened. 'You will be here all the time, won't you, Tiggy?' If the terrier trio escaped and demolished these lovingly prepared creations she would get lynched.

'Of course I will, love. You know you can rely on me.' She beamed and patted Lottie on the arm.

But, that was the problem. Tiggy was about the most unreliable person in Tippermere. She was lovely, generous, kind, but all those things weren't the same as reliable. One whiff of something happening elsewhere and she'd forget all about her duties.

'You are getting changed into something more appropriate, I presume, Charlotte?'

Lottie jumped as a prod to her arm and the commanding voice announced her gran's arrival. She looked down at her jeans and clean polo shirt (which was actually ironed and didn't have a trace of horse slobber on it).

'But this is appropriate.' She looked back at her gran. 'When I was little I remember you wearing your dog-walking clothes and wellies.'

Elizabeth sniffed. 'It had been a wet spring.'

Lottie tried not to grin. Today Gran was dressed like the Queen Mother about to attend a garden party or Royal Ascot. She blamed Sam, who was clearly having a very bad influence on her.

Sam believed very strongly that appearances mattered, and you had to dress and act the part. So she never compromised. Wherever she was, she was Sam, footballer's wife. She was in love with all things sparkly and so she always wore jewellery. She also considered long, polished nails an essential, along with the type of high heels that Lottie would have fallen off. Given a choice between riding a horse with a reputation for bolting and a pair of Sam's shoes she'd go for the horse every time.

In complete contrast, Lady Elizabeth was as traditional as they came, with a leaning towards the eccentric. Her favourite footwear included Hunter wellingtons and sensible flat shoes, and she had always considered a tweed skirt and a Barbour jacket suitable for most occasions. Until Sam had come along.

Sam clung to her beliefs that Elizabeth spent her days sipping sherry and entertaining the gentry, despite strong evidence to the contrary – including constant calls for G&T's and the complete absence of visitors apart from the vicar, farmers, and gamekeepers.

But Elizabeth, it appeared (and Lottie still wasn't sure if this was a little private joke at Sam's expense or not), had now decided she should act the part when making a public appearance. Lottie knew that Sam would be impressed.

'It's only the village show, Gran. I always dress like this.'

'And very nice you look too.' Tiggy, who was dressed in a very full gypsy skirt, which billowed out over her ample hips, and an off-the-shoulder broderie anglaise top that showed off her pink, freckle-smattered cleavage, beamed at Elizabeth, who carried on undeterred.

'One should keep up appearances. What will the vicar's wife think when you present prizes dressed like that?'

Lottie frowned. The Very Reverend Waterson always insisted that he was delighted to open the show (despite the committee assuring him that it was absolutely no problem at all for them to find a celebrity to perform the task), and informed Lottie that his unassuming wife Jane would be devastated if she were ever not asked to help with judging. Lottie couldn't imagine the pleasant and uncomplaining woman ever thinking anything derogatory of anybody. 'I'm sure she won't mind at all, Gran.'

'On your own head be it.' Elizabeth tapped her stick against the table leg and Lottie cringed, wishing she'd stop. The last thing they wanted was the whole thing giving way and a mass of fondant icing raining down on the grass. 'You youngsters. In my day a lady would act with some decorum and dress the part.'

'Oh wow, babe, isn't this fab?'

Lottie could have sworn Elizabeth rolled her eyes as Sam, a designer-clad vision, was dragged into the marquee by an enthusiastic Scruffy, who was luckily on a lead.

'Oh your Ladyship,' Lottie kicked her on the ankle as she threatened a bob. 'I bet it's nearly as good as one of them garden parties, isn't it? Look at them flower arrangements over there. No Scruffy,' she giggled, 'you can't eat them. Don't you think he looks smart, Lottie? Me and Roxy gave him a bath and look, she painted his little toenails all by herself, bless.'

Lottie, Tiggy, and Elizabeth all looked down at Scruffy's feet to see nails and hairy toes daubed liberally with bright red sparkly nail varnish. Elizabeth snorted in a very unladylike way, then deftly morphed it into a more polite cough.

'I am off to check where they have placed the bandstand this year, Charlotte. I do hope it is out of general earshot.'

'Aww, isn't she lovely, Lottie? I wish I had a gran like her, and she's so proper posh. The way she looks down her nose and everything.'

Lottie groaned. 'I better see what she's up to, or she'll be telling them to move marquees and everybody will be here soon.'

'Okay, babe. Oh I can't wait for you to see Roxy and her little Rupert. She's made her pony so pretty. You'll be amazed.'

Amazed, Lottie decided, probably wasn't the word for it.

* * *

'I do find this so difficult, dear, don't you?' Jane, the vicar's wife, hovered at the side of Lottie, a basket of rosettes in her hand. 'I'm always so afraid of hurting people's feelings.' She straightened the ribbons of the third-place rosette nervously. 'Mr George, the butcher, came to me after the show last year and accused us of showing favouritism. He said we'd picked the cutest child not the waggiest tail, and it wasn't fair that his Amy had got orange hair and braces. We were discriminating against her unfavourably, he said, and after all it was God that had made her that way.'

'She'd also got a dog with fleas and a habit of dragging its bottom along the floor,' Lottie pointed out reasonably.

'Oh, I know. But I couldn't say that to him. He's normally such a nice man, but he was quite aggressive. I was rather worried about what he might put in my sausages. Oh look, isn't that puppy adorable?'

Lottie looked at the gangly puppy, which was indeed cute, then she glanced up. 'But that's Mrs Warburton's daughter and she always wins best chutney, and her husband is on the town-planning committee. They'll all say we're after something.'

'How about that one? It's the scruffiest dog I've ever seen, but look at its tiny painted nails and it's so happy.'

'That,' Lottie groaned, 'is my best friend's dog.'

Roxy, spotting that she was being observed, started to jump up and down. She waved wildly, shouting as loudly as she could, 'Auntie Lottie, Auntie Lottie, look at me,' which didn't help at all.

The problem was, Lottie decided, she knew all of them and whatever they decided there would be trouble.

'We could ask them about pet care?' Jane said, as dogs and owners started to walk around the makeshift ring with their parents shouting frantic instructions.

'Not fair on the youngest or least educated.'

'Ask them to get their dogs to jump over a little obstacle?'

'Size-ist.'

'Waggiest tail?'

'Well we did think that maybe we should go for the *dog we'd most like to take home* this year, because last year somebody complained it wasn't fair for dogs that didn't have tails.'

'Well maybe if we just ask them why?' Jane said, going pale as a bouncy Dalmatian caught up with the dog in front and tried to mount it.

'Might have to separate them first.'

When they finally got the parade of dogs in a fairly neat line, Lottie was already dying for a stiff drink.

'Why would we want to take your dog home, dear?' Jane patted an elderly Labrador on its head.

'Cos my dad says he needs shooting.'

'Oh heavens.' She stopped and looked at Lottie for help. 'I'm sure he doesn't mean that.'

'Says he's a right bugger.'

'Oh.' Jane patted the dog again and moved on to a Cavalier spaniel with mournful eyes.

'And, er, why would we want to take your dog home?'

The little girl stared, her eyes opened wide and then Lottie realised that her lower lip had actually started to wobble. She dithered, mesmerised. It was far too early for upset – they hadn't even started to award rosettes yet.

'You can't, you can't take my Molly home – she's mine.' Tears spilled and ran at an alarming pace down the previously happy face and with a distressed wail she wrapped her arms around her dog. 'Mummy, mummy, don't let her have Molly.' Scrambling to her feet, she ran right out of the ring, towing the dog behind her. 'Mummy, mummy.'

'Oh no, I didn't mean . . .'

She really did have to get this over as quickly as possible, thought Lottie, glancing at her fellow judge, who was close to tears herself. 'Maybe we should just pat them on the head?'

Jane nodded, biting her bottom lip.

Patting seemed to work and Jane had cheered up by the time

they'd worked their way around the ring without causing any more upset. And, after persuading the little girl that nobody was going to steal her pet they awarded first prize to the Cavalier, as it couldn't be disputed that the dog was undeniably the one that its owner most wanted to take home.

Lottie was just heading over towards the cake tent, to make sure that Tiggy was still standing guard, when she got waylaid by a giggling Tab, who had a beaming Jamie with her.

'Oh my God that is just so funny, you have got to see.'

Lottie looked at her in amazement. 'What is?'

'Pandora!' She started giggling again.

'What do you mean Pandora? I didn't even know she was here. I mean I know we invited everybody, but I didn't expect her and Seb to hang around.'

'You didn't?' It was Tab's turn to be surprised. 'Then I wonder who arranged that.' She turned around and pointed over to the far side of the ring, where there were two identical gazebos side by side.

Lottie peered. Even from this distance she could see that one had 'Gypsy Rose' (otherwise known as Mrs Jones' sister) in it, as was traditional, and the other had . . . Pandora.

'But what—'

'She insisted on signing autographs, love.' Billy put an arm round Tab, and his other around Lottie, and stared across. 'Seems to think she's a proper celebrity, so your gran parked her over there with raddled Rose. Said they were both away with the fairies, and she was well out of it over there, and' he chuckled, 'look at that queue old Rose has got. We'll see how long Pandora can stick hearing the same bloody fortune told over and over again. Ay up, look, Rose is sneaking a tipple.'

Everybody in Tippermere knew Rose, and there was always a competition to see who could get the most outrageous fortune from her. Being as fond of a tipple of cider as she was, the stories got more far-fetched as the day went on, and everybody knew that if you fed her a whiff of scandal she'd run with it. Pandora would be torn between covering her ears and listening in.

'Last year she told Dom that he'd got a secret sex life and she knew he liked his women pinned down and helpless so that he could have his wicked way,' giggled Tab.

'She didn't!'

'She did, Amanda told me. And she told Amanda that she would have five children by different fathers. She said still waters run deep and even Amanda didn't recognise the powerful passion she had inside her yet. Amanda said nothing was going to gurgle inside her, including another baby, after this one.'

Lottie laughed. 'She swore she'd never get pregnant again. I think she's threatened to give Dom a vasectomy herself.'

'Poor Rose.' Tab was fascinated by the fortune teller, who was jingling her gigantic hoop earrings and jangling her bangles more animatedly by the minute. 'Do you think she's really a gypsy?'

Billy guffawed. 'Gypsy, my arse. Her dad worked at the abattoir and her mum was a dinner lady at the village school, love. More alcohol than gypsy in her bloodstream.'

'I think it's the combination of cider and weed that makes her so potty,' said Tab. 'I might ask her to tell my fortune. She told Sam she was a princess in a previous life and that she'd rise again from the ashes.'

'Isn't it a phoenix that does that?'

'I don't know, but Sam was happy. She said she knew deep down that she should be wearing a tiara and talking all posh like her ladyship.'

'Well Pandora isn't happy.' Lottie nodded over at Pandora, who had put her sunglasses on and was tapping her foot irritably as she glared at the crowd waiting to have their fortune told.

'Right, enough gossiping, come on you lot, shift your arses.' Billy rubbed his hands together in anticipation.

'Oh God, what have I forgotten to do now?' Lottie honestly

thought she'd done enough judging for the day. She'd also agreed to supervise the pony rides, but she didn't think that was for at least another hour.

'Rory sent me over to gather forces.' He looked pointedly at Jamie. 'Tippermere forces. It's us against you outsiders in the tug of war.'

'We don't normally have a tug of war, Dad.'

'Well we do today, love. Rory's got quite a book running on it and the losers are in the stocks, and if you think I'm letting that sanctimonious vicar throw a wet sponge at me you've got another thing coming. So flex your muscles, girl. That man hasn't forgiven me for telling him that he had as much chance of being an extra in this film as he did of filling the church pews on a Sunday.'

'Hang on, I've got an idea.' And before anybody could stop her, Tab was off, dragging Jamie with her.

Ten minutes later, Lottie looked at Rory and Xander facing each other over a scarf tied to the middle of the rope and hoped that this wasn't going to get personal.

It all looked rather one-sided though, with the vicar (persuaded to support his flock by Tab) being the only member of the Tippermere team who didn't look like he regularly worked out. Her father, Billy, might not have been as young and athletic as he had been but he added weight as the anchor. Rory, Mick, and Dom looked the sportsmen that they were and with a handful of farmers and huntsmen thrown in they looked pretty formidable.

The outsider's team was formed mainly from film crew, one or two of whom were used to manhandling heavy cameras or props, but the majority never lifted much more than a coffee cup.

'Pick up the rope.' Elizabeth, who had sensed fun and homed in like an Exocet missile, issued the order as though she did this every day and Lottie wondered if she'd given Rory the idea in the first place. She really wouldn't put it past her gran to decide Seb needed another dent in his armour of self-importance.

'*We* should have David.' Jamie who was half hidden behind Xander pointed towards the end of the Tippermere line. 'David Simcock. He's from Kitterly Heath not Tippermere.'

Elizabeth gave him one of her withering looks then reluctantly agreed. 'Well, go on Charlotte, join in to balance the numbers.'

'But Gran, I need to get ready for the pony rides.'

'Nonsense, nobody is interested in that at the moment. *This* is the main event. You boy, yes you.' She waved at a guy who was more often seen in the catering van serving burgers and currently had one hand on the rope and the other on his mobile phone. 'Put that away. Charlotte, if you do not hurry up I will go and get Victoria. At least it will stop her demolishing the cakes.'

Lottie sighed and squeezed into the line behind Rory. If Victoria, known to everybody but Elizabeth as Tiggy, was eating the cakes rather than guarding them she'd kill her. Or rather the villagers of Tippermere would.

'Take the strain.' Elizabeth was enjoying herself. 'Pull.' And she blew a whistle, which Lottie didn't even know she had, with as much force as she could muster.

Lottie was still recovering from the ear-splitting sound, and the teams were throwing their collective weights back when there was a high-pitched squeal. It was followed by a shriek of 'Uncle Worwy, Uncle Worwy look at me,' and the bellow of a pony who had just spotted the love of its life.

Lottie dropped the rope as Rupert the pony, with Roxy bouncing on his back, ploughed through what had been the judging ring, demolishing the flower arrangements as he went.

'Oh hell.' Rory let go of the rope, and the rest of the Tippermere team, unbalanced, lurched forward, sending the outsiders sprawling on to their backsides.

Lottie tried not to giggle as Rory set off at a jog; the chestnut pony zig-zagged across the lawn like a sailboat trying to make headway against a strong wind, dodging all attempts at capture as he headed resolutely on towards his goal, his best friend, Bilbo, who had just emerged from the stable yard.

Alice gave an unexpected squeal and started to giggle and a nauseous Amanda looked up in surprise that turned to horror.

It wasn't that the roly-poly ponies moved fast, it was more their determination to go that caused the problem. Spotting, and hearing, Rupert, Bilbo gave a series of welcome nickers that sounded like a hiccupping machine gun and putting his head down he set off to meet his friend midway. Amanda, staggering to keep up, tripped over the verge between gravel drive and lawns and waving her arms wildly to keep her balance she forgot all about hanging on to the pony.

'Oh heavens, hang on, darling.' Dom was already sprinting, leaving a laughing Lottie and Rory in his wake.

An hour later, Lottie was surprised to spot Rory and Xander behind the barbecue, having obviously called some kind of truce.

She'd given up on the idea of giving pony rides, as all the prospective customers were casting murderous looks at Bilbo and Rupert. She'd heard a few mutterings about the Stanthorpes being stark, staring mad, and several comments along the lines of '*if they think I'm going to let my little Harriet sit on one of those wild animals they've got another thing coming.*'

Amanda was safely installed in the tea tent with a slice of carrot cake (not Lottie's – she'd warned her friend not to risk that) and a nice cup of chamomile tea. Alice was being led astray by Roxy, who had finally agreed to let go of Rory's leg – which she'd clung to for half an hour – and Rupert and Bilbo were safely locked up in their adjoining stables.

'Hasn't it gone well, babe? Did you see my Roxy? Isn't she doing amazing with her riding? It was so good of Rory to go and catch her, though. She told him that when she grows up she's going to be a princess and he can be her prince, they can get married and have lots of little princesses. He looked really chuffed. He'll make a fab dad won't he, babe?' Sam passed Lottie a glass of champagne and giggled. 'Here you go, doll. I thought you looked like you needed this.'

Chapter 27

'So, what's your problem, mate?' Rory decided that once you got to know him, Xander actually seemed an okay type. 'Here.' He handed him a burger and took the proffered can of beer.

'Cheers. No problem,' Xander shrugged, 'though I think you staged that runaway pony so you didn't have to admit defeat in the tug of war.'

'Bollocks, we could take you lot on any day. You know what I mean, though. I've been watching you, you move as fast as that hairy little bugger did every time you see the press.'

'Just call me camera-shy.' Xander grinned and took a bite of burger.

Rory raised an eyebrow, then stirred up the charcoal on the barbecue, sending a shower of sparks out.

'Okay, look.' He fed the rest of his food to Ella, who was sitting patiently at his feet listening to the conversation as though she understood every word, her eyebrows wriggling in concern. 'When I said I understood what you were going through when Black Gold died, I meant it.'

'You said.' Rory shrugged. 'Riding accidents happen.'

'But I could have avoided that one. I should have stopped him, swapped ponies. And it was my fucking fault for riding the line.

333

That rider had a reputation for smacking the ball straight at you, he needs shooting.'

'But he's rich?'

'You got it.'

'Autopsy?'

'Heart.' Xander picked up the dog and watched as she licked his fingers clean.

'So it could have happened any time.'

'That doesn't help, to be honest.'

'No, I suppose it doesn't.'

'But it wasn't just that. The papers did have a field day, and there was enough hate mail to keep me in bog roll for the rest of my life – really bad. My girlfriend couldn't cope with it – she wanted to be going out with the guy everybody loved, not the moody bastard that everybody hated.'

'Yeah, I've seen that before.' Rory winced, but he knew it was the price of fame. You soon found out who your real friends were, the people who loved you, when things went wrong.

'I'd pulled out of the team, so no job, no adulation, complete loser, eh? The newspapers loved it. They all kicked off again and my ex sold more than one story saying how I'd changed. She slagged off polo, went for the cruelty angle, despite the fact she'd been at every bloody match for three seasons chasing the players before I was stupid enough to fall for her.'

Rory gave up on trying to resuscitate the charcoal.

'Then my parents split.'

'I thought they had years ago? Pandora's your half-sister, isn't she?'

'She is, but Dad never left Mum, well not back then. He wasn't daft, just a dickhead. Pandora takes after her mum and would you marry somebody like that?'

Rory laughed. 'Well according to the papers I would.'

'She's probably responsible for getting that photo of the two of you in the paper.'

'So I heard.'

It was Xander's turn to raise an eyebrow, and Rory winked. 'We have contacts. So why did your Dad decide to go now, then, after all this time?'

'A mix of stuff, I guess. Mum had a nervous breakdown, went to pieces, so it gave him the perfect excuse. He'd had enough. I mean she always was a bit different, a bit eccentric.' He gave a sad smile as he fondled Ella's silky ears. 'She would have fit in well here, if Dad had let her stay, but he was a selfish bastard. Anyway she really went to bits, I was getting death threats and some of them were going to their address, and Dad was playing away again. Not that he ever didn't. But the one he's found this time is different. She's got money as well as looks, which I think Mum realised. Pandora will blow a gasket when she finds out. So,' he sighed, 'life was a bit shit, and without polo to keep my mind off things I started drinking more than I should, so that added more fuel to the fire. Newspapers were having a field day, which is why I want to keep out of the limelight now. I can't risk them starting to dig again and printing stuff about Mum – she doesn't deserve it and,' he paused, 'Dad will turn nasty, he'll think I've dumped to the press on purpose to get people on my side, make him pay up. If that happens he'll do a Pandora and refuse, just to make a point.'

'Pay up?'

'He's refusing to pay all Mum's medical bills, or look after her. He just wants to dump her and move on.' He gave a wry smile. 'It's what he does best. Trouble is, she's used to being cared for. She totally relied on him providing for her, and in return she did everything he wanted, waited on him hand and foot. It might not be very PC these days, but it worked for them. My problem now is working out how to cover the bills until we get to court and get some kind of settlement.'

'Why not get back into polo, go abroad? You'll be off the radar.'

'I sold all my best ponies to cover her care. She was admitted into a private clinic then, wham, he buggered off and left her without a penny.'

'Joint account?'

'You're kidding, aren't you? Dad had control of everything. He just saw her as the little woman and she trusted him to sort it all. I'd need somebody to offer me a ride to get back in, but to be honest I think I need a break from the game. I've lost the thirst, if you know what I mean.'

Rory did – if you weren't hungry to win then it showed. It was all downhill from there.

'I can't let him get away without looking after her, he owes her that much. But until we get to court I've got to be careful.'

'You should talk to Tom about that – he's an expert at keeping a low profile.'

'Tom?'

'Tab's dad. He was a model, did the whole escape-to-the-country bit, but he's an okay kind of guy. Surprised you've not met him yet, though he's a real hermit when it suits him. You don't think Pandora had anything to do with your headlines?'

'Probably.' Xander shrugged. 'Wouldn't put it past her, and I've got a sneaking suspicion she scared my ex off. Though I think she did me a favour there.'

'So you didn't have a reason to turn down her offer of a job on this shoot?'

'Nope. I've always felt a bit sorry for her – all she ever got from Dad was money. He was a shit, and it wasn't her fault was it? So I've stayed in touch and, to be honest, I thought maybe this time there was no ulterior motive, she was just being nice. But there was no way out, no easy way to say no, which could be just how she planned it.'

'And she knew you fancied Lottie?'

'Oh come on mate, I—'

'I know you did, and it just looks, from where I'm standing, that Pandora wants to rattle her, cause trouble between us.'

'Oh she does like to stir things, it's in her nature; she doesn't like people to be happier than she is.'

'I'm not saying you're still after Lottie, but . . .' He gave Xander a long stare.

'She's a lovely girl, who wouldn't fancy her? You're a lucky man, Rory. I hope you know that. But I'm not the enemy, I'm no marriage wrecker.'

'You leave that to Pandora, eh? There's no need to answer that.' Xander didn't. 'To be honest, mate, I really hate all this filming.'

'I know. I can't say I'd be impressed if I was in your shoes.'

'Even before the helicopter incident I was getting pissed off with it all. I'd love to be able to tell Seb to bugger off.'

'But you can't, can you?' Xander gave a wry grin, 'and I'm not just saying that so I can hang around your wife.'

'Not saying what?' Tab bounced between the two of them, as though she was expecting trouble. 'Hey, any burgers left? We're starving.' She stroked Ella on the head and gave Rory a hug so he didn't feel left out.

'Too late, we've just had the last two. You'll have to eat Lottie's cake.'

'She warned us not to.' Tab grinned, then pointed. 'Hey, look at the WI tent. That is so cool.'

The tent was billowing like Mrs Jones' skirt had when Roxy had crawled under and released the air out of her balloon. And it wasn't just the tent.

The slight breeze that had been welcome earlier on in the afternoon had been replaced by hefty gusts of air that were scattering the embers of the barbecue and tugging at the marquees so that they flapped alarmingly.

'Wind's picking up.' Rory batted at the embers with his spatula as they flew onto the pile of napkins, threatening to ignite them. There was an abrupt swirl of wind, which he hadn't been expecting, and the whole pile took off, tumbling across the grass, with Ella in pursuit.

'Look at that, look at that.' Tab tugged on Jamie's t-shirt and they all looked across the ground to where Pandora's signed photos were being tossed about unceremoniously. She shrieked, one hand clutching the small tent, which seemed intent on taking to the skies, the other waving helplessly as she made a futile attempt to grab her precious pictures. The adjoining tent was airborne one minute, showing glimpses of Gypsy Rose, who was snoring, clutching a large bottle of cider to her chest, and then back down the next.

'Do you think we should help?' Tab looked at the three men, none of whom seemed inclined to move.

'Bet you ten quid Rose has got an indecent red thong on under that skirt. One more gust and we'll get a flash.'

'No way. You've got insider knowledge.' Xander looked at the barbecue. 'Got a lid we can put on this thing?'

The carefully strung bunting pulled free of its moorings, sending the dogs into a frenzy as they all tried to jump on it, and the crowds fled from the marquees, which were creaking rather alarmingly as they swayed in sympathy with each gust.

'I suppose we'd better do something,' Rory sighed. 'Go on, Tab, you and Jamie help the gypsy and poisonous Pandora, and we'll make a start on the bigger stuff.'

The film crew might not have been particularly handy when it came to tug of war, but they excelled at packing stuff away. It was part and parcel of their job.

By the time Jamie and Tab made their way over to rescue Pandora, she was close to hysterical and they had to prise her fingers off the tent pole. As her red hair whipped around her face and her kohl spread so that her eyes were as wide as a frightened cat's, Lottie was very tempted to take a picture and sell *that* to the tabloids. But that would have been mean.

Nobody said anything, as she clutched the few photographs

that had been rescued to her chest and demanded to know why nobody had checked the weather forecast, but they were all relieved when she pleaded a migraine and let Seb pack her into the car and take her back to the hotel for a long soak in the bath and a foot massage.

'I rather think that James will be good for young Tabatha, don't you?' Elizabeth who had been supervising proceedings with Bertie at her side, waved a finger in the direction of the pair. Tab was laughing as Jamie fought to fold up a trestle table that was refusing to co-operate. 'That girl has always taken life far too seriously.'

'She was a goth, Gran, they don't smile.' Lottie, who had been just about to steal a cupcake before she put the remainder in a box stopped herself short. Elizabeth had a raised eyebrow that said she knew.

'Insecurity is most unattractive, I always find, but that boy has a settling way about him.'

'Tab's not insecure!' Tab had always walked with a confident swagger, never hesitated to rise to a challenge and had the power to scare every man under thirty that was unfortunate enough to cross her path.

'Attitude is created for a purpose, Charlotte. Honestly I do wonder where your powers of observation are at times. You are perfectly capable of knowing that one of your blessed horses is out of sorts, but stubbornly refuse to acknowledge human traits.'

'I'm not stubborn.' She pushed the lid down firmly on the cakes, before one of them jumped out straight into her mouth.

'Tabatha will find a happy outlook much more helpful in life.'

'She's been happy for a while, it's not just Jamie.' Lottie thought Elizabeth was being slightly unfair. True, Tab had been a stroppy teenager and slightly scary as she hit her twenties. But the crisp outer shell had started to melt as she'd grown into her own skin. She'd be twenty-five soon and when Lottie looked at her she wished she was that age again.

'I do hope that he doesn't return to his mother when filming draws to a close – he's a nice young man. He needs his independence.'

'And if he does you'll have pushed them together for no reason.' Elizabeth arched an eyebrow. 'I know you engineered that, Gran. Tab only had eyes for Xander until you interfered.'

'I did not interfere – besides what interest would Xander have in a child? She needed a distraction, and I wanted them to do something for me. I do not do anything without a reason, Charlotte. I thought you would have realised that by now. At least you do notice some things, even if Alexander's intentions completely bypassed you.'

Heat rushed to Lottie's cheeks. 'Gran!'

'Ah, so you did notice eventually. I am surprised that man lets his sister manipulate him like she does, but he is rather a product of his emotions as his mother was. Too kind for his own good.'

'Sorry?' Talking to her gran could be like unknotting a necklace chain, link after link entangled, and you were frightened of tugging too hard in case it snapped. Never to be the same again.

'Well that woman did persuade him to come back here, knowing full well that he'd have to deal with you.'

'Did she?'

'Honestly, Charlotte. If an old woman like me knows that, then I'm sure your deductive powers are up to the task. I rather think she wanted him here to upset the apple cart, as it were.'

'Apple cart?'

'Your marriage, dear. And on one hand the poor boy couldn't resist returning to Tippermere on the off chance he might see you, and on the other felt that his sister might genuinely be trying to help him. That woman is only ever going to do things for her own ends, though. I do rather think he was quite shocked to actually find you here.' A small smile played on her lips. 'Now I know exactly what you're thinking, so you can stop right there.

I do things for the good of the estate and my family. Pandora is only interested in herself, an island of need.'

Lottie wasn't sure she liked her marriage being referred to as an apple cart, it sounded far too wobbly.

'Everything okay, darling?' As if on cue the other half of her apple cart arrived and gave her a big sloppy kiss and a bum squeeze. 'We're done here. Good job that bloody wind died down or we'd have never managed.'

'I know.' As each gust of wind had billowed its way across the grounds, gathering up bunting, sweet wrappers, and paper plates as it went, Lottie had thought they faced an impossible task. But it had left as quickly as it arrived, leaving behind the very messy, but tranquil, remains of the show. 'Everybody has been brilliant, I can't believe how quickly it's all been tidied away.'

'Those lads have worked wonders,' Billy clamped an arm around Rory's shoulder and winked at Elizabeth. 'Bloody good job the Drakelow drama queens have disappeared, though.'

'Dad, you shouldn't call them that.'

'Bollocks, you know me, love. I say it as I see it, and that Seb is as bad as his wife. Right,' he rubbed his hands together, 'time for a pint, I reckon, everybody coming?'

'We will follow on, William. Charlotte and I need to talk.'

Billy and Rory looked at Lottie, who shrugged. 'Do we?'

'We do. Go on then, hurry along, boys.'

They didn't need to be told twice, they never did when it came to booze or a party. Maybe that was partly why she loved her husband so much, because of the similarities between him and her father. And maybe that was why lately she'd been so scared of messing it all up.

Since Gold's death, she and Rory had actually been as close as they'd ever been, drawn together by the tragedy, and the prospect of change. All those worries about how she might mess up his life had disappeared. They were a team again. Probably because the whole having-a-baby debate had been crushed by something far more pressing, she hadn't had even a passing thought about the issue. Or she'd at least been able to bury her head in the sand and pretend it would go away.

Today the insecurities had flooded back with the force of a hurricane, after he'd rescued Roxy. Only a fool would have missed the look of pure happiness on Rory's face as the little girl had clung to him adoringly.

Lottie watched her father and husband walk off companionably and wondered what she'd done to upset Elizabeth now. She didn't like 'talks'.

'I think today went rather well. Well done, dear.'

So maybe she hadn't done anything wrong.

'Let's have a little walk.'

Maybe she had.

'Now, tell me what else is bothering you.'

There was definitely something. 'Like what? I'm fine.'

'You are twitchy, Charlotte.' Elizabeth paused. 'You and Rory work well together as a team.'

Lottie was pretty sure she hadn't shown any reaction at all, but Gran had decided she was on the right scent.

'He was quite determined to get to the root of those nasty articles in the tabloids, quite cross at the way he'd been portrayed.'

'I know.' Lottie wished she'd had a chance to change from her respectable to her comfy shoes before walking. Her feet were crying out for riding boots. 'I miss Pip. She was great at sorting stuff out like that.'

'I miss her too dear. Such a clever girl.'

Elizabeth slipped her hand through Lottie's arm, the other one on her stick as they walked slowly across the lawns towards the lake.

'Pandora's clever too.' Lottie sighed. 'I'm still not quite sure what she wants more, Rory or Tipping House.'

'Rory is strong enough to resist that type of woman, Charlotte. He was quite wonderful rescuing Roxanne today, wasn't he? The children are rather smitten with him.' Her tone had softened.

'I know.' Lottie studied her feet. 'He loves the kids, especially Roxy.'

'Does he want to start a family, dear?'

'Probably.' She took a deep breath, hoping it would dislodge the feeling of indigestion, which she knew was actually something else.

'And you don't?'

'It's not that I don't, it's . . .' Elizabeth waited, knocking the heads off daisies with her stick as they strolled. Lottie ground to a halt and looked at her grandmother. 'I'd be an awful mother.'

'And why do you say that?'

'I don't even like babies. I like cuddling puppies more than babies.'

'But those are other people's babies, Charlotte. Your own are rather different. I'm sure you would cope splendidly. Your mother was the same. She never really thought of having her own children until she had you, and she was an excellent mother. She adored you.'

'And she left me.' It burst out of Lottie before she could stop it.

'Ah.' Elizabeth started to walk again and Lottie hurried after her. 'She left all of us, my dear.'

'I know, sorry.' Lottie put a hand over her mouth. She was being selfish. 'It's just,' she had to say it, 'I don't want to lose Rory as well.'

'Oh Charlotte, my dear, why on earth would you lose Rory?'

'I know he wants children, and,' she fondled Bertie's ears, 'I'm just not sure, and what if he finds somebody else to have his baby? I mean,' she was feeling glummer by the moment, as unburdening herself was not providing the cathartic release she was expecting. 'I know he might be immune to Pandora,' or might not be, who knew? 'And he might not mind too much at the moment, but what if he gets fed up of waiting? I might never change my mind, and that's not fair on him.'

'If he's the man I think he is, he won't get fed up, my dear.' Her tone softened. 'Why do you underestimate him? If you have your reasons, I'm sure he will understand. You have talked properly about this, I presume?' She shook her head at the look on Lottie's face. 'Oh honestly, Charlotte. Men cannot mind-read you know, whatever they would like us to believe. You really do need to be quite plain speaking with them. And as for fair, to be fair is to be open-minded, and I rather think you are taking quite a shuttered view.'

'But everybody keeps saying he'll make a wonderful father.'

Elizabeth took Lottie's hand in hers. 'Ah yes, that mysterious thought-pervading *everybody*. This is not about *everybody*, this is about you, both of you. They might be right, my dear, who knows? And what does 'wonderful' mean? There are many kinds of wonderful, but only one life that's right for you. I used to stand here when I was young with a head full of romantic notions.' Lottie couldn't imagine her gran having any kind of notions. 'I always imagined that Mr Darcy might appear from this lake one day, dear.' She smiled a secret, and slightly sad, smile. 'I thought that would be rather wonderful, but your dear grandfather couldn't swim, so maybe it wouldn't have been quite so splendid after all.' She flicked at the grass with her stick and her normal, slightly acidic, tone returned. 'Now, I think I have had quite enough excitement for one day. You may walk back with me, and then go and find your husband. And Charlotte?'

Lottie looked up.

'Do not rush into any decisions about the house or your marriage. It is always surprising just how much time you have. A bad decision is always far harder to reverse than a good one. Now, where's that dog got to?'

* * *

'How can anybody say life in the country is boring?' Jamie put a pint down in front of Tab and squeezed in next to her.

344

'Oh boy, do I need this.' Tab took a long slurp, then wiped the back of her hand over her mouth.

'So ladylike.' He grinned.

The Bull's Head was packed to the rafters, making conversation pretty much impossible unless you were prepared to do a Billy-style bellow. But Jamie didn't mind. He was just happy pressed thigh to thigh with Tab, and he was more than happy to have an excuse to whisper in her ear.

'Is it always like this?'

'Oh yes, everybody has cake and burgers at the village show, then comes here afterwards to get plastered. Did you see the state of Pandora's red hair? It was all on end – she looked like a lit match.' Tab giggled. 'And she was screaming that she'd broken a nail, she was yelling at Seb for not rescuing her earlier, and telling Rose she was a fat drunken dollop who needed to get a life. Not that Rose was conscious. She probably won't wake up until tomorrow lunchtime. Her husband always comes to collect her in his tractor – just throws her in the trailer.'

'She's got a husband?' Jamie was astounded.

'Oh yes, they've got a smallholding and keep pigs and geese. She says her hubby was a pig in his previous life.'

'And she was a goose?'

'No, he's always called her a silly goose, though. Think he got her one for Valentine's Day one year as a joke. They do stuff like that; they're a bit weird, but I like weird.'

'Weird can be good.' Jamie stared into his drink. 'I'll miss this place when we pack up; it won't be that long now.'

'Will you miss me?' Tab traced a teasing finger along his inner thigh and he clamped a hand over it.

'Yep.' He looked sideways under his lashes and she was watching him intently. A smile playing over the mouth he'd grown quite fond of, lips he wanted to kiss. Being pressed up close to Tab always had a strange effect on him.

'Come on, I'm going to take you home, Jamie boy.'

'Home? But, your Dad . . .' He could hear the alarm in his voice. Wanting to kiss her was one thing, but meeting the parents after two drinks, no proper dates, and not even lip-to-lip contact, let alone the sharing of bodily fluids, seemed a bit extreme.

'You stupid twat. Christ, you don't think I still live with him, do you?'

He didn't like to mention that he still shared a roof with his librarian mother, except when he was on location.

'I'm in the place above the stables. Lottie and Rory let me move in when they had to put the wedding business on hold. Come on, it's a bit too cutesy for me, but it'll do.'

Jamie didn't notice if it was cutesy or not. Going up the narrow staircase with Tab's pert bum only inches from his face was like clambering those last few tortuous steps to the summit.

On one hand he didn't quite want to get there, because once he did that was it. He'd reached the top, scaled the insurmountable, the only way was down. But on the other hand he knew it was now or never.

He was trying to work out whether she really meant what she'd suggested, or whether this was just another laptop session, when she flung open the door at the top then spun around, her oh-so-kissable lips only inches from his, her dark gaze suddenly unsure.

So he kissed her. Put his hands on her slim waist, closed his eyes and went for it.

God, she tasted good – exactly like he knew she would.

'Jamie?' He opened one eye and there wasn't a trace of apprehension left in hers. 'Kick the door shut.'

He peeled off her t-shirt and she was bra-less. Nipples the colour of fudge – dark against her incredibly pale skin. Oh shit, this was going to be a disaster. His cock was already straining against the zip of his jeans and his brain wasn't co-operating at all. No way could he even try and count backwards or do any of

346

those things that were supposed to put off the inevitable.

At the first touch of his tongue her nipple puckered to a hard nub and her stomach contracted.

'Have you got *any* underwear on?' The words tumbled out and sounded like he was talking under water.

'Have a look.'

He looked. She had. The skimpiest bit of black lace he'd ever seen, and it was so not what he expected that he nearly came there and then. He was still wondering how the hell he was going to do this when she stripped his top over his head, unbuckled his belt, and was working on his flies.

'Don't. Sorry. I mean don't touch me.' The words stuttered out in an agonising staccato that he couldn't control.

It was too late. His cock sprang out like a jack-in-a-box and Tab's eyes opened wide. 'Oh my God, that is so much bigger than I thought it would be.'

'This is not the time to talk about size,' he said through gritted teeth, and did what seemed like the wisest thing, pushed her back onto the enormous bed that dominated the room.

The second he was on her she stopped teasing, stopped talking. Her eyes were dark pools, her lips swollen beneath his.

He'd meant to take his time, but when she opened those long, slim legs he lost all sensible thought and was in there like some teenager on a first date.

'Bloody hell.' Jamie ran his fingers through his hair, pushing it out of his face and propped himself on one elbow, looking down at Tab. 'Bloody amazing, bloody fucking hell.'

She smiled, a Mona Lisa smile.

'Was it alright, did you . . .?'

Tab grinned and traced a finger down his spine.

'Sorry, I mean I know it was a bit quick.'

'Sh.' Tab put a finger on his lips and studied his features slowly, thoroughly, for the first time. 'It was perfect.' She'd done it. If she was totally, perfectly honest, the earth hadn't exactly tilted on its axis, but something had shifted.

'Do you think we need to do it again to be sure?' He was staring at her boobs and she could feel a prickle as her nipples tightened. His mouth came down, sharp teeth tugging, and the prickle spread down to her stomach.

What Jamie lacked in finesse, she decided, he more than made up for with enthusiasm and stamina. 'Wow, yes, right there, that is so cool, really, really, amaz—'

Then she forgot all about what she was about to say when he hit just the right spot.

Chapter 28

The horsebox juddered and there was a yell that Lottie was sure even the riders out on the course would have heard.

'Ow! Bugger, stop it.' Tab obviously wasn't happy.

Lottie looked at Rory and giggled. 'Do you think I should go and help her?'

The horsebox rocked more violently.

'What is it with her and that horse? God knows what they're up to in there.'

'It's not Tab's fault. Joker is in love with her.'

Rory shook his head and had a final look at the course. Lottie had declared it terrifying when they'd walked it together earlier, and then hastily added that it was of course 'a piece of piss for you and Joker, just awful if I had to do it'.

He knew that the big horse was more than capable of clearing every jump comfortably, his only worry was that the way Joker covered the ground so effortlessly, if he didn't have his wits about him they'd take a wrong turning. Roaring Rob would have him for dinner if he did, after he'd disembowelled him.

'He'll get round, he's brilliant.' If he said it enough times he'd believe it.

Lottie kissed him. 'Stop being grumpy, you're brilliant too, darling.'

'What do you think Tab is doing to him?'

'He gives her love bites.' She grinned and stood up. It really wasn't fair to leave Tab to get Joker ready on her own. 'It took her ages to persuade Jamie that it was a horse, not another man. He said it was a worse excuse than saying the dog ate her homework – more original, but worse. But she doesn't like telling him off.'

'Jamie or Joker?'

'Joker. She said he makes his ears go all floppy and his bottom lip wobbles if she gets cross with him.' There was a bang on the side of the horsebox that made both of them jump.

'I can hear you bloody laughing at me. I hope he dumps you in the lake, Rory Steel, you ungrateful sod. Now open this ramp and let me out before he starts sticking his tongue down my throat.'

They dropped the ramp and Joker sauntered out, flapping his ears; not even the immaculate plaits and shining coat could make him look a proud thoroughbred. He just looked slightly comical and quite adorable.

Tab looked dishevelled. Her normally sleek hair was tousled and damp, where the horse had chewed and nuzzled it, and he'd half pulled her shirt out of her jodhpurs.

Rory grinned. 'You look like you've either had a good shagging or gone five rounds with Mike Tyson.'

'I'll go for Tyson, if you don't mind. Here, take him.' She tapped the end of Joker's nose and the whites of his eyes showed as he tried to see. 'If you do that again then that's it, we're over, finished. Okay?' He shook his head violently so that all his painstakingly neat plaits rocked from side to side, boats bobbing on the crest of a wave.

Rory double-checked his tack, then tightened his body protector and put his hat on.

'You'll blow them away,' said Lottie, giving him a rather

awkward hug around his body armour. 'Oh, I love you, and I love you too Joker.'

'More like suck them to death.' Tab, despite her protestations, had grown incredibly fond of the big bay horse, and sneaked him a Polo mint as Lottie gave Rory a leg up into the saddle.

'This is so exciting. Oh hell, my phone's ringing.' By the time Lottie managed to prise her mobile out of her skin-tight jodhpurs it had stopped vibrating. She ran to catch up with Tab, Rory, and Joker, who were making their way towards the start of the cross-country course, staring at the caller-ID on the phone display as she went. 'That's strange. It's Uncle Dom. What does he want? He knows we're here. Oh, I'll ring him back once you've gone through the start gate. I'm not going to miss that for anything. Oh golly, look at the way he's flapping his ears. Do you think that means he's excited?'

She was still shouting love you and go for it, when Joker launched his large frame onto the course, lolloping off at a ground-swallowing gallop.

Despite a 'call me' text, Dom was refusing to answer his phone, which was annoying. Lottie hated it when you were trying to ring somebody back and they just wouldn't answer. With every redial it got more frustrating.

'It can't be that urgent, can it?'

Tab shrugged, too busy trying to keep track of her precious Joker as he headed towards the lake, then faltered on take-off. 'Oh bugger, I hope he doesn't really dump Rory in the lake. You don't think he was listening to what I said, do you? Shall we go to the other side of the course?'

Lottie dithered. She desperately wanted to support Rory and Joker on their first major outing together, but Uncle Dom's call was unsettling. He was a bit like Gran. He didn't do anything without a reason. She was rocking from foot to foot when her mobile burst into life. But it wasn't Dom.

351

'Where the hell are you? I've covered the whole bloody course looking for you.'

'Dad?' She frowned. 'What course?'

'The cross-country, what do you think, you ninny? I've seen Rory twice – can't miss that big clown's face.' She presumed he was talking about Joker, not her husband.

'We're near the start.'

'Well get your arse over to the horsebox pronto, love. There's a good girl.'

'Dad?' But he'd rung off. He was pretty much permanently attached to his mobile phone, but was as blunt on it as he was face to face. He'd said what he wanted to.

'I better go, Tab. Are you alright for a bit?'

'I'm fine.' Tab was already striding off, shouting behind as she went. 'I want to see him over the coffin – if he's let Joker have his head he'll never hold him back. Catch you later.'

Billy was sitting on the ramp of the horsebox looking hot, sweaty and not at all happy when she got there. 'Sorry, love.' He stood up wearily, which immediately sent her stomach into her boots. 'Bad news. Your gran's been rushed into hospital and Dom said he thinks we should be there. Thought it easiest if I came over in the car and got you.'

'Hospital?'

'Yes, hospital.'

'But there's nothing wrong with her. I saw her yesterday. I was talking to her.'

'Yes, well, that's what she wanted us all to believe. Come on, love.'

Billy didn't speak again until the car had bounced its way over the uneven field and was on smooth tarmac. 'She'd summoned Amanda for coffee this morning and had a dizzy spell. Admitted she's been having funny turns, getting lightheaded – for heaven's sake put your foot down, it's not a bloody Sunday.' Billy was near enough to touch the bumper of the car in front – he wasn't what you'd describe a patient driver. 'And having pains in her neck. These bloody drivers are a pain in neck, shouldn't be allowed on the road. Amanda was worried, insisted Dom took her to hospital and,' he leant on the car horn, 'they think it's a heart attack.'

'Oh God.'

'She's okay, love.' He put a hand briefly on her knee, then returned it to the horn. 'Bit more befuddled than normal, but she's already got the nurses on their toes. Insisted she had to see you, though, and they won't let her out.'

'So it is serious.' Lottie bit down hard on her lip, the sweet taste of blood flooding her mouth and making her feel sick.

Billy didn't answer straight away. But when he did, his gruff voice was soft. 'She's an old lady, love. We tend to forget because of the way she is, but I've noticed she's not been getting around like she used to.'

Lottie scrunched her eyes shut. It was her fault. She'd dragged her off on that walk after the village show. Elizabeth had been slower than normal, had wanted to turn back. Had been tired, and she hadn't paid any attention. She shouldn't have let her walk so far, and she shouldn't have been moaning on about her own silly problems. Oh no, what had she said? She should have noticed her gran was feeling off, and she really shouldn't have been going on like that. The whole idea of her running the estate was to stop Gran stressing.

'It's nobody's fault.' Billy shot her a glance that said it all. Soft, caring, making her want to burst into tears. 'She's a good age, love. Now come on, shoulders back, stiff upper lip eh, like she'd want.' He winked. But it didn't hold the normal joviality.

* * *

'I do wish everybody would stop fussing. Sit down, Charlotte. Here. Come on, no here, on the side of the bed. I haven't got anything catching, you know.'

353

Lottie didn't think she had. She just thought she looked small and frail in the big white bed.

'The rest of you can go. Go on, run along. And you can take that look off your face, Dominic, I want to talk to Charlotte. She'll tell you if I expire, won't you dear? Not that I intend to.'

Lottie sat down and pleated the edge of the sheet.

'Don't worry, I am not about to launch into a death-bed confession, dear. Oh don't look at me like that. I felt a bit off colour and asked Dominic to bring me in for a quick check up. Now, I think it's time we talked about children, but not how to make them. I think you youngsters know far too much about that.' She placed her hand over her granddaughter's and Lottie stared at it.

Elizabeth's skin was papery thin, almost translucent, sea green-blue where the veins ran through, and at the base of her thumb it was mottled brown, wrinkled like an autumn leaf that would soon crumble. The once-soft, gentle touch was slightly dry, almost weightless. A lump formed in Lottie's chest, like urgent indigestion demanding attention, the pressure building. She mustn't cry.

'I was like you when I was young, Charlotte. Not a maternal bone in my body. I'd always wished I'd been born a boy – they had far more fun. When I bore my children it was out of a sense of duty, one did that in those days, but from the day they were born they were mine. Nothing ever belongs to you like your child. Men can play with your heart and your sensibility, but a child can snap it in two. A child will bring you grief, but they will also give you the best moments of your life. I would have gladly given my life for Alexa's if the good Lord had let me trade. Losing her left a scar that never healed.'

Lottie glanced up through her eyelashes to see that Elizabeth's eyes were closed.

'That child was a force of nature, as wilful as an uncut colt, but it is the fearless that leave the strongest mark. She had her insecurities, like all of us, and you were the greatest one, Charlotte.'

Her eyelids sprung open, her piercing blue gaze rested on Lottie.

'Me?'

'Oh yes, the thought of having a baby terrified the poor girl.' A smile twitched at the corner of her mouth, then faded as though it was too much effort. 'Alexandra was my greatest success, Charlotte, and you are hers. I had never seen her unsure until she looked on you for the first time. But the moment she touched you it went. I've been thinking about what you said, and you really have to understand that your mother didn't abandon you, child. To think that would be cruel and unjust. She would never, ever willingly have left you.'

Oh please don't say you're going to leave me as well, thought Lottie, crossing the fingers on the hand that was at her side, hidden from Elizabeth's sight.

'I'm not going anywhere yet.' Her tone was dry. 'You shouldn't fear the future, child. You are not your mother. If you have a child then you will probably be around until it is quite fed up of you.' She coughed and Lottie cringed. 'It is surprising how quickly youngsters need to find their own feet. They are surprisingly resilient. Just look at young Roxanne.' The corner of her mouth lifted briefly and Lottie couldn't help but smile.

'There's no stopping Roxy, she's a mini Sam.'

'And Samantha is a splendid mother, despite outward appearances, and has a very warm heart.'

'I know.'

'She has time for people.'

Lottie suddenly felt guilty; there had been plenty of times recently when she'd felt hassled and short of time, and had blamed herself for letting Sam drag her off to watch the filming. But the other girl had a busy life too. Yet she'd been making time for Lottie, filling the gap that Pip had left. Talking sense and supporting her whenever Pandora had made life uncomfortable.

'Is that why you got the ponies for Roxy and Alice? Because you knew Sam would come and see me every day?'

'Samantha is a good ally, Charlotte. Her words come from her heart and from common sense rather than from a need to impress. She can see what is false, see through pretence rather well, and she stands by her friends. I know you miss Philippa as much as I do, and you miss young Michael rather more. We all need somebody to listen and tell us we are taking the right path.'

'I know.' I need you too, thought Lottie. More than I need anybody.

'History does not always repeat itself, dear. That is a fanciful notion. You are already older than your mother was when she was taken from us, and those scandalous newspapers reports about Rory and Pandora are not a repeat of your father's headlines when you were a child. It is simply Pandora trying to bring her film, her fantasy, to life. Life imitating art, and very badly, if I may say so.'

'I never said I thought Rory was after her.' Lottie went back to her origami of the bedsheets.

'No, but you fear that will happen if you tell him the truth about how you really feel about having children. You have to trust the strength of your relationship, Charlotte. Trust him enough to be completely honest, open your heart.' She smiled. 'It is a far bigger sin to assume your fears are grounded than to declare them and risk confirmation. Be brave, my dear. Look at me.'

Lottie glanced up.

'Let one crow of doubt in and the whole flock may follow. Don't let them. You've faced so many challenges, proved you are strong, so don't doubt the strength of the man you chose. Rory is not your father. Although I must say, William did a splendid job of bringing you up, even if we did have our differences at times.' Her voice was drifting off again, lost in thought. 'He would have had to change, grow up, even if Alexandra had been here. You do realise that, child? Change is an important part of growth.' She squeezed Lottie's hand. 'You're like her, you know, so like her in some ways. Strong and resourceful. I'm so proud of what you've done at Tipping House.'

'But you don't think the wedding business is good enough, do you? That's why you let Pandora come here? You wouldn't have introduced me to Jamie if you hadn't wanted it to happen.'

'Twaddle, dear. I have never wanted to see our home turned into a film location. All that nonsense is ridiculous. Your wedding business is a splendid idea, very fitting, but I rather thought we should take the opportunity to make it bigger and better.' Lottie could have sworn she'd brightened up. 'Out of the flames will rise your phoenix – if you will let it. Just imagine what will happen after this film is screened. I'm sure you will have interest rekindled. James arriving seemed quite fortuitous. Not that I foresaw Pandora's involvement – she really is the most unpleasant young lady. So unfortunate. But it's all about spin, my dear, isn't that what they call it? In my day we called it being one step ahead.'

'And that's why you agreed to it?' Lottie tried to keep the smile fixed on her face, but the tightness of her jaw, the pounding of her heart, had to be visible. Gran had such belief in her, had worked so hard, Lottie couldn't admit that soon the dream could be over, that however well the wedding business rebounded, it could be too late to save Tipping House.

'Of course, and of course it has kept you occupied, which is not a bad thing. I do hate idle hands.' She patted Lottie's hand. 'I know you will always do the right thing, Charlotte. But don't let anybody rush you into anything. You always have more time than you think. Signing away your life is easy, living it is harder. And now, dear, I do feel rather tired. It's all the excitement. Hospitals are such wearing places – one is much more relaxed at home. You go off and find young Rory – practise making babies.' She closed her eyes.

Lottie frowned. What did she mean about signing away her life? 'I'll come back later, just to check how you are, when I've done the horses and, er, the baby-making practice.'

Elizabeth opened one eye. 'You should talk to young Tabatha, and that Jamie, talk to them about the fire.' She sighed. 'They make such a splendid couple. I really must find out if that court-ship has progressed. Tomorrow, when I'm feeling brighter.'

'What do you mean, the fire?'

But the eye was very firmly shut again and Elizabeth showed absolutely no sign of having heard.

'See you later, Gran.' She didn't often kiss her gran these days. Elizabeth didn't do demonstrative, but she felt a sudden need. She would have loved to have hugged her, held her close, but maybe that was a step too far.

'Of course. Now leave an old lady to her sleep.' Lottie had her hand on the door when Elizabeth spoke again. 'Charlotte, remember one thing. You have something Pandora doesn't. Family and heritage. It's the first that's most important. You should never forget your family and friends, Charlotte. They will always be there for you. Our family is our strength.'

* * *

Rory was the first person Lottie saw when she came out of the room. He was still in his mud-spattered breeches, his curls flattened to his head by his riding hat, and he was the most welcome sight she'd seen all day. She was just about to jump on him when a man with a clipboard bustled in and cleared his throat.

The consultant peered over his glasses at them until they'd stopped fidgeting and then launched into what sounded like a rehearsed speech.

They thought it had been a heart attack, or more than one. A warning sign. She had to rest, in bed, in hospital. She was elderly, frailer than she seemed, and they shouldn't be taken in by her manner and words. She'd be exhausted when they went. She needed tests – they'd keep Dominic informed. He didn't know when she'd be well enough to go home. She might need care. It was best if they let her rest now and came back tomorrow. She was comfortable and in the best place. Then he checked his notes and rushed off to another emergency.

* * *

'Okay, darling?'

'I think so.' Lottie wasn't really sure how she felt. 'She looked so old.'

'She is old.' He opened the car door for her, did up the seatbelt.

'But old, old. You know, small, fragile.' She'd looked tiny in the big stark room. Adrift in an ocean of white. Helpless. 'How long have you been here?'

'I came as soon as I finished my round. Tab said she'd sort Joker. Are you sure you're okay?'

'I think I just want to go home and have a cuddle.'

'I can sort that.'

'Gran said the other day that I have to find my 'wonderful', and I have to talk to you about what I want and making babies, and I need to talk to Tab and Jamie. Not about making babies, about fires.'

'Quite a list.' The corner of his mouth quirked up in the way that made her stomach do a happy dance and made her want to kiss him.

'She will be okay, won't she?'

'I hope so, darling.'

Lottie knew when they got back to Tipping House that she should be tired, that she should rest. But she couldn't stop talking, about anything. As long as she didn't have to stop and think.

'Was Joker good?'

'He was fabulous, never had a horse like him.'

'Dad reckons he'll pull your arms out of their sockets in the show-jumping ring.'

359

'Rubbish.' Rory grimaced. 'He doesn't half motor on, though, if you let him, and he's a big horse.'

'Is Tab on her own looking after him?'

Rory grinned. 'Well I've got a feeling she might have some company.'

'Come on, let's go and check the horses. I need some fresh air, and you do, too, don't you Harry?'

Harry wagged his tail and lifted a paw, waiting for the command to go.

'I can do them, Lots. You stay here.'

'I want to, and then you need a long bath or you'll be so stiff you'll fall off tomorrow.'

They were making their way back from the stables, the dogs milling around with their noses to the ground, when Lottie spotted a car making its way up the long driveway. It was Dom.

'I can't hang about,' he had wound down the window and stopped a few yards from them, 'Amanda's been on her own with Alice for hours, so I really do need to get back, she'll be worried. Mum said you should have this.' He waved an envelope in the air. 'Forgot to give it to you earlier. Heaven only knows why she has got letters in her handbag, but she was quite insistent that you read it before we visit her tomorrow. I'll pick you up at 11am, unless I hear otherwise from the hospital. I presume you're off competing, Rory?'

Rory raised a questioning eyebrow, so Lottie answered for him. 'Of course he is. They've done really well today, haven't you?' She took the letter.

'Good luck at getting round. I've heard it's a tight course for a big horse.' And with those words of encouragement, Dom neatly turned his car around and headed home.

Chapter 29

Dominic had known. He lay awake, Amanda's warm body along-side his, and knew. He'd always faced his problems alone, preferring to keep his feelings to himself, until he'd met Amanda. Then he'd discovered that sharing them with her made him stronger.

He needed her comfort now, but didn't want to wake her up. She'd had enough sleepless nights and uncomfortable days as she'd battled through the early stages of her pregnancy, being as sick as a dog every single day, but not complaining.

It had been the same when she'd been carrying Alice, and the idea of doing it all again had frightened him. He didn't want to see her suffer. But she'd been determined, and with her soft calm voice had told him it would be worth it. One more child.

He hadn't been the one feeling like death warmed up every day for months, but he could understand why she was willing to go through it all again. The brain forgot, forgave, or the popula-tion wouldn't be growing at the rate it was. Most people would stop at one, otherwise.

Alice was as easy to love as her mother – thoughtful, quiet, and undemanding. So unlike her grandmother.

He shifted slightly so that he could wrap his arm around

Amanda. He knew what he was doing. Concentrating on life instead of death, avoiding thinking about his stern, aristocratic mother. Lady Elizabeth Stanthorpe. She'd never been one to show emotion, to be demonstrative. It was all about the stiff upper lip, carrying on regardless, but he'd never felt unloved. A squeeze from her hand, the nod of approval – they came, and the little gestures meant so much.

Dom, never one to show emotion himself, felt the unshed tears burn at the back of his eyes. For a moment, when he'd gone to say goodbye, her grip had been firm. Her fingers curling around his hand like talons, but it had been fleeting. When he bent to kiss her, an unheard of gesture, the same hand had rested on his neck. Keeping him there. And he knew, as her words whispered their way quietly into his head.

'There's a letter in my bag, Dominic. Charlotte needs to read it. I know I don't have to ask you to promise, you've always been a good boy. You've never let me down. I'm so glad you found Amanda, she will always be there for you. I did worry when you were younger and alone.'

'She's wonderful. I'm lucky.'

'*You* are wonderful too, Dominic. Go home to Amanda, she will be wondering where you are.'

'But—'

'There's only one thing you can do, Dominic. Tell them I need to go home, I must go home. Please.' She didn't let go. 'Tell them.'

'I'll try. We'll see you tomorrow, Mum.' He moved, back slightly, searched those once-sharp eyes, which were watery, misted. Old.

'You will.' She paused to cough. 'See me.' Then she closed her eyes and released her hold on him. And he knew.

Dom had kept his hand resting on his mobile phone all night and when it vibrated gently into life below his fingers, he knew what time it was before he glanced at the clock. Four in the morning – prime dying time. He'd told them to ring whatever time it was, any change, good or bad. But nobody rang in the middle of the night with good news.

Amanda murmured as he slipped out of bed and went downstairs to take the call.

'Dom.'

'Shush, darling. Get some sleep, I won't be long.'

* * *

The call was brief. Dominic was dressed and waiting at the door to Tipping House, with Lottie and Rory alongside him, when the ambulance arrived.

With the moon casting a cold shimmer over the lake Lady Elizabeth Stanthorpe arrived back at her beloved home and was tucked up in bed with her Bertie at the foot and her granddaughter and son on either side.

She sighed, a gentle flutter of sound, a butterfly beat in the stillness. 'That's better. Much better.'

Chapter 30

'She never liked goodbyes.'

'No.'

'Do you think she knew she was going to . . .?' Lottie sensed rather than heard her Uncle Dominic's sigh.

'I do. That's why she wanted to get home so urgently. She knew her heart was damaged. Mother hadn't got it in her to live a half-life. She wouldn't have wanted to carry on if she couldn't live life to the full, walk the dogs, and give us grief.' He tried to smile. 'Lying incapacitated in bed wasn't quite her style, was it?'

He squeezed her hand and they watched together as Lady Elizabeth Stanthorpe was laid to rest.

The church had overflowed. Everybody in the village, almost without exception, turned out – some loved her, some admired her, some respected her, but all had been impacted by her presence in Tippermere. Those that couldn't squeeze into the pews stood in the summer sun, listening to the words that drifted out through the open doors.

Now they lined the small graveyard. There had been no new-fangled requests from Elizabeth for her mourners to dress in bright colours, there were no modern songs serenading her departure. Elizabeth died as she had lived her life, with old-fashioned dignity, but with a certain mischievousness that was reflected in her demands that Bertie attend the service, that Roxy and Alice arrive with their ponies, and that Pip be included via Skype over a rather intermittent Wi-Fi connection that left her singing out of sync with the rest of the congregation.

As Lottie stared at the dark, newly dug earth she couldn't quite get to grips with the fact that Elizabeth had actually gone. That they would never, ever see her again.

The time between her death and the funeral had passed in a haze. She'd been stumbling through thick fog, unable to see or understand what was going on around her. But Rory had steered her through it, managed any problems with the film crew, sorted the horses, and made sure that somebody was with her every second of the day.

Now Lottie shook hands, accepted kisses, and murmured words of regret, and all she could think was – she's gone. The one constant in her life. *Our family is our strength*, Gran had said, but it was Elizabeth who'd been strongest of all. And now the strongest link had been broken.

Rory squeezed her hand, a constant reassuring presence through the meticulously organised wake. Elizabeth had left detailed instructions on her funeral, the wake, everything, Lottie realised, apart from how they coped afterwards. She'd not said what to do when everybody had gone. How to cope the next day when you turned around, expecting her to be there. What you did when you had a question nobody else could answer, how to comfort Bertie as he wandered around inconsolable and lost.

There was no manual to help when you spotted her wellingtons in the boot room. Smelled her distinctive cologne that clung to the house with a ghostly embrace. Spotted the walking stick abandoned in the hallway.

It was early evening before peace descended on the Tipping House Estate. Bertie had finally settled, stretched out in front of

Elizabeth's favourite chair, his head on his paws, his eyebrows lifting and his tail beating the floor at the slightest sound. Ever hopeful.

'The letter.' Lottie frowned. She'd forgotten all about the letter that Dom had delivered.

'Tomorrow.' Rory pulled her tighter against his body. 'You're tired.'

'I can't just sit here thinking about . . .' She pulled free, sending the dogs scurrying in all directions, and went in search of the letter, which she knew she'd put somewhere safe after reading it.

When she'd first read it, in bed after returning from the hospital, she'd skimmed over the words. Expected Elizabeth to be around to suggest what she should do.

The heat of tears unexpectedly filled her eyes and she brushed them away with the back of her hand wearily. She couldn't just keep crying. Gran would be cross.

Harry followed her around with a look of hope in his brown eyes, his tail doing a slow wag. 'You've already been for a run.' The wags speeded up. 'Oh there it is, on the kitchen table.' She made her way back to Rory, who moved the terriers off the seat to make room for her, and unfolded the letter. 'I want you to see this. We need to talk about it.'

'Okay.' The word was long and drawn out and she glanced at him.

'You look totally knackered.'

'I am.' He ran his fingers through his hair and gave a tired grin. 'Pooped.'

'That's a bit of a girly word.'

'I feel a bit of a girl right now. Come on, then, show me the letter.'

There were two pages in the envelope. The first, an enquiry about The Tipping House Estate on behalf of an unnamed potential buyer. The second was an email from Pip, who had done some digging, as instructed by Elizabeth.

Rory hadn't read either. If he was completely honest he'd completely forgotten about the mystery mail as events had taken over. He had been caught up in consoling Lottie whilst grieving himself, caught unawares by the thump to his gut, by the sheer weight of emotion that had enveloped the whole house. The phrase 'tearing the heart out' had suddenly meant something.

He took the pages from Lottie. She'd not told him what they contained – just said they needed to talk about it. Now he read them, and then read them again, to be sure.

'Fucking hell, that's her game is it?' He gave a low whistle. 'Pandora wants to buy this place?'

'I told you she did. She wants you and this place. She wants everything.'

He glanced sideways at her, but she didn't look like she was about to cry. She looked cross and determined, like Elizabeth.

'Well she definitely isn't having me. I'm all yours.'

Lottie gave the first signs of a smile. 'She's not having any of it, the cow.'

'Do you think she even has the money?'

'Well Seb might have.'

'I bet she's not even told him. He'd never want to live here. He hates fresh air. Are you sure Pip has got her facts right?'

'Have you ever known her be wrong? She should be a private investigator not a journalist. Anyhow, look, she says here that it wasn't hard to find out who had asked the agent to write and enquire. She just rang them up and acted ditsy.'

'Ditsy?' He laughed. 'Doesn't sound like a word you'd apply to Pip.'

'Thick, dippy, you know she just acted stupid and said she was ringing on Pandora's behalf to check if they'd had a response from us yet.'

'But how did she know . . .'

'Gran just had an inkling that it was Pandora,' she paused to let the wobble go out of her voice. 'Look she says that in her message to Pip, she also says if it isn't Pandora, then it doesn't matter, we should just ignore it.' She purposefully didn't read out Elizabeth's exact words, reading them would bring her back. She wrote in exactly the same way she spoke. Precise, to the point, but correct. If she read them, she'd hear her in her head and that would be it.

'Maybe we should just ignore it anyway, even though it's Pandora?'

'No.' Lottie sighed and let Harry join the pile of dogs on the sofa with them. 'I need to confront this and stop it once and for all.'

'But you could just say no.' Rory frowned. 'I mean, you're already in discussions with those other people who want to buy it, so she's too late anyway.'

'No, look at the name.'

Rory looked and wasn't any the wiser.

'Rory, it's the same people that the solicitors have been talking to. Pandora is the buyer we've been negotiating with.'

'You're kidding? Shit.'

'When I saw Gran at the hospital she insisted I didn't rush into anything. This is why, Rory, she knew. It didn't make sense at the time. I wondered what she was going on about when she said something about signing my life away being easy. She kept saying I had more time than I realised and not to rush, and she said it when we chatted after the village show as well. She was trying to warn me. We've got to stop. No way could we be Pandora's tenants, can you imagine it?'

Rory stared. 'No way. We've not committed to anything, have we?'

'Nope. It's not quite got to that stage yet.'

'Then there has to be alternative, another buyer, anything.'

She looked him in the eye. 'Gran thought Pandora was somehow connected with the fire too.'

'Fire?' She had Rory's full attention now. 'She tried to burn our bloody home down?'

'Well Gran didn't exactly say that.' Lottie had to be honest. 'But she said Pandora had been talking to the guy who we think did it, and she got Tab and Jamie to do some digging on Facebook 'cos that's where he's been boasting about the fire serving us right, and about knowing a film star. What if she put him up to it?'

'You're kidding me?'

'No, but I need to know why she did that. Gran also reckoned that Pandora had been trying to cause trouble between us.'

'So she wasn't after my sexy body after all?' He grinned.

'Well I think she is, actually, and she did make sure that story about the two of you got in the paper.'

'And she sent Xander in to woo you.'

'Woo, who says woo these days?'

Rory grinned. 'So it could be her behind the story of your childhood romance too.'

'We didn't have a childhood romance. She tricked Xander into coming here. He didn't know we lived here till it was too late. He used to hate me at school, he didn't mind coming back to Tippermere, but the last thing he expected was to bump into us.'

'Oh yeah?' Rory laughed and squeezed her. 'Hated you? Fancied the pants off you, more like. I told him to get over it.'

'Ahh so that's what you were nattering about over the barbecue.'

'That and some other stuff. He's okay when you get to know him.'

'I told you he was. We need to get everybody together and talk about this.' *Family is our strength. Friends and family.* The fight died away in Lottie as abruptly as it had come. She was drained, empty, she didn't want to fight, she wanted to curl up and cry.

Rory stood up and held out a hand. 'We do, soon, and I think we should rope Xander in as well.'

'Xander?'

'Xander, I've got a feeling he'll be happy to help. Now come on, it's bed time.'

'Rory?'

'Lottie?' He sat back down and pulled her onto his lap.

'I do love you.'

'I know.'

'I think Mum loved me.'

'I know she loved you, Lottie. How could she not? Your dad told me that she would have done anything for you. He said he'd never seen her as happy as when she was playing with you.'

'Did he? Really?'

'I think the thing he most regrets is not being able to share you with her, not being able to show her the wonderful woman you've grown up into. He said he's not a praying man, but if he was he'd just ask that she could look down and see.'

'Oh.'

'He did say it when we were drunk on whisky, mind, when Tiggy was driving me home, and he did say he's not really a church-going man, but he meant it.'

'Rory, if we had a baby and, and, well if anything you know, happened to me, and it was just you and the baby,' she looked up to check he was listening, 'how would you feel? I mean being landed with a kid that you had to look after on your own.'

'Well I wouldn't feel I'd been landed, for a start, if it was our child.' He kissed the top of her head. 'I'd be so bloody glad, Lottie, that I'd still got a tiny part of you left, something to remind me, somebody to love, who was as close to you as I could ever have been.'

'That's good.' She yawned, a sudden wave of fatigue washing over her like a warm blanket. 'I think I'm ready for bed now.'

'Good.' He stood up, then swept her into his arms. A big, warm protective hug and she nestled in against his firm, familiar torso. 'Come on, sleepy, even Harry has admitted defeat and gone without us.'

* * *

370

Grief had paralysed Lottie when her horse had died, but this time it was different. She had walked around in a daze until the funeral, but now seemed to be full of a strange energy that wouldn't let her rest.

The tack room had a spring-clean, the horses were groomed until their coats gleamed, even if they were going straight out into the field, and poor Harry was worn out as he considered it his duty to shadow her wherever she went.

When she cleared Rory's coffee cup away before he'd even had a sip, he put his hands on her shoulders and gently but firmly steered her back to the table.

'No, stop. Sit still, we need to talk.'

She started to play with a spoon.

'Lottie listen. There's only a few more days of filming left. They'll all be gone soon.'

'Not if Pandora has her way.'

'So we make sure she doesn't get her way.'

'Gran said not to rush, but we can't stall for ever just waiting for a miracle, can we?'

'Fight back, Lottie,' he leant across the table, eased the spoon from her fingers, and took her hands in his, 'that's what you're good at. If you need to confront her, then do it, then we can start again. Okay?'

'Again?'

'Elizabeth got you all the ammunition you needed. Don't let her down, Lottie. Come on, let's talk to Tab, ask what she found out.'

'Now?'

'Why not? I'll give her a shout. I left her tidying the muck heap, so she'll jump at the chance to do something else.'

Tab jumped. Tidying the muck heap was her least-favourite job in the whole world. She was at a complete loss as to under-standing why it had to be a neat packed-down rectangle, when surely the word 'heap' said it all.

'There isn't really that much to tell.' Tab took a slurp of tea and after pressing a few keys one-handed, waved her mobile phone under Lottie's nose. 'He's such a stupid twat, look at him.' They all looked. 'He wouldn't add either of us to his friends list at first, but then I added a profile pic of two girls with their boobs out and there you go. What a dickhead.'

'So, did he talk to Pandora?'

'Oh yeah, best buddies. Like this.' She crossed her fingers. 'The best bit about Gazza, our pyromaniac, is he doesn't know how to keep his gob shut. It's all a big ego boost for him. He's been boasting about the fire and putting us in our place, going on about mega-star Pandora and how she fancies the pants off him. He's such an arsehole. No, really, he is.' She scrolled down the posts.

'But she didn't actually get him to start the fire?' Rory wasn't that interested in looking at all the posts. He didn't get social media, apart from Twitter, which made him laugh. He'd got plenty of friends and if he wanted to talk to them he rang them.

'Oh no.' Tab shook her head firmly. 'I'm pretty sure they'd never heard of each other until after. It looks like she got in touch after she'd seen it in the paper, and she commiserated with him. He was getting all this grief from other people, who'd booked their weddings here and had them cancelled. You know, they were blaming him. I mean he was giving as good as he got, but look at it.' She scrolled down the page so that they could see the abusive comments and the threats he'd hurled back. 'But Pandora flattered him.'

'Why?'

'Elizabeth,' she flinched and looked at Lottie guiltily, 'and Pip reckoned she was just stirring it, she wanted him to talk to the papers about how bad the fire had been so that more of them would cancel their bookings and it would scare people off.'

'And we wouldn't get any new bookings.'

'I suppose so. I think she kind of persuaded him that he'd

done the right thing.' She shrugged and turned the phone off. 'Elizabeth reckoned that Pandora wanted to get more questions raised about the fire, to try and point the finger at you so that you didn't get the go-ahead from the insurance company. Just before she . . . Well, she asked me and Jamie the other week to see if we could find anything out, and Pip was helping. She is just so clever at this stuff.'

Lottie smiled. 'I miss Pip. She was brilliant at digging up the dirt. Gran really missed her too . . .' The smile faded, Rory squeezed her hand.

'She, er, wanted us to see if Gazza knew any of those couples that were taking you to court too, you know, for their money back.'

'Do it. You and Jamie. See what else you can find out. Then we're going to work out how to turn the tables.'

* * *

'I knew she was a conniving cow, babe. Soon as I saw her.' Sam gave Lottie a big hug, then wriggled her way between Amanda and Tab on the sofa. 'Squeeze up, there's room for a little one. Oh, sorry, babe, didn't see you there.' She looked from Xander, who was sitting quietly in the corner, to Lottie and raised an eyebrow.

'Don't mind me.' He shrugged and gave a lopsided smile.

'It's not your fault, though, is it, hun? You didn't know what she was up to.'

'No, but I knew what she was like. I should have worked it out sooner.'

'We just thought Xander should know all the facts.' Rory looked at Lottie, who nodded. He'd spent a lot of time with them, since Elizabeth's death. The film had been winding down, most of the scenes that needed his expertise had been shot, but he'd been reluctant to go. Lottie understood; it was hard when you hadn't quite worked out where home was, where you belonged.

He'd proved a dab hand at helping with the youngsters, and given Rory some tips on how to improve Joker's fitness as well as his tendency to run through the bit when it suited him. And Tab had been glad to have some time off with Jamie. She'd even had a day out with him and met his mother, who, she told Lottie, was nothing like he'd described.

'I thought she'd be all mousey and middle aged, with her nose buried in a book, and know lots of long words, but she's really nice, you know. Dead pretty, with this short, spiky blond hair. She's cool.' Which from Tab was as good as it got.

Lottie looked around the room. They'd miss Xander when he went, and Tab would miss Jamie. It hadn't all been bad.

'The thing is, I didn't just want to tell you about what Pandora has been up to, and what Gran found out. I mean I wanted you to know why there have been all those horrid reports in the newspapers.'

'Tomorrow's litter-tray lining, love. What?' Billy raised an eyebrow, 'well, we used to say today's headlines, tomorrow's fish-and-chip paper, but you lot don't have chips these days, do you? A bit of deep-fat frying never did me any harm, mind you.'

Tiggy patted his tummy and giggled. 'Of course not, love.'

'Er, yes.' Lottie glared at her father, and tried to remember what she was saying. 'Well, yes, I wanted you to know that she was behind all those photos, and all those reports about wedding cancellations. She'd made sure that a couple of reporters offered those girls money for their stories, and they didn't have a story unless they could say we'd been unfair.'

'You mean all them distressed brides saying you wouldn't give them their deposits back, all that nastiness, that was her doing?' Sam frowned.

'It looks like it, and then she'd stirred things up to try and stop the bookings for next year. That was why,' she looked at Sam again, 'she was snooping, she wanted pictures of the damage inside so she could say how bad it still was and how we'd never re-open. But anyway, what I'm really getting to is what Gran wanted.' She took a deep breath and clutched Rory's hand a bit tighter. 'The last time we talked,' she mustn't cry, this was good, not sad, 'she told me not to rush into anything and we've just found out why. She knew that the insurance company had nearly finished looking into things and she was sure we'd be okay.' She took a deep breath. 'We've just heard that the police have formally charged that man with arson and we've got the go-ahead from the insurance company, they're going to pay out, so we really don't have to sell. If we can stop people cancelling their weddings and get more bookings as quickly as possible then we should be able to scrape by.' She crossed her fingers out of sight. 'The bank should extend the loan if I can make a good enough case.'

'Bloody hell, I'll drink to that, love.' Billy raised an imaginary glass. 'If we don't all die of thirst first.' He winked.

'Oh babe, that's smashing. Aww, isn't it brill? Lady E was so clever,' Sam sighed.

'Not that we ever would have sold, that is.'

Lottie looked gratefully at Rory. 'Gran said we should make use of everything that's happened, you know, use the filming to kick-start things again, make it bigger and better. That's why she agreed to the filming in the first place, to get us some publicity for when we re-opened.'

'Crafty mare.' Billy shook his head.

'I just, er, wanted everybody to know, and maybe help.'

'Of course we'll help, babe, won't we, Mand? Can we have them topless waiters this time? You know, make it a bit more flash than the opening bash we had last time.'

Lottie tried not to roll her eyes. 'We're going to have a wrap party for the film, and make as big a thing of that as we can, so, er, maybe you can help plan it.'

'Fab. Oh wow, it will be amazing, babe, I promise.' Sam clapped her hands, and then delved into her massive tote bag for her notepad.

'I mean you don't have to all help, and you can go to the pub now if you want,' she looked at Billy.

'Carry on, love. But obviously not for too long.' Everybody laughed.

'Amanda's the one who's brilliant at planning, so . . .'

'We have to do this in the way Elizabeth intended.' Amanda blushed as she mentioned Elizabeth's name, and looked at Lottie in silent apology.

'It's fine, darling, carry on.' Dom, his voice soft, patted her knee. 'Mother will be listening in, making sure we don't forget her. Woe betide anybody who doesn't do things the way she expected.'

'We need a massive press release as soon as we have a launch day, and then we have to use everything connected to the film to our advantage, the good,' she glanced at Lottie, 'and the bad. I think that was her plan, wasn't it, Lottie?'

Lottie nodded. It wasn't until she'd had a long chat to Amanda that she realised just how much effort Elizabeth had put into supporting her, saving the business.

'And we can use those ridiculous pictures of Pandora clinging to a horse, can't we?' They all looked at Tab, who gazed at the ceiling, a look of innocence on her face.

'What pictures?'

'Well somebody might have, er, taken a couple of snaps before they joined in the rescue.'

Xander chuckled. 'She will roast you alive and set the solicitors on you, I'm sure there'll be a clause about no photos of the set.'

'But it wasn't the set, was it? And you weren't filming at the time. I was an innocent bystander, a fan, capturing the moment.' She grinned at Jamie. 'I'm a massive fan.'

'Innocent, my arse,' Billy guffawed.

'Well, I er, hope you don't mind, but I started to compile a file.' Amanda plucked a folder from her tote bag. 'Elizabeth suggested it . . .' She looked apologetically at Lottie again.

Lottie gave a wry smile. 'She really was amazing, wasn't she?' Her words were little more than a whisper. 'I had no idea she was doing all this for me.'

'She loved you, Lottie, and she was keen that we all pull together and support you. She knew just how big an undertaking Tipping House is.' She frowned. 'You don't mind, do you? She only talked to me and Dominic because we're family.'

Lottie blinked back the tears. 'You're all wonderful, I don't deserve . . .'

'Nonsense.' Billy waved brusquely at the folder. 'Carry on, Mandy love. Anybody going to pass some beers round? I'm spitting feathers here. Can't plot an uprising with a dry throat.'

There was a general shuffling around while Rory and Jamie took drink orders, then Amanda cleared her throat again.

'I've got cuttings here of all the articles and interviews about the film, and Pandora, and,' she glanced up from under her eyelashes at Xander, 'Xander, if you don't mind? There's some super photos and some of all the crowds that came to watch. I've even got some video footage of Tab and the dogs when they, er, galloped across and nearly flattened Seb, and some of little Roxy and Rupert at the village show. In fact, there's some rather funny clips from the show and I haven't a clue who took them. Elizabeth thought it might be rather fun to set up a YouTube channel?'

'I just hope the film isn't a flop. Aren't we rather putting all our eggs in one basket?'

'It won't be a flop.' Amanda shut her folder decisively. 'It's already garnering plenty of attention.' She smiled. 'Pip has way better contacts than even Pandora does, you should see what some of the reviewers are saying – and they've only seen the rushes.'

Chapter 31

Pandora put her hands on her hips and narrowed her eyes as a black Jaguar F-type purred its way along the driveway and glided smoothly to a halt in front of the stone steps leading up to Tipping House, scarcely scattering a single gravel stone.

A very pretty, petite woman slid gracefully out of the car. She stood up and straightened her skirt before propping her sunglasses on her sleek brown bob and gazing up at the house, which the afternoon sunlight had warmed until it had a delicious golden honeycomb glow.

'Jamie, Jamie!' Jamie sighed and abandoned the cables he'd been tidying. 'Get that,' she gestured, 'moved.'

Jamie wasn't sure if she was referring to the woman or the car. It was hard to tell with Pandora. 'But we've finished filming for the day, I thought I heard Seb say . . .'

'I don't care what you heard Seb say.' She glared as the woman reached back into the car and withdrew a leather portfolio case, before closing the car door with a reassuringly expensive clunk. 'We pay to use this place *all* day. Seeing as you're such good friends with her, you can tell Lottie . . .'

'You can tell her yourself.' There had been days recently when Jamie had started to wonder what the hell had ever made him think working for Pandora was a good idea, especially now he knew she'd used him just like she used everyone else.

He had just been another pawn in Pandora's game. Even the scriptwriter had been kicked out of her bed now he'd outlived his usefulness.

He watched as Lottie ran down the steps, the dogs at her heels, and then wrapped her arms round her visitor. A wide, welcoming smile on her open face.

Some people were just nice, he concluded, and others weren't.

Lottie faltered when she realised that Jamie and Pandora were watching.

'Everything okay?'

'Actually no.' He could almost hear Pandora sharpening her claws. 'You can't leave that car there, it needs moving.'

'Oh, I thought you'd finished for the day, Seb said—'

'We have.' Jamie looped the end through the cable and dropped it onto the pile.

'Well, er, that's good, then. This is Anna. She's one of Amanda's friends. She's starting work on the renovation. Isn't it exciting?'

'You've got the go-ahead from the insurance company? That's brilliant, Lottie.' Jamie, who already knew that they'd finally had the all-clear to start repairs decided to spell it out for Pandora's benefit. It was like watching the paint drain out of a bucket. Despite a good layer of make-up and the benefits of an all-over fake tan, Pandora visibly paled. He couldn't help embellish. 'I bet you can't wait to get the wedding business going again. Sam said they were,' he paused, 'awesome.'

'Renovation? Go-ahead?' The words came out staccato, rapid gunfire.

'Anna helped us out when we first set the business up. You should see what she did to the place. She's amazing.' Lottie linked her arm through the other girl's.

'Amazing.' Pandora stared, then gathered herself together. Jamie could have sworn she actually grew an inch as the tone of her voice froze over. 'Well I do hope you're not going to ask us to stop filming.'

Sam appeared in the doorway, 'Oh we won't be any bother at all, babe. It's all inside, isn't it?' She clapped her hands. 'I can't wait to see what you're going to do, Anna. I bet it's going to be *so* tasteful.'

Pandora ground a heel into the lawn and Jamie cringed.

'Oh no, of course not. If you need to film just carry on. We're making a start, then once you've gone it'll be all go. It's fab, isn't it?' Lottie beamed, and looked happier than Jamie had seen her in months. She'd lost weight, but she still looked huggable. Something you could never accuse Pandora of. 'I can't believe it's finally all over and the insurance company have given the go-ahead.'

'Fab.' Pandora looked from Lottie to Sam, then raised an eyebrow when she saw Tab in the doorway. 'I see you've got the cavalry with you.'

'We're all in this together. Oh actually, while you're here, there's something I wanted to say . . .' Lottie shoved a hand in her pocket, then tried the other one, returned to the first and triumphantly pulled out a piece of paper. 'I wanted to talk to you about this.' She waved the letter between them. 'This is from you, isn't it? It's from an estate agent acting on behalf of a buyer. My solicitor sent it. It *is* you isn't it? You were trying to buy my house.'

'So?' Pandora shrugged. 'I haven't done anything wrong.' She looked Lottie up and down. 'I was going to keep it as a nice surprise for you, but who cares? What if it is me? It isn't against the law. And I'm not trying to buy your house, dear,' she folded her arms, 'I *am* buying it. All this talk about renovation is a little late, although of course I might still lease it back to you. Look at it this way, I'm doing you a favour. Let's face it, you really are hard up, aren't you? How on earth would you keep this place going on your own? Just look at you. If we hadn't come along and filmed here you'd have been in a right mess.' She took a step

380

closer. 'Some people don't know a stroke of luck when they see it. I'm successful, and when your lease expires I can make it into something, rip up all those disgusting moth-eaten rugs and brighten the place up instead of living in the past. I really don't know what your problem is.' She sniffed. 'I'm sure you'll be much happier in a place that's more within,' she paused, 'your means. What do you need? A few stables, a field or two?' She glared at Anna. 'The money we've paid you for filming won't go far, you know. This woman,' she waved a dismissive hand, 'would sell you a few overpriced soft furnishings and you'd be broke again.'

'Oh well, I am really grateful that you came and filmed here. I mean it's been super, hasn't it? But I don't think you understand.'

Sam grinned. 'It's been fab. I just loved those little polo horses and I can't wait to see my Roxy in the film,' she gave Pandora a warning look, 'like Seb said she would be.'

'Oh be quiet, you stupid woman.' Pandora glared at Sam then switched her attention back to Lottie. 'It's you that doesn't understand.'

'Tipping House isn't for sale. It never has been. You aren't buying it and I don't know where you got that idea from. I don't care if it's got moth-eaten rugs and, for your information, I like living in the past.'

Pandora gave a short laugh. 'How sweet. Well I'm sorry, but I think you'll find it's too late to back out. Your solicitors have agreed to sell, I've arranged a deposit, so sadly you can rent from me or you'll have to take your moths elsewhere.'

Lottie shook her head. 'No, Pandora. It's not me who's leaving. As soon as the insurance company contacted us, the solicitors were instructed to stop negotiations.' She shrugged. 'We're not interested. We've not accepted any deposit and we didn't sign the contract.'

'Don't be ridiculous. You can't pull out. I've told you it's too late.'

'I have. We have. It isn't for sale.'

'You're delusional, an idiot. I'm calling my solicitor and he'll tell you, it doesn't matter if you have got your money.'

'She's rather a nice delusional idiot, though.' Jamie grinned, and got the type of glare that would have sent him scurrying for cover six months ago. Whether he'd got immune, or simply manned up (as Tab would say) he wasn't sure. And he didn't care. He cared even less when Tab scampered down the steps, linked her hand through his arm, and kissed his cheek.

'How touching.' The glare had been followed by a withering look.

'We want to ask you about Gareth Timms as well.' Lottie found that now she'd started, she couldn't stop.

'Who?' Pandora stared blankly at her.

Tab grabbed Jamie's tablet, jabbed at it angrily, and then waved it under Pandora's nose. A nearly naked, tattoo-covered, twenty-something, showing the start of a beer belly and sporting only an elephant willy warmer thrust his trunk in Pandora's direction. Lottie, who'd joined them on the grass, opened her eyes wider and tilted her head, trying to work out just what she was looking at.

'Oops.' Tab giggled and tapped off the startling profile picture, which she'd enlarged by mistake, and pointed to a post. 'He says he knows you.'

'Oh, him.' Pandora shrugged and studied her nails, barely suppressing a yawn, but Jamie could see the tightness in her jaw, the pinch of her lips. 'Is there a point to this? I really am quite busy, you know, some of us work and I do have a call to make.'

'He's the one that started the fire, Gazza,' Lottie pointed to one of the tattoos, which proudly announced his name and wondered if he'd had it put there in case he forgot who he was, 'the one that tried to wreck my business. He says you know him.'

'Know?' She gave a short, harsh laugh. 'I'd hardly say I knew him, he's just a fan.'

'Well he says here that . . .'

'Oh, honestly, does it matter what the Neanderthal says? Sorry, is there some law about conversing with people like that? Not that I'd imagine you'd ever lower yourself that far.'

'There's no law, babe.' Sam decided that staying on the steps was a better bet, as her heels were new and they did have gorgeous diamantes down the back, and she was bound to sink even if the grass was bone dry. 'But he has been arrested now, and I mean, you knowing this guy and then wanting to buy the place looks a bit iffy, doesn't it, if you see what I mean?'

'I hadn't heard of him until after your fire, if you see what *I* mean.' Pandora scowled.

'But you did get him to talk to the papers and stir things up.'

'It's up to him what he says, he's a grown,' she sniffed, then pushed the tablet away with the type of look on her face that said she'd just eaten something unpleasant, 'man.'

'Very grown.' Tab grinned, and enlarged the profile picture again.

'You planned this all along, didn't you, Pandora?'

'I had nothing to do with the fire, you can't blame me for that, Lottie.'

'No, but you did suggest to the insurance company that I was desperate for money.'

'Well you are.'

'So you don't deny it?'

'You can't prove anything.'

'And you got all those people to ring up and cancel their weddings, and demand their refunds back. That was your doing too, wasn't it?'

'And how do you propose to pay back all those people, dear, poor Lottie? All those court cases, all that bad publicity.'

Lottie frowned. 'Court cases? How do you know about those? Nobody knows about that. It *was* you that got Timms to encourage them to take me to court for the money, wasn't it? He would never have thought of that on his own, and he knew nearly all of them.'

'No, he really isn't the brightest of men, is he? But all I was doing was offering friendly advice, so what are you going to do,' she laughed, 'sue me?'

'No, but those people aren't taking us to court now. We've settled. Some of them are having their deposits refunded, but most of them have changed their minds, and they want their weddings here after all.'

'You're lying. All of this is a lie, isn't it? Isn't it? You're wrong, you're wrong about all of it. I'm having Tipping House and there aren't going to be *any* weddings. Do you hear me?'

'Darling, Pandora.' Pandora hadn't noticed Seb, or a whole group of the film crew, approach. They'd crept closer, drawn by the sight of their star getting more rigid by the second, her voice rising to an ever-higher pitch. She shrugged off the hand he'd put on her arm. 'I think we should go. Calm down.'

'Calm down?' She turned her fury on him. A lesser man would have shrunk back, but not Seb. 'Calm down? And then I can be fucking comatose like all these inbred idiots?'

'Stop it, Pandora. You're making a fool of yourself.'

'And it was you who sent Jamie here. It was all your idea to film at Tipping House, wasn't it?' Lottie didn't need to ask, but she had to.

'Oh that's nonsense.' Seb spoke with utter conviction. 'She didn't even want to come here. I had a hell of a job convincing her. Didn't I?'

'Oh for heaven's sake, of course it was my bloody idea. How else could I prise you away from your precious studio and city-living?' Pandora stared at Seb. 'What are you doing here anyway, haven't you got things to do? Has one of your minions snitched?'

'Not snitched.' Seb gave a wary sigh. 'I heard you yelling at Lottie – everybody on the set did. In fact, I imagine everybody in the bloody county has heard you.'

'Well you can go away. I'm quite capable of fighting my own battles.'

'Of that I have no doubt, darling. So let's get this straight, you picked this location?' Seb took a step back from his wife. 'But we had the script . . .'

'It was me who found the script, if you remember. I brought it to you. To be honest, it stinks, it's a pile of utter drivel.' She laughed. 'Do you honestly think this shit will sell? But it was perfect for this place. I wanted this place. I needed it. Don't you understand me at all?'

'I thought it just grew on you. You weren't keen on coming here, you hadn't planned . . .'

'Of course I planned it. Oh you really can be dense at times, darling. Didn't you think it strange that the other location you wanted fell through at the last minute?'

'So it wasn't a coincidence coming here? I thought you were up to something from the moment you admitted you knew Lottie lived here, but not this. It's utter madness.' Xander had wandered over with the rest of the crew to see what the fuss was about, and his voice was dangerously soft. But Pandora was oblivious.

'Coincidence? Don't be ridiculous.' She gave a harsh laugh. 'There's no such thing as coincidence, darling brother.'

'Why did you make Xander come?' Lottie felt a bit rude butting into what now seemed like a family argument, but she had started it, and it was *her* home that they were arguing about.

'Why do you think I enlisted my brother, you silly cow? Men are ruled by their dicks, they're all the same, and we all know where his was leading him.'

Which effectively alienated all her potential male allies, thought Lottie, wondering just how much hate could exist in one person. There was no stopping Pandora now, though, who was looking at Lottie as though she had just crawled out from under some stone. 'He had a massive schoolboy crush on you. You're not telling me you never noticed him following you around with his tongue hanging out? God knows why, you were so plain,' she paused, 'and fat. But I knew it would make him,' she pointed at Rory who was a step behind Xander, 'stupid and jealous.'

'But not stupid or jealous enough,' said Lottie quietly.

'You just think you're so clever, don't you? You thought you were better than me, with your posh relatives and all your little horsey friends. Well, you're not. I'm the one who has made some-thing of myself. I'm the one who's famous. I could take him,' she pointed at Rory, 'from you any time I liked. And you know what?'

Lottie knew they were about to hear the answer whether they wanted to or not.

'I *am* somebody. I don't even need a place like this to make people respect me. I don't want your silly house for myself, or your gormless husband. He might be fit, but who wants a man who spends all his money on horses?'

Lottie looked at her in astonishment, not quite sure what to say.

'Oh honestly, why are you making such a fuss about a decrepit old heap of the past? You've buried yourself in this bloody place, where all the men smell of horseshit and the most exciting thing you have to talk about is raising money for the church roof. Do you know how pathetic you all look in your stupid country clothes with all those dirty mongrels spreading dirt and disease in your homes? This place needs to be gutted. It's such a shame that stupid man didn't do a proper job.'

Harry looked up at Lottie and wagged his tail, and Ella pawed at Xander's leg. He stooped to pick her up and Pandora swapped her attention to him.

'And you're just as bad as they are. It's no wonder that girl was fed up of you. I told her she was wasting her time. You're just like your mother, pathetic.'

Xander grabbed her arm. 'You spoke to Miranda?

'Take your hands off me.' If looks could kill, thought Lottie, Pandora would be serving multiple life sentences for murder.

Medusa had nothing on her. 'Of course I spoke to Miranda,' she cocked her head on one side, her voice suddenly sweet. She was Jekyll and Hyde, and Lottie marvelled at how she could switch so smoothly from pure poison to sweetness and light. 'She is such a darling girl, but she wasn't good enough for you. You were being so moody and difficult, the poor thing didn't know who to turn to. So I helped out, I thought a complete break would be good for you.'

'You cow. You can't just step in and ruin people's lives.'

'Oh don't be melodramatic. You weren't really bothered about her, and it wouldn't have lasted anyway.'

'Pandora, she dragged up all the dirt she could on me, made me look a complete shit, sold out to the newspapers. Don't you care at all?'

Pandora shrugged. 'Of course I care, but you wouldn't have come here if you'd still been shacked up with her, would you? I needed you, dear brother. It's always been rather annoying how you've chased all these other insignificant women and ignored me.'

'Nobody could ignore you.'

'Well maybe not ignored, but you've not been as attentive as you should. You would have got bored of her anyway. Just as you would have got bored of Lottie, except she doesn't want you anyway, does she? I honestly thought you'd have managed to succeed in at least one thing in life and get her into bed, but you couldn't even do that.'

'Pandora.' It was a warning, but she wasn't about to take notice.

'Nobody wants you, do they, Xander? Not really. Except me, I understand you, *I* want you.'

'I'm sorry?' His tone was incredulous.

'Don't you realise? I always loved you, Xander, we were a team. You should be with me.' She faltered, her voice stuttering as she realised what she'd said, and saw the look of horror on his face.

'You're insane. You're my half-sister, for God's sake. Father might have made some pretty big mistakes like that, but I damned well don't.'

'We belong together. We used to get on so well when we were here before. You looked after me and you loved me too. I know you did.'

'Pandora,' he paused, 'I didn't love you, I felt sorry for you. That's why I tried to be friends. I thought the way Dad treated you was unforgiveable, but I can't change it. Oh God.' He shook his head then looked back at her, a frown of confusion spread across his features. 'How can you be like this? Who are you?'

Seb laid a hand back on his wife's arm. 'Pandora, we need to talk. I don't understand any of this, and I need to.'

She turned to him, her eyes shiny bright, pin-pricks of pink on her normally pale cheeks. 'We don't need to talk.' There was a trembling edge to her voice that could have been excitement or threatening tears. 'Ring the solicitor, Seb.' He shook his head. 'Seb, I said ring him.'

'No darling, it's over. You're not buying Tipping House, well not with my money anyway. We need to talk.'

She shrugged him off angrily, her voice a low hiss that carried across the silent air like an electric current. 'But I want it, I need it. I've worked for this and I deserve it. I have to buy Tipping House.'

'We don't need a house like this.'

'*We* don't, I do.'

'Give me one good reason. Why Pandora? Why the hell do you need a place like this?'

'For Daddy.'

Everybody froze. Stared.

'For Daddy?' Seb's arm dropped to his side.

Pandora looked at Seb. Of all people, he had to support her. 'If *her* horrible father,' she pointed at Lottie, 'had let Daddy buy Folly Lake Manor when he wanted to we could have stayed here, all of us, and been happy. He wanted to live here. He loved

Tippermere. And her family stopped him. It was her fault he couldn't have that place, but he can have this one, her home. I've got it for him. He loved it here. Don't you understand?'

'No he didn't.' Xander's tone was soft, but certain. 'Father doesn't love anything, he just wanted to be somebody; he thought he could buy status. It was just for his portfolio, something to show off about, you idiot. He couldn't give a shit about Tippermere.'

'Liar. He did love it, and he would have loved me, but instead he got cross. We had to leave, he sent us away because he couldn't buy the right place here. Mummy told me. She told me. Lottie ruined my life and now I'm going to ruin hers and show Daddy. He'll come back, he'll come back to me.'

'No he won't. We would have left anyway, he was always moving on.' Xander shrugged. 'And he sent you away because your mother kept coming round and making demands. He had appearances to keep up, Pandora, he wanted everybody to think he was the loyal husband and your mother wouldn't leave him alone.'

'It's not true. You don't know him, you don't understand. When I tell him about Tipping House he'll realise how much he loves me, he'll be proud of me. When I saw it in the papers I knew I could get it, I just knew.'

'Oh Pandora, he doesn't love anybody, can't you see that? The reason I'm hiding from the press isn't because of the polo, it's because I've got to fight him in court. He doesn't even want to give my mother, a woman he's been married to for years, any money after he's abandoned her. I'm sorry, but why would he care about you? Why would getting this place make any difference? He doesn't give a shit, Pandora, he's a selfish bastard, he can buy places like this whenever he wants, and,' he paused, 'he's engaged. He's already found a new woman.'

'Liar, shut up, you're just trying to hurt me.'

'He's besotted, for the first time in his life I think he actually does care about somebody as much as he cares about himself.

389

She's rich, she's pretty. He's never coming back, Pandora. You'll never see him again, whatever you do.'

'Shut up.' Pandora put her hands over her ears. 'He will, he will come back.'

'You stupid cow, you don't know what he's like at all, do you? You can't make anybody love you, Pandora.'

'I can, he'll love me, he will, I'll show you.' She whirled around. 'Seb, you understand, don't you? Tell him, tell them.'

'No, Pandora. I don't understand. Please, come back to the hotel, talk to me. You and me, come on.'

'You have to understand. I have to have this place. Tell her, Seb. Tell Lottie she has to sell it to me.'

'Darling.'

'No, let go. Give me your phone, I need to ring the solicitor, he'll tell you.'

It was Seb they felt sorry for, poor, confused Seb, who hadn't got a clue how to cope with such an emotional outburst. Seb, who suddenly looked lost and vulnerable. Try as he might, he couldn't persuade Pandora to move, so they slowly retreated. Rory, Tab, Jamie, and Xander headed towards the comfort of the peaceful stable yard, and Lottie, a shocked Anna, and Sam went into Tipping House. The next time Lottie dared look out of the window, Seb and Pandora had gone.

* * *

Seb had never seen his wife pack so quickly. Well, he'd never seen her instruct one of the make-up girls to pack so quickly. Within an hour of her filming her last scene, she had her suitcases and trunks lined up by the trailer door and was checking the cupboards.

The last few days of the filming had been the worst of his life. It had taken every ounce of his persuasive powers to coax Pandora into completing her scenes, and many hours of talking – employing every logical reason that he could summon up – to convince her that she didn't want Tipping House. She'd never wanted it. They had the perfect life and her father was a cruel, vindictive man, who had no part to play in it.

Eventually she had reluctantly agreed that he was right, and that she would return to the set. In public she was as callous and uncaring as ever – denying that she ever had more than a passing interest in the decaying lump of the past that was the Tipping House Estate, and that she was acting a part. But, in private, when they returned each evening to the hotel, she played the part of wounded martyr to the hilt, saying that giving up her dream was a sacrifice she was making just for him. By the time he called 'cut' for the final time, Seb was mentally and physically exhausted, and vowing that he never wanted to see a horse, polo stick, or field in his life again.

Pandora slammed the final cupboard shut. 'It will be such a relief to leave this shit hole. I honestly think we should consider moving to Spain.'

'That was in the script dear, not real life. The rock star persuading his wife.' He'd been totally shocked by Pandora's outburst and admission that not just the script, but the whole film had been driven by her need to seek revenge on the people she felt had slighted her as a child, and by her desperate need for her father's approval and love. He had never had the slightest inkling that his wife was desperate for parental affirmation, or that she was anything other than one hundred per cent self-confident. And now he wasn't sure whether his admiration for her had increased, or been demolished. Only time would tell.

But he'd been proved right. He had told Xander that she would tire of the country and flee back to city living, that she'd recognise the truth in the fiction, and so she had. Or at least he hoped she had, and it wasn't just that her plans had been thwarted. Just as the fictional rock star had tired of his wife's obsession with rural living and rugged men, so had he. How he would ever rectify the huge issue she had with her absent father he honestly wasn't sure. If they'd been in America, many hours of expensive therapy would have been the obvious solution. Maybe their next stop should be the United States.

'Well sometimes life imitates art,' her voice was still higher-pitched than normal, external proof of the internal turmoil she was determined to disguise, 'and I think that scriptwriter might have a point. In that final scene where Spike insisted that we were done here, and showed up Dan for the serial shagger he really was, it made me think. Some of these men are little better than animals, you know. One can get bored of sex, mud, and looking at scenery, and I do rather like living somewhere a bit more civilised. The climate is better in Spain, the men know how to dress, and there aren't any horses.'

He sighed. Maybe life for Pandora had always been an act, a brave face, and maybe in coming to Tippermere he was finally gaining an insight into who she really was. 'I'm sure there are in the rural areas.'

'Not where we will be going.' She pecked him on the cheek, barely making contact. 'Such a shame you have to stay on right until the end. Never mind. You can call me. Right, I think that's everything. I will see you back in London. Oh the bliss of proper shops and talking to normal people again.' She paused in the doorway. 'I envied Lottie when I was at school. She was popular even though she never even tried. People took notice of her and I was the poor little invisible girl. I never stopped dreaming about coming back and taking it all from her. I wanted to be a lady, to have people look up to me, respect me, and I wanted Daddy to love me.' Her voice had an almost wistful edge to it, and Seb softened his tone in response.

'But people do respect you, darling, they adore your films.'

'They respect the films, not me. *I* want to be important. When I read about the fire it just seemed like fate. It was a sign that it was the right time to come back here and sort things out. I spoke to that awful Gazza man and it was easy – it all just fell into place as though it was meant to be.'

'Your life is different, Pandora. You don't need a place like Tipping House, and you don't need Rory, Xander, or your father. Do you?'

Pandora flicked her hair back over her shoulder. 'Oh don't be ridiculous, I *do* need a place like Tipping House. But a bigger, better place. I'll call you when I find one in Spain.'

Chapter 32

Everybody in Tippermere was relieved when they found out Pandora had rushed back to London as soon as she'd shot her last scene, two weeks before the end of filming. Seb, feeling obliged to celebrate a wrap, had stayed behind. A situation they were both more than happy with.

He was used to working on films that didn't have his wife in a starring (or any) role, which meant he was at liberty to plead the need to stay on location or return home at whatever ungodly hour suited him. In fact, it suited them both.

Seb and Pandora always attended the most glamorous and prestigious events, arm in arm, but the rest of the time went their separate ways with unvoiced relief.

Packing his wife into a chauffeur-driven limo, Seb had heaved a huge inward sigh of relief. Then he'd gone out and 'got bladdered', as Billy put it, after finding him in a ditch after the man had taken a wrong turning.

It had become a regular occurrence over the next two weeks; relishing his new-found freedom from a demanding and unpopular wife he'd become a familiar face in Kitterly Heath.

The first time that Sam and her friends had come across him in their favourite wine bar, he'd been swaying on a stool, chatting up the bisexual barman, totally smashed. Seb, it transpired, had a wild side. He was lining up the glasses in front of him neatly, some habits it seemed, were too deeply embedded in his psyche to ignore, even when drunk.

'I know you, don't I? You're the one who was winding Panda up.' He balanced his chin on a hand, attached to a wobbly arm, and swayed. 'That footballer's wife. What the fuck are you doing in here all alone? Is he playing away? Ha, ha geddit?'

'I live here, babe. Just up the road, and my Davey doesn't play on a Thursday, hun. Aren't you the funny one?' She patted his arm. 'Didn't know you had a sense of humour. You kept that quiet, didn't you, you old devil.' She looked round. 'Your Panda isn't here, is she?'

'I wouldn't be calling her Panda if she was. She's Pan-dor-a.' He sniggered. 'She's gone home, got sick of the country. I knew she would. Life imitating art, y'know. I said to Xander she'd realise. The script said she'd get fed up and she has.'

'But that's just the script, isn't it, babe?' She waved at the barman. 'Normal please, doll, and one for Seb here. It didn't look to me that she got fed up, more like her little scheme didn't work out.'

Seb harrumphed. 'Whatever.'

'Did you know she was trying to buy Lottie's place?'

'Never tells me anything, scheming bitch, but you've got to admire her, haven't you? Do y'know they microwave the wine in here?' He snorted and took a gulp.

'I tried it once at home, babe, put it on for thirty minutes instead of seconds.' She giggled. 'Well how was I to know? I just had the number thirty in my head. Had to chuck some cinnamon in it and tell Davey it was mulled wine. He told me it was criminal to do that to a Chateauneuf du pape.'

'You're kidding?'

'No, he did. Actually said "criminal" like it was really bad.'

'I meant kidding about cooking it.'

'Oh no, babe. I'm not joking. Well, we always drink bubbly or cocktails, don't we, girls? Just picked up the nearest bottle, how was I to know it was a special one? Didn't taste that brilliant to me.'

'Well that's because you boiled it, you stupid cow.'

Sam sighed and picked the bottle of champagne up. 'I was just starting to like you, babe, and now you've screwed that up as well.'

* * *

Sam loved a good party, and the best kind were the ones she organised herself, with a free rein to be as outrageous as she wanted. If Lottie and Amanda hadn't been quite as pre-occupied, they'd have got involved themselves to put a lid on her enthusiasm.

'Don't you worry about a thing,' she'd said to Lottie, grabbing the hastily prepared plan that involved a few drinks, balloons, and some canapés. 'Leave it to me, babe.'

Lottie needed cheering up. Sam had seen how much her horse's death had upset her, and to be followed up with losing the woman who'd always been there in the background, quietly steering things, had left her devastated. Lottie had put a brave face on it, but it was evident to Sam that she was just going through the motions.

Sam missed Lady Elizabeth as well, everybody in Tippermere did, and she couldn't imagine the size of the hole that had been left in Lottie's heart and home. But she plodded on resolutely, wading like a sleepwalker though treacle, determined to succeed as Elizabeth would have wanted.

'Are you sure there's nothing I can do?' Amanda, now past the sickness stage of her pregnancy, had felt obliged to help. Sam loved the very sensible and ladylike Amanda nearly as much as she loved Lottie – but she didn't want this celebration to be sensible, she wanted to see off the film crew with a bang. A grand finale.

'You've got your hands full with Alice, babe.' Which wasn't entirely true, as Alice, despite her tender years, was nearly as sensible as her parents. 'And I know what it's like when you're forever dying for a wee. I'll give you a shout if I need you. I know you've got amazing contacts, babe. Here, you couldn't give me a list of people who can get me this stuff could you?' She handed over her own plan, shoving Lottie's in her tote bag.

Amanda went pale when she saw the list. 'I'll see what I can do, although some of this is a bit outside my normal . . .'

'Aww, thanks, babe. I knew I could rely on you.'

* * *

'Now look at you, my little princess. Look Davey, isn't she gorgeous? I could eat you up.' Sam leant forward and nibbled Roxy's arm, and with a squeal the little girl ran off. 'You don't think I look over the top, do you hun?'

David Simcock, dressed in a fitted designer DJ that hugged his six foot ten toned frame to perfection, put his hands on Sam's waist and holding his wife at arm's length he let his gaze drift over her from the bottom up. 'You look stunning, love. Beautiful.' He kissed her cheek, carefully, wary of the many layers of make-up. 'If I wasn't already married I'd be down on one knee.'

Sam giggled. 'Oh, get you.'

'Good job Pandora isn't here or she'd be scratching your eyes out.' He held his arm out. 'Ready to show them how to have a proper party?'

'Bloody hell.' Tab's eyes opened wide at the sight of a bow-tie-wearing topless waiter who was heading straight for her with a tray of champagne. Jamie laughed, he'd been pressed into service by Sam earlier in the day and had a good idea of what the evening had in store. He wished they had a Sam in their town instead of a crowd that were more bag-lady than WAG. Even the so-called 'stars' he worked with on a daily basis paled into insignificance compared to the force of nature that was Samantha Simcock.

'Wow.' They were in the marquee proper now. 'That is so, so amazing. Look.' A pointing Tab was already heading towards a chocolate fountain, where Roxy and Alice were standing armed with bamboo sticks.

Roxy had five marshmallows on her spear, chocolate was dripping from her fingers, and her cheeks were already chocolate-smeared. She even had it in her hair. In contrast, Alice was as clean and tidy as always. She had two slices of banana and was looking at the chocolate dubiously as though it were forbidden fruit.

'This is our fountain, Tabifa, Mummy said that one's for gwown-ups and I can't touch it.'

Tab looked at where Roxy was pointing. 'Oh my God, I've died and gone to heaven.' And Jamie wasn't sure if that was down to the contents of the fountain or the waiter standing next to it.

'No you've not.' Roxy looked mystified. 'You're still here.' Then she lost interest in Tab and attempted to stick another marshmallow on her already overladen stick. The stick arched over, and as the chocolate hit the top of the first spongy cube it gave up its fight to stay in one piece. 'Oh bug.' She glanced up at Tab. 'I'm allowed to say bug, just not the ger bit as well, Mummy said.'

'Course you are, sweetie pie.' Tab didn't care what she said, she was already heading towards the stream of Sangria, and a loin-cloth-attired Tarzan who was supplying glasses.

'Oh heavens,' Amanda didn't know whether to cover Alice's eyes or her own, 'she'll be up all night if she eats that chocolate. Did you know Sam had all this planned? She never mentioned semi-naked men or sugar rushes to me.'

Tab didn't take her eyes off Tarzan, just held out her hand for a glass.

Jamie grinned. 'She said she didn't want to bother you or Lottie with the finer details. Where is Lottie, by the way?'

'Arguing with the fire juggler that a tent isn't the place for naked flames.'

'Just naked men.' Tab, who had reluctantly decided that this Lord of the Jungle was more of a man's-man than a lady lover, had downed her drink and was staring wide-eyed at the rest of the party-goers and entertainment.

'Only Sam could make a tent look like this.'

'Marquee,' said Lottie, who after temporarily confiscating the lighter fuel had returned it on condition that all flames stayed outside. 'It's amazing, isn't it? She said it was a good excuse to go a bit theatrical, seeing as it was a wrap-up party. Her words not mine.'

'You know you wanted me and Jamie to carry on digging?'

Lottie nodded. 'Not that it really makes any difference now. I don't think Pandora will ever come back.'

'I think *he* might, though.' Tab nodded over towards the bar, where Seb was holding court with two of Sam's friends. 'I didn't like him at all at first, he's so bloody bossy and prissy, but he's grown on me a bit. He's got a wicked sense of humour.'

'I think Xander quite likes him too.'

'Mm, anyhow, all those brides-to-be that were in the newspapers complaining were the same ones that had attacked Gazza on his Facebook page. Bit of a coincidence, isn't it? I gave Pip the list to check out and she reckons Pandora persuaded him to tell them it wasn't his fault, it was all yours, that you owed them and they should go to the newspapers and complain.'

Lottie sighed. 'It doesn't take much to turn people nasty does it? Harder to get them to be nice.'

'I'll miss this place.' Xander grinned and took the bottle of beer that Rory offered. 'And all you mad people.'

'What are you going to do next, then?' Lottie, who'd been wondering just how many calories there were in a chocolate-covered slice of banana dragged her attention away from the fountain and plonked herself on Rory's lap. She was dying to kick off her heels, but knew that Gran would frown down from Heaven.

'Tour the world? No, I'm kidding. I don't know, but being around you lot has kind of reminded me how much I miss riding. I need to get back in the saddle.'

'I don't see why you can't hang around for a bit, if you've got nowhere to go.'

'I think you should stay here, babe.' Sam topped up Lottie's champagne glass and poured herself another. 'You can give polo-riding lessons, can't he? That'll be popular, or I know, you could give my little Roxy lessons. I mean, she does love Rory but now he's got this new horse and sponsor and everything he's going to be busy. And Lottie won't be able to do all that mucking out and riding now she's got to get the wedding business going again. Aww look at Roxy, she's a right card isn't she? Covered in chocolate.'

'Well, actually Rory did have this idea,' Xander paused as though unsure whether he should say more.

Lottie glanced up at Rory and he winked. 'I suggested he take over Mere Lodge.' She frowned. The small eventing yard had been Rory's base before they'd moved into Tipping House, and he'd rented it out to their friend Mick O'Neal. 'Mick's given in to Niamh's pleading – she said she needs to be nearer to her mam.' He rolled his eyes and Tab giggled at his appalling Irish accent. Lottie, on the other hand, felt like she was about to burst into tears at the news.

'But he can't go.' She hadn't quite meant it to come out like that, but Rory understood. He squeezed her waist.

'He'll be back, it's only for a few months.'

Lottie missed Mick. Since he'd got back together with Niamh he'd been away from Tippermere more than he'd been there.

She'd seen him on New Year's Eve when he'd set up the fireworks with Rory, then he'd been there for Elizabeth's funeral, there for her with his wise words and all-seeing dark gaze. 'She knew you were ready to take over, treas.' He'd held her at arm's length for a moment, wiped away a tear from her cheek. 'And she knew you'd got a good man by your side. Rory will take care of you. You make a good team. Remember what I told you, about your feet bringing you back to where your heart is? Well, your heart is here, my love, but I've still got the wandering feet. Your Gran was a good one, good enough to hang about until you were ready, but she was tired.' He kissed the top of her head. 'Be happy that she can rest now, and be happy for everything she's given you.' She'd looked for him at the wake, but he was nowhere to be seen. He'd disappeared again.

'I'm not sure he will be.'

Rory chuckled. 'He said you'd say that. But I reckon there's no harm in Xander looking after the place for a few months, is there? Room for his ponies, and I was thinking as you might be er . . .' He glanced down at her stomach and Sam squealed.

'You're not? She isn't? Oh my God, babe, why didn't you say?'

'No.' Lottie giggled as Sam's face fell. 'I'm not pregnant, but we have kind of decided that maybe it would be nice to, you know . . .' she looked up at Rory's face. 'Gran would have liked it.'

Rory nodded. 'Elizabeth would have loved it.'

'Oh wow, can I tell Davey?'

'No Sam, you cannot tell anybody.'

'Oh babe, what made you decide to go for it?'

Lottie rested her head against her husband's chest. It was complicated. It had taken Elizabeth to show her how important her family was, to make her see that her mother had loved her and not willingly gone, that her father had never resented having to alter the course of his life to look after her. That Rory loved her enough to let her decide.

'I know Gran would have loved to see the house filled with children again, but it's not just for her.' She breathed in the familiar, comforting smell that was pure Rory. 'It just seems the right time for us. It's what we both want, isn't it?'

'Aww, isn't that fab? Oh my God, I think Roxy has just ducked Alice in the chocolate fountain. Roxy, Roxanne!'

Lottie giggled. 'Sam's been ace, hasn't she, doing all this?'

'I don't know about ace, but she's in her element.' Rory grinned as they watched her and David rescue Alice from the fountain.

'Gran realised I missed Pip, you know. That's why she got the ponies for Alice and Roxy. She knew it would give Sam an excuse to be at Tipping House more. She wanted her to be here for me.'

'Probably. She was an amazing woman, your gran, just like you are.'

* * *

Lottie nestled against Rory and looked up at the black night sky. The party had been wonderful, but this was better. Being outside with just Rory for company, the warm evening air draped around her shoulders.

'It'll be strange without them, won't it?'

'The crew?' Rory laughed. 'I don't know about strange, it'll be bloody wonderful.'

'They weren't that bad.'

'They weren't that good either.' They stood side by side and looked over the lake, the sound of the party echoing in the background. The moon casting a ghostly light on the water. 'But Xander will still be around, and Seb is talking about coming back here when the film comes out. He said he'd send tickets for the premiere.'

'Do we have to go? We'll have to dress up and see Pandora again.' Lottie tried not to pout.

'Up to you, darling. But it won't do any harm to get in the papers. We'll have to take a big banner with us, *Tipping House Estate, home to the stars, book your wedding quick.*'

'That's a lot to fit on a banner.'

'I was planning on an enormous banner. Me and Xander can fix it the length of the red carpet.'

'You like him, don't you?'

'I do. I have to admit I wasn't keen at first.' He wrapped his arms around Lottie's waist and pulled her closer. 'When he was after you, but he seems an okay type of bloke, and he's a good rider. He's grown on me.' He paused, studied his wife. 'I miss Mick too, you know. I think the eejit is slightly fonder of you than me, but we had some good times.'

'I think they'll stay in Ireland. He only left because Niamh did.'

'Who knows, but we've got an open invitation to go over. Do you think we should sneak back and get some practise in?'

'Practise?'

'Baby-making, you know, just check we know what we're doing?'

Lottie giggled and kicked off her heels. 'Race you.' Then she was running as fast as she could towards Tipping House. Home.

Acknowledgements

Thank you to all the wonderful HarperImpulse team, without whom there would be no Tippermere. Particular thanks to Kimberley Young, to my long-suffering and hard-working editor Charlotte Ledger, and to Cherie Chapman.

My thanks to Sarah Clegg, an amazing sporting artist and photographer, and good friend, for introducing me to the wonderful game of polo, and thanks to members and players of the Cheshire Polo Club who provided an insight into the game.

To Samantha and Andrew Lane, thank you so much for sharing the incredibly cute Ella with me.

To all the amazing readers who asked me to write this third Tippermere book – you have no idea how much you brighten my days and inspire me.

And last but not least to Paul who keeps me smiling, and to Alex who uncomplainingly suffers my blank looks and lack of dinner making.